C000133036

Collected Stories and Sketches: 5
A Ring upon the Sand

Etching by William Strang, 1898

R.B. Cunninghame Graham

Collected Stories and Sketches

Volume 5

A Ring upon the Sand

*Edited by Alan MacGillivray, John C. McIntyre
and James N. Alison*

Kennedy & Boyd
an imprint of
Zeticula Ltd
The Roan
Kilkerran
KA19 8LS
Scotland
http://www.kennedyandboyd.co.uk
admin@kennedyandboyd.co.uk

Redeemed, and Other Sketches originally published in 1927
Writ in Sand originally published in 1932
Mirages originally published in 1936
This edition copyright © Zeticula 2012
Frontispiece from *Etchings of William Strang* by Frank Newbolt, Newnes, 1907.

Contributors:
R.B. Cunninghame Graham: The Life and The Writings
        © Alan MacGillivray 2011
Introduction to *Redeemed, and Other Sketches* © James N. Alison 2012
Introduction to *Writ in Sand* and *Mirages* © John C. McIntyre 2012
An Argentine Child's Wake, with Music and Dancing © John C. McIntyre 2012
Spanish-Argentine Vocabulary in Four Sketches and Tales by R.B. Cunninghame Graham
        © John C. McIntyre 2012
Cover photograph © Martin Muirhead 2012
Cover design by Felicity Wild
Book design by Catherine E. Smith

ISBN 978-1-84921-104-8

"Nothing remained ... .of all that microcosm of human life, its dangers, beauties, disillusions, loves, hatreds and jealousies. Nothing was left to mark the passage of the great town of canvas that had arisen in a night, fallen in an hour and passed away, like life — nothing, except a ring upon the sand."

(*Writ in Sand*, "Writ in Sand")

Contents

Preface to the Collection

Robert Bontine Cunninghame Graham first came to public attention as a Radical Liberal Member of Parliament in the 1880s, when he was in his thirties. The apparent contradiction between his Scottish aristocratic family background and his vigorous attachment to the causes of Socialism, the Labour movement, anti-Imperialism and Scottish Home Rule ensured that he remained a controversial figure for many years right up to his death in the 1930s. Through his father's family of Cunninghame Graham, descended from King Robert II of Scotland and the Earls of Menteith, he had a strong territorial connection with the West of Scotland. On his mother's side, he had significant Hispanic ties through his Spanish grandmother and a naval grandfather who took part in the South American Wars of Liberation. His own world-wide travels, particularly in the Americas, Spain and North Africa, and his amazingly wide circle of friends and acquaintants in many countries and different walks of life gave him a cosmopolitan breadth of experience and a depth of insight into human nature and behaviour that would be the envy of any writer.

And it is as a writer that we now have primarily to remember Graham. His lasting political monuments are the Labour Party and the Scottish National Party, both of which he was deeply involved in founding. Yet he has to share that credit with others. His literary works are his alone. He wrote books of history, travel and biography which were extensively researched but very personal in tone, so that, although highly readable, they might not easily withstand the objective scrutiny of modern scholarship. Rather it is in his favoured literary forms of the short story, sketch and meditative essay, forms often tending to merge into one another, that Graham excels. Over forty years, between 1896 and 1936, he published fourteen collections of such short pieces, ranging over many subjects and lands. With such a wealth of life experience behind him, Graham did not have to dig deep for inspiration. Probably no other Scottish writer of any age brings such a knowledge and awareness of life's diversity to the endeavour of literary creation. However, the quality of his achievement has not as yet been fully assessed. One reason is not hard to find. There has never yet been a proper bringing together of Graham's separate collections into a manageable edition to provide the essential tools for critical study. Consequently literary attention has never been really focused on him, something for which the climate of twentieth-century Scottish, and British, critical fashion is partly responsible. Neither the Modernist movement nor the Scottish Renaissance seems to be an appropriate pigeonhole for Graham to inhabit. He has instead had to suffer the consequences of being too readily stereotyped. Perhaps entranced by the glamour of his apparent flamboyant persona of 'Don Roberto', the Spanish hidalgo, the Argentine gaucho, the Scottish laird, the horseman-adventurer, a succession of editors have republished incomplete collections of stories and sketches selected more to reinforce an image of Graham as larger-than-life legend rather than as the serious literary man he worked hard to be.

The purpose of this series is to make Graham's literary corpus available in a convenient format to modern readers as he originally intended it. Each collection of stories is kept intact, and they appear in chronological order with Graham's own footnotes, and retaining his personal idiosyncrasies and eccentricities of language and style. It is not the intention of the editors to make magisterial judgements of quality or to present a fully annotated critical edition of the stories. These purposes would go far beyond the bounds of this series in space and time, and must remain as tasks for future scholars. We merely hope that a new generation of general readers will discover Graham's short stories and sketches to be interesting and stimulating for their own sake and in their own right, diverse and revealing of a strong and generally sympathetic personality, a richly-stocked original mind and an ironic, realistic yet sensitive observer of the amazing variety of life in a very wide world.

Alan MacGillivray
John C. McIntyre

Robert Bontine Cunninghame Graham

The Life

Robert Bontine Cunninghame Graham belonged to the old-established family of Cunninghame Graham, which had its ancestral territory in the District of Menteith lying between Stirling and Loch Lomond. The family had at one time held the earldom of Menteith and could trace its ancestry back to King Robert II of Scotland in the fourteenth century. The title had been dormant since the seventeenth century, and the Cunninghame Grahams showed no real interest in reviving it. In fact, Graham passed his childhood officially bearing the surname of Bontine, because, during his youth, owing to a strange legal quirk relating to the entailing of estates and conditions of inheritance, the name 'Graham' could only be borne by Robert's grandfather who held the main Graham estate of Gartmore. Robert's father, William, an army officer, had to take another family surname, Bontine, until he inherited Gartmore in 1863. As a young man thereafter, Robert does not seem to have bothered which name he used, and when he in his turn inherited Gartmore, he kept Bontine as a middle name.

Graham was born in London in 1852. His half-Spanish mother preferred the social life of London, while his father had his responsibilities as a Scottish landowner. Accordingly, Graham's boyhood years were spent moving between the south of England and the family's Scottish houses at Gartmore in Menteith, Ardoch in Dunbartonshire and Finlaystone in Renfrewshire. Before going to preparatory school, he spent a lot of time with his Spanish grandmother, Doña Catalina, at her home in the Isle of Wight and accompanied her to Spain on a number of visits. This was his introduction to the Spanish way of life and the Spanish language, in which he became proficient. At the age of eleven he went to a prep school in Warwickshire, before going to Harrow public school for two years. He apparently disliked Harrow intensely and in 1866 was taken from it and sent to a Brussels private school which was much more to his taste. It was during his year there that he learned French and had instruction in fencing. After a year in Brussels, Graham's formal education ended and he spent the next two years until he was seventeen between his homes in Britain and his grandmother's family in Spain, developing along the way his passion for horses and his considerable riding skills.

Graham's adult life began when in 1870, with the support and financial encouragement of his parents, he took ship from Liverpool by way of Corunna and Lisbon for Argentina. The primary motivation was to make money by learning the business of ranching and going into partnership on a Scottish-owned *estancia*, or ranch. This was seen as a necessity, given that the Graham family had fallen into serious financial difficulties. Graham's father, Major William Bontine, had sunk into madness, the final consequence of a severe head injury in a riding accident, and had engaged in wild speculation with the family assets. Consequently, the estates were encumbered with debts and the Major's affairs had been placed under the supervision of an agent of the Court of Session. As the eldest of three sons, Robert had to find his own fortune and eventually pay off his father's debts. Much of his travelling in the following decades, both alone and later with his wife, Gabriela, had the search for profitable business openings at its heart.

Between 1870 and 1877, Graham undertook three ventures in South America. The ranching on the first visit came to nothing, although, being already an accomplished horseman and speaker of Spanish, he very quickly adapted to the life of the gauchos, or cowboys. He also observed at first hand some of the violence and anarchy of the early 1870s in Argentina and Uruguay; he contracted and recovered from typhus; and finally he undertook an overland horse-droving venture before returning to Britain in 1872. The following year he returned to South America, this time to Paraguay with a view to obtaining concessions for cultivating and selling the yerba mate plant, the source of the widely drunk mate infusion. In his search for possible plantation sites, Graham rode deep into the interior and came across the surviving traces of the original seventeenth and eighteenth century Jesuit settlements, the subject, many years later, for one of his best books. He had little success in his efforts and returned to Britain in 1874. After a couple of years travelling, mainly in Europe, but also to Iceland and down the coast of West Africa, Graham set out again, this time with a business partner, bound for Uruguay, where he contemplated ranching but actually set up in the horse trading business, buying horses in Uruguay with a view to driving them into Brazil to be sold to the Brazilian army. This (again) unsuccessful adventure was later described in the novella, "Cruz Alta"

(1900). Graham again returned to Britain and took up residence at his mother's house in London, becoming a familiar man about town and a frequenter of Mrs Bontine's literary and artistic salon, where he began to develop his wide circle of friends and acquaintances in the literary and cultural fields. It was his experiences in South America in the 1870s that formed his passion for the continent and directed so much of his later literary work. Out of this came the appellation of 'Don Roberto', which is now inescapably part of his personal and literary image.

Paris was another of Graham's favourite places, and it was there in 1878 that he met the woman whom he very rapidly made his wife, much to the apparent hostile concern of his family, particularly his mother. The mystery and (probably deliberate) uncertainty surrounding the circumstances of his marriage cry out for proper research among surviving family documents. One can only sketch in the few known facts and legends. Graham met a young woman who was known as Gabriela de la Balmondière. By one account she had been born in Chile with a father of French descent and a Spanish mother. She had been orphaned and brought up in Paris by an aunt, who may or may not have had her educated in a convent. By another account, she was making a living in Paris as an actress.

After a brief acquaintanceship, she and Graham lived together before coming to London and being married in a registry office in October, 1878, without family approval. In time everybody came to accept her as an exotic new member of the family, although there seems to have been some mutual hostility for several years between her and Graham's mother. It was not until the 1980s that the discovery of Gabriela's birth certificate showed that she was in fact English, the daughter of a Yorkshire doctor, and her real name was Caroline, or Carrie, Horsfall. Why Graham, and indeed the whole Graham family, should have gone on through the whole of his and her lives, and beyond, sustaining this myth of Gabriela's origins invites speculations of several kinds that may never be resolved.

After a few months of marriage, Robert and Gabriela set out for the New World, first to New Orleans, and then to Texas with the intention of going into the mule-breeding business. Over the next two years they earned a precarious living by various means both in Texas and Mexico, until the final disaster when a Texas ranch newly acquired by Graham and a business partner was raided and destroyed by Apaches. The Grahams finally returned to Britain in 1881 with substantial debts, and lived quietly in Spain and Hampshire. The death of Graham's father in 1883, however, meant that Robert finally inherited the main family estate of Gartmore with all its debts and problems, and had to live the life of a Scottish laird with all its local and social responsibilities.

The restrictions placed upon Graham by his new role could not confine such a restless spirit for long, and in 1885 he stood unsuccessfully for Parliament as a Liberal. The following year he was elected the MP for North-West Lanark, the beginning of an active and highly-coloured political career that continued in one form or another for the rest of his life. He spent only six years actually in Parliament, a period in which he soon revealed himself as more a Socialist than a Liberal, espousing a number of Radical causes and becoming deeply involved and influential in the early years of the Labour movement, being, along with Keir Hardie, one of the co-founders of the Labour Party. The high point of his time in Parliament was when he was arrested and committed to prison, accused of assaulting a policeman during the 'Bloody Sunday' demonstration in Trafalgar Square on 13th November, 1887. From his maiden speech onwards, he wrote and spoke out forcefully on behalf of Labour causes and finally in 1892 stood unsuccessfully for Parliament directly as a Labour candidate. Even out of Parliament Graham continued to be active politically. Although he gradually ceased to be a leading figure in the new Labour Party, his new-found talent as a polemical journalist, in great demand in the serious papers and journals of the day, enabled him to remain in the public eye with his concern about social conditions and his unfashionable anti-Imperial attitudes. He was opposed to the Boer Wars, as he was also to the new imperialism of the USA, shown during the Spanish-American War of 1898, which affronted his strong attachment to Spain and Latin America. His commitment to Scottish Home Rule led him in his later years to find a new role as a founder of the Scottish National Party.

After leaving Parliament in 1892, Graham and his wife were free to travel more frequently, sometimes together but more often pursuing their diverging interests apart, and always on the look-out for possibilities of improving their finances. Spain and Morocco were the main areas of their travel. Graham also began to diversify in his new-found interest in writing into the prolific production of travel books and collections of short stories and sketches. Yet nothing could stave off for ever the inevitable consequences of his father's irresponsibility. The debt-ridden estate of Gartmore had eventually to be sold, and the Grahams settled for financial security on the smaller family estate of Ardoch on the northern side of the Firth of Clyde. Even so, a worse blow was to befall Graham. Gabriela had never been physically strong and was prone to pleurisy (not helped by her chain-smoking habit). She died in 1906 on the way back from one of her many visits to the drier warmth of Spain. Her marriage with Robert of more than a quarter of a century had been childless, but they were a close couple and Robert missed her greatly.

As his life advanced into late middle age and old age through the new century, Graham developed his writing with more collections of short stories and works of biography centred on Mexican and South American history. His astonishingly wide circle of friends in all fields of society and his continuing political activities kept him close to the centre of society and often in the public gaze. At the outbreak of the First World War, though he had been critical of the warmongering attitudes that had marked the years from 1910 to 1914, Graham, at the age of 62, volunteered for service and was charged with two missions to South America, one in 1914-15 to Uruguay to buy horses for the Army, and the second to Colombia in 1916-17 to obtain beef supplies. The first mission enabled him to recapture some of the excitement of his early years on horseback in South America, although it made him desperately sad as a horse-lover to think of the dreadful fate awaiting the animals he bought. The second mission turned out to be unsuccessful, owing to a lack of shipping.

After the war, Graham continued to travel, now more for relaxation and for the sake of his health. He had a new close companion and friend, a wealthy widow, Mrs Elizabeth ('Toppie') Dummett, whose artistic salon in London he frequented and who travelled with him on most of his journeys. Back in Scotland, Graham continued to spend summers at Ardoch, and was well known round the Glasgow and Scottish literary scene, as well as being involved in Scottish political controversy. Among his literary friends were the poet Hugh MacDiarmid (C.M.Grieve) and the novelist and journalist, Neil Munro. Graham made a point of attending the dedication of a memorial to Munro in the summer of 1935. Graham was then eighty-three years old. A few months later, Graham set out on what he probably knew would be his last journey, back to Argentina, the scene of his first youthful adventures. In Buenos Aires, he contracted bronchitis and then pneumonia, and after a few days he died. His funeral in Buenos Aires was a large public occasion attended by the Argentine President, with two horses belonging to Graham's friend,

Aimé Tschiffely, the horseman-adventurer, accompanying the coffin as symbols of Don Roberto's attachment to the gaucho culture that had been such an influence on his life and philosophy.

Robert Bontine Cunninghame Graham is buried near his wife Gabriela in the family burial place at the Augustinian Priory on the little island of Inchmahome in the Lake of Menteith. A memorial to him is now placed near the former family mansion of Gartmore.

The Writings

It may not be too much of an exaggeration to say that the greatest blessing bestowed upon Robert Bontine Cunninghame Graham in his boyhood years was an incomplete formal education. Two years at prep school, two years at Harrow and one 'finishing' year in Brussels gave him little of the classical education deemed essential for the well-born Victorian gentleman. Instead he reached the age of eighteen with considerable fluency in Spanish and French, and an undoubted acquired love of reading gained from the books in the libraries of his family's Scottish houses and his mother's house in London. His extensive (if difficult to decipher) letters home to his mother from abroad make this latter fact clear. The proficiency in Spanish and French gave him immediate entry into two major literatures of the modern world in addition to English, a more bankable asset for the modern writer-to-be than any familiarity with the classical writings of Greece and Rome.

It is conventional to ascribe the beginnings of Graham's writing career to the period after he left Parliament and was settled back in Gartmore, in the last decade of the century. However, the habit of writing had undoubtedly been acquired by him over many years preceding, when he was writing long letters home about his experiences in the Americas, and, later on, writing speeches and articles as part of his work as a strongly involved and committed Radical Liberal Member of Parliament.

Nevertheless, we can only begin to speak of Graham as a true writer when in the years after 1890 he began to publish both fiction and non-fiction on a regular basis. Probably beginning with an essay, "The Horses of the Pampas", contributed to the monthly magazine, *Time*, in 1890, Graham went on to write extensively for the *Saturday Review* and other periodicals. There were essays, sketches and short stories, and, later, books of travel and history. Graham's confidence in himself as a writer can be seen to grow during this period, especially when he acquired the literary and critical friendship of the publisher, Edward Garnett.

What makes Graham very different in his writing from any other late Victorian upper-class traveller and man of action is his conscious awareness and absorption of the realistic spirit and literary techniques of contemporary European writers. His main subjects initially are his beloved South America and Spain, as filtered through his personal experiences as a younger man, and aspects of life in Britain, perhaps especially Scotland. Yet he describes these with, in the main, a detached unsentimental insight gained from his reading of the short stories and sketches of Guy de Maupassant and Ivan Turgenev. Equally, after reading *La Pampa*, a set of vignettes of gaucho life written in French by Alfred Ébélot, on the recommendation of his close friend, W.H. Hudson, he came to see how his memories of life among the gauchos could be structured into short tales blending close detailed observation and brief narrative. Yet it would not be true to think of Graham as always being a totally controlled and dispassionate writer. There is both fire and anger in those of his pieces that set out to confront rampant and racist imperialism, social injustice and cruelty directed against helpless human or animal targets.

There is perhaps a tentative quality about Graham's first two books. *Notes on the District of Menteith* (1895) is a highly personal short guidebook to the part of Scotland he knew at first hand surrounding the ancestral home. It almost seems to be a practice for the real thing, before going out into the territory of the big book. Similarly, *Father Archangel of Scotland, and Other Essays* (1896) is an initial attempt at the short story collection, in which Graham shares the contents with his wife, Gabriela.

Graham's first true full-length book conceived as a single narrative is his account of personal experiences in Morocco, *Mogreb-El-Acksa* (1898). The book, whose title translates as 'Morocco the Most Holy', deals in the main with Graham's time there in the later months of 1897. Paradoxically, for a man who travelled so extensively throughout his long life, it is one of the only two real travel books that Graham ever wrote. The other is *Cartagena and the Banks of the Sinú* (1920), which arose out of Graham's mission to Colombia in 1916-17. It is clear that he came to see his experiences in the wider world primarily as a fertile and energising source for fiction.

Between 1899 and 1936, Graham published thirteen collections of sketches and short stories. Generally, his approach for these collections was to bring together stories and short pieces of a rather heterogeneous nature, with settings ranging from his favourite locales of South America and Spain, and increasingly North Africa, to Scotland, London, Paris and more distant parts of the globe. Some of the stories are crafted narratives; others may be little more than detailed descriptions of life and manners with a minimum of narrative, or even personal essays on a range of diverse topics. Although his tone is mostly detached and often ironic, the persona of the writer is never far away and at times Graham's partialities emerge clearly through the text.

The first two collections, *The Ipané* (1899) and *Thirteen Stories* (1900), give the impression of being the most diverse, partly because of the throwaway nature of their titles. 'Ipané' is merely the name of an old river boat that appears in the title story of the first collection. The book has a random quality about it with no sense of a central thread behind the choices.

Thirteen Stories, as a title, suggests an equal randomness. Indeed the main story in the collection is in fact a novella, "Cruz Alta", which takes up fully a third of the length of the book on its own, the other stories being very diverse in their settings and themes. However, the collections that follow in the years before and during the First World War have titles that seem to show a more directed thinking by Graham about their central thrust or themes. *Success* (1902) and *Progress, and Other Sketches* (1905) imply an inspirational quality. *His People* follows in 1906, and *Faith* (1909), *Hope* (1910) and *Charity* (1912) seem to be linked as a group within Graham's mind. *A Hatchment* (1913) and *Brought Forward* (1916) bring to an end the first cycle of Graham's fictional output. Thereafter, there is a gap of eleven years before the final late collections, *Redeemed, and Other Sketches* (1927), *Writ in Sand* (1932) and *Mirages* (1936), the titles of which seem to suggest a disengagement from the serious business of life. And yet perhaps too much weight can be attached to the titles of these works. In all of them, the stories are equally varied and exotic in their sources, and Graham never lets himself be pinned down by a reader's or critic's desire to pigeonhole him as a fiction writer on a particular subject or theme.

It is in his historical writing that Graham does reveal himself as having a specific interest and purpose. Beginning in 1901, he published a sequence of works, mostly biographical, dealing with aspects of South American history from the time of the sixteenth-century Conquistadors right down to his own lifetime. For the writing of these books, he undertook extensive research into the original source documents, a labour in which his knowledge of Spanish proved to be invaluable. The largest group of historical biographies deals with prominent figures in the conquest of South America by the Spaniards. *Hernando de Soto* (1903), *Bernal Diaz del Castillo* (1915), *The Conquest of New Granada* (1922), *The Conquest of the River Plate* (1924), and *Pedro de Valdivia* (1926) show his interest in most areas of Latin America, not merely his own beloved Argentina. Indeed, his travel book, *Cartagena and the Banks of the Sinú* (1920), includes a sketch of the history of Colombia from the Conquest onwards. In that same year Graham also published his biography of the Brazilian religious revolutionary leader of the 1890s, Antonio Conselheiro, under the title, *A Brazilian Mystic*. Two biographies of later figures in South American history are *Jose Antonio Paez* (1929), dealing with one of the heroes of the liberation of Venezuela from Spain in the 1820s, and *Portrait of a Dictator: Francisco Solano Lopez* (1933), about the leader of Paraguay through the disastrous Triple Alliance War of the 1860s. How popular these books about a continent and culture little-known in Britain could ever be is questionable. In writing them, Graham was undoubtedly trying to counteract the contemporary craze for writings about the British Empire, an institution about which he held distinctly unfashionable views. Probably the most enduring of his historical works has turned out to be *A Vanished Arcadia; Being Some Account of the Jesuits in Paraguay, 1607 to 1767* (1901), for reasons more to do with its later cinematic connections than any historical appeal. A historical biography of more personal significance to Graham was *Doughty Deeds* (1925), an account of the life of Graham's own direct eighteenth-century ancestor and namesake, Robert Graham of Gartmore.

Graham's wife, Gabriela, had literary aspirations of her own and published a number of works, frequently infused by the deep religious feeling that developed as she grew older. Her main work was a two-volume biography of Saint Teresa, to which she devoted years of travel and research. Graham clearly played a major role in encouraging her in her writing, and helped in its publication. He had collaborated with her in *Father Archangel of Scotland, and Other Essays* (1896). After her death in 1906, he arranged for the posthumous publication of a new edition of *Santa Teresa* (1907), her poems in 1908, and a new collection of her shorter writings, *The Christ of Toro and Other Stories* (1908).

This survey has touched on all the books that Graham published in his lifetime. Selections have been made by some of his many admirers from his considerable output of short stories and sketches, usually focusing on specific subject areas of his work, such as South America, Scotland or his passion for horses. One unfortunate effect of this may have been to stereotype Graham as a particular kind of writer, an exotic breed who sits uncomfortably in a literary climate dominated by the Modernists of the earlier twentieth century. The extravagant larger-than-life image that has built up about him has perhaps skewed our perceptions of his writing, which is more European in its sensibility than British Edwardian or Georgian. Paradoxically, despite his class origins and cosmopolitan experience, Graham can also often seem to be closer in tone and outlook to twentieth-century Scottish writers like George Douglas Brown, Hugh MacDiarmid or Lewis Grassic Gibbon, writers whose work he almost certainly knew well. There is a great deal of scholarly work waiting to be done on Graham as a Scottish writer, not least the unquantifiable task of bringing into print the large body of his articles, journalism and letters that have never been properly investigated. The full canon of his work has still to be established. Until that is done, it is not possible to make any true assessment of the literary significance of Robert Bontine Cunninghame Graham.

Alan MacGillivray

Note to Volume 5

This fifth and final volume of Cunninghame Graham stories and sketches brings together the three collections he published in the last decade of his life. *Redeemed, and Other Sketches* appeared in 1927, followed in 1932 by *Writ in Sand*, and in 1936, the year of his death, by *Mirages*. There is a sense of winding down in the pieces presented. The characteristic Graham astringency and irony are less intense, and there is more conventional sentiment. However, some of the familiar targets for his distaste and anger are still being picked off. Graham shows himself to be fully alive to the increasingly menacing world of 1930s Europe. If he had lived, there is little doubt about where his sympathies would have lain. Graham died on the 20th March 1936. Exactly four months later, the Spanish Civil War began.

Alan MacGillivray
John C. McIntyre
James N. Alison

Redeemed, and other Sketches

"Cuando Tocolote canta, Indio muere
No lo creo, pero sucede"

Central American Aphorism

R. B. Cunninghame Graham

To

Elizabeth Dummett

Introduction

In 1927 when Cunninghame Graham published the medley of sixteen sketches entitled *Redeemed,* he was revisiting a format which he had not used for eleven years. His Preface acknowledges this fact and apologises for breaking the farewell promise made in *Brought Forward* that he would not trouble the public further with his writings. This preface is in fact an engaging reminiscence in its own right. It recalls a likeable gaucho rogue, Candelario, who had once served as Graham's foreman in an early ranching venture in Argentina, and was constitutionally incapable of honouring his promise not to rustle unbranded cattle on his employer's behalf. Out of this portrait Graham neatly shapes his own plea that his readers should forgive him for breaking his pledge to give up 'short stories'. He was, said G K Chesterton, 'the Prince of Preface Writers'.

As in Graham's eleven previous sets of sketches, these pieces vary widely in location, period, form and pace, mingling autobiography, historical reconstruction, fictional narrative, travelogue, journalism and philosophical musings. Reflecting Graham's family connections and his recent travels there is significant Hispanic content. Six sketches are set in Spain, three in South America, three in England, two in Scotland, and one each in Italy and Morocco. Four of the items, "El Alcalde de Móstoles", "Los Llanos del Apure", "Animula Vagula" and "Inveni Portum", were given more accessible titles, presumably with the author's consent, in the omnibus collection *Rodeo* (1936) edited by Aimé Tschiffely, which appeared posthumously. These new versions were "War to the Knife", "The Plains of Venezuela", "The Orchid-Hunter" and "Harboured". Graham, who was aged 75, dedicated *Redeemed* to Elizabeth Dummett, a sociable and kindly widow who shared many of his interests, was a skilled horsewoman and proved an indispensable helpmeet in his later years. The prevailing mood of the volume is signalled in its Spanish epigraph, which is a Mexican proverb about the credulity of the indigenous Indian conviction that the owl is a portent of death: 'When the owl sings the Indian dies. I do not believe it, but it does happen.'

In one way or another virtually all of these sketches, however lively their style, express their author's resigned alertness to intimations of mortality.

In the title piece the word 'redeemed' is freighted with typical Graham ironies, carrying conflicting senses of religious salvation, payment of a pawned pledge and, in a political context, annexing lost territories. During the 19th and early 20th centuries expansionist Italian patriots had used the term *Italia Irredenta* to identify areas on the Austro-Hungarian frontier which they regarded as properly Italian in history and culture. Their inflammatory ambition was to annex (redeem) these territories, by force if necessary. On the outbreak of the First World War savage mountain warfare swept the valleys and passes of the border region. In this sketch Graham delivers a sustained caustic commentary on its unhappy impact, ten years later, on a small Alpine community in the Trentino-Alto Adige zone which had been forced to change its national allegiance. 'Redeem' in its syntactic variants is repeated sarcastically ten times in the course of his diatribe, and the language flares exuberantly into phrases such as, '[...] an agony of patriotism in the parturition of their perorations'. Ominously, for this is 1926, the cry of 'Viva il Tuce' is heard in the land.

What Graham deplores is that an isolated, inoffensive culture has been corrupted by the intrusion of nationalism and peacetime exploitation in the name of progress. Not for the first time in his sketches a luxury tourist hotel is depicted as a grossly vulgar symbol of this decadence. For him the one saving grace is that the seasons return in their reassuring fashion, and the creatures and wild flowers of the valley observe their natural cycles. Man is certainly transient and vile, but the earth abides, even over the neglected graves of unknown, redeemed — and redeeming — soldiers.

"Promoted" is another sketch in the volume which exploits the ironies of an enigmatic one-word title. Though differing in tone from "Redeemed", it also deals with bloody conflict. A fast-moving graphic narrative, it is a semi-fictional reconstruction of a nasty episode in Spanish history. In 1568 a rising broke out in the Alpujarra hills of Andalusia in which the Moriscoes, the Moorish communities still surviving a century after the Reconquista, rebelled against increasingly vicious religious persecution by the Christian church and state. A small battle-hardened force of Spanish troops disembarks from a Genoese galley at Motril and yomps over lands devastated by fighting until it reaches Lanjarrón south of Granada where a Turkish ally of the Moriscoes, Mamet Ali, is holding out in an impregnable clifftop redoubt. The narrative viewpoint is that of the Spanish Christians: the Turk is 'a devil and son of a devil', and the rebels are to be slaughtered as 'Moorish dogs'. Very curiously, the climax of the account, in which the chaplain, a militant Franciscan friar, suicidally leads the charge which breaks the siege, seems to be lifted directly from a similar incident in Graham's earlier sketch "Mudejar" (*Brought Forward,* 1916). The irony of the title is that the fanatical Fray Juan who has always been regarded by his CO as potential officer material is 'promoted' only by his death — to Heaven.

The presence of six Spanish sketches in this volume is testimony to Graham's deep feeling for the country, its peoples and landscapes, and its troubled history. In "El Lebeche" he is again dealing with southern Andalucia but the period is contemporary. The essay is a moment in time sensitively observed in atmosphere and mood. El Lebeche, a spring wind blowing north from the Sahara, periodically deposits unwelcome dust, rain and steamy mist on the region's sunny Mediterranean coasts. The resort which Graham describes, possibly Malaga as it was in the Twenties, is caught in its depressing throes. He comments tartly on the modern cityscape with its jerry-built holiday villas, ornamental gardens, tourist hotel, tramways, motor cars and 'all the flotsam and jetsam of a southern town'. It is ill adapted to cope with this climatic nuisance. On the other hand he seems to endorse the underlying, older Oriental ways of life which survive in the mud and fog. These ways are largely horse-drawn, depending on mules, donkeys and high-wheeled carts. Their endurance has biblical echoes invoking Calvary, the Son of Man in Jerusalem, 'Providence and their hard lot', Maria Santisima (i.e., Andalusia) and this vale of tears. Key to the sketch is the powerfully positive culminating image of a local goatherd guiding his flock towards their pastures. In these dreich surroundings he seems cheerful and contented as he disappears into the mist cradling one of his kids and crooning a harsh Arab-sounding song, 'quavering and wild as the cry of a curlew on a Scottish moor'.

In "La Virgen de la Cabeza" Graham employs the traditional trappings of a traveller's tale. On a bitter Andalusian winter's day a stagecoach party has been riding west to Granada along the flanks of the Sierra Nevada. Benighted by heavy snowfalls and fearful of wolves, the group takes shelter in a crowded village inn where 'around the ample hearth tongues were soon loosened and experiences exchanged'. The Cervantine setting of the inn is deftly conveyed with its communal table, hearty food, roaring fire and mixed clientele of villagers and travellers. The talk being naturally of the wolves, a muleteer recalls with a swagger his terrifying encounter with a pack in the Alpujarra cork woods. *In extremis* he had invoked the help of a potent Andalusian saint, Our Lady of the Head, swearing to do penance and donate a valuable candle to her shrine. His prayers were effective, but as he unwarily confesses to his amused listeners, he had reneged on his promises to Our Lady, feeling sure that she would not need his meagre offering. The village priest who is in the audience sternly rebukes him for his backsliding and at the same time extends his compassion to a cold and wretched girl prostitute on the periphery of the group, 'We are all of the same family'. The priest's words might serve for a closing benediction upon the motley company as the winter evening becomes clear and calm, but 'far away in the recesses of the woods a wolf howled mournfully'.

North of Andalusia, the region of Castile-La Mancha in central Spain is the location of three related sketches, "Oropesa", "At Navalcán" and "El Alcalde de Móstoles". Its high austere plains with their fringing sierras experience torrid summers and freezing winters. Perhaps their aridity was an appealing inversion of the great sodden mosses lapping on Graham's lost Gartmore back in Scotland. Probably he also relished the popular view of himself as the latterday Quixote seen tilting over La Mancha in William Strang's fine etchings.

"Oropesa" is Graham's richly colourist attempt to convey the essence of these uplands; their landscapes, climate and inhabitants. He suggests that the severities of the landscape have over the centuries generated a distinctive breed of hard, simple peasantry — Cervantes' Sancho Panza being a caricatured example. The author's focus on the hill town of Oropesa probably arose from his friendship with Bernardino de Velasco, the playboy Duke of Frias, Count of Oropesa, a flamboyant and impoverished young Spanish grandee. Particularly striking is his description of the melancholy shambles of the once magnificent ducal chapel and library. In concluding he draws back on a serene panorama of twilight on the distant sierras, 'like mountains in some planet long extinct, whose shadow has just reached the earth'. In a later collection (*Writ in Sand*, 1932) Graham offers the tribute of a moving obituary to

Bernardino in "Fin de Race"

The longest sketch in the selection, "At Navalcán", is also its only explicitly autobiogaphical narrative. Addressed as 'Don Roberto', Graham rides out with his friend Nicolas, the head gamekeeper of the Duke of Frias in order to visit Navalcán, an out-of-the-way village in the woods of Oropesa district where the old Spanish ways of life still flourish. As they arrive, the whole community is giving itself wholeheartedly to wedding celebrations. He observes it all with relish — the dancing and the rituals; the feasting and the music. He recognizes the antiquity of the proceedings with their traces of Moorish origins, and the blending of peasant exuberance with an innate Castilian elegance in the participants. This is a rare instance of a Graham sketch in which unclouded feelings of celebration and happiness prevail. Finally, as the pair ride away from Navalcán in the moonlight, 'Don Roberto' concedes to the gamekeeper that he has never witnessed festivities such as these in England.

"El Alcalde De Móstoles" presents what, for Graham, is a relatively straight narrative of a celebrated episode in the history of Castile-La Mancha. On the second of May (el Dos de Mayo) 1808 Andrés Torrejón, the stolid mayor of the small town of Móstoles near Toledo, was aroused by news of a brutal massacre in Madrid to declare personal war on the French invaders. Invoking the Scottish parallel of the Fiery Cross, Graham describes how the news of Torrejón's audacity spreads rapidly throughout Spain, triggering, he suggests in a sweeping simplification, Wellesley's Peninsular campaigns and ultimately Napoleon's defeat in Russia. His description of the appearance and character of the mayor resembles closely that of Cirilo the ex-alcalde in "At Navalcán". As in "Oropesa" Graham's assumption seems to be that stubbornly independent men such as these (and in Graham's writings they are mostly men) — the plainsmen of La Mancha, the gauchos of Argentina, the hillmen of the Alpujarras, the llaneros of Venezuela, the Arab shepherds and the islesmen of Skye — are all in a sense admirable, archaic outcroppings of their own particular habitats.

The Arabic title "Dar-el-Jinoun" means House of Demons. This tantalising essay is a soft-focus impression of a pastoral Moroccan landscape in an area where the cultures of North Africa and southern Europe have historically been at their closest. Characteristically Graham does not spell out that his 'strange little town' is 1920s cosmopolitan Tangier and its littoral, but he scatters hints, identifying for example the ruins of Roman 'Tingis, a city old when London was a wattled village'. In folktale mode he tells of the bizarre creation, expansion and subsequent decay of a luxurious European mansion built in an extravagant neo-Moorish style on the outskirts of the old town. Latterly the local Arabs shun the desolate villa as the home of Djinns; but for Graham it is yet another melancholy emblem of the vanity of human wishes. Surfacing in this fable are traces of Graham's own experiences and social contacts in Tangier. The Moorish villa had been built by Graham's eccentric friend Walter Harris, resident correspondent for *The Times* newspaper in Morocco. Harris's encounters with the murderous warlord, Muli Ahmed er Raisuli, are graphically described in his *Morocco That Was* (1921), a work which clearly influenced this sketch. Graham also contemplates the Tangier shores in "A Blessing", another pastoral piece — but with a quietly cruel final twist (*A Hatchment,*1913).

The selection *Redeemed* contains three items located in South America: "Los Llanos del Apure" in Venezuela, and the paired "Animula Vagula" and "A Hundred In The Shade" in Colombia. The genesis of these probably owed something to Graham's family associations with Venezuela and to his visit there in 1925; and to a wartime mission to Colombia in 1917, which also yielded his travel book *Cartagena and the Banks of the Sinú* (1920) and the biography *José Antonio Páez* (1929).

The Llanos of Graham's sketch are the vast savannas in western Venezuela drained by the river Apure, a tributary of the Orinoco. He describes it lyrically as a beautiful but unforgiving primeval landscape subject to extremes of climate, a paradise populated by fierce wildlife and largely unpolluted by man. It seems more harsh than the pampas of Argentina; and its Hispanic denizens, the Llaneros, even more formidable individualists than the gauchos. The piece is not narrative in form but it contains a vignette of Páez, a partisan leader of the llaneros who fought with Bolívar against the Spaniards in Venezuela and was a friend of Graham's grandmother. It unfolds into a colourful dawn-to-dusk commentary on a day in the life of the Llanos.

"Animula Vagula" and "A Hundred in the Shade" belong to the category of colonial travellers' tales made popular by the Edinburgh periodical *Blackwood's Magazine* (though these two were not published in that outlet). This fashion had achieved its masterpiece in Joseph Conrad's *Heart of Darkness* (1899). In common with Conrad's novella Graham's tales incorporate the device of a secondary narrator's account of a steamer voyage up a great river through alien territory. In the temporary enforced companionship of the journey the passengers, 'various waifs and strays', reveal something of their personalities and the bleak isolation of their lives. The setting of both seems to be the long Magdalena River flowing north through Colombia into the Caribbean.

The title "Animula Vagula" comes from the anonymous and riddling fragment of Latin verse traditionally reputed to be the dying Roman emperor Hadrian's farewell to life. It poses the mystery of where the soul goes when it leaves its friendly host, the body. Graham's story is a subtly layered interrogation of the limits of human sympathies and obligations. The travellers hear an anecdote concerning the corpse of a young white man which had recently turned up at a riverside post. What sort of man was he, and who really cared? Who was to take responsibilty for his identification and burial? The Indians who brought him in? The local Colombian officials? Or the enigmatic Orchid-hunter who is telling the tale and may be his fellow countryman? Having raised these disturbing questions the hunter leaves the ship to pursue his own exotic, lonely trade in the jungle. This fine sketch shows Graham at his most Conradian.

The Orchid-hunter also makes an appearance in the second steamship tale, "A Hundred in the Shade", but only in a brief reminiscence. The main yarn is that of an American who for some reason he does not himself understand feels impelled to unburden himself of a romantic confession of how 'twenty years ago to the day' in New Orleans he lost the love of Daphne, a superior English courtesan who finally preferred the security of marriage to a mining engineer. The implication of the title is that the oppressive environment of the river and the ship may have driven him to the revelation. In both of these pieces the impersonal voice of Graham provides the framing narrative.

As noted earlier, and not surprisingly perhaps for someone of Graham's age and habitual cast of mind, the shades of *memento mori* gather throughout the selection. Three items, 'Inveni Portum", "Wilfrid Scawen Blunt" and "Long Wolf'" are in one way or another particular obituaries, whilst "Inch Cailleach" and "Euphrasia" are more general elegiac musings in Scottish country places.

When Joseph Conrad died in 1924, Graham attended his funeral in Canterbury. The two had enjoyed enduring friendship and respect in matters artistic, philosophical and personal. They also shared a pessimistic world view which is expressed in the title of Graham's obituary. *Inveni*

Portum is a Latin tag derived from a Greek epigram, a much favoured epitaph of weary resignation from life, and befitting Conrad's life as a seaman:

'Fortune and Hope farewell! I've found the port;
You've done with me: go now, with others sport.'

The narrative traces the course of the funeral — a pleasant rainy summer's day in the historic old city, and the seemly formalities of the Latin Mass. As the cortege drives to the country cemetery Graham movingly recalls Conrad's achievements as a writer, his ruggedly commanding appearance and his matching personality. At the graveside he feels that his old friend has reached his final harbour and fancies that he will sometimes hear the wild gulls calling overhead.

The intriguing eulogy for Wilfrid Scawen Blunt who died in 1922, starts and ends in a Sussex wood beside a large mound which marks the grave of another of Graham's cherished friends. In memorialising Blunt Graham must have realised that he was in effect musing about himself, for he clearly regarded him as a soulmate and alter ego — horseman, traveller, scholar, impoverished county gentleman of ancient lineage with a forlorn and decaying manor house. Blunt sustained the style of an Arab sheikh much as Graham affected that of gaucho and hidalgo; both were fearless critics of British imperialism. This delightful tribute is lyrical, sentimental and tinged with affectionate whimsy: ' [...] it would please him if he knew that in the moonlight rabbits came out to play around his grave and the owls fly silently over his resting place.'

"Long Wolf" recalls a forgotten warrior of the Oglala Sioux tribe who fought against Custer at the battle of the Little Big Horn in Montana, in 1876. He later joined Colonel Cody's travelling Wild West show and died in London in 1892. Graham, who did not know him personally, composed the sketch long after his death. It is prefaced by a complicated note from Kermit, son of former President Theodore Roosevelt, revealing how the piece came to be written. Scanning a quiet corner of the large Brompton cemetery in south London, Graham comments ironically on the lives of the incumbents and notes the neglected grave of Long Wolf, a 'wilding' out of place among the tombs of these prosperous Londoners. Speculatively he conjures up in contrast the Indian's early days in the harsh, elemental society of the prairies before the West was invaded by whites. Finally he toys with the thought that the wolf sculptured on his headstone might come alive at night and howl, perhaps, in his memory.

Seventy years after its publication this reverie had an extraordinary delayed impact which might well have amused Graham. A Worcester woman Elizabeth Wright came upon it 'in a dog-eared book in a local antiques market' and decided that something would have to be done. As a result of her efforts on behalf of the displaced shade of Long Wolf, his remains were exhumed in the presence of Sioux representatives and brought home in 1997 for honourable burial in the tribe's ancestral burial ground at Wounded Knee in South Dakota.

A beguiling feature of these three elegiac pieces in *Redeemed* is that Graham chooses to end each of them with small, possibly consoling, intrusions of the wild — gulls, rabbits, owls and the wolf.

In this selection only two sketches have a Scottish setting, "Euphrasia" and "Inch Cailleach". "Euphrasia" is a pensive piece of reportage on the condition of a 1914-1918 war memorial somewhere on Skye. At Dunvegan there is a Celtic cross monument with a Gaelic text closely matching Graham's description. In yet another instance of the author's taste for ironic word play, *Euphrasia* is both botanical Latin for the attractive weed Eyebright and an obsolete medical term for the strange feeling of cheerfulness which sometimes precedes death. Graham highlights the contrast between the untended shoddiness of the memorial and the natural beauty of the location, particularly the abundance of eyebrights in the surrounding meagre fields. His thoughts are coloured by glimmers of Celtic Twilight, with references to Cuchullin, the Fingalians and their heroic steeds; and he recalls the area's historic associations: Haco's Norsemen en route to battle at Largs, and the islesmen who fought for Montrose, Claverhouse and Wellington. Though the names on the memorial are mostly of men who died far away, he fancies that their spirits may look homewards 'to some Valhalla in the mists that roll round Sligachan'. His final very sentimental consolation is that however much the monument and its names may be forgotten and neglected, the seasons will come and go, and in the west wind the little eyes of the eyebrights will turn towards the cross. We are back here in the mood of the conclusion to the title sketch "Redeemed".

With "Inch Cailleach" Graham comes very near to his old ancestral lands, for this topographical piece lovingly explores a small wooded island on Loch Lomond some ten miles from his former estate at Gartmore. The title comes from the Gaelic *innis na cailleach,* island of the old woman (or nun or demonic hag). He records the local tradition that the island might have been the site of an early nunnery. Certainly the secluded peaceful environment is well suited to the life of meditation and prayer, but on the ground there are no material traces of the nuns: 'the dim sisterhood had left no record'. Encircled by oak thickets the island's old burial ground suggests a different kind of history for it holds the rough-hewn gravestones of McGregor and McFarlane clansmen whose sword emblems commemorate their wild, outlawed way of life. As in "Euphrasia" Graham summons up Ossianic lore of the heroes Fingal, Cuchullin, and the hound Bran, and fancies that their nocturnal spirits may visit the island to commune with the nameless dead. His theme is once again the transience of all human endeavours: only the quietly invasive beauty and harmony of the natural world persists. The sketch ends in a benevolent rhetorical blessing: 'Let them sleep on [...] let them rest [...] till the shrill skirl of the Piobh Mor shall call them to the great gathering of the clans'. It is noteworthy that Graham and his wife are buried together within a ruined monastic site on a similarly secluded island near Gartmore, Inchmahome on the Lake of Menteith.

As suggested earlier, there can be no denying that melancholy suffuses the seventeen items in *Redeemed,* but that fact does not of itself weaken the selection's appeal. The modulations of this mood within and between sketches are striking and subtle. Indignation, nostalgia, despair, romance, desolation, friendship, pessimism, historical sensitivity, misanthropy, whimsy, respect for the natural world, sentimentality, admiration, reverence for animals, wonder and curiosity — all of these feelings and attitudes, and many more, give texture to Graham's writings. For the most part his command of language and form can support this range of responses.

Writing between two World Wars the most powerful comfort that he has to offer us is the perhaps naive reassurance that somehow or other the natural world can assert itself as a self-healing system against the ravages of human folly. Such indeed might be Graham's vision of 'Redemption', and in this respect he could be seen as an innocent precursor of our contemporary ecologists, at once romantic and pessimistic, who have promoted the *Gaia* hypothesis.

(JNA)

Contents

Preface

In the dark ages, in South America, I had a capataz, called Candelario Carmona, a courteous, kindly man who could ride anything with hair on it, and a good guitar player, but obstinate as a male mule.

He could never see an orejano animal without putting my brand upon it.

As there is widespread ignorance amongst the educated proletariat, of matters of importance, I may explain that the term Orejano is used in South America for a beast without a brand. In Western Texas such a one is called a Maverick, after a certain Colonel Maverick, who, as the legend goes, looked on all animals as potentially his own.

In certain circumstances it is allowable to brand an orejano, but to Candelario all circumstances were good.

The neighbours used to laugh and say either the grass in Don Roberto's camp is the sweetest in the whole district, or else his capataz uses a lazo made from the hide of a long cow.

Justice, but not in my house, says the proverb, and as I knew her to be blind and half suspected her of deafness in the most of cases, I did not wish to fall into her hands. So when a good-sized calf or colt, with the skin peeling off a half-healed brand upon its hip, mysteriously appeared amongst my animals, I used to lecture Candelario on the error of his ways.

He promised faithfully, swearing upon his children's heads, and he had seven of them, that he would never lift a lawless lazo on an animal again during the whole course of his life.

I doubt not that he took me for a fool, for he was one of those who, had he owned even a yoke of oxen, would soon have had a plentiful supply of calves from them. So, in despite of all that I could say, I found my cattle and my colts increasing mightily, especially when I had been away upon a journey for a month or two.

When I remonstrated and reproached him for having broken faith, he used to look at me, with a sly look out of his eye, just like a horse that kicks at the stirrup as you are mounting him, and say, "If a man happens to be born with a big belly, it is of little use to bind a sash round it." This, and the string of proverbs that he used to pour out, whether they bore upon the subject or had no connection with it, such as, "A naked woman does not save her modesty by keeping on her gloves," did not prevent him following his old ways. So with the best grace I could assume I let him ride his hobby, seeing moreover it was to my advantage, and recognising how difficult it is to teach old dogs new tricks.

I might have ended my career a great cattle king, for I have known such, who, starting life from just as small beginnings as my own, finished up millionaires, but with this difference, that they required no capataz to brand other people's cattle for them. Fate willed it otherwise. For several years Candelario used to write to me, that is, he got the owner of the nearest pulperia, a Spanish Basque, who never could make nouns and adjectives agree in gender, to do it for him.

Droughts, floods, fandangos, Indian incursions, locusts and the like, things just as interesting as the divorces and adulteries that fill the newspapers, and less demoralising, I learned of, after I had laboriously spelled out the Basque's caligraphy and phonetic rendering of the tongue.

These letters ceased, after one saying certain malicious bastards, for he was certain Holy Mother Church had never coupled up their parents, had falsely put about a rumour that he killed his neighbour's cows on nights without a moon. I knew his heart (he said), and how repugnant to his sense of honour such a deed would be. Moreover, such things were difficult to prove, for were a man to demean himself to such an action, he would be sure to cut the brand out of the hide, and certainly on his way home would lead his horse in the bed of some stream or other, to cover up his trail. That was the last I ever heard of him, and in what Pampa he now rides that is to me unknown. Only I hope he has good horses and finds grass growing for them all the year round, and water flowing from some celestial spring or other, for I presume, if heaven is heaven, it must be surely what we have loved on earth, a little sublimated. As time went on, gradually Candelario's corporeal image vanished from my mind, for time and toleration are the only solvents nature has placed at our disposal. They, give them time, dissolve everything, even our prejudices.

So Candelario's attitude became more comprehensible to me as time went on, and toleration grew with it. Not for a moment had I ever thought that Candelario branded all these animals out of the love and the affection that he bore to me, still less to increase my welfare and give me what is called in England a status in the land.

For the first time or two, I have no doubt, he did it carelessly, for when a man has a good horse between his thighs, knows he can throw the lazo, and fell opportunity presents itself, it is a hard thing to refrain.

Temptation cometh neither from the east nor from the west, but like the poor, is always with us. Sometimes a bottle and at other times a wench, a title, ribbon, tip for a block of shares, or, best of all, a little cheque discreetly given for imaginary services or future villainy. So, as a general rule, mankind does not put up a very stiff resistance to any form in which temptation manifests itself, but goes down talking, trying to save its face. Moreover, anyone who has been cajoled, trapped or persuaded into any kind of promise, usually looks upon himself more as a victim than as a criminal, when he succumbs to fate.

Promises made to oneself are harder to evade, for all of us are bond slaves to that conceit that makes us think ourselves compounded of some different kaolin to every other man.

Thinking upon a vow I registered eleven years ago (Postume, Postume!), not to write any more short stories, it seems to me that possibly the reflections that I used to cast on Candelario's female ancestry when he broke faith with me, were injudicious and perhaps not fully proven. I fancy now that if we were to ride out together "campeando" animals, and a good-looking orejano was feeding in a glade in a "rincon" beside some river, that I should look at him and set my horse into a gallop with a shout, and in a minute more two raw-hide ropes would settle round the horns.

R B Cunninghame Graham

Redeemed

The great hotel, a cross between a railway station and a Swiss chalet distorted in a dream, magnified and made vulgar beyond the ordinary inartistic vision of mankind, stood up and challenged the stern Alpine scenery.

Snow streaked the mountains that towered behind it, far into the summer, giving an air as of a monstrous iced pudding to the yellow cliffs. The territory in which the caravanserai neared [sic=reared] its spiky roof was all redeemed. Purchased with blood, as every territory, redeemed or otherwise, is purchased from its former owners, when it changes hands. Blood had been shed in every Alpine valley, upon the stony plains, and on the mountain sides.

Blood had purified the flowers. Fumitory, meadow-sweet, hepatica, harebells, prunella, gentian, arnica, and all the infinite sub-alpine flora, from tiny eyebright to rank-growing leopardsbane and viper's bugloss, had been sanctified, baptized in blood. They were all redeemed, and raised their eyes to heaven rejoicing that one national flag had been substituted for another, and that the world had made a step upon the road towards perfection.

Botzen had been altered to Bolzano, Brixen to Bresanone, a melodious change, that perhaps was worth while what it must have cost in bloodshed and in loss of life. Flaxen-haired, stolid little children learned their lessons in a foreign tongue. Throughout the valleys of the district, peasants, brought from Naples and from Sicily, drilled and equipped in shoddy uniforms, had slaughtered peasants equally unbecomingly arrayed, from Austria, Bohemia, Carinthia, and all the kaleidoscopic kingdoms, States, Banats, and Sandjaks of the whilom empire that, someone said, was composed of as many pieces as a patchwork quilt.

These brethren in the faith of Christ, who till the time that they first met in strife had been generally ignorant of each other's existence upon earth, had fought like wolves to redeem or to defend a territory that most of them had never heard of in their lives.

Lousy and footsore, in hunger and in thirst, they had given all they had to give, their blood. As they lay wounded, waiting for death, behind the rocks, in mud-holes and in woods, the birds of prey had picked their eyes out, wolves had gnawed their limbs. Their fellow-sufferers, the gallant horses, still more helpless and more innocent of all offence than they themselves, had suffered the same fate.

In lonely cottages, hundreds of miles away, in the hot rice-fields, amongst the orange-gardens of Trinacria, in lonely Alpine villages, old men and mothers mourned the loss of Hans, Giovanni, Giacomo, and Fritz, who should have ploughed the fields and reaped the crops, but who lay rotting in the mire or shrivelling in the sun.

Generals in uniforms, plastered with bits of ribbon, like a collection of military postage stamps, had received honours of one kind or another for their share in the sorry business. Orators sweating in the sun had worked themselves into an agony of patriotism in the parturition of their perorations, and had been acclaimed by frantic crowds. Parties had fallen, and been replaced by other parties, just as venal as themselves, parties who, till they had got their hands upon the national treasury, had been the foremost advocates of peace, humanity, and justice for mankind. Then they had all turned patriots, except those who had found a better way to fill their pockets, by preaching hatred betwixt man and man.

Even all just or unjust wars must have an ending. So peace, with all its horrors, as the South American General referred to it, in bidding good-bye to his troops after a campaign, descended on the land, and all was as it had been before, but that the flag was changed. Girls still drove cattle to the pastures, and in the village streets old women still sat spinning, whilst mothers searched their children's heads for wonders of the insect world.

The church bells sounded as of yore, calling the faithful to give thanks unto the god of battles, who in his infinite solicitude for their welfare had done so much towards their happiness.

Crocuses peeped out shyly in the spring. Arums unfurled their mottled leaves in damp, shady places. Almond and plum trees displayed their fairy glory in the keen mountain air. The upland pastures became sheets of delicate embroidery, as daisies, buttercups, and speedwell traced their designs upon them, infinite, intricate, yet so inevitable that only nature could have worked so marvellous a sampler.

War had but little raged in the mountain commune, although so many of its sons had fallen in other districts fighting for liberty or in defence of their beloved country from the invader, according to the standard under which they had chanced to be enrolled. Such of the villagers as struggled back, broken in health and mutilated, were looked at more in the light of wretches worthy of compassion, than of heroes. They themselves spoke little of their battles; never of glory or of patriotism, but loved to dwell upon the wonders they had seen, as railways, steamships, and the great cities through which they might have passed.

The village might have slumbered on indefinitely, insanitary, picturesque, and mediæval-looking, with cobbled streets and cow-byres underneath the houses, so that the sweet breath of the animals served to counteract a little the garlic-scented respiration of the Christians who lived above them, had not a tourist from some great centre of progress, culture, charity, art, prostitution, drink, wealth, and poverty happened to pass through the valley on his motor-bicycle. His eye, always cocked like a pointer's ear at game, for any chance to make an honest or dishonest penny, at once took in the natural advantages the place presented for an hotel.

Sheltered from all the winds, except the south, well wooded, and with mountains forming an amphitheatre behind it, the village stood on a little platform that looked out upon the lake.

The climate, mild and equable during the summer, was not too hot for golf or tennis or any of the pastimes that have made men healthy and developed intellect to such a point that Plato, Newton, or Descartes would be quite unremarkable amongst their votaries.

A spring, fetid enough to heal most of the imaginary ailments that afflict people in a high state of culture, had been found by a chamois hunter, the kind of man whom nature and providence usually select as the recipient of their confidences.

Thus all was ready for the fructifying touch of capital — that capital that is a blessing or a curse, according as it happens who possesses it. Lorries and carts soon began to arrive upon the site the syndicate had chosen for the great hotel. Black-coated, supernaturally important-looking men, with measuring tapes and with theodolites, went through their mysteries, tracing out on the ground a plan that looked ridiculously small. Workmen from every portion of the kingdom poured into the valley, and wages rose at once throughout the district. A general federation of amalgamated labour unions was formed. The villagers learned for the first time how miserable they had always been under the tyranny they had not felt, till it was pointed out to them.

Called on to execrate the mayor, the doctor, priest, and the owner of the shop, they always did so at the meetings of the local trades union to which they were called on to subscribe; but being of a gentle, kindly nature, long bound in conventions of a primitive and human polity, when in the streets they met their tyrants they greeted them with their accustomed smiles, took off their hats, and clamoured eagerly to "kuss die hand."

One or two shoddy villas sprang up, owned by the members of the syndicate, and by degrees the villagers became ashamed of their ancestral costume, except those who were enrolled as guides or paid to stand about to keep up local colour in the streets. When the hotel was finished and had been duly opened by the governor of the emancipated district, with the assistance of the bishop of the diocese, who prayed to the Almighty to ward off lightning or inundations from it, to make the hotel a focus of true Christian progress, and prosper it financially, the national flag was duly hoisted over the consecrated edifice. Then the whole village was invited to inspect the premises. Dressed in their homespun clothes, emitting a strong scent of the wool from which they had been made, their hob-nailed shoes skating and sliding upon the slippery floors, they strayed about with open mouths admiring all the specimens of Art Nouveau with which the mansion was adorned.

The imitation Spanish tiles, the callipygic Venuses, holding up torches that stood on each side of the staircase, the fountain with the gold fish swimming about the artificial rocks that lined the basin, the palm-trees in their terra-cotta pots, the lifts, the porter in his uniform, the chambermaids, some of whom came from the village, dressed up in smart new frocks, with muslin aprons, with bows of ribbon of the national colours pinned in appropriate places, the racks of postcards, depicting the quiet Alpine valley, in cobalt, in lemon yellow, and a green so vivid as to almost turn the eye inside out, and all underneath a sun comparable alone to that of San Fernando de Apure, all was fairyland. Being by nature a well-mannered race, they interfered with nothing, but exclamations of Gross-artig, Wonderbahr, Gemütlich, interspersed with Viva il Tuce! Viva l'Idalia! for the tongue of their redemption was not yet quite familiar to them, were heard on every side.

Then they filed out, decorously, and in order, not leaving even a sandwich paper or a broken bottle to mark their passage, as would have happened in lands more civilised. The mildness of the climate, the scenery, and the fame of the spring, now known as La Sorgente del Camoscio, attracted visitors in crowds. Their advent had the usual effect upon the villagers, who rapidly became mere parasites on the hotel. The girls, who formerly had gone about in the rough costumes that their ancestors had worn from the remotest times, now were all shingled, dressed in shoddy imitations of the prevailing fashions, painted and powdered when they could afford it, and not infrequently drifted off to towns to try their luck in the one calling that needs no apprenticeship.

The children carried faded flowers in their hands, and when they saw a stranger they would offer them with a professional little grin that they soon all acquired.

The men made walking-sticks and carved objects out of wood, with which the shops were stocked to overflowing, for all the guests in the hotel, having but little else to do, took away something or another with the name of the village stamped upon it as a souvenir.

Inside the hotel, life went on pretty much as we may suppose it goes on amongst the fish in an aquarium, with the exception that the human specimens were summoned to their meals with greater regularity. All nationalities met on a basis of general futility. Windows were rarely opened, and as the central heating was maintained as piously as the fire of Vesta, a smell as of a monkey-house prevailed, tempered a little by the scent of powder and the perfumes with which the women drenched themselves, although protesting it was quite out of fashion and the last thing that they would use. Americans, English, French, Germans, Italians, and representatives of almost every nation upon earth, vying with one another in their commonness, sat about the great hall of the hotel at little tables, plethoric, scarlet-faced, and semi-torpid after lunch, like anacondas when they have devoured a deer. Palms of the genus Chamærops Hotelensis and Aspidistras, that plant which like the sparrow resists life in conditions that surely nature never intended either for plants or birds to live in, made up a flora fit for the artistic aspirations of the guests.

A jazz band brayed out its cacophonies regardless of the negro rhythm, and only striving to produce the maximum of noise, almost unceasingly, most of the day and night. The lack of rhythm did not inconvenience any of the clients, who jigged and jiggled as long as the musicians discoursed their melodies.

Stout ladies, who had brought their salaried dancing dogs with them, waddled or tottered round the room, gazing up into their victims' faces with a leer.

Half-naked girls squeezed themselves up against rich, tottering old men, as lizards flatten themselves out upon a wall where the sun kisses it. Legs seem disjointed at the knee in the last negro importation from America. Hips waggled just like the rumps of a troop of cattle waggle as a man sees them seated on his horse when they start jogging on the road.

The scene resembled nothing so much as a Candombe danced by our coloured brethren in Colombia or Brazil, but without their abandonment or their lewd joy in life. Photographed by flashlight, it might have been hung up outside a cage of chimpanzees, to show how true man had remained to the primeval type, after a million years.

When once the great glass doors of the hotel had closed upon the servile, yet sniggering servants, and the stench of petrol left behind, the Alpine valley stretched out towards the hills, unspoiled and beautiful. The sunlight played on the dark, yellow cliffs, turning them in the evening into vast braziers. At daybreak as the sun rose, it turned the selfsame cliffs to prisms with a myriad of tints, shrouded and chastened in the white mist that hung like a fine steam about them.

Birds twittered in the trees, and cattle that had slept upon the highest place that they could find amongst the stone-strewn upland pastures, rose lazily to graze. Campion and centaury opened their petals to the dawn after their long night's rest. Spirals of blue smoke ascended from the cottage chimneys, and far away amongst the hills the cow-bells tinkled, and the voices of the herd-boys, raised to an artificial pitch as they talked to each other from one side of the valley to the other, came floating down the breeze.

All seemed idyllic, and like what Eden may have been when animals alone were its inhabitants.

It seemed impossible that so much blood had been poured out to redeem people who required no redemption, but only wished to listen to their lives, as a tree sheds its leaves in autumn and renews them in the spring.

Green hillocks here and there showed where the dead who had fallen fighting had been buried namelessly, without a stone to mark their resting-places. All these redeemers (or redeemed) were as forgotten, as much forgotten, as if they never had been. But, in the little cemetery by the low-eaved church there stood seven wooden crosses rapidly falling into disrepair. One bore the lettering Austrian Soldier, another Unknown German, and a third An Italian, name unknown. The other four had no inscription, save Soldiers, not identified. These seven nameless ones, sleeping in the sweet mountain air, under their mouldering crosses, in the quiet churchyard, enamelled with its Alpine flowers, had achieved their redemption, as it were, unwittingly, sealing it with their blood.

They sleep so soundly, it may well be, that they will never hear the call of the last trump.

Redeemed

Los Llanos del Apure

Man has not staled their wildness, and they still stretch out along the Orinoco, the Apure, and the Arauca to the far-distant Meta, just as they first came from the Creator's hand when on the seventh day He rested from a work that He must surely now and then regret. A very sea of grass and sky, sun-scourged and hostile to mankind. The rivers, full of electric eels, and of caribes, those most ravenous of fish, more terrible than even the great alligators that lie like logs upon the sand-banks or the inert and pulpy rays, with their mortiferous barbed spike, are still more hostile than the land.

In the four hundred years the Llanos have been known to Europeans man has done little more than to endow them with herds of cattle and with bands of half-wild horses and of asses that roam upon them just as their ancestors roamed the steppes of Asia from the remotest times. Islets of stunted palm-trees break the surface of the plains, as the atolls peep up in the Pacific Ocean and also bear their palms. The sun pours down like molten fire for six months of the year, burning the grass up, forcing the cattle to stray leagues away along the river banks, or in the depths of the thick woods. Then come the rains, and the dry, calcined plains are turned into a muddy lake, on which the whilom centaurs of the dry season, paddle long, crank canoes dug from a single log.

The Llanos, with their race of half-amphibious herdsmen, but little differing in features and in hue from their ancestors, the Achagua Indians, have been the scene of great events. They have had their days of glory, when they were almost household words in Europe during the great struggle for the independence of the Spanish Colonies, a hundred years ago. At the Queseras del Medio, by their aid, Páez, Prince of Llaneros, and almost the last good lance that villainous saltpetre has left to history, broke the cavalry of Spain. Out of the woods, sheltered behind the smoke of the dry grass they had set on fire, the saddleless, wild horsemen, half-naked, with but a rag or two tied round their bodies by a thong of hide, swooped on the uniformed, drilled, disciplined, brave, heavy-handed

Spanish troopers, like the riders of the Valkyrie. Páez, himself as wild and savage in those days as any of his men, rode at their head upon a half-tamed colt. Those were not days of tactics, for personal prowess, perhaps for the last time in history, ruled everything. It must have been a glorious sight to see their charge, the flying hair, the tossing manes and tails, the dust, the shrill screams of the attacking horsemen, the answering shouts of "Viva España" of the Spanish troops, the frightened taotacos whirling above them uttering their harsh note, while in the sky the vultures sailed aloft, like specks against the sapphire blue, knowing a banquet was being set for them. To-day the Llanos that furnished the troops with which Páez so ably seconded Bolívar in his long fight for independence are almost depopulated. No one seems to know the cause.

Though much of the population has gone, enough remains to herd the cattle, the vast Llanos' only wealth. Unlike the Gauchos and the Mexicans, the Roman Butari, the Arabs of North Africa, the Western cowboy (before fell cinemas made a puppet of him), any old saddle, any clothes, content the dweller on the plains of the Apure. His horse is almost always thin, often sore-backed, and always looks uncared for, while the ungainly pace at which he rides, a shambling "pasitrote," or tied camel waddle, moving both feet on the same side at once, deprives him of all grace. Still few can equal, none excel, him for endurance. Nothing daunts him, neither the peril of the rivers, with all their enemies to mankind ever awake, to tear or numb the unlucky horseman who may come near their fangs or their electrically charged bodies, or any other danger either by flood and field. He, of all wielders of the raw-hide noose, alone secures it, not to the saddle, but to his horse's tail, fishing for, rather than lassoing a steer, playing it like a salmon with a rope a hundred feet in length, instead of bringing it up with a smart jerk, after the fashion of the Argentines or Mexicans. Abominably slow and tedious in his methods to the eyes of commentators; still it is never wise, in matters of such deep import, to criticise or to condemn customs that use and wont have consecrated.

If the Llaneros have changed outwardly, the Llano has remained the same. No puffing steam engine or petrol-reeking car defile [sic] its surface. Diligences it has never had, and the sole method for a caballero when he wants to traverse it is on a horse. Some indeed may have ridden mules. Camels and asses, with llamas, yaks, bullocks, and buffaloes, no doubt can carry man upon their backs, but on the horse alone can he be truly said to ride. So the Llanero still rides the Llano on his pacing horse, the reins held high, the stirrups dangling from his naked toe, his eyes fixed on the horizon, as a sailor, on his watch, looks out across the sea. The mirage still hangs castles in the air and cheats the eye in the terrific heat with pools of water, always just out of touch, as happiness is ever out of reach in life. The Promised Land is always a day's march ahead of us.

Unchanging and unchanged, the Llanos swelter in the sun as they first sweltered at the creation of the world, and as La Puebla saw them in the expedition that Maestre Diego Albeniz de la Cerrada describes, he who wrote, as it were in a mirage, his observation so minute, his gift of artistry so great, and with his dates, and trifles of that nature, all awry. So distant are the Llanos from our vainglorious, noisy, and evil-smelling civilisation, as to be almost unaware that such a thing exists. They await the coming of the thing called progress, just as a girl may dream about her marriage night without exactly knowing what it means.

Meanwhile, through palm woods looking exactly like those of the Argentine Gran Chaco, through jungle and through woods, in dust, in rain, under a sun that blisters, if you touch an iron stirrup, the post of the republic carried in canvas bags on two grey mules accompanied by an apocalyptic horse, trails wearily across the plains. If in their pilgrimage the mules, the old white horse, and the dark half-breeds chance to light on a Velorio, or a wedding at a rancho on the road, they join in it, for after all to-morrow is another day, and time is certainly not money, under the rule of him whose fellow-citizens style "El Benemerito."

Even the garden by the Tigris could hardly have been fairer or more bird-haunted than the banks of the Apure, with its myriads of egrets making the trees as white as is a northern wood after a fall of snow. Legions of aquatic birds as black as jet sweep down the rivers in battalions, succeeding one another as if some feathered general was marshalling them to fight.

Flocks of flamingos rise from the waters, as Aphrodite rose up from the waves, rosy and beautiful. Piero di Cosimo alone could have dealt with them in paint, and if the painter of the "Death of Procris" had but visited the Apure, among his pelicans, his flamingos, and his swans, he would have placed new species, as fit to grace his theme and far more gorgeous than the birds of the old world. In the freshness of the dawn, when a white mist bathes all the woods upon the rivers in a thin vaporous haze through which the trees show faintly, as a rich purple or green burnous tinges the fleecy whiteness of an Arab's haik, nature exults in the new birth of day.

The Llano for a brief moment turns to a tender green and stretches out like an interminable fresh field of corn. From the recesses of the woods along the river banks comes the harsh screaming of the parrots, and birds and insects raise their morning hymn of praise. Stilled are the voices of the prowling animals of prey, insistent during night. The jaguar no longer snarls, or whets his teeth against the tree trunks. The red, howling monkeys start their chorus, sounding as if a lion was raging in the everglades, and the shy tapir after a night passed feeding on the sedges and the grass swims to his lair, his head and back just showing, like a river horse, leaving a silvery trail behind him to mark his silent passage through the stream. Wild cattle troop back to the woods, before the vaqueros intercept them with their swift horses and their unerring noose.

Without an interval of crepuscule, the sun rises at once fierce, fiery, and inexorable, streaking the sky with rays of orange and of scarlet for an instant, then bursts upon the world like a fell enemy before whom fly all living things except the saurians, who bask somnolently upon the sand-banks, immune against his rays. Just at the break of dawn fish leap in shoals into the air, making the water boil, their silvery bodies for a moment springing like crescent moons into the air and falling with a splash into the deep. His well-greased lazo ready coiled in front of his right knee, his brown, bare toes sticking out through his alpargatas, clutching the light Llanero stirrup with its crown-like prolongation underneath the foot, the Llanero scans the horizon as his horse paces rapidly along, leaving a well-marked trail upon the dewy grass. He sits so loosely in the saddle that one would think if his horse shied it must unseat him, but that he also shies. High on his vaquero saddle, so straight and upright that a plummet dropped from his shoulder would touch his heel, he reads the Llano like a book.

Nothing escapes his sight, as keen as that of his Achagua Indian ancestors. Signs on the ground, almost undiscernible, he marks. If his horse, trippling along at its artificial gait, stumbles or pecks, he curses it, objurgating its female ancestry, gives it a sharp pull with the bit, digs in his spurs, interrupts for a moment the interminable "galeron" that he is crooning in a low voice, and pointing with his whip says, "Three horses passed along here early in the night. One is the big cream colour that always strays, for he is a little lame in the off hind foot, see where he has stepped short upon it." With an unerring eye he sights a steer with a strange brand. "That is one of General Atilio Pacheco's animals," he says, and turning to his companion, smiling, remarks, "If he stays too long in these parts he may stay for ever, for God is not a bad man, anyhow."

As the sun rises higher in the heavens, the light distorting everything, magnifying or diminishing, according as its rays are refracted, dried tufts of grass appear as large as clumps of canes, and animals on the horizon as small as turkey buzzards. Then the vaquero heads for home, after assuring himself that no bullock has been killed by a tiger in the night, or has got wounded from any cause and requires treatment to prevent maggots from breeding in the wound. Clouds of dust rise on the horizon. The morning breeze dies out entirely during the hottest hours, and the plain shimmers in the heat. Bancos and mesas, those curious sand formations that intersect the Llanos like striations in a rock, give back refracted heat to meet the heat descending from above. All nature groans. Only the lizards and iguanas seem to revel in it. Homing vaqueros, their "pelo de Guama" hats coal-scuttled fore and aft against the enemy, lounge in their saddles. Their horses plod along, with drooping heads, too weary even to swish their tails against the flies. At the straw-thatched houses the riders get off with a sigh and seek the shade of the "caney."

As the heat waxes and the air quivers as if it came from some interior furnace, a deathly silence broods upon the plains. A sense of solitude creeps over everything, as if the world had been consumed by some unlooked-for cataclysm that had destroyed mankind. The weary horses, who endure the burden of their lives either parched with thirst, or forced to live a half-amphibious life during the periodical inundations, exposed year in, year out, to the perpetual torment of mosquitoes, horse-flies, ticks and all the "plagas" of the insect world, with the off-chance of sudden death from the fangs of tiger or caiman, seek shelter where they can, under the scanty foliage of the Moriche palms. Cattle have long ago retired as far as possible into the reedy swamps. Nothing is stirring; not a sound breaks the afflicted silence of the sun-cursed plain, but the perpetual calling "Oh, ah ho" of the small, speckled doves. Gradually the heat decreases, a breeze springs up, and nature, after her long struggle with the sun, revives.

The animals, who have passed the hot hours under whatever shade that they could find, recommence eating and birds show signs of life.

Parrots scream harshly. Flights of macaws, yellow and red and blue, the great white patches round their eyes making them look as if they all wore spectacles, soar like particoloured hawks, uttering their croaking cry. The interval of freshness is all too brief, for night falls without twilight on the Llanos; and the sun dips down under the horizon just as he does at sea.

Before the darkness closes in, flights of birds migrate towards the woods, fire-flies dart to and fro among the dark metallic leaves of the jungle fringing the river, and from the recesses of the forests the nightly chorus of the wild animals, silent through the day, breaks out. Then comes the miracle; the miracle of miracles, unknown to those who have not journeyed on those interminable steppes or sailed upon the Apure or the Orinoco. No words can paint the infinite gradation of the scale of colour that leaves the spectroscope lacking a shade or two. Green turns to mauve, then back to green again; to scarlet, orange, and vermilion, flinging the flag of Spain across the sky. Dark coffee-coloured bars, shooting across a sea of carmine, deepen to black; the carmine melts into pale grey. Castles and pyramids spring up; they turn to cities; the pyramids to broken arches, waterfalls, and ships, with poops like argosies. Gradually pale apple-green floods all the heaven; then it fades into jade. Castles and towns and ships and broken arches disappear. The sun sinks in a globe of fire, leaving the world in mourning for its death.

Then comes the after-glory, when all the colours that have united, separated, blended and broken up, unite and separate again, and once more blend. A sheet of flame, that for an instant turns the Apure into a streak of molten metal, bathes the Llano in a bath of fire, fades gradually and dies, just where the plain and sky appear to join as if the grass was all aglow.

Animula Vagula

"You see," the Orchid-hunter said, "this is just how it happened; one of those deaths, that I have seen so many of, here in the wilderness."

He stood upon the steamer's deck a slight, grave figure, his hair just touched with grey, his flannel Norfolk jacket, which had once been white, toning exactly with his hat and his grey eyes.

At first sight you saw he was an educated man, and when you spoke to him you felt he must have been at some great public school. Yet there was something indefinable about him that spoke of failure. We have no word to express with sympathy the moral qualities of such a man. In Spanish it is all summed up in the expression, "Un infeliz." Unlucky or unhappy, that is, as the world goes; but perhaps fortunate in that interior world to which so many eyes are closed.

Rolling a cigarette between his thin, brown, fever-stricken fingers, he went on: "Yesterday, about two o'clock, in a heat fit to boil your brain, a canoe came slowly up the stream into the settlement. The Indian paddlers walked up the steep bank carrying the body of a man wrapped in a mat. When they had reached the little palm-thatched hut over which floated the Colombian flag, that marked it as the official residence of the Captain of the Port, they set their burden down with the hopeless look that marks the Indian, as of an orphaned angel.

" 'We found this "Mister" on the banks,' they said, 'in the last stage of fever. He spoke but little Christian, and all he said was, "Doctor, American doctor, Tocatalaima; take me there."

" 'Here he is, and now who is to pay us for our work? We have paddled all night long. The canoe we borrowed. Its owner said that it gains twenty cents a day, and we want forty cents each, for we have paddled hard to save this Mister.' Then they stood silent, scratching the mosquito bites upon their ankles with the other naked foot—a link between the *Homo sapiens* and some other intermediate species, long extinct.

"I paid them, giving them something over what they demanded, and they put on that expression of entire aloofness which the Indian usually assumes on such occasions, either because thanks stick in his gullet, or he thinks no thanks are due after a service rendered. They then went off to drink a glass or two of rum before they started on their journey home.

"I went to see the body, which lay covered with a sack under a little shed. Flies buzzed about it, and already a faint smell of putrefaction reminded one that man is as the other animals, and that the store of knowledge he piles up during his life does not avail to stop the course of Nature, any more than if he had been an orang-outang."

He paused, and, after having lit the cigarette, strolled to the bulwark of the steamer, which had now got into the middle of the stream, and then resumed:

"Living as I do in the woods collecting orchids, the moralising habit grows upon one. It is, as it were, the only answer that a man has to the aggressiveness of Nature.

"I stood and looked at the man's body in his thin linen suit which clung to every angle. Beside him was a white pith helmet, and a pair of yellow-tinted spectacles framed in celluloid to look like tortoiseshell, that come down from the States. I never wear them, for I find that everything that you can do without is something gained in life.

"His feet in his white canvas shoes all stained with mud sticking up stiffly and his limp, pallid hands, crossed by the pious Indians, on his chest gave him that helpless look that makes a dead man, as it were, appeal to one for sympathy and protection against the terror, that perhaps for him is not a terror after all; but merely a long rest.

"No one had thought of closing his blue eyes; and as we are but creatures of habit after all, I put my hand into my pocket, and taking out two half-dollar pieces was about to put them on his eyes. Then I remembered that one of them was bad, and you will not believe me, but I could not put the bad piece on his eyes; it looked like cheating him. So I went out and got two little stones, and after washing them put them upon his eyelids, and at least they kept away the flies.

"I don't know how it was, for I believe I am not superstitious, but it seemed to me that those blue eyes, sunk in the livid face to which a three or four days' growth of fair and fluffy beard gave a look of adolescence, looked at me as if they still were searching for the American doctor, who no doubt must have engrossed his last coherent thought as he lay in the canoe.

"As I was looking at him, mopping my face, and now and then killing a mosquito — one gets to do it quite mechanically, although in my case neither mosquitoes nor any other kind of bug annoys me very much — the door was opened and the authorities came in. After the usual salutations — which in Colombia are long and ceremonious, with much unnecessary offering of services, which both sides know will never be required — they said they came to view the body and take the necessary steps; that is, you know, to try to find out who he was and have him buried, for which, the heat at forty centigrade, no time was to be lost.

"A stout Colombian dressed in white clothes, which made his swarthy skin look darker still, giving him, as it were, the air of a black beetle dipped in milk, was the first to arrive. Taking off his flat white cap and gold-rimmed spectacles — articles which in Colombia are certain signs of office — he looked a little at the dead man and said, 'He was an English or American.' Then turning to a soldier who had arrived upon the scene, he asked him where the Indian paddlers were who had brought in the canoe.

"The man went out to look for them, and the hut soon was crowded full of Indians, each with his straw hat held up before his mouth. They gazed upon the body, not sympathetically, nor yet unsympathetically, but with that baffling look that Indians must have put on when first the conquerors appeared amongst them and they found out their arms did not avail them for defence. By means of it they pass through life as relatively unscathed as it is possible for men to do, and by its help they seem to conquer death, taking away its sting, by their indifference.

"None of them said a word, but stared at the dead man, just as they stare at any living stranger, until I felt that the dead eyes would turn in anger at them and shake off the flat stones.

"The man clothed in authority and dusky white returned, accompanied by one of those strange out-at-elbows nondescripts who are to be found in every town in South America, and may be best described as 'penmen'— that is, persons who can read and write and have some far-off dealings with the law. After a whispered conversation the Commissary, turning to the assembled Indians, asked them in a brief voice if they had found the paddlers of the canoe. None of them answered, for a crowd of Indians will never find a spokesman, as each one fears to be made responsible if he says anything at all. A dirty soldier clothed in draggled khaki, barefooted, and with a rusty, sheathless bayonet banging on his thigh, opened the door and said that he knew where they were, but that they both were drunk. The soldier, after a long stare, would have retreated, but the Commissary, turning abruptly to him, said: 'José, go and see that a grave is dug immediately; this "Mister" has been dead for several hours.' Then looking at the 'penman,' 'Perez,' he said, 'we will now proceed to the examination of the dead man's papers which the law prescribes.'

"Perez, who in common with the majority of the uneducated of his race had a great dread of touching a dead body, began to search the pockets of the young man lying so still and angular in the drab-looking suit of white. To put off the dread moment he picked up the pith helmet and, turning out the lining, closely examined it. Then, finding nothing, in his agitation let it fall upon the chest of the dead man. I could have killed him, but said nothing, and we all stood perspiring, with the thermometer at anything you like inside that wretched hut, while Perez fumbled in the pockets of the dead man's coat.

"It seemed to me as if the unresisting body was somehow being outraged, and that the stiff, attenuated arms would double up and strike the miserable Perez during his terrifying task. He was so clumsy and so frightened that it seemed an eternity till he produced a case of worn, green leather edged with silver, in which were several brown Havana cigarettes.

"The Commissary gravely remarking, 'We all have vices, great or small, and smoking is but a little frailty,' told Perez to write down 'Case, 1; cigarettes, 3,' and then to go on with the search. 'The law requires,' he said, 'the identification of all the dead wherever possible.

" 'First, for its proper satisfaction in order that the Code of the Republic should be complied with; and, secondly, for the consolation of the relations, if there are any such, or the friends of the deceased.'

"Throughout the search the Indians stood in a knot, like cattle standing under a tree in summer-time, gathered together, as it were, for mutual protection, without uttering a word. The ragged soldier stared intently; the Commissary occasionally took off his spectacles and wiped them; and the perspiring Perez slowly brought out a pocket-knife, a box of matches, and a little bottle of quinine. They were all duly noted down, but still no pocket-book, card-case, letter, or any paper with the name of the deceased appeared to justify the search. Perez would willingly have given up the job; but, urged on by his chief, at last extracted from an interior pocket a letter-case in alligator skin. Much frayed and stained with perspiration, yet its silver tips still showed that it had once been bought at a good shop.

" 'Open it, Perez, for the law allows one in such cases to take steps that otherwise would be illegal and against that liberal spirit for which we in this Republic are so renowned in the Americas. Then hand me any card or letter that it may contain.'

"Perez, with the air of one about to execute a formidable duty, opened the case, first slipping off a couple of elastic bands that held the flaps together. From it he took a bundle of American bank-notes wrapped up in tissue-paper, which he handed to his chief. The Commissary took it, and, slipping off the paper, solemnly counted the notes. 'The sum is just two thousand,' he remarked, 'and all in twenties. Perez, take note of it, and give me any papers that you may have found.' A closer search of every pocket still revealed nothing, and I breathed more freely, as every time the dirty hands of Perez fumbled about the helpless body I felt a shudder running down my back.

"We all stood baffled, and the Indians slowly filed out without a word, leaving the Commissary with Perez and myself standing bewildered by the bed. ' "Mister," ' the Commissary said to me; 'what a strange case! Here are two thousand dollars, which should go to some relation of this unfortunate young man.'

"He counted them again, and, after having given them to his satellite, told him to take them and put them in his safe.

" 'Now, "Mister," I will leave you here to keep guard over your countryman whilst I go out to see if they have dug his grave. There is no priest here in the settlement. We only have one come here once a month; and even if there were a priest, the dead man looks as if he had been Protestant.'

"He turned to me, and saying, 'With your permission,' took his hat and left the hut.

"Thus left alone with my compatriot (if he had been one), I took a long look at him, so as to stamp his features in my mind. I had no camera in my possession, and cannot draw — a want that often hinders me in my profession in the description of my rarer plants.

"I looked so long that if the man I saw lying upon that canvas scissor-bed should ever rise again with the same body, I am certain I could recognise him amongst a million men.

"His hands were long and thin, but sunburnt, his feet well shaped, and though his face was sunken and the heat was rapidly discolouring it, the features were well cut. I noted a brown mark upon the cheek, such as in Spanish is called a 'lunar,' which gave his delicate and youthful face something of a girlish look, in spite of his moustache. His eyebrows, curiously enough, were dark, and the incipient growth of beard was darker than his hair. His ears were small and set on close to the head — a sign of breeding — and his eyes, although I dared not look at them, having closed them up myself, I knew were blue, and felt they must be staring at me, underneath the stones. In life he might have weighed about ten stone I guess, not more, and must have been well-made and active, though not an athlete, I should think, by the condition of his hands.

"Strangely enough, there seemed to me nothing particularly sad about the look of him. He just was resting after the struggle, that could have lasted in his case but little more than thirty years, and had left slight traces on his face of anything that he had suffered when alive.

"I took the flat stones off his eyes, and was relieved to find they did not open, and after smoothing his fair hair down a little and taking a long look at the fast-altering features I turned away to smoke.

"How long I waited I cannot recollect, but all the details of the hut, the scissor canvas bed on which the body lay, the hooks for hammocks in the mud-and-bamboo walls, the tall brown jar for water, like those that one remembers in the pictures of the *Arabian Nights* in childhood, the drinking gourd beside it, with the two heavy hardwood chairs of ancient Spanish pattern, seated and backed with pieces of raw hide, the wooden table, with the planks showing the marks of the adze that fashioned them, I never shall forget.

"Just at the door there was an old canoe, dug out of a tree-trunk, the gunwale broken and the inside almost filled up with mud. Chickens, of that peculiar mangy-looking breed indigenous to every tropic the whole world over, were feeding at one end of it, and under a low shed thatched with soft palm-leaves stood a miserable horse, whose legs were raw owing to the myriads of horseflies that clustered on them, which no one tried to brush away. Three or four vultures sat on a branch of a dead tree that overhung the hut. Their languid eyes appeared to me to pierce the palm-tree roof as they sat on, just as a shark follows a boat in which there is a dead man, waiting patiently.

"Over the bluff, on which the wretched little Rancheria straggled till it was swallowed up in the primeval woods, flowed the great river, majestic, yellow, alligator-haunted, bearing upon its ample bosom thousands of floating masses of green vegetation which had slipped into the flood.

"How long I sat I do not know, and I shall never know, but probably not above half an hour. Still, in that time I saw the life of the young man who lay before me. His voyage out; the first sight of the tropics; the landing into that strange world of swarthy-coloured men, dank vegetation, thick, close atmosphere, the metallic hum of insects, and the peculiar smell of a hot country — things which we see and hear once in our lives, and but once only, for custom dulls the senses, and we see nothing more. Then the letters home, simple and child-like in regard to life, but shrewd and penetrating as regards business, after the fashion of the Northern European or his descendants in the United States.

"I saw him pass his first night in the bare tropical hotel, under a mosquito-curtain, and then wake up to all the glory of the New World he had discovered for himself, as truly as Columbus did when he had landed upon Guanahani on that eventful Sunday morning and unfurled the flag of Spain. I heard him falter out his first few words in broken Spanish, and saw him take his first walk, either by the harbour, thronged with its unfamiliar-looking boats piled up with fish and fruits unknown in Europe, or through the evil-smelling, badly-paved alleys in the town.

"The voyage up the river, with the first breath of the asphyxiating heat; the flocks of parrots; the alligators, so like dead logs, all basking in the sun; the stopping in the middle of the night for wood beside some landing-place cut in the jungle, where men, naked but for a cloth tied round their loins, ran up a plank and dumped their load down with a half-sigh, half-yell — I saw and heard it all. Then came the arrival at the mine or rubber station, the long and weary days, the fevers, the rare letters, and the cherished newspapers from home — those, too, I knew of, for I had waited for them often in my youth.

"Most of all, as I looked on him and saw his altering features, I thought of his snug home in Massachusetts or Northumberland, where his relations looked for letters on thin paper, with the strange postmarks, which would never come again. How they would wonder in his home, and here was I looking at the features that they would give the world to see, but impotent to help."

He stopped, and, walking to the bulwarks, looked up the river, and said: "In half an hour we shall arrive at San Fulgencio. . . . They came and fetched the body, and wrapped it in a white cotton sheet —for which I paid — and we set off, followed by the few storekeepers, two Syrians and a Portuguese, and a small crowd of Indians.

"There was no cemetery — that is to say, not one of those Colombian cemeteries fenced with barbed wire, in which the plastered gateway looks like an afterthought, and where the iron crosses blistering in the sun look drearier than any other crosses in the world.

"Under a clump of Guáduas — that is the name they give to the bamboo — there was a plot of ground fenced in with canes. In it the grave was dug amongst some others, on which a mass of grass and weeds was growing, as if it wished to blot them out from memory as soon as possible.

"A little wooden cross or two, with pieces of white paper periodically renewed, affirmed that Resurrecion Venegas or Exaltacion Machuca reposed beneath the weeds.

"The grave looked hard and uninviting, and as we laid him in it, lowering him with a rope made of lianas, two or three macaws flew past, uttering a raucous cry.

"The Commissary had put on a black suit of clothes, and Perez had a rusty band of cloth pinned round his arm. The Syrians and the Portuguese took off their hats, and as there was no priest the Commissary mumbled some formula; and I, advancing to the grave, took a last look at the white sheet which showed the angles of the frail body underneath it, but for the life of me I could not say a word, except 'Good-bye.'

"When the Indians had filled in the earth we all walked back towards the settlement perspiring. I took a glass of rum with them, just for civility . . . I think I paid for it . . . and then I gathered up my traps and sat and waited under a big Bongo-tree until the steamer came along."

A silence fell upon us all, as sitting in our rocking-chairs upon the high deck of the stern-wheel steamer, we mused instinctively upon the fate of the unknown young Englishman, or American. The engineer from Oregon, the Texan cow-puncher going to look at cattle in the Llanos de Bolivar, and all the various waifs and strays that get together upon a voyage up the Magdalena, no doubt each thought he might have died, just as the unknown man had died, out in the wilderness.

No one said anything, until the orchid-hunter, as the steamer drew into the bank, said: "That is San Fulgencio. I go ashore here. If any of you fellows ever find out who the chap was, send us a line to Barranquilla; that's where my wife lives.

"I am just off to the Choco, a three or four months' job. . . . Fever? — oh, yes, sometimes, of course, but I think nothing of it. . . .Quinine? —

thanks, yes, I've got it. . . . I don't believe in it a great deal. . . Mosquitoes?
— no, they do not worry me. A gun? — well, no, I never carry arms . . .
thanks all the same. . . . I was sorry, too, for that poor fellow; but, after
all, it is the death I'd like to die myself. . . . No, thanks, I don't care for
spirits. . . . Good-bye to all of you."

We waved our hands and crowded on the steamer's side, and watched
him walking up the bank to where a little group of Indians stood holding
a bullock with a pack upon its back.

They took his scanty property and, after tying it upon the ox, set off
at a slow walk along a little path towards the jungle, with the grey figure
of our late companion walking quietly along, a pace or two behind.

Redeemed

Wilfrid Scawen Blunt

Right in the middle of a ride cut in the woods, a ride he must have shot and ridden over a thousand times, under a great grass mound, looking like an ancient tumulus of some prehistoric chief, sleeps Wilfrid Blunt.

Sweet chestnuts, birches, and scrub-oak trees fringe the ride. Under their branches is a row of yew-trees, planted by himself. In future years, when they are tall and dark, they will stand sentinels in a long line on each side of the grave, and in the winter nights the owls will sit amongst their branches, calling and answering one another, a nightly threnody.

Thistles and tufts of campion, dog's mercury, and enchanter's nightshade grow so thickly that they carpet all the grass. Rabbits limp noiselessly across the open ride; in the keen east wind the autumn leaves shiver down, mottled and red and golden yellow; silence broods over the whole wood, although the house is not three hundred yards away.

After his agitated life, in which he played so many parts, sculptor and poet, traveller, lover, politician, diplomat, and man of fashion, and at the last a Sussex squire, loving the trees, the speech and people of his native place above all things on earth, he lies at rest.

The old-world Jacobean house with its yew hedges, paths of broken flags, and steps that lead to the front door, between whose crevices spring tufts of ragweed, garlanded by a thick growth of traveller's joy clinging to the balustrade, is empty and forlorn; but over all, in everything, still lingers and will linger many a day the traces of his strange, complex personality. So that, although the shrine is empty, the spirit haunts it, and, after all the spirit, not the body of the saint, makes the shrine sacred to the true adept.

So strong is the impression of the vanished owner stamped, that when you see the old familiar objects hanging in the stone hall, the peacock's skin, the Arab saddle bags, the lazo and the bolas, the mameluke bits, and the great brass coffee-pots disposed about the walls, it seems impossible that in the panelled room you will not see the figure of the squire dressed in his Arab clothes, his full white beard spread like a Viking's on his chest, reading a ponderous tome in vellum, seated by a fire of logs piled in a Sussex grate.

The Morris tapestry, the great oak tables, the newelled staircase with its door across the landing, the priest's secret chamber, the prints of horses, horses, and still more horses, from the Godolphin Arab down to his own Mesaud, hang on the walls.

All is unchanged; the Darnley [*sic* = *Darley*] Arab, and the spotted Polish stallion, with the old French print of the execution of the spy, who puts aside his dog with his left hand to save it from the bullets, a print on which its owner never looked without a pang, they all are there.

The thick yew hedges, and the Attar roses growing between old lines of box in the walled garden outside the dining-room, and the innumerable weather-boarded sheds and barns that cluster round the house, seem full of something that is no longer there, yet still pervades the atmosphere as strongly as in life.

If in all England there is a house that is the embodiment of him who owned it, the little Jacobean mansion with its lichened walls, its stone-slabbed roof, its air as of a camp, inside, and outside, of an age when men built slowly, to please the eye and to defy the assaults of time, Newbuildings is the place.

The piles of Arab blankets in the corners of the rooms, the newest books and magazines upon the tables, speak of a man who touched life at a hundred points. Although so various, still at the core a country gentleman, a mighty lover of good horses, and breeding many of them from his famed Arab stud, yet not a country gentleman who brought London to the country after the modern way, but one who lived much as his forefathers lived for generations back.

Withal, as Easterns say, a great protector of the poor; not over much concerned about their rights, but sympathising heartily with their wrongs and with their poverty. Amongst the mass of mediocrities that constitute, have constituted, and will for ever constitute mankind, unless there is a new creation conceived upon a different plan, he moved amongst his fellow-men, somewhat aloof and unapproachable, lashing their base ambitions with a steel whip, and yet with many a foible of his own, for without weaknesses no man can be strong.

Born out of his generation, as are the most of men who achieve anything but mere material success, he yet was a true Englishman, a very Englishman of the Elizabethan breed, with something in him of the

Renaissance in his love of sport and culture, a combination rare to-day, for now the sportsman is so often nothing but a sportsman, the man of culture nothing but a prig.

Science, as manifested in the power to take a good, dull man by air to Baghdad and bring him back again an ignoramus still, with but the local ulcer in his cheek to show for it, left him, I fancy, all unmoved.

Culture to him, as to the Orientals, with whom he lived so much and sympathised so deeply, was an affair of spirit and of mind not to be measured by material progress, or, even by the arts. An Arab with his simple life, his scanty fare of dates and coarse bread toasted on the embers, and his perpetual speculations on the attributes of God, was a far greater object of his admiration than is the modern plutocrat, living in luxury and paying thousands for a picture that he is ordered to admire, without a thought beyond materialism.

He held the greater portion of the ills to which humanity is heir are irremediable, and that the best mankind can do is to endure them silently, trusting in Allah's mercy and compassion, without expecting that he will alter nature's laws on our behoof.

No man was ever less a Pagan or a Hellenist than was this cultured English gentleman, with his love of adventure and his deep sympathy for the oppressed in every portion of the world.

In type of body and of mind he was essentially a northerner, except that he detested compromise, so dear to northerners, as fervently as any member of the Latin race.

Bread was bread, verily, to him, and wine was wine; the two could never mix their essences and become the hotch-potch dear to politicians, and hence the secret of his aloofness from our public life, failure to comprehend it, and its amazement at his attitude. At the same time, there never lived a man more fitted to enjoy and understand all that was best in English country life, for he loved hospitality, enjoyed a gallop on the downs, or a hot corner in the woods, as much as any chuckle-headed Sussex squire of the whole neighbourhood. I cannot see him seated on the bench at Quarter Sessions; but if he ever went there I am sure his sympathies were with the poachers and the tramps, being himself a sportsman and a super-tramp, taking the whole world as his beat.

Something there was of the Old Testament in his mental bias, either inherited or perhaps superinduced by his long intercourse with the Arabs, the most biblical of men.

Thus in the fine old house plenished with Chippendale and Jacobean furniture, devoid of most of the appliances of modern life, surrounded by his slow-witted Sussex dependents, who all adored him, seeing his real kindness of heart beneath a somewhat stern exterior, he seemed a paradox.

His quiet surroundings, the unbroken calm in the old, solitary house, disturbed but by the cooing of the fantail pigeons in the yard as they sat sunning themselves before their doors in the barrel stuck up on a pole, the smell of elder flowers that the breeze now and then wafted through open windows (scawen, he used to say, was Cornish for an elder), all spoke of rural England, that rural England that has almost disappeared. It was his pride to keep the old-world air about his mansion-house, although his thoughts must have so often wrapped him in the travellers' melancholy, and now and then he must have wished to feel the sun burning between his shoulders, to hear the gurgling of the kneeling camels and the shrill neighing of the horses, tethered and picketed.

If he occasionally let his thoughts stray towards the East and longed to smell the acrid scent of the camp-fire of camels' dung, he kept his counsel, for no man ever wore his heart less on his sleeve than he did, knowing the world is full of jackdaws, and that when hearts lie open, they delight to peck at them.

Still to his house there came a never-ending string of pilgrims, Arabs and Persians, Turks, Indians, and all sorts and kinds more or less materialised dwellers in Mesopotamia, generally each with his tale of woe and of oppression, real or fancied, and all with open palms.

Long hours he listened to them, for he was surely born in Tarshish in the next house to the Apostle of the Gentiles, suffering fools, if not gladly, at least patiently, and, I imagine, dealing out largesse with an unsparing hand.

If he believed all that they told him is difficult to say; but possibly his passion for the liberty of down-trodden nationalities, and his hatred of imperialism, sometimes rendered him their prey.

Certain it is that almost all that he foretold in regard to the East thirty or forty years ago, has become justified by events.

His was a voice as of a Cassandra prophesying in the wilderness, in the days when he warned England that Egypt would be free, that Ireland would become a nation, and that our Indian Empire was seething with revolt.

Had he been listened to, the measures that have been wrung from us by force would have been graciously bestowed; but then who looks for vision in a statesman or a man of business and does not find himself deceived?

Little by little he withdrew from public life, leaving a world that had not understood him, and that he himself had often failed to understand, for your keen intellect and piercing vision often betray their owner, making him see the mirage floating in the air so clearly that he fails to catch the string of camels plodding laboriously through the sand, as his eye dwells on the castles and the towers so soon to be dissolved.

Sussex eventually claimed him for its own, and though his active mind was always occupied with Eastern politics, his stud and his estate, the welfare of his tenants and all the engrossing details of a country life enmeshed him, as they always have enmeshed men of his class and race in their declining years.

His house became, as it were, a place of pilgrimage to which young poets, rising politicians, breeders of Arab horses coming from many lands, and his old friends resorted, to revel in his pungent conversation, receive advice, to buy a horse occasionally and to be received with the large hospitality worthy of one who had been so long a dweller in the tents.

No man gave forth more freely of the best he had at his command, and years and travel, with an enormous store of miscellaneous reading, had made his mind a very granary of recondite information that he was always ready to impart.

Modest about his own achievements, to the point that few of his old friends had ever heard of the recumbent statue of his brother wrought with his own hands, in Crawley Priory, he seldom talked about his Eastern journeys except to intimates, and even then quite unassumingly. Time will do him justice, for time alone holds a judicial scale between a man and the warped judgments of his contemporaries.

His weaknesses will be forgotten. Your petty minds only see petty objects. Genius is far beyond their purview.

Fame surely will reserve a niche for the tall figure in its Arab clothes, that for so many years moved through the panelled rooms in the old Jacobean house, pausing to take a book up now and then, or to adjust a bunch of the many-coloured asters in which he took such pride, and always followed by a Blenheim spaniel or by a King Charles.

His pilgrimage is over, all his activities are stilled. His love of justice and the clear vision he enjoyed into the causes of events that have of late shaken all England to the core, will be remembered, and his *Love Sonnets* take their just place beside the works of the long line of English makers whose names are chronicled in gold.

Now in the Sussex earth that he so loved he rests in his last camp. In the long ride in the deep woods winds stir the trees: the sun pours down in summer, and in the winter the snow spreads its mantle on the grass. It is all as he wished it should be, for it would please him if he knew that in the moonlight rabbits came out to play around his grave, and that the owls fly silently over his resting-place and light upon the trees as noiselessly as snowflakes light upon the ground.

If there are things we shall remember after we are dead, as he himself sang in his verses on the Pampa, he will remember these. His Eastern wanderings, the strife of politics, his agitated life with all its friendships and its bickerings will fade away; but as he lies face upwards to the stars, he will remember, perhaps perceive, with some new sense unknown to those who labour in the flesh, all that is passing round him. The summer sun, the frost that cracks the trees at night, making the moping birds sit miserable, waiting for the dawn; the fierce north wind, the hoar frost on the leaves coating them with a translucent panoply of fairy scales; the changing seasons, the recurring miracle of day and night, the moon's cold rays, the Pleiades, Orion and his belt; all the familiar constellations, the Pole Star, and Sohail, that he must have gazed at often as he lay awake camped in the desert, all the continual marvel of the growth of vegetation, he will remember. At least I hope so; and if he cannot see them as they pass around him, just as they passed in life, oblivion, the best gift the gods have to bestow, will bring him peace at last.

Long Wolf

Introductory Note by Kermit Roosevelt

My interest in Mr. Cunninghame Graham's writings was first aroused through reading the dedication in Mr. W. H. Hudson's delightful collection of short stories, gathered under the title *El Ombu*. It runs as follows:

To my Friend
R. B. CUNNINGHAME GRAHAM
(*"Singularisimo Escritor Ingles"*)
Who has lived with and knows (even to the marrow as they would themselves say) the horsemen of the Pampas, and who alone of European writers has rendered something of the vanishing colour of that remote life.

My father had been for many years an eager reader of all that Mr. Cunninghame Graham wrote, and I well remember his appreciation of the following letter which he received from him shortly after Buffalo Bill's death:

"March 27th, 1917.
"Cartagena de Indias,
Colombia.

"The Honourable,
Colonel Theodore Roosevelt.

"Dear Colonel Roosevelt:
"I saw by chance to-day in *Harper's Magazine* that a national monument is to be raised to my old friend Colonel Cody; that it is to take the form of a statue of himself on horseback (I hope the horse will be old Buckskin Joe), that he is to be looking out over the North Platte, and that you have kindly consented to receive subscriptions for it.
"When Cody and I were both young I remember him at the Horsehead Crossing, in or about the year 1880 I think, and subsequently saw him next year with the first germs of his great show in San Antonio de Bejar, Texas. (God bless Western Texas, as we used to say in those days — it is a thirsty land.)
"Cody was a picturesque character, a good fellow (I hope the story of his game of poker on his death-bed is not apocryphal), and a delightful figure on horseback. How well I can see him on his beautiful grey horse in the show!
"Every American child should learn at school the history of the conquest of the West.

"The names of Kit Carson, of General Custer and of Colonel Cody should be as household words to them. These men as truly helped to form an empire as did the Spanish Conquistadores.

"Nor should Sitting Bull, the Short Wolf, Crazy Horses *[sic = Horse?]* and Rain-in-the-Face be forgotten.

"They too were Americans, and showed the same heroic qualities as did their conquerors.

"I would not have Captain Jim of the Modocs fall into oblivion either.

"All of these men, and they were men of the clearest grit, as no one knows better than yourself, were actors in a tremendous drama, set in such surroundings as the world never saw before, or will see again.

"*Anch' io son pittore*, that is to say, I too knew the buffalo, the Apaches, and the other tribes of the Rio Grande.

"May I then trouble you with my obolus, a cheque for £20 towards the national monument to Buffalo Bill?

"I envy him his burial-place.

"May the statue long stand looking out over the North Platte.

"If in another world there is any riding — and God forbid that I should go to any heaven in which there are no horses — I cannot but think that there will be a soft swishing as of the footsteps of some invisible horse heard occasionally on the familiar trails over which the equestrian statue is to look.

"Believe me, dear Colonel Roosevelt,

"Yours most sincerely,

"R. B. Cunninghame Graham.

"P.S.—I congratulate you most heartily on the force which you are raising. It is like you, and if I had been blindfolded and asked who was raising such a force, I should have answered unanimously, Teddy Roosevelt.

"After eleven months in the Argentine, buying horses for the British Government, I am at present in Colombia on a mission connected with cattle, on the same account.

"R. B. C. G."

I thought at the time that here was the writer that could make Buffalo Bill and his era live and speak and act for our children and our children's children. After the Armistice I made the suggestion, and it was at first favourably received, but upon thinking it over Mr. Cunninghame Graham decided that, since his roaming in North America and participation in our frontier life had been largely confined to our South-West and to Mexico, he did not feel inclined to take up a work which would necessarily deal largely with the bleak frozen winters of the North-West, to which he was a stranger.

Accompanying his final decision, as a grateful earnest of his interest, and appreciation of the West, he sent the following sketch, which, instead of reconciling us to the decision, can only serve to make us regret it the more.

Kermit Roosevelt.

Long Wolf

In a lone corner of a crowded London cemetery, just at the end of a smoke-stained, Greco-Roman colonnade, under a poplar tree, nestles a neglected grave.

The English climate has done its worst upon it. Smoke, rain, and then more smoke, and still more rain, the fetid breath of millions, the fumes of factories, the reek of petrol rising from little Stygian pools on the wood pavements, the frost, the sun, the decimating winds of spring, have honeycombed the headstone, leaving it pitted as if with smallpox, or an old piece of parchment that has long moulded in a chest.

Upon the stone is cut the name of Long Wolf and an inscription setting forth he died in 1892 in Colonel Cody's Show. Years he had numbered fifty-nine. The legend says he was chief — I think a chief of the Ogalla [sic] Sioux, if memory does not play me false.

In high relief upon the cross, our emblem of salvation, a wolf is sculptured, the emblem of the tutelary beast he probably chose for himself in youth, during his medicine fast. It may have been that the name grew from some exploit or some incident in early life. Most probably the long wolf meant more to him than did the cross that Colonel Cody has erected over his dead friend and comrade in the wild life they understood so well. If the Long Wolf resents it, they can discuss the matter where they now ride — for that they ride, perhaps some Bronco Pegasus, I feel certain, as heaven would be no heaven to them if they were doomed to walk.

From whence the Long Wolf came so far, to lay his bones in the quiet corner of the Brompton Cemetery where now he sleeps, that is to me unknown, as absolutely as the fair field where the fledged bird had flown was to the poet. All that I know is that the bird was fledged, flew for some nine-and-fifty years, and now rests quietly in his forgotten grave.

The tombstones stand up, white in marble, grey in granite, and smoke-defiled when cut in common stone. They stand like soldiers, all in serried rows. The occupiers of the graves beneath them sleep on undisturbed by railway whistle or motor-horn, by blasts of steam, by factory sirens, or the continuous rumble of our Babylon. These were familiar sounds to them in life. If they could wake and should not hear them, their ears would pine for what had filled them all their lives. Upon each stone is set the name and age and virtues of its occupant. A pious text informs the world that a devoted wife and mother died in the sure and certain hope of a glorious resurrection. All charitable folk will hope her faith has been rewarded in the empyrean that she now inhabits, just as her virtue was rewarded here on earth, for to be forty years a devoted wife and mother is its own reward.

A little farther off, a general, his battles over, reposes in his warrior's cloak. He needs it, for the white marble makes a chilly couch in our high latitude. A champion sculler, with his marble boat and broken sculls, has gained his prize. A pugilist is cut in stone in fighting attitude, and farther off there sleeps a publican.

Men, women, children, gentle and simple, poets and statesmen, soldiers, sailors, and solid merchants, once held in honour upon Change, young girls, wives, husbands, mothers, fathers, and representatives of every age and class of man, take their repose under the dingy grass. Their very multitude surely must give them some protection, and a sense of fellowship . . . for they all died in the same faith, with common speech and aspiration, in their own fatherland.

Under the poplar-tree, its leaves just falling, golden in the autumn frost, there lies a wilding. No one is near with whom in the long nights of rain and winter he can exchange a word.

The prosperous citizens, in their well-cared-for tombs, with their trim beds above them often gay with flowers, even in death appear to look askance at the new Christian, with his wolf above the cross. No one to place even a bunch of violets on his grave, although the pious hand that buried him, perhaps in foresight of the loneliness certain to overtake the Long Wolf, lost in the thick ranks of palefaces, has placed in two glass cases (one of them is cracked) some artificial pansies — perhaps for thought, perhaps for recollection — all is one, for thought and recollection fade into one another almost insensibly.

On what forgotten creek, in what lost corner of the Dakotas, where once his race lorded it over buffalo and mustang, the Long Wolf first saw light, I have as little knowledge as of the composition of the mysterious thing that gave him life, accompanied him throughout his days, and then departed into the nothingness from whence it came.

I see the teepees set by the river's side, with the thin smoke that rises from the Indians' parsimonious fire curling out through the poles. The wolfish-looking dogs lie sleeping at the lee side of them; children play in the sun the strange and quiet games that Indian children play. Out on the prairie feed the horses under guard. Amongst these quiet children Long Wolf must have played, lassoed the dogs, or shot his little arrows at the birds. From his youth upward he must have been a rider patient and painstaking as the Indians are with horses, without the dash and fire that characterise the Western men and Mexicans.

At seventeen or eighteen, when he had assumed the name that now so strangely differentiates him from all those with whom he lies, he must have taken part in many a war-party. Upon the trail, strung out in a long line, he must have ridden with the other braves, silent and watchful, holding the horse-hair bridle with the high, light touch that every Indian has by nature and so few Europeans can acquire. He must have suffered hunger, thirst, fatigue, and all the dangers incidental to the life of those days on the plains long ere the railroad crossed them and when the buffalo migrated annually, in countless thousands, followed by the attendant packs of wolves. What his adventures were, how many scalps he took, and what atrocities he saw committed, only he himself could tell and Indians keep no diaries except in memory.

Little by little, as the West was day by day invaded by the whites, the buffalo grew scarcer and game was difficult to kill, he and the tribe would find their means of livelihood filched from them and their position insecure. Whether the chief took part in the great fight upon the Little Big Horn, or later joined the Ghost Dancers in their pathetic struggle, is a sealed book to all but him who brought the Long Wolf over in his company, and he has joined the chief on the last trail.

It is best perhaps we should know nothing, for, after all, what most concerns those who pass by his grave, rendered more lonely than if it had been dug out on the prairie, by the crowd of monuments of alien folk who crowd about it, is that he lies there, waiting for the last war-whoop, uncared-for and alone.

Whether his children, if he had any, talk of his death in the strange city, buried in fog and gloom, so vast and noisy, with its life so circumscribed by customs and by laws, remains a problem never to be solved. How and of what disease he died is long forgotten by the men who pass his tombstone so unheedingly. His spirit may have returned to the region of the Red Pipestone Quarry, or ride in some wild heaven, where buffalo are ever plentiful, grass green, and water ever running, that the Creator of the Indians must have prepared for them, as he is all-wise and merciful.

It may be that it still haunts hovering above the grave under the poplar-tree. I like to think, when all is hushed in the fine summer nights, and even London sleeps, that the wolf carved on the tomb takes life upon itself, and in the air resounds the melancholy wild cry from which the sleeper took his name.

'Twould be mere justice; but as justice is so scarce on earth, that it may well be rare even in heaven, 'twere better ears attuned to the light footfall of the unshod cayuse and the soft swishing of the lodge-poles through the grass behind the travois-pony should never open.

The long-drawn cry would only break the sleeper's rest, and wake him to a world unknown and unfamiliar, where he would find no friends except the sculptured wolf.

Let him sleep on.

Oropesa

Out of the immensity of the Castilian steppe, there rises, just on the confines of Estremadura and Toledo, an old brown town crowned by a feudal castle with its crenellated walls. The town must have grown round the castle, as the Dukes of Frias and of Escalona, Counts of Oropesa and of Haro, settled their vassals for protection in the long feud with the neighbouring Counts of Maqueda, just such another little town crowned by a castle, now mouldering to decay.

Time has swallowed up their rivalry; but the Castilian plain has defied time and in the autumn still keeps the character given to it in ages past in the old saying, "Even a lark when it goes to Castile must take its food with it." Little is altered on the great plain on which the sun plays like a fire. When all the waving wheat-fields are cut and threshed it is converted into a European Sahara. Dried thistles and the stalks of mullein desiccated in the fierce heat alone stand up to break its surface, taking on strange, fantastic shapes and looming up like dead, gigantic trees, seen in the mirage of the noonday sun. Time has done nothing either to the long strings of hooded carts, each drawn by a line of horses or of mules, led by a donkey and accompanied by a fierce yellow dog. Stretching across the plains, they wend their way through heat and dust, like trains of camels in the desert, their drivers either asleep inside the carts, or seated on the youngest of the mules, with the strange pretext that its legs grow stronger if it carries weight upon its back.

Villages built of sun-dried bricks rise here and there out of the plain, each with its church large enough for a considerable town. In the deserted streets pigs stray, and at the doors, sheltering against the walls to seek the shade, stand donkeys and an occasional mule, fastened to iron rings or wooden hooks driven between the bricks. Silence, a silence compounded of isolation and of heat, for the air shimmers and seems to flicker, broods over everything, and through the clouds of dust upon the roads pass carts and still more carts, and donkeys with men sitting sideways on their backs. Now and again a solitary horseman rides past at the Castilian pace, perched high upon his Moorish saddle, his feet encased in shovel-shaped iron stirrups, the thick, white dust deadening his wiry little horse's footfalls as effectually as if it had been snow.

Far off, the Sierra of the Gredos, its jagged outline cutting the sky at sunset into teeth, connects the Sierra de Guadarrama with that of Guadalupe and gives the plains a look of an evaporated sea, as desolate as those that seem to lie between the mountains in the moon. Dry rivers only marked by sheets of dazzling white stones, where in the winter rages a torrent, only serve to make the landscape still more African. Upon their banks, despite the universal dryness, long lines of rushes still preserve their greenness, and an occasional white poplar stands up and like a palmtree challenges the sun. Small flocks of sheep crouch with their heads all close together, seeking shade from one another, and a few fierce, black bullocks find a precarious pasturage among the stubble of the wheat-fields, guarded by men dressed in brown dusty clothes, their great black hats drawn down over the handkerchiefs with which they bind their heads. They stand as motionless as the dried thistles, milestones upon the path of time, stretching back to the patriarchal ages, when their ancestors must have kept sheep and cattle on the self-same plains, dressed in the same brown rags and leaning on their leaded quarter-staves, with their slings wrapped around their waists. Well did the Roman writer epitomise the land in the phrase, *Dura tellus Iberiæ*, dry, thirsty, and sun-scourged, just as it is to-day. Only at sunset when the lights fading from a deep orange, by degrees turn violet and greenish grey upon the jagged peaks and granulated slopes of the Gredos, does an air of mystery creep over the vast expanse of plain, so clear and so material in the fierce light of day. Then the rare bushes take on fantastic shapes, making the traveller's horse snort and shy off from them, as if they really were the beasts of prey that they appear. When the brief twilight gives place to the inimitable sapphire of the Castilian night, and the stars shine out like diamonds set in blue enamel, no sound but the faint tinkle of some mule's bell passing on the road disturbs the solitude. As night wears on, the shifting constellations mark the passing hours. Shepherds and mule-drivers camp round their fires, as did the camel drivers in Yemen, when the Arabs first observed the stars and named them, Altair, Algor, Sohail, and Fomalhaut. The noonday fire gives place to piercing cold, and in the morning, when the sun rises, turns once again to heat.

These plains, with their hard climate and scant vegetation, their fierce white atmosphere, that precludes all sense of mystery, have produced a race of men hard, unimaginative, but honourable and simple, capable of bearing all the extremes of heat and cold, and all the miseries of life with equanimity. Their ancestors formed the famous Spanish infantry that followed Charles V, that emperor of light horsemen, and swept through Italy like a devouring flame. They froze in Flanders, and across the seas were the backbone of the scant legions of Pizarro and Cortes. The scarcity of water and the inherited sense of insecurity that had come down to them from the days when one village was inhabited by Christians and the next by Moors, who butchered one another for the love of God, imposed a mode of life upon them unique in Europe, and most likely in the world. No snug farm-houses, with their trees and granges, their lowing cattle and folded sheep at night, were ever seen on the Castilian plains.

Huddled in villages or in such little towns as Oropesa, the cultivators lived far from their fields. At daybreak, seated on their donkeys, carrying their wooden ploughs upon their shoulders, they sallied forth to plough, to tend their scanty vines, or reap their corn. Their donkeys, hobbled, fed at the edges of the unfenced fields, picking up a thrifty livelihood. If they had oxen, they too were led out from the town. At noonday the cultivators ate a little bread and garlic, or a stew yellow with saffron, heated up in an earthen pipkin over a fire of thistle-stalks and bones. During their noonday siesta their patient oxen stood and ruminated, for luckily the angels did not often sweep down and goad them to their toil, what time their owner slumbered, as was the case with San Isidro Labrador, the patron of Madrid. Canonisation cannot have often been attained on easier terms, although it surely might have been bestowed more equitably on the oxen than on their owner, sleeping in the shade.

Over the plain the town of Oropesa and its castle brood. Its winding, ill-paved streets recall the Middle Ages or a town in Morocco or Algeria. In the great castle now turned to civic uses the Counts of Oropesa long held sway. Theirs was the right of *Horca y cuchillo*, gallows and sword, that corresponded to the pit and gallows of the Scottish nobles of the past. The title formed one of the group of titles held by the Dukes of Frias, themselves as Counts of Haro having been created Grand Constables of Castile upon the field of Najera. One of the greatest of the families of Spain, the equals of the Osunas, Albas, and Medina Celis in point of rank and of antiquity, the whole town speaks of them. Their arms are everywhere; on mouldering gateways and on the low-browed houses, over the castle drawbridge and on the doorway of the great church built by Herrera, the architect of the Escorial, and now an empty shell in which the archives of the house of Frias are left a prey to rats.

Hundreds of boxes bulging with papers fill a chapel. Deeds from the time of Juan II and Enrique IV; the Catholic Kings, signed "I, the King" and "I, the Queen"; deeds telling of the siege of Breda; plans of the fortresses in the kingdom of the Two Sicilies; letters from early Spanish navigators; from Popes and Cardinals; from the Emperor Charles V, Philip the Second, Don John of Austria, with Papal Bulls, Contracts of Marriage, Grants of Arms, and all the flotsam and the jetsam of a great feudal archive, whose owners have suffered by their incapacity to conform to the exigencies of a commercial age, lie scattered on the floor or are stored in great loosely tied-up packets, left carelessly on shelves. Books in all languages; rare first editions, mixed up with modern novels and with magazines, are piled up everywhere under the leaking roof, exposed to the fierce sun of summer and the winter rains that beat through windows destitute of glass. Books upon hunting, horsemanship, and hawking, such as Lopez de Ayala's *Aves de Caza*, and a first edition of Moreri's *Dictionary*, in twelve enormous tomes, lie cheek by jowl with first editions of Scott's novels, Byron's poems, and countless lives of saints. Great choir-books bound in leather stamped with the arms of the Dukes of Frias, their capital and initial letters finely illuminated, their pages set with miniatures of kings and emperors, lie heaped on one another in enormous piles. The children of the town, in conscience and tender heart, tear pages out of them when they want little lanterns for a festival. Their mothers now and then pull out a page or two of the first book that comes to hand, to wrap up groceries, giving a modern reading of the adage, "All take their firewood from the fallen tree."

At the east end of the great Græco-Roman church, behind the place where once stood the high altar, is an enormous picture by Juan Ricci. Our Lady, in the front plane, receives the homages of two noblemen with just that little touch of sweetness in her smile and air of femininity that one generation in Castile had not quite banished from the Italian style. In contradiction to the Spanish taste, that even in Murillo's most sugary compositions hold no air of meretriciousness, but accentuates the peasant birth of our Lord's mother, Ricci portrays a lady with just that touch of good society about her virginhood that shows his origin and the date when he worked. Two or three personages who look too well attired for shepherds, stand, not in adoration, but with an air of being heavenly courtiers, who could at need turn a neat compliment. In its flamboyant frame of chestnut-wood that time, damp, and the sun that beats upon it almost directly, have scarcely harmed, the picture, finely painted as it is and worthy of a place in the Vatican when Alexander Borgia was Pope, yet seems a little out of place in the sad, stately aisle of the old Spanish church. Far better would a dark introspective saint by Zurbaran, or a grim martyrdom by José Ribera, with all the limbs of the poor victim twisted in agony, *ad majorem Dei gloriam*, have fitted the air of desolation and neglect of the deserted fane. On the side altars, dusty and fly-blown images of saints, sculptured in wood, and gilded, stand disconsolately, some of them still with rosaries hung round their necks by pious votaries before the church was given over to the owls and rats.

A picture of a Christ, bloody and realistic and realising to the full the Spanish saying, "To a bad Christ, much blood," has almost faded off the panel that time and damp have cracked. Heaps of birds' feathers lie beneath the dome, and from the organ-loft some of the pipes have fallen into the nave and serve for trumpets to the children in their games. Nothing of all the glory of the immense and stately church remains, except the air of melancholy grandeur that clings to everything in Spain, even though in decay. Pigeons and owls and bats are now the only congregation of the decaying church of the great family of Frias, once famous in the history of Spain.

Their castle on its rocky eminence above the church, though used as a town-hall and inhabited by the cacique of the district, still dominates the town that lies a maze of winding, ill-paved streets, full of old houses, with low horseshoe entrances, iron balconies, and coats of arms above the doors, all garnished with their hitching rings for mules. Castle and church and old brown mouldering town stand out so clearly that they appear fantastic in the clear atmosphere. Far off across the plain the Sierra de Gredos rears its serrated peaks, and as the evening sun turns them to pinnacles of jacinth, opal, amethyst, and jade, that by degrees melt into a faint blue, they appear mountains in some planet long extinct, whose shadow just has reached the earth.

Redeemed

La Virgen de La Cabeza

All day the diligence from Baza to Granada had ploughed its way through heavy snow. At daylight, as it set out from Baza, the curious little town might just as well have been in Russia as in Spain. Long icicles hung from the heavy, red-tiled eaves of all the houses. The church towers looked like ornaments upon a wedding-cake, and in the plaza, the cannons with which the Catholic Kings besieged the place, that are preserved as monuments, were buried almost to their mouths. Outside the town the carts and trains of mules that fill all Spanish roads, as they have done for centuries, and will do, God willing, still for centuries, plodded along, just as they plodded in summer through the dust. Their drivers, muffled to the eyes in their striped blankets, trotted beside them, instead of sitting in their usual fashion, sideways on their backs.

The six apocalyptic horses, after a brief scuffling gallop, subsided to a gentle trot, then to a walk, their feet buried above the fetlocks in the light, powdery snow. The lumbering diligence swayed like a collier in a seaway, lurching to one side, then to another, following a boy who rode in front upon a mule to point out the best places in the road. The sun rose frostily, painting the distant sierra of the Alpujarras pink, but brought no heat with it. Now and then bits of the road, swept bare by the fierce winds, were sheeted thick with ice, so slippery that both the driver and his mate had to cut brushwood to strew upon it before the coach could pass. Occasionally, deep in the snow-laden pine woods, or from the recesses of the sierra, a wolf howled with that wild, marrow-curdling note, once heard never to be forgotten, especially if far from houses and alone. The horses knew it too, pricked up their ears, huddled a little closer to each other, and broke into a shambling trot for a few yards. At the post-houses in the wretched Alpujarra villages as the tired, sweating team was being changed, the passengers, benumbed and chilled, stamped about on the snow, smoking and drinking aguardiente after their meal of greasy sausages coloured with saffron, potato-soup, and the white flaky pastry that the Moors left in Spain.

Upon the frozen drinking-troughs, broken at one end with an axe to let the horses drink, the women had thrown corn for the chickens, who ate it standing on the ice. Post-house succeeded post-house in the short winter's day, as in a nightmare of cold and misery. At last, just as the setting sun once more threw a faint flush upon the mountains, they reached a village in the hills. With the same satisfaction that a boatload of shipwrecked mariners may feel upon arriving at some wretched fishing village, the inmates of the diligence looked at the flickering light in the dark archway where they had drawn up with a jolt. "Any port in a storm," observed the driver. "Granada is still ten leagues away. Better to stay here and make penitence with Uncle Nicolas Rodriguez than to be frozen or be eaten by the wolves."

In the great kitchen before a fire of olive logs and brushwood the travellers gradually got their brains and bodies thawed. A huge iron pot swung in the chimney from a chain. Watching it, with their noses almost in the embers, lay several fierce dogs, their bloodshot eyes half open as they watched the travellers file in. All round the stone-floored vaulted room mule-drivers were either sitting on their packs or fast asleep, looking like corpses as they lay with their heads covered in their cloaks. A doorway always open, across the passage by which the diligence had entered the hotel, led to the stables where a long line of horses, mules, and donkeys munched their chopped straw and corn.

Men passed to and fro perpetually, either to part their fighting animals, who stood all touching one another, or to buy corn from Uncle Nicolas, which they took in a saddle blanket to their beasts. The mules and asses all stood saddled; their packs so high and bulky that as you looked down the long line of animals they seemed like islands towering above their backs. The smell of mules and horses, mingling with the odour of the cooking and the clouds of tobacco smoke, produced that incense peculiar to all Spanish wayside inns.

Among the muleteers and other guests, for travellers were always dropping in, two country girls, short, broad, and merry-faced, their eyes as black as sloes, their hair as thick and as abundant as a Shetland pony's tail, attended to the cooking or fetched glasses of aguardiente amid the perpetual harshly screamed-out orders of the hostess. As they passed by the men they received a shower of quodlibets that might have disconcerted girls less used to them. They took all smilingly, just as they had taken from their birth hard work, short commons, exposure to the weather, and all that Providence had chosen to dispense.

Dinner was served to the travellers by the diligence at a long wooden table covered with a clean, rough cloth. All up and down the board were set great lumps of home-baked bread, small fluted tumblers, and bottles of red wine, giving the whole an air as of Leonardo da Vinci's picture of the "Last Supper." As they consumed potato-soup, the stew of beef and bacon with cabbage and chick peas, the whole made savoury with bits of high-spiced red sausages, one or two dwellers in the little hamlet dropped in to hear the news: the apothecary, the barber, and the priest, a tall and handsome man of fifty, wearing the "manteo" with the air that only priests of his nationality ever can assume.

Seated around the ample hearth, tongues were soon loosened and experiences exchanged. No one had ever seen so fierce a storm so late in February, except of course one that they all remembered in their youth, when storms in every quarter of the world must have been almost continuous. Uncle Nicolas, the host, had seldom seen the wolves more plentiful. As he said this the others nodded their heads gravely, being aware, the wind carried off feathers and words before it. One man had lost a colt, another a young cow, and Uncle Nicolas himself three or four goats and a fat pig. The goats he did not care about so much; but the loss of the pig lay near his heart, for it had been cared for like the children of the house, and he had not enjoyed a single sausage, not to speak of bacon or a ham, after all the corn it had consumed. A strong, athletic muleteer, raising himself upon his elbow, after having made a cigarette and spat upon the floor with emphasis, said but a fortnight past upon the road he had encountered three devils straight from hell, as fierce as tigers, all thirsting for his blood. He, with four mules, was on the road from Albuñol to Orgiva. In a deep hollow near a cork wood suddenly they appeared and set on him. "I was alone," he said, "and had my quarterstaff; but then, you know, no blow a man can strike a wolf ever disables it, except it falls on the foreleg. I had no time to tie my mules, and it was lucky, as it proved, I did not so do. The accursed government has rendered gunpowder so dear that my trabuco was unloaded, although I had it with me on my saddle. Jesus! What could I do but whirl my quarterstaff about to keep the fiends at bay.

"Yes, I was frightened. Why deny it? Miles from a house and with night coming on and not a living thing beside me but the four laden mules. Then in my terror I remembered there was one who, if she willed it, could protect me from the wolves. 'Nuestra Señora de la Cabeza,' who has her sanctuary outside Motril, upon La Esplanada, she whom men found upon the beach among the lilies, dark-featured, like ourselves, and most miraculous. So as I fought, the wolves drawing always closer to me, I vowed a candle of the purest wax to her and swore to go barefooted up the hill to pray to her, if she would succour me.

"She must have heard me, for as I stepped backwards I was surprised to see my mules, who first had seemed about to gallop off, now all were standing still, with their ears pricked forward and pawing with their feet. A miracle, I saw it in a trice, and vowed another candle twice as large as the first that I had offered and swore to make the pilgrimage stripped to my shirt and drawers. Slipping between the animals of God, I patted them, and either because La Morenita had whispered in their ears or from the instinct of self-preservation, they turned their heels round towards the wolves. So well they kicked and lashed at them, whinnying a sharp hin-hin, as their hoofs struck those enemies of man, that they all fled, limping and howling, leaving me and the mules alone upon the road.

"I owe my safety, after God, first to La Morenita, who from her mansion in the skies puts out her tongue at every other virgin, as well she may, for which of them has lilies that appear each spring in the same place where she was found, even when plucked up by the roots? Then to my mules, who fought for me at peril of their lives. The case is difficult, so I shall only give one candle to Our Lady of the Head, and as for going to her in my shirt and drawers, that would be hardly decent, as she is a lady. As to bare feet, that matters little, for from my childhood I have gone bare-footed and stones and briars harm me as little as if I were a goat and not a Christian. La Morenita never will find out the difference, for in the skies 'tis ten to one that there is not a pair of scales. What do the saints in glory want with so much wax? Surely there must be bees enough in paradise to make them fifty thousand candles, each bigger far than mine."

A laugh went round the other muleteers, that the priest stifled with an uplifted finger. "Peace, heretic," he said. "Oh, man no better than a stealer of the sacrament, would you then cheat our Blessed Lady of Motril, who but so recently has saved your life, out of a miserable pound of wax and put your soul in peril?"

"Pardon me, father," said the muleteer, "I am a poor man with a large family, and so I thought La Morenita might not have heard of it and that the candle that I promised her might as well go in bread for my own

Christianity; but since it seems that I have sinned, God bless her swarthy face, she shall have a donkey load of wax."

The moon had risen, and through the chinks of the rough wooden shutters long beams of silver mingled with the glare from the roaring chimney, and all the company sat gazing into the fire, their garments dried, with the agreeable feeling of being safely harboured after storm. Turning towards a girl whose flimsy, brightly coloured clothes, paint, powder and sham jewellery showed that her calling and election had been determined, at least in this world, "Draw nearer to the fire, my daughter," said the priest, "and warm yourself. Storms and misfortunes, nights like this, and the words of our Blessed Lord Himself, remind us that we are all of the same family." Then going to the door he opened it, letting the moonlight stream into the room and play on the stone floor.

"The night is clear," he said," the wind is calmed, and the peaks of the sierras look like loaves of sugar. It may be that our Lady of the Lilies, whose holy name has been to-night bandied about rather irreverently, has been with us unseen and stilled the elements." He stood a moment gazing into the night, his figure sharply silhouetted between the moonlight and the fire. Far away in the recesses of the woods a wolf howled mournfully.

Inch Cailleach

The Island of the Nuns lies like a stranded whale upon the waters of the loch, with its head pointing towards the red rocks of Balmaha. Tradition tells of a nunnery on the island in times gone by, and certainly it must have been a fitting place to build a convent on. A deep, dark strait cuts it off from the world. No spot in the whole earth could be more fitted for a conventual life of meditation, or for the simple duties performed in simple faith, such, as string out a life like beads upon a rosary, till the last prayer is said.

Fell opportunity, that has so often turned saints into sinners, could have had no place upon the rocky islet in the lake. The voices of the sisters singing in the choir must have been scarce distinguishable from the lapping of the wavelets on the beach, or blending with them, made up a harmony, as if nature and men were joining in a pantheistic hymn. Nuns may have lived upon the island with, or without, vocation, have eaten out their hearts with longing for their lost world, or, like the Saint of Avila, in mystic ecstasy have striven to be one with the celestial spouse. All this may well have been, but the dim sisterhood has left no record of its passage upon earth, except the name Inch Cailleach, beautiful in its liquid likeness to the sound of the murmuring waves, and the wind sighing in the brackens and the bents.

Ben Lomond towers above the wooded island, with its outcrop of grey rocks, and in the distance Ben Vorlich, Meall nan Caora and Bein Chabhair seem to protect it from all modern influence by their grim aspect and aloofness, for even their rare smiles when the sun hunts the shadows across their rocky faces, still are stern. If the lone, wooded inchlet once sheltered nuns, or if the name was merely given it to commemorate some ancient Highland Cailleach, who had retired there to gaze into the mists upon the hills, or dream of Fingal and Cuchullin as she sat nodding over a fire of peat, certain it is that nature must have put forth her best creative power to form so fitting a last resting-place for the wild clan, whose bones are laid beneath the mossy turf round the great sculptured stones.

Right on the top of a long shoulder of the island, within the ruined walls of the old chapel whose broken pillars, moss-grown finials and grooved door-jambs lie in a growth of bilberries among the invading copse, the Gregarach for centuries have interred their dead. They and the wild McFarlanes — was not the moon known as McFarlanes' Bowat? — rest from their labour at the sword. Quietly they lie, they who knew never a quiet hour in life. Equal in death and equal in misfortune when they lived, had they consulted all the heralds and their pursuivants they could not have hit upon a device more fitting than the cross-handled sword that is cut roughly on so many of their tombs. Bitterly they paid for the slaughter of Glenfruin, with two hundred years of outlawry, and with the hand of every man against them. Well did they deserve the title of the Clan Na Cheo, for the mist rolling through the corries was their best hiding-place, the natural smoke-screen that protected all the Clan Gregor from their enemies. On the leafy Island in the great lake alone they found a resting-place, and though the long grey stones by which they swore are few in number, the grassy hillocks that dot the burial-ground encircled by the ruined walls are numberless. Nowhere could men have found a spot so fitting for a long sleep after their foray in the world. The soughing wind among the thickets of scrub-oak, of hazel and of birch, the fresh, damp scent of the sweet-gale and staghorn moss, the belling of the roe at evening, the strange, sweet wildness of the steep, isolated island with its two headlands and its little plain, now buried deep in wood, must lull the resting children of the mist.

A steep and winding path leads from the pebbly beach, and crosses and recrosses a little rill, brown but transparent, as it wends its way towards the lake in miniature cascades and tiny linns, in which play minnows. It makes a tinkling music for the sleepers among the ruins of what was once Inch Cailleach parish church. It passes now and then a fir, whose bright red trunk stands out aflame among the copse, and bears the cones from which Clan Alpine took its badge. Here and there clumps of scarlet dockens mark the way, like stations of the Cross upon a Calvary. Hardly a footstep has beaten down the grass, for up above, in the lone circle of grey stones, lie men whose names were written in characters as evanescent as the smoke-scrolls an aeroplane traces upon the sky. Clearly imprinted on the peaty soil, roe tracks call up the memory of men who passed the best part of their lives in following the deer. The silence of the woods is only broken by the flight of some great capercailzie, as its wings beat against the leaves when it first launches into flight, or by the cushats cooing, deep and full-throated as the bell-bird's call in the Brazilian wilds.

The loneliness, the sense of isolation, although the world is just at hand, and tourist-laden steamers ply upon the loch, passing but a few hundred yards away and breaking up the picture of the wooded island reflected in the lake, as in a mirage, with their paddles, are as absolute as if the islet was situated in the outer Hebrides.

The very scent of the lush grass, set about thickly with the yellow tormentils, with scabious and bog-asphodel, strikes on the nostrils as from an older world, in which the reek of petrol and the noise of factories were unknown. Many a procession of ragged warriors, in the past, their deerskin buskins making scarce a sound upon the stones, must have toiled up the winding path to lay their dead within the little burial-ground, and then, the ceremony over, stepped noiselessly away into the sheltering mist. The nuns, McGregors, and McFarlanes all have passed away, and are as if they never had been, yet they have left an aura that still pervades the leafy isle. Nothing is left of them but the vaguest memory, and yet they seem to live in every thicket, every copse, and as the burn runs brattling to the lake it sings their threnody. When all is hushed at night and owls fly noiselessly, their flight hardly disturbing the still air, and the rare nocturnal animals that all-destroying progress (or what you call the thing) has left alive, surely the spirits of the nameless sleepers under the mossy turf rise like a vapour from their graves, commune with Cuchullin and with Fingal, pat Bran's rough head, and fight old battles once again; until at the first streak of dawn they glide back to their places, under the sculptured stones.

Let them sleep on. They have had their foray, they have chased the roe and followed the red deer. The very mists upon the mountains are far more tangible than they are now. Let them rest within the ruined walls of the dismantled chapel buried in the copse, that has shown itself more durable than the stone walls that lie about its roots. Bracken and heather, bog-myrtle, blaeberry and moss exhale their odours, sweeter than incense, over the graves where sleep the nameless men. The waves still murmur on the beach, the tiny burnlet whispers its coronach. Under their rude tombstones men whose feet, shod in their deerskin brogues, were once as light as fawns, are waiting till the shrill skirl of the Piob Mor shall call them to the great gathering of the clans.

Redeemed

El Alcalde de Móstoles

In the year 1808 Napoleon was at the height of his renown. All Europe lay beneath his feet. England and Russia alone were still unconquered; but in due course he hoped to deal with them. Austria, Prussia, Holland, and Italy were provinces of France. Spain, that had for centuries been inaccessible to conquerors, was beaten to her knees. King Joseph, known to the Spaniards by the name of Pepe Botellas, held his court in Madrid, surrounded by a few sycophants and renegades. All patriotism seemed dead. Murat and his Mamelukes kept down the city with an iron hand. Goya was taking notes of everything, crystallising the odious tyranny of the French, in his immortal "Horrors of War," — horrors that have never been surpassed, either in reality or paint.

The country, delivered over to the mercies of the invading troops, was seething with revolt, but wanted someone to stand out and lead. Only the partisan El Empecinado was in arms in Navarre and the Basque provinces. For all that, no Frenchman's life was worth ten minutes' purchase outside cantonments or the camp. The country people cut their throats like sheep with their long knives, and often threw their bodies into their wine-vats to get rid of them. In after-days, to say a wine had a French twang was long a jest among the peasantry. Still they went on, stabling their horses in the churches, violating nuns and stealing priceless ornaments from the cathedrals and the monasteries. Spain stirred convulsively under the heel of the detested Gabacho, as the people liked to call the French. That which was to prove her strength, and had done so in ages past, was now her weakness, for the intensely local patriotism had formed each town and village into a community apart, slow to combine with one another. "Mi tierra" meant for them, not Spain, but every separate village and a few miles around.

At last the turbulent populace of Madrid, irritated past bearing by the Mamelukes who represented to them not the French only, but their hereditary enemies, the Moors, rose in revolt. Armed with their knives alone, they fell upon the Mamelukes in a narrow street, stabbing their horses and butchering the riders when they fell. Two heroic officers of artillery, Velarde and Daoiz, opened fire with a piece of cannon on the French. Their heroism was wasted — that is, if sacrifice is ever wasted — and the revolt was crushed that very afternoon, in what Murat referred to as a "bath of blood." The two young officers were shot, and by their death secured their immortality in Spain. Madrid was stunned, but the news soon was carried to the neighbouring little towns, by men escaping from the massacre.

Out on the Castilian steppes, fifteen or sixteen miles from Madrid, there lies a little town called Móstoles. It lies, almost as one might say, *à fleur d'eau* on the great brown plain. The high-road to Portugal passes down its long main street. Even to-day it has but thirteen hundred citizens. In summer the houses, built of sun-dried bricks covered with plaster, are calcined by the sun. The winter winds, sweeping down from La Sierra de Guadarrama, scourge it pitilessly. For nine months of the year dust covers everything, falling on man and beast, on the few moribund acacias in the plaza, turning all to the colour of a rabbit's back. During the other three it is a slough of mud that wheel-borne traffic and the long strings of donkeys and mules struggle through painfully. Far off the Sierra of Guadalupe and the Gredos are just visible as faint blue lines hardly to be picked out from the clouds, except in certain states of atmosphere. In the short, fierce summer the mirage spreads illusory pools over the surface of the plain, and in the winter mornings, after a sharp frost, the woods along the foothills of the Guadarrama hang upside down upon the sky. Along the road are dotted many other little dusty towns, all with their little plaza, great church, large enough for larger congregations than they ever hold, their apothecaries with leeches in a glass jar at the door, and fly-blown patent medicines in the window, and barber's shop, that serves as news exchange.

Upon the second of May of the year 1808 news filtered through to Móstoles that there had been a massacre in the capital. The seventeen kilometres of high road could easily be covered on a good horse within two hours, and it is not to be supposed the rider spared the spur.

As it was written, one Andres Torrejon happened to be Alcalde of the place. An honest countryman of six-and-sixty years of age, in all his life he had never had occasion to show what he was worth. What he was like to the outward visible eye is but a matter of conjecture. Most probably a square-built, round-faced Castilian farmer, his cheeks stubbly with a week's growth of beard — the village barber shore but on a Sunday morning — sparing of speech, yet full of sayings fitted to every accident of life. His dress, that has but little varied, even to-day, knee-breeches of dark cloth, his jacket short, showing a double-breasted flowered waistcoat of a sprigged pattern, his linen dazzlingly white, a black silk handkerchief bound like a turban round his head, the whole surmounted by a hard-brimmed, black felt hat, kept in place underneath his chin by a broad band of silk. His interior grace, his honesty, tenacity of purpose, and his enthusiasm, slow to be excited, but when once moved as irresistible as a landslide after rain, he has left stamped upon Castile. It will endure as long as her vast plains wave green with corn in spring, turn leather-coloured under the fierce sun of summer, and in the winter when the keen frosts burn up all vegetation, stretch out desolate, with but the withered stalks of thistles standing up ghost-like in the waste.

The nerves of all true patriots were on edge. Never since the days of the Saracens had the invader's foot trodden Castilian soil. The news of the last outrage brought all the people out into the plaza before the parish church of the Ascension, a mosque, tradition says, in the days Spanish peasants always refer to as "the time of the Moors." All over Spain the people's nerves were twitching, but yet the heavy hand of Murat had deprived them of all spirit of revolt.

It happened, luckily for Andres Torrejon, that the Ex-Secretary of the Admiralty under Charles IV, Juan Perez Vilamil, was living in the town, having refused to recognise King Joseph and his usurping court. Long did the Alcalde and Vilamil talk over what was the best course to pursue. Then, after praying in the church, the Alcalde called a meeting of his rustic senators. The people thronged outside the council-room, the very room in which to-day is set into the wall the tablet that commemorates what was resolved on that eventful afternoon in May. The peasant councillors sat round the council board, with their Alcalde in the chair. Perez and Gomez, Camacho, Lopez and Galvan, all peasants, their hands furrowed with toil and weather, their shoulders rounded with the plough, their faces tanned to a deep brown by the hard climate of Castile, and their eyes twinkling deeply in their sockets, like the eyes of mariners, of Arabs, and of all those who pass their lives upon illimitable plains, scorched by the wind and sun, all waited for what "Uncle Andrew" had to say.

Rising with due deliberation from his seat, after having taken off his hat and placed it carefully beside him on the table, the Alcalde told of what had happened in Madrid. His actual words are not recorded, only the substance of his speech. As he spoke of the massacre, the shooting down of women and of children in the streets, the execution of the prisoners drawn up opposite a wall, and of the people who had died trampled beneath the horses of the Mameluke infidel, his hearers' hands stole to their sashes, and muttering "Death to the Gabacho," they spat upon the floor. Sitting impassively like figures carved in walnut-wood, the peasant council suffered under Napoleon's heel. Now and again one of them would assent in a half grunt, and anyone who did not know them might have thought they were unmoved. As they sat with their heads a little sideways, their mouths half open, and their breath coming in short gusts that heaved their chests under their heavy rustic clothes, just as a barge heaves on a canal after a steamer passes, they seemed like animals about to spring upon their prey. The Alcalde recapitulated all their country's wrongs. The cuckold Charles IV a prisoner in France, the queen, a harlot left under the dominion of her lover of the day, the troops unpaid and led by officers who did not know their duty, and worst of all the miserable French puppet king, lording it on the throne of Charles V. "Spain wants a leader, someone to show the way, to gather up the scattered bands of guerrilleros and above all a straight and downright declaration that the country is at war. No one has yet stepped out to lead us, although they slaughter us like flies, scorn us and spit on us; on us Castilians, whose forefathers furnished the famous Spanish infantry that swept through France and Italy like fire. Who would think we were the heirs of those who fought at San Quentin?"

The people of the town pressed round the iron-grated windows of the council-chamber, silent, but gazing on their rustic councillors, strung up with fury, cursing their impotence. At last the speaker, tightening up his sash, wiping the foam and moisture from his lips, took a long breath, and after looking round to Vilamil, who nodded at him, said, "Friends and neighbours, I have served you faithfully for years. The time has come that I must now serve Spain. Therefore I, Andres Torrejon, duly elected the Alcalde of this town of Móstoles, do declare war against the French."

For a brief moment there was silence, silence so absolute that the breath of the people peering through the gratings of the windows sounded as loudly as when a horse upon a frosty morning pants up an incline. Then, rising to their feet, the conscript peasants surrounded the Alcalde, grasping him by the hand, and shouting, "War, war to the knife;

death to the assassins of Madrid." The people in the little plaza caught up the cry of "War, war to the knife. Uncle Andrés has declared war upon the French!"

In the closing darkness of that night of May Andres Torrejon sat down and penned his memorable pronouncement, the first and last that he was fated to indite, but one that made his name immortal throughout the Spanish-speaking world. "Our country is in peril, Madrid is perishing, the victim of the perfidy of the French. Spaniards, hasten to save her. May 2nd, 1808. El Alcalde de Móstoles." Nothing could have been more simple and direct, with just the touch of the ridiculous that gives sublimity. His next act was to send the son of his old colleague on the council, Simon Hernandez, on a good horse to take his proclamation to the Alcaldes of the neighbouring towns. At once he mounted, and first reaching Navalcarnero, left the fiery cross. Alcorcón, Navalmorál, and Escalona all received the message, and all of them at once declared war on the French. The messenger crossed the Alberche and pushed on westwards, riding without a stop across the plains all through that fateful night in May. In two days' riding he reached Badajoz, his horse still fresh, after having covered nearly two hundred miles. The city rose at once, and sent on word to Cáceres. Cáceres passed on the signal and by the end of May all Spain had risen, not like an ordinary country rises in such circumstances, but town by town, village by village, each declared war upon the French.

The rest is history, the coming of the great "Lor Vilanton" as he was called in the Spain of those days, with the English troops, and the long war of the Peninsula. The hour had struck, and from that moment Napoleon's star began to pale, Moscow completed that which Móstoles began, and when the French recrossed the swift Borysthenes, slaughtered like sheep by the pursuing Cossacks, their ruin (after God) they owed to the Alcalde of the little town, sun-dried and wind-scorched, in the Castilian plains.

Redeemed

El Lebeche

A dense sea fog covered the hills as with a shroud. The ruined Moorish castle that dominates the town, frowned through the mist upon the Christian city as if it still resented its subjection to the Cross. Great drops of moisture fell from the palm-trees. The fields of sugar-cane formed one coagulated mass, their leaves matted together with the damp. The red hibiscus and geraniums mocked the weather, their scarlet blossoms shining like lights upon a fairway that led to some uncharted port. The highway running through a line of villas was a sea of mud. The passing motor-cars raised showers of dirty water that fell upon the rare foot-passengers, just as the wrath from heaven falls on the righteous and the unrighteous, with divine impartiality.

The mountain streams that traverse the great suburb, La Caleta, had become raging torrents, bearing upon their flood dead cats, old orange frails, fragments of earthenware, and all the flotsam and jetsam of a southern town.

Lines of dejected donkeys and of mules, all dripping wet, pursued their homeward Calvary along the road between the double line of tramway rails. Behind them, on an apocalyptic horse or thin white mule, perched sideways on the "aparejo," huddled in a threadbare blanket with heels drumming ceaselessly against their flanks, their drivers faced the clinging mist, scarcely less miserable than their four-footed fellows that they urged along. The sea boomed like the echo of great guns discharged centuries ago, whose sound had been arrested in some uncongenial atmosphere, and had been liberated by the fog. In a recess between the gutter and the great retaining wall of some rich Indiano's villa lay a tired donkey with its head propped up on a stone. Dripping with moisture that, mingling with dried sweat, formed ropy lines upon its shrunken flanks, its pack-saddle still upon its back, it lay waiting the coming of A Son of Man to it and to its kind, who should ride into the Jerusalem of all the animals. Orange and lemon trees, dripping and draggled-looking in the unfamiliar gloom, gave an air as of the garden of the Hesperides slowly submerging when Atlantis sank into the sea.

The people's flimsy clothes, the unsubstantial villas, built for fine weather with their ample porticoes, their flights of marble steps, and fountains still playing futilely against the mist, added, by their unfitness with their surroundings, to the discomfort that had descended on the bright southern land. Tramways emerged from the misty atmosphere, as unexpectedly as ships loom up, menacing and imminent, in a fog at sea. Their jingling bells seemed muffled, and when their passengers descended they slipped off unperceived and were swallowed up as noiselessly as a stone dropped into the snow. It was the sort of day that makes one think the creator of the world may, after all, have been some sort of Bolshevist, or else had worked during a fit of indigestion that he was anxious to pass on to all his puppets with their immortal souls.

The tourists in the great hotel, well warmed and sheltered, raised a perpetual litany against the weather, the country, Providence, and their hard lot in having left their homes to find themselves faced with the same conditions they had left behind. Outside, exposed to cold and wet, dripping and miserably clad, the passers-by on the high-road uttered no word of protest, enduring everything, hunger (the national disease), the want of shelter and the long miles they had to tramp before they reached their miserable homes, with all the Oriental patience of the race. Now and then on the oily waters of the swelling sea a fishing-boat's sharp-pointed lateen pierced through the mist, and then sank out of sight, just as the back fin of a shark emerges from the water, and as quickly disappears.

Interminable lines of donkeys and of mules passed by as in a nightmare. The high-wheeled mat-covered carts, drawn by a string of horses, piloted always by a little donkey, followed by a dejected dog, creaked on, swaying and surging to one side and the other, their driver's head just visible as he lay stretched out at full length to shelter from the rain. Trees, houses, the hills, and all the features of the landscape had disappeared, and nature seemed to suffer through the excess of her fecundity. When all the pack mules and the carts had passed and disappeared into the mist, a herd of milch-goats plodded along, their dangling udders almost trailing in the mud, towards their pasturage.

Behind them stalked the goatherd, wrapped in his tattered blanket, with a broad-brimmed hat upon his head. Tall, sallow, weather-beaten and athletic, he walked cheerfully along, cracking his sling at intervals and carrying a kid whose head peeped out beneath his arm. He crooned a fitful Arab-sounding song with a strange interval, and now and then broke off to munch a piece of bread, his face wreathed in an almost religious smile, for bread is something sacred to people of his class in the land of Maria Santisima.

The mist, the cold, the wind, all were as nothing to him, for he had bread, and appetite with bread is not vouchsafed to men for nothing in this vale of tears.

Then he, too, and his goats passed on and vanished, but from the recesses of the gloom there floated back snatches of his harsh song, quavering and wild as the cry of a curlew on a Scottish moor.

Redeemed

Dar-El-Jinoun

The sandy Sáhel stretched out for a mile or two along the shore of a sea, never at rest under the east wind that tormented it, fretting its surface with white tide-rips, that from the beach looked like a flock of gulls. The little Arab town upon its hill, dazzlingly white, but for its slender mosque tower covered with green tiles, its flat-topped houses rising tier on tier, framed in the picture to the west. A jutting cape clothed with a scrubby growth of kermes oak, palmetto and lentiscus, crowned with a mouldering watch-tower, cut off the Sáhel from the outside world, upon the east.

Wild mountains rose jagged and serrated to the south, and the low sandy plains, where Spain was lost under Don Roderick, shut it in to the north. A grove of fig-trees, planted in a circle, rose like an oasis in the thorny vegetation that fringed the sandy grass which ran a quarter of a mile or so in depth, between the foothills and the sea. In the oasis of the fig grove during the noonday heat the Arab herd-boys, watching their goats, their scraggy cows, or their lean colts, that still retained, in spite of hunger and in-breeding, something of the grace their ancestors had brought from the Hejáz, or Nejd, played upon flutes cut from a cane, or plaited strings out of the fibre of the dwarfish palms. Their plaintive little tunes, quavering and fitful as the singing of a fledgling bird, appealed rather to the soul than to the outward ear. Only Theocritus could have done justice to the scene, when underneath the trees the goats lay dozing, and the colts stood resting a hind-leg and swishing their long tails half drowsily, while the boys breathed into their rustic flutes.

Upon a rocky hill that rose out of the waste of gnarled, goat-eaten brushwood still stood the ruins of a castle built by the Portuguese, "in the epoch of their glory." Time had done little to deface it; but the Arabs, always prone to take their goods where they find them, had used it for a quarry. Below it, a few feet above the beach, a deserted battery still held guns, marked with the name of George III, but prone upon the ground, their carriages long ago used to light the shepherds' fires. The cracked cement held tufts of wild flowers, and lizards peered out shyly through the interstices. Beneath the castle lay a Moorish cemetery to mark the resting-place of the Mujehadin who had died in battle fighting against the infidel. Its rough, unsculptured stones, that looked as if they had been taken from a Scottish drystone dyke, marked where the dead were sleeping, and warned the horseman who crossed the burial-ground at speed, his grave was open for him. Three caroub-trees, secular, but green and vigorous, overhung a well. The only trees upon the plain, they had resisted all the fury of the perpetual east wind, that dwarfed and stunted all the other vegetation in its blast. A sluggish little river formed a bar in miniature where it flowed into the sea, at one end of the plain. Salt-pans were dug beside its banks, the heaps of salt piled up beside them, dazzlingly white and scintillating in the sun. The walls of Tingis, a city old when London was a wattled village, were strewed about in piles; but the great docks for galleys built by the Romans, when they had crossed the straits into North Africa, still stood intact, though silted up with sand.

Over the whole little plain brooded an air as of an older world, an Arcadia, tempered with an occasional tribal fight or cattle raid, to show that the shepherds were still Arabs, holding as an article of faith that the sword writes plainer than the pen. Still, though the ships of every nationality sailed through the straits all day, only a few miles distant from the coast, the people passed their lives unchanged since Abraham's servant saw Rebekah, with her jar poised upon her shoulder, waiting at the well. Long lines of white-clad figures passed noiselessly along the beach at dawn upon their way to market in the town. They passed so noiselessly, carrying their slippers in their hands, for leather costs more than the skin upon the feet, that when they vanished in the distance only their footsteps in the wet sand showed their reality. All day the long procession from the hills of Angera wended its way toward the town. Men drove their mules and asses, laden with country produce and with firewood, and women staggered, bent double underneath great loads of straw or broom to heat the ovens in the town.

Two tidal rivers barred their way. If they were deep as the tide was making, a man headed the caravan and sounded with a cane. The rushing water piled up on the weather quarters of the mules, and donkeys struggled through with men holding them up against the stream. The women bravely ventured in, with their clothes tucked up underneath their chins, but saved their modesty by covering their mouths. At eventide the people all returned looking more phantom-like and unsubstantial even than at dawn. The younger men danced on the sands like fauns, and boys threw their curved clubs at rabbits that had come out to graze upon the grass.

When night had once descended and when Sohail, Algol, Altair and all the stars the Arabs named in far Chaldea centuries ago shed their soft beams upon the world, a peace, not passing human understanding, fell upon the plain. The murmur of the surf on the white beach, the quiet of the district with its air of having been untouched since first the Arabs straggled over it upon their way to the Castle of the Crossing when they invaded Spain a thousand years ago, seemed designed to protect it virgin and inviolate, to all eternity. Yet it was destined (who shall divine what Allah has in store even for his faithful?) to see a palace rise beside the well and its three caroub-trees. Slowly it rose, not in a night like Jonah's gourd but despite the efforts, laudable enough perhaps taken from the point of view of race preservation, of Spanish workmen to do as little as they could in as much time as possible, the frequent floods that cut off all connection with the town, and cattle raids that made the roads unsafe to travel for days together. The hedge of aloes planted on a mound, with a deep ditch to seaward, cut off a portion of the plain planted with trees that looked at first destined to shrivel in the fierce east wind that hitherto had triumphed over all vegetation but the lentiscus scrub.

Courtyard succeeded courtyard, and by degrees the house itself took shape, to the astonishment of the Arabs, who said it was a veritable palace of the *Arabian Nights*. Built in the Moorish style, with battlemented walls so dazzlingly white, that the eye at noontide could as little gaze on them as on the sun itself, the name just suited it. A loggia with low arches faced the well and the three caroub-trees. So close they grew to the arcaded loggia that they seemed with their leafy canopy part and parcel of the house. Workmen from Fez had decorated several rooms with the same pious sentences and stalactites their ancestors had left in the Alhambra, and when the lights were lighted they shone through the pierced stucco work, setting the room aglow. When all was finished, the Oriental carpets on the floors, the silver-mounted guns and yataghans, and all the flotsam and the jetsam that Oriental life holds out with both hands to those with taste and money who pass their lives one foot in Europe the other in the East, completed the astonishment of the Moors who visited it. After its first fight with the prevailing wind and when the hedge of cypresses got up, the garden that had arisen out of the bare plain, as if by magic, was a paradise. Palms and gravilleas, camphor and Judas-trees, with all the flowering shrubs of every climate, shot up in a few years, and people who remembered the low wind-swept plain, to their amazement walked in a shady wood, when they revisited the place. The wind no longer howled, but rustled softly overhead, among the trees. An air of calm and of repose hung over everything, and by the pools in which the goldfish sailed about, sheltered from the sun by the pink water-lilies, Moors used to come and sit with the same sense of great content that the sound of a plashing fountain in the sun induces in their race. The house became a meeting place for all the flower and cream of the strange little town, at that time a miniature Constantinople, with its ambassadors and ministers from every nation upon earth, all with portfolios and no duties to fulfil.

Ladies in European fashions, looking strangely out of place in the surroundings, sat in the Moorish rooms on cushions, their high-heeled shoes refusing to adapt themselves either to the picture or the position as they sat. They strayed about the gardens, asking the names of the exotic plants and straight forgetting them. Some thought it would be quite amusing to live in such surroundings, others deplored the fate of the poor Moorish women, immured for life within four walls. Both attitudes of mind were probably as far removed from what the fair philosophers imagined as was possible. Adjectives that must have exhausted their scant vocabularies, as charming, sweet, delicious, lovely, scented the atmosphere with a kind of mental patchouli. One might have thought oneself in a celestial pastrycook's.

Horses were always neighing at the gates. Occasionally they broke loose and fought with one another, rearing and screaming as they pawed the air. Mules dozed patiently under their high red saddles, the boys who held them generally sleeping peacefully seated on the sand. Nor were there wanting incidents to show that Oriental life was as near at hand as that of Europe, with its sauntering ladies and paste-board ministers of Albania, Andorra, San Marino, and the other little States, once dear to Offenbach. Raisuli as a young unknown man with but five followers once passed the night, sleeping below the caroub-trees around the well, happy to feast upon a sheep procured for him at the nearest aduar. Years afterwards the master of the house, after a long captivity at the hands of the same man whom he had welcomed and who had slept beneath his trees, was liberated under the cover of the night in the grove of fig-trees on the plain.

The villages of Sinia and Menár had many a tribal fight, and while they fought, inside the house ladies and gentlemen took tea, admired the curiosities, and went into the garden to see if some rare plant or other was in flower. Thus house and garden rose out of the sand, flourished and appeared destined to endure. It was written otherwise, either because Allah was jealous of the little paradise, or because nothing is destined to endure. To-day, fallen from its high estate, dreary and bat-haunted, the paint hanging in flakes from the once dazzling walls, the house lies desolate. Across the loggia, the bougainvillea, once the glory of the porch, a splash of purple on the whitewashed walls, looking like a stain of wine on a white tablecloth, lies prone and draggled in the dust. The fishponds are all dry, the goldfish dead, the little rills of water burst and leaking on the paths. The fountain is half full of empty sardine tins and broken glass. The fruit-trees stand neglected and unpruned. Only the palms, their heads in fire, their feet in water, flourish and raise their feathery branches, reminding one of a deserted lighthouse still keeping watch over a ruined port. Grass grows in the courtyards once so full of life, and a green shutter in the house bangs to and fro in the east wind, sounding in the deserted garden like a signal-gun booming through a fog. Wild boars root in the beds once tended carefully and stocked with flowers. Even at noontide the place is melancholy. In the long nights when rabbits play about upon the grass and porcupines pace through the shrubberies, it must be a veritable Dar-el-Jinoun, for only djinns could thrive in such a house.

Redeemed

Promoted

At the sound of the boatswain's whistle, the galley-slaves lay on their oars. Turks, Moors, and Christian criminals, they formed a curious amalgam of the rascality of Southern Europe and Northern Africa. Stripped to the waist, with their heads shaven closely to the skin, they sat six deep, chained to the bench on which they tugged the ponderous oars. A gangway, raised above the towers [sic=rowers], ran the whole distance of the rowing benches, and on it stood the boatswain with a heavy whip that he used unmercifully. If one of the slaves died at the oar, he was at once heaved overboard and the five left had to perform the same work as before, with a man short. In storms, or actions, or a chase after some other vessel, the boatswain ran to and fro, putting bread steeped in wine into their mouths.

When the way that the galley had on her had ceased, she let her anchor go and floated like a nautilus on the quiet waters of the little harbour of Motril, a cable's length from shore.

Her pennant, trailing in the water and the great ensign at the jackstaff on the poop, showed her to be one of the Dorias galleys from Genoa. On board her, under the command of Captain Don Julian Ramirez, straight from the Flemish wars, came a detachment of the famous "tercios," to fight against the Moriscoes, whom persecution had driven to revolt. All the hill villages of the Alpujarras around Granada were held for the new sultan who, once a Christian under the name of Fernando de Valor, had gone back to the simpler faith of Allah and his prophet and butchered every Spaniard he could find. Don John of Austria himself was in command against them. Boats left the galley, full of men, their horses swimming after them, led by a rope. They formed upon the beach and let their horses roll in the sand before they saddled up. Then, when the last boatload had got ashore, the detachment of some fifty men slowly set out towards Motril leading their horses, who were stiff and cramped after ten days at sea from Genoa. Their captain led his own horse as he walked at the head of his company.

They crossed the beach close to the spot where, in a bed of lilies, was found the sculptured image of Our Lady of the Head, revered throughout the district for many a miracle it has wrought, although the unbelievers shoot out their lips and say, it once adorned the prow of some wrecked ship. When they arrived at the old town the wild inhabitants swarmed out to welcome them, the children, swarthy and ragged as the Moors, shrill-voiced and critical, and in no wise awed by the grim warriors, upon whom they freely passed remarks not always complimentary. As they marched slowly through the sandy streets, towards the plaza where they were to camp, the population crowded to their doors, and, from the iron-grated windows, peered women dressed in the formal costume of the time, but much behind the fashion of Madrid. Though nothing in the world was so detested in their eyes as a Moor, still the close intercourse between the ever-jarring races had endued them with so much of the Arab character that many of them drew their shawls across their mouths when the troopers stared too closely at them.

All eyes were fixed upon the captain, who, thin and war-scarred, one hand upon the hilt of his long Milan rapier, gravely saluted the Alcalde as he gave his horse to a man to hold, who stepped out from the ranks. The men in their trunk hose, buff jerkins, tall russet boots and bright steel bassinets, were low in stature as a rule, but active and well knit, swarthy and with the look about them that only life exposed to constant danger ever gives. Some carried crossbows of steel fitted with little windlasses, for no living man was strong enough to bend them with the naked hand. Others bore harquebuses that still were fired with the pyrites wheel, for flintlocks were but just coming into use. All carried pikes and swords of the same pattern as their captain's, though of a common make, heavy, but serviceable. Broken to war for years in Holland, the soldiers, who had been accustomed to give or take but little quarter in their campaigns against the northern heretics, were just the kind of men to deal with their hereditary foes, the Moors. The people of Motril poured into their willing ears tales of the cruelties committed by the revolted Moriscoes on the Christian villagers, that set their blood on fire. Their captain scarcely could prevail on them to rest, before the horses were fit to take the road.

On the third morning, after a mass held in their camp and an unneeded exhortation not to spare the Moorish dogs, they filed out of Motril. Their chaplain, Fray Juan de Dios, a tall, pale-faced Franciscan friar, strong and athletic, with his habit tucked up in his belt, marched with the crossbowmen on foot, carrying a crucifix. Captain Ramirez and his lieutenant, Hugo Mondragon, said that the friar was wasted, and that so fine and tall a man ought to have been a soldier. They often asked him, half in earnest, half jestingly, to change his habit for a uniform, promising if he did so to promote him to the rank of "alferez" at the first opportunity. To all these jokes, the friar used to reply that he could do better service in his own regiment and that the Lord would not forget to promote him, if he should see fit.

At daybreak Captain Ramirez left the town, the ragged population turning out to see him on the road, and then returning to its usual avocation of consuming time, as time was what it had the most of to consume. A fresh, soft breeze blew off the sea, wafting a light mist towards the ochre-coloured hills, around whose tops it hung in wreaths, but without shrouding them from sight as in the north. The company crossed the half-dried-up river, that only ran in channels here and there, the horses whinnied, glad to be freed from the confinement of the ship and danced and passaged sideways when the water splashed against their legs. Gradually Motril sank out of sight, as they wound through the sugar-fields that circle round the town. When the church tower had disappeared and all the miserable reed-built, straw-thatched huts were passed, Captain Ramirez threw out skirmishers on each side of the troop and sent two mounted men in front. Each crag and copse upon the way might hold an enemy and all the farms upon the road were quite deserted, the cattle driven to the shelter of the walls of Adra, Salobreña, or Motril and the crops left standing in the fields. As they ascended the rude track towards the Alpujarras, bearing towards the east a little, they passed by Albuñol, its white and Moorish-looking houses refracting back the morning sun so as almost to blind the soldiers, long accustomed to the low skies of the Low Countries. The soldiers muttered to each other, "Spain once more; praise to the Lord, she never changes, and though bread, meat and all the rest may lack, we have the sun to warm us. Long live the Sun!" When the track passed Polopos, they entered the great cork woods of the lower foothills of the sierras, and looking to the vast expanse of country descried Almuñecar in the distance and Salobreña on its rocky eminence. Torrox, still held by the enemies of God, nestled against the very breast of the wild hills, encircled by its walls. Its slender mosque tower was just visible, and near the walls the tents of the besiegers, sent by Don John of Austria to reduce the place, clustered like toadstools round the trunk of a dead tree.

Now and again they passed dead bodies half eaten by the wolves, and halted for Fray Juan to say a prayer over them, while the men cursed the spawn of Mahomet. Lanjarron lay half in ruins, and from the cellars crept starved wretches who had been too terrified to venture out to make their way towards the coast. From them the captain learned that the first strong place held by the rebels was but a half-day's march away among the hills. The people said it was impregnable without siege cannon, perched as it was, like an eagle's eyrie on a crag, with a deep chasm in the rock before the only gate. Night was approaching, and in an orange garden where half the trees had been cut down they made their camp. So wild and desolate the landscape looked in the fast failing light, it seemed they and their horses were the only living things in all the world. Far off, the sea shone like a sheet of frosted silver, without a sail to give relief to its immensity. The red earth glowed like a blazing furnace under the last rays of the setting sun. Great bands of scarlet, fading into magenta and dissolving into a faint purple, barred the sky. Lakes seemed to float above the mountain-tops as in a mirage; lakes so translucent and diaphanous that, as they melted into faintest saffron and disappeared to form again in fine gradations of violet, black, brown, aquamarine, and palest opal, it seemed as if the atmosphere challenged the spectrum to follow all its shades.

The sentinels drowsed at their posts, blowing their match occasionally to keep it burning. When it flared for an instant, its bluish gleam lit up the bivouac and disclosed the groups of soldiers, sleeping with their feet towards the fire, and underneath the orange-trees, the horses picketed, munching their barley, or resting a hind-leg, with one ear pointing forward and the other backward, to catch the slightest sound. Of all the camp, only the friar was wakeful, telling his beads, and rising now and then to pray upon his knees. The officers, who slept but intermittently, smiled at each other as they looked at him, and muttered, "Not only he, but all the friars in Spain are praying for us." The false dawn saw the camp astir, with the dew dropping off the orange-trees, matting the horses' manes and tails and running from the barrels of the harquebuses. Before the morning star had fairly disappeared, the men had cleaned their arms, looked to the crossbow strings, fed their horses and after a brief prayer from the friar, commenced a long ascent over a steep staircase of rock, the horses scrambling like cats to keep their foothold, and striking fire out of the stones. Soon peasants driving their flocks before them appeared upon the road, with tales of all the horrors of the revolt, for both sides fought like famished wolves, holding their lives as nothing, if they might only kill an enemy. On every side the smoke of burning villages filled the air, and in the distance shots resounded through the hills.

Spurring along the road and looking anxiously from side to side among the bushes, a courier from Don John of Austria's headquarters at Isnalloz rode up to them. Victory was certain, but several rebel chieftains still held out and the campaign was bound to last for months. A Turk, one Mamet Ali, held the strong little fortress of Hisnr-el-Birk, only a league away, with about five-and-twenty men. From it he sallied out at intervals to raid the district, slaughtering the villagers like sheep, and violating all the women and girls. The courier did not know the Spanish name of the stronghold, but said it did not matter, for hereabouts we all speak Arabic. He tightened up his girths, crossed himself, mounted and moved off, calling out as he went, "Mamet Ali is a devil and the son of a devil; look out for him." Then, spurring on, he vanished in a cloud of dust, his horse's footfalls echoing back for a long time in the still air.

Captain Ramirez called a halt, dismounted all his men, who fed their horses and ate a scanty meal. Then he sent out two scouts. On their return they said the castle was but a mile or two away. The bridge across the chasm had been cut. The trestles still remained, and in the bushes they had found some planks they thought might stretch across. The captain saddled up at once, and dashing forward, drove the Moors into the fort. No time was to be lost, for bolts and arrows whistled among them, wounding several of the men. The captain's first care was to send the horses to the rear, out of the missiles' way. Then he called out for volunteers. All answered his demand, and carrying brushwood cut down with their swords, to shelter them, they bridged the chasm, losing a man or two slain by the stones the Moors cast down on them. The Turk stood on the walls directing everything. No shot could touch him. The soldiers said he was in league with Satan, or had a hundred lives. When all was ready and the fire of the harquebuses and the crossbowmen kept back the enemy from the bridge, there was a pause. The hardy soldiers, who had faced perils all their lives in the Italian and Dutch wars, in Mexico and in Peru, stood hesitating, for it seemed certain death to venture on the planks exposed to fire and to a rain of stones.

The captain was tightening up his belt to lead his men to victory or to death, when he was put aside, firmly but gently. His eyes ablaze, his face pale as a corpse, his habit tucked up to his belt, carrying a sword in one hand and in the other holding a crucifix, Fray Juan de Dios rushed across the bridge amid a shower of stones. The soldiers, yelling "Santiago, close up Spain; death to the Moorish dogs!" rushed after him and battered down the door. For half an hour the fight raged furiously without a thought of quarter, the soldiers striking down the Moors, who fought to their last breath, stabbing their enemies upon the ground in their death agony. Mamet Ali, still without a wound, fought stubbornly up the stone stairway to the roof, then bounding on the parapet, hurled a last curse against the Nazarenes and sprang into the abyss. Down in the courtyard, after his losses had been counted, Ramirez wiped his sword upon the cloak of a dead Moor. "The dogs fought well," he said to his lieutenant. "Where is the friar? for after God we owe the victory to him. This time he shall be made alferez if I have to go to Rome to get the Holy Father to absolve him from his vows. I will promote him this time, no matter what he says." His second in command looked at him sadly, saying, "It is in vain. He was promoted half an hour ago in his own regiment. . . . Come and see where he lies."

Ten paces from the gate he lay, his eyes wide open, the fire of combat gone from them, and a contented smile upon his face. A little stream of blood, already nearly dried, had trickled from his lips, as a great rock crushed in his chest. His sword, broken and bloody, was by his side. With his last breath he had grasped the crucifix in his right hand.

At Navalcán

We had been riding through the open park-like oak forests that had been sown with corn, now reaped, at the fast jog known as the Castilian pace. It had not rained for months, and the rough trail lay inches deep in dust as white as flour. The greyhounds following us lolled out their tongues like long, red rags, and trotted on resignedly close to the horses' heels. Not a bird stirred in the torrid heat. The air seemed as if heated in a furnace, and a few cattle here and there stood motionless in the dry streams, as if they knew that there was water underneath the surface, although they could not reach it. The bark upon the cork-trees scattered among the oaks seemed bursting. Even the lizards appeared to run across the track as if they did so under protest, scared by our horses' feet.

Nicholás checked his lean, roan mare, and stopping in a long account of his adventures in the Manigua of Cuba, where in days past he had served against Maximo Gomez and Maceo, pointing to a conglomeration of brown, dusty houses that clustered round the tower of a church, a mile or two away, said "There is Navalcán. They will be dancing in the plaza already, Don Roberto," he said; "let us push on and see them in their old dresses, for in Navalcán they are still Spaniards as God made them in days past. Old Cirilo's daughter was married this morning, and we shall be in time to see the fiesta if we spur on a bit."

He settled himself back upon his saddle, and with his face tanned by the tropics and his native sun, his suit of dark grey velveteen, and his short jacket, over which he wore a leather shoulder-belt with a great boss of brass stamped with the arms of the Dukes of Frias, for he was their head gamekeeper, he looked just like the yeoman on the good grey mare that he was riding "a la gineta" who [sic] Cervantes has immortalised.

We spurred our horses, passed by the ruined Roman bridge with its high arch spanning the dried-up river, stopped for a moment under a gnarled oak-tree, for Nicholás to point out where he had killed a wolf last winter, and diving down a steep path like the bed of a torrent, entered the outskirts of the old-world town. Men upon donkeys and on mules, with now and then a horseman sitting high on his semi-Moorish saddle, his feet encased in iron shoe stirrups, passed us, all going to the feast. Pigs ran about the streets, as much at home as Peter in his house, as Nicholás observed. Children, ragged, bright-eyed and dirty, stared at the passers-by from the doors of houses, as Kaffir children might stare at a strange white man passing before their kraal.

We clattered up a steep and stony lane, the horses' shoes striking a stream of sparks from the rough stones, and got off at the house of one Cirilo, an ex-alcalde of the town. Short, stout, dressed in black velveteen, a broad black sash wound three or four times about his waist, a stiff and broad-brimmed black felt hat upon his head and alpargatas on his feet, he seemed descended apostolically from Sancho Panza, both in appearance and in speech. Our horses were led by one of Cirilo's sons, just in the way Cervantes describes, when the Knight of the Rueful Figure and his squire arrived at many another such a little town as Navalcán. Assembled in the chief room of the house, adorned with a few pictures of the saints, a curious piece of old embroidery in a black frame, and several trophies of the chase, were all the notabilities. Much did we salute each other, inquiring minutely after the state of health of all our separate families, and being assured that the poor house in which we sat was ours. The mistress of the place and her two tall daughters stood about, talking and bringing wine, lemonade, and cakes of meal and honey, with the same white, flake pastry that the Moors left in Spain and that is to be seen to-day in every house in Fez and Tetuán.

They stood about, sitting down only occasionally and as if under protest, for in old-world places such as Navalcán, women, all unknown to themselves, have still continued the old Arab custom of never sitting down to eat together with the men. Being strangers in that remote and time-neglected village, we also in a way acted as newspapers. "What of Morocco and the accursed war? Neighbour Remigio has a son there fighting the infidel. He cannot use the pen, so that his father does not know if he is alive or dead." Then with a touch of that materialistic scepticism that is at once the strength and weakness of the race, "The big fish make their harvest out of it, I suppose, for in disturbed rivers fishermen find their gain." Cirilo took off his hat and wiped his forehead, conscious that by the enunciation of a proverb he had clinched the matter for all time. Our hats he had begged us to take off, and placed them on a chair, for a guest's hat in old-world towns in Spain is handled with respect.

The conversation ran a good deal on the price of pigs, of mules, sheep, horses, and other matters that men of culture take their delight in talking of the whole world over. All governments were bad, and politics the ruin of a country, yet none of them ever in his life lifted a hand to change a government, but talked of politics for hours. The clergy, too, were rogues who did no work of any kind, were drones and cumberers of the earth, yet they went religiously to mass, and when the parish priest came round to drink a glass of wine with us, all rose up courteously to do him reverence. A native of Asturias, a province he described as quite a paradise, the priest gave it as his opinion that England was by degrees emancipating herself from the bonds of the heresy that Henry VIII and his accursed concubine, Ana Bolena, had promulgated. I said I thought it might be so, and that when all was said and done Ana Bolena had paid dearly, both for her carnal lapses and her heresy. As one who is enunciating an eternal verity, Father Camacho rejoined in a grave voice, "Sir, she is burning in hell fire for all eternity." I left it at that, hoping the faggots might be after all made of asbestos and the poor sinner's sufferings mitigated by the intervention of Jehovah's other self, Allah, the Merciful, the Compassionate.

After a round of the strong, harsh, red wine that in those parts is jocularly referred to as "Peleon," that is, the fighter, whether from its effect upon the stomach or the brain is doubtful, washed down with sweet and sticky lemonade, Cirilo said the dancing in the plaza had begun. The ceremony in the church had taken place at eleven in the morning, so that the happy pair were actually joined in holy matrimony, or as the country people say, "married in Latin," and in their new estate were welcoming their friends.

Outside the door the strains of the dulzaina, the Arab pipe the Moors left in Spain, accompanied by the sacramental drum, mixed with the blare of a brass band. The little winding streets were like the beds of torrents, with great live rocks coming to the surface, worn smooth and slippery by the passing feet of mules and horses since Navalcán was Navalcán. Men passed who might have stepped out of past centuries, all in the old Castilian peasant's dress, made of black velveteen, short jackets, open waistcoats and frilled shirts. They wore black broad-brimmed hats over silk handkerchiefs bound round their heads with the ends hanging down like tails. Where the streets were free from rocks the white dust lay so thickly that the feet of the passers-by, all shod with alpargatas, made no more sound than if it had been snow on which they walked. Now and again, above the music of the band, came a wild cry from one of the excited village youths, so like the neighing of a horse, it seemed impossible that it was not a stallion calling to a mare.

A mass of country people filled the middle of the square. Only one man, a neighbouring proprietor, was dressed in modern clothes. The women, for the most part, wore gay-coloured petticoats, giving them a look of humming tops as they moved to and fro. Over their skirts they had a long lace apron, worked in elaborate openwork designs, that in most cases had been generations in their families. Under their short basque jackets their loose white blouses, elaborately worked and frilled, swelled out like pouter pigeons' crops. Their heads were bare, and their thick hair, as black as jet, was parted in the middle, brushed close against their cheeks, and plaited into two long pigtails, hanging down their backs. All wore gold earrings worked in filigree, and round their necks strings of gold beads, heirlooms from older days. Their feet were shod with dark, brown leather shoes, latched on the instep and cut in open patterns by a rustic shoemaker. Though they were peasants they all walked with the incomparable carriage of the women of their race, with the slight motion of the hips that sets the petticoats a-swinging, just as a horse's tail swings very gently to and fro at the Castilian pace.

The dancers formed a long line down the middle of the square, the men and women standing opposite each other. The bride and bridegroom stood in the middle of the line. The bride, tall, handsome, dark, and active on her feet as a wild colt, wore a silk skirt almost concealed under the folds of old-fashioned coarse lace that had belonged to her great-grandmother. Upon her head she wore the "Cresta," a high knot of ribbon shaped something like a coxcomb, to show she had never made a slip of any kind. This badge, the people said, was getting rarer than it used to be for brides, a circumstance that they attributed to the decay of morals, that had been going on continuously for the last five hundred years. This bride upheld the ancient purity of Castilian morals in spite of being five-and-twenty years of age. It somehow made one think about the girl who had received the prize of virtue five years running, and in the comic opera remarked, "Oui, cinq fois rosière, c'est joli, mais cristi! que c'est dur."

The bridegroom, a tall, swarthy youth, who had already an anticipatory air of cuckledom *[sic]* about him, between excitement and

120

the wine that he had evidently drunk was streaming down with sweat. Still, when the band, placed just beneath the village cross, struck up a lively Jota he capered nimbly, first with one girl, then with another, snapping his fingers like a pair of castagnettes, with his arms held above his shoulders and waving to and fro. A thick, white dust covered the dancers' old-fashioned dresses, as it were with flour, and falling on the women's black and glossy hair, gave it a look of being powdered, not unbecoming to them.

When the band stopped from sheer exhaustion and the dulzaina players' cheeks were for a spell deflated, great pitchers of rough earthenware full of the heady country wine were handed round among the crowd. They drank, first looking towards the bride, and wishing her long life and many children, then drew the backs of their brown, toil-stained hands across their mouths, tightened their sashes, and after taking one of the black and coarsely made cigars the bridegroom went about offering to everybody from a brown paper parcel, fell to a-dancing, with the cigars behind their ears. Wild goats or antelopes could not have been more active than the youths and maidens; the swing and perseverance of the band were wonderful. The elders stood about in groups, smoking the rank, ill-made cigars that a paternal Government in Spain provides at its own prices to its citizens.

The band ceased suddenly, without a warning, just as a gipsy song ends, on a long-drawn-out note. The men, after the fashion of their kind the whole world over, collected into groups and criticised the girls as they walked to and fro with their arms round each other's waists. Great tables were laid out in the patio of a house, with rows of pitchers filled with wine and round hard rolls upon the spotless tablecloth, making one think of Leonardo's "Last Supper," and hope no Judas would intrude upon the feast. In the house where the happy pair were going to reside their friends and neighbours all had brought their offerings. Jugs, pots, pans, washing-basins, hoes, spades and axes, great skins of wine, salt, sugar, coffee; innumerable bundles of cigars, adzes and planes, saws, gimlets, and almost every article of rural life lay piled upon the floor. A load of wood, sacks of potatoes, with jars of olives and of oil, recalled a wedding such as Theocritus might have celebrated.

Then, entering the house, the bride received us, and all the strangers, who had not come provided with their household offerings, presented five or ten dollars to the bridegroom, who thanked them fluently in such well-chosen language as few dwellers in the north, men of much more education than himself, could hope to compass. He handed all the money to the bride, who put it carefully into a bag she carried by her side and thanked the givers, who once again wished her health and happiness, with many children and long-drawn-out years, with self-possession and the grave air of dignity that comes so naturally to the Castilians. Cirilo hoped that she would imitate her mother, who had thirteen children, and his daughter, smiling at him, rejoined that she would try.

In an inside apartment, that in Spain is called an alcove, without a window and stiflingly hot, was placed the marriage bed. Full five feet from the ground it stood, with mattress upon mattress piled mountains high, a great lace valence worked by the bride herself in antique patterns of men on horseback, tall cypresses, and crosses here and there, swept down and touched the floor. The coverlet was lace, made by the mother of the bride and by her sisters, and the four curtains hanging from the posts were of a curious kind of needlework, exactly like that made by the Moorish women in North Africa. In a dark outhouse, outside the bridal chamber with its four-poster bed, were laid a plank or two, covered with several sheepskins and a rug. This Spartan couch tradition had provided for the bridegroom, who had to occupy it till the last guest retired.

Once more Cirilo took us to his house, and once again regaled us with wine and lemonade, cakes, coffee, and with old-world sweetmeats, made of the kernels of a pine-cone, stewed in honey, into a sticky little slab. We mounted at his door, with all his family holding the stirrups and the reins; wished him farewell with a cascade of thanks, and picked our way through the dark streets, our horses plunging wildly now and then, for from each door the citizens were sending rockets whizzing through the air, and serpents ran along the stones, exploding loudly and shedding a blue glare upon the ground.

Outside the town, when we had got a pull upon our horses, the moon had risen, making the bushes take fantastic shapes, and look like animals, ready to spring upon us. The mountains of the Gredos looked unearthly in the moonlight, the shrill cicalas kept up a continuous singing, and neither Nicholás nor I said anything for a mile or two, till turning round he asked me, "Have you seen anything like that in England, Don Roberto?" To which I answered "No."

Inveni Portum

Joseph Conrad

A light warm rain fell upon the old-world streets. The houses, with their casement windows, timbered upper stories and overhanging eaves, still kept the air as of an older world. The gateways, with their battlements and low archways through which the medieval traffic once had flowed, with men-at-arms and archers, strings of pack-horses, monks, nuns, and pilgrims come to worship at the shrine of Becket, were now mere monuments.

Time had but mellowed without defacing them, although the damp had made the stone peel off in flakes, giving it a look of scales. Long stretches of the city wall still stood, covered with a growth of wallflowers and of valerian, loved of cats. Houses and yet more houses crowded in upon the cathedral, usurping what by rights should have been a grassy close, guarded by elm-trees or by limes, with nests for rooks, who with their cawing supplemented the murmuring masses in the adjacent choir, for surely rooks in a cathedral close must ever praise the Lord for their quiet, sheltered lives. Grouped round its dominating church the city huddled as if it sought protection against progress and modernity. Bell Harry in his beauty seemed a giant lighthouse pointing heavenwards. It was indeed a haven where a man who had had his fill of this world's din might well retire to and find rest, for the incoming cricketers were evidently but birds of passage, and when they all departed once more the town would sink back to repose. Although the streets were decorated with flags and floral arches and filled with sun-burned athletes, and the companions of their beds and bats, with cohorts of the clergy come up from their parsonages, greeting effusively Old Brown of Brasenose or Smith of Wadham, whom they met annually at this, the week of weeks — for cricket is a sport that clergymen can attend without offence — nothing could take away the air of medieval quiet that broods upon the town. The peaceful landscape, with the slow Medway winding through its fields of lush, green grass, full of contemplative cows, its apple orchards, its rubble churches, with their truncated spires and air of immortality, is restful to the eye. The town itself, resting from its long strife with time, brings quiet to the soul.

On every side are relics of the past — gates, barbicans, and walls, the grassy mound of the Dane John, about whose origin so many legends cluster, the square, squat tower, all that remains to show where once the church of Mary of Magdala stood, the crypt where exiled Huguenots performed their maiméd *[sic]* rites, the helm and gauntlets of the Black Prince of Wales and Gascony, above his tomb in the cathedral, speak of the past; the resting past, for in the present, as in the days when past was present, there can be no peace. The quiet old city seemed indeed a fitting place in which to harbour one who long had battled with tempestuous seas, had heard the tropic rollers kissing the coral reefs and felt the sting of spindrift coating his beard with salt. So to the chapel of the older faith he held, not only as a faith, but as a bulwark against Oriental barbarism, we bore his coffin, buried under flowers, laid it before the altar railings, and his friends, Catholic and Protestant alike, with those who hold that God will not damn those whom He created with the potentialities of damnation in their bodies and their souls, for the mere fun of damning, all listened to the "blessed mutter of the Mass," devoutly on their knees. Within that little fane, with its images of saints, enough for faith, for faith works miracles, even upon the optic nerve, perhaps, but not enough for art, all became Catholics for the nonce. When all is said and done, of all the faiths it is the most consolatory, and tears stood in the eyes of many of the heterogeneous congregation. What, after all, is better for the soul than prayer to an unseen God, in an uncomprehended tongue? When the priest got to *Ite Missa est* no one appeared to have found the service wearisome, for somehow it seemed to join us to the friend whom we should see no more, a little longer.

Then, through the streets all hung with flowers, as if to honour him whom we were taking to his anchorage, we took our way out to the cemetery. We passed through ancient archways, skirted the crumbling walls, caught glimpses of the cathedral towers up winding streets, marvelled at the number of the churches, and marked the advertisement of something or another, carried out in the vile bodies of three poor Christians, decked with huge, grinning cardboard heads, as in a pantomime.

I think there was little that we did not see, from the collected band of cricketers, who, standing at the chief hotel, saluted as we passed, as reverently as if the funeral had been that of one of their own mystery, to dogs, that nearly sacrificed themselves beneath the wheels, a skewbald horse that drew a gipsies' caravan, and bullocks going to the slaughterhouse, for when the soul is stirred the external eye looks upon the world more keenly than when we sit at home smoking a good cigar. Those sorts of drives in funeral carriages appear to last for ever, in fact one almost wishes that they would, for it is well that now and then a man should see *memento mori* written up plainly before his eyes, for him to read and inwardly digest. As we rolled slowly on into the open country the engine of the motor hearse slowed down to the jog-trot of the old-time funeral horse, so heavily the hand of custom bears upon the reins of everything. I fell into what in the north we call a "dwawm," that state in which the mind is active and as if freed from its subjection to the flesh. Time put the clock back for some five-and-twenty years or so, and I saw him who now lay in his coffin underneath the flowers, his battle over and his place assured in the great fellowship that Chaucer captains, struggling to make his way. What were his trials, what his disillusions, and what he suffered at the hands of fools, only himself could tell, and he was never one who wore his heart upon his sleeve for critics and for daws to peck at. For leagues we journeyed, as it appeared to me, passing men tedding haycocks in the field, Boy Scouts in brakes, and now and then a Kentish farmer in an old-fashioned dogcart.

All the dead man had written and had done welled up in my mind. *Nostromo*, with its immortal picture of the old follower of Garibaldi, its keen analysis of character, and the local colour that he divined rather than knew by actual experience, its subtle humour, and the completeness of it all, forming an epic, as it were, of South America, written by one who saw it to the core, by intuition, amazed me just as it did when I first read it, *consule Planco*, in the years that have slipped past. Then came *The Nigger of the Narcissus*, into which he put the very soul of the old sailing ships, and that of those who sailed and suffered in them, as he himself once sailed and suffered and emerged, tempered and chastened by the sea. *Youth* and *The Heart of Darkness*, and then the tale of *Laughing Anne*, so deep and moving in its presentment of a lost woman's soul, all flitted through my mind. Lastly, *The Mirror of the Sea*, with its old Danish skipper who intoned the dirge of ships, past, present and to come, haunted my memory. So dreaming with my eyes wide open, all the long

125

years of friendship rolled back again, and my lost friend appeared, as I remembered him — was it a hundred years ago, or was it yesterday? For death annihilates perspective, blots out all sense of time, and leaves the memory of those that we have lost blurred in the outline, but more present to the mind than when Time, seeming but an invention of the poets with his unmeaning hourglass, and his unnecessary scythe, still rolled on, as it seemed eternally, just as a man when dozing on his horse during a tedious night march, or jogging on behind a troop of cattle in the sun, thinks that his whole existence has consisted but of an ache between the shoulders and a dull throbbing at the knees. Waking or sleeping, or in a mixture of the two, but with my senses wide awake enough, I seemed to see my friend.

His nose was aquiline, his eyes most luminous and full. It seemed his very soul looked out of them, piercing the thoughts of those whom he addressed; his beard, trimmed to a point, was flecked with grey a little and his moustache was full. His face, of the dull yellow hue that much exposure to the tropic sun in youth so often causes, was lined and furrowed by the weather. His dark and wiry hair age had respected except that it had grown a little thin upon the temples, leaving his forehead bare. His cheek bones, high and jutting out a little, revealed his Eastern European origin, just as his strong square figure and his walk showed him a sailor, who never seems to find the solid earth a quite familiar footing after a sloping deck. His feet were small and delicately shaped, and his fine, nervous hands, never at rest a minute in his life, attracted you at once. They supplemented his incisive speech by indefinable slight movements, not gestures in the Latin sense, for they were never raised into the air nor used for emphasis. They seemed to help him to express the meaning of his words without his own volition in a most admirable way. Something there was about him, both of the Court and of the quarterdeck, an air of courtesy and of high breeding, and yet with something of command. His mind, as often is the case with men of genius — and first and foremost what most struck one was his genius — seemed a strange compact of the conflicting qualities, compounded, in an extraordinary degree, of a deep subtlety and analytic power, with great simplicity.

As he discoursed upon the things that interested him, recalled his personal experiences, or poured his scorn and his contempt upon unworthy motives and writers who to attain their facile triumphs had pandered to bad taste, an inward fire seemed to be smouldering ready to break out, just as the fire that so long smouldered in the hold of the doomed ship in which he made his first voyage to the East suddenly burst out into flames. His tricks of speech and manner, the way he grasped both of your hands in his, his sudden breaking into French, especially when he was moved by anything, as when I asked him to attend some meeting or another, and he replied, "Non, il y aura des Russes," grinding his teeth with rage. England, the land of his adoption, he loved fervently, and could not tolerate that anything with which he had been once familiar should be tampered with, as often happens when a man adopts a second fatherland, for to change that which first attracted him seems a flat blasphemy.

As the car drew up at the cemetery gate with a harsh, grating noise upon the gravel, I wakened from my dream. The rain had cleared and the sun poured down upon us, as in procession, headed by the acolytes and priests, we bore the coffin to the grave. A semicircle of Scotch firs formed, as it were, a little harbour for him. The breeze blew freshly, south-west by south a little westerly — a good wind, as I thought, to steer up Channel by, and one that he who would no longer feel it on his cheek, looking aloft to see if all the sails were drawing properly, must have been glad to carry when he struck soundings, passing the Wolf Rock or the Smalls after foul weather in the Bay.

Handsomely, as he who lay in it might well have said, they lowered the coffin down. The priest had left his Latin and said a prayer or two in English, and I was glad of it, for English surely was the speech the Master Mariner most loved, and honoured in the loving with new graces of his own.

The voyage was over and the great spirit rested from its toil, safe in the English earth that he had dreamed of as a child in far Ukrainia. A gleam of sun lit up the red brick houses of the town. It fell upon the tower of the cathedral, turning it into a great, glowing beacon pointing to the sky. The trees moved gently in the breeze, and in the fields the ripening corn was undulating softly, just as the waves waft in on an atoll in the Pacific, with a light swishing sound. All was well chosen for his resting-place, and so we left him with his sails all duly furled, ropes flemished down, and with the anchor holding truly in the kind Kentish earth, until the Judgment Day. The gulls will bring him tidings as they fly past above his grave, with their wild voices, if he should weary for the sea and the salt smell of it.

Redeemed

Euphrasia

On a mound in an upland field, right in the middle of a waste of ragwort, black knapweed, and a sea of myriads of eyebright, looking like stars upon a winter's night, there stands a War Memorial. The poorly carved Iona cross, and cast-iron railings with their gate looking as if bought at an ill country ironmonger's, serve but to render its loneliness still more pathetic, contrasted with the overwhelming landscape. "Agus Bheannaich an Sluagh no Daoine Uile a Therig iad Fein gu Toileach (Nehemiah, xi. 2)" runs the Gaelic text upon the plinth. Rendered in English it states, the men whose names are cut upon the stone gave their lives willingly. I do not doubt it, for they were born and passed their youth on the same soil and in the selfsame atmosphere, sharp and invigorating, tempered with the acrid reek of peat, that nurtured Fingal, Cuchullin, Fergus and the heroes that the Celtic Homer sang.

At the foot of the lean field where stands the cross, there winds a long sea-loch with nothing on its shores except a ruined castle to show that man has sailed its waters, since King Haco's fleet visited it, six hundred years ago. As it was when he saw it from his rude birlinn, with his oarsmen bending to their task, their shields ranged on the galley's sides, their swords bestowed beneath their feet upon the vessel's floor, so it remains to-day. The tide still leaves great fringes of brown kelp and yellow dulse upon its slippery rocks; seals still bask on the islands; the dogfish hunts the shoals of herrings, and the Atlantic clean, snell air comes up between South Uist and Benbecula, just as the "Summer Sailors" felt it on their tanned cheeks, stirring their yellow hair, in the days when in their long ships they scourged the Hebrides.

Green, flat-topped mountains tower up on the far side of the loch; great moors, on which grow nothing but the cotton grass, sweet gale and asphodel, stretch towards the fantastic range of the dark, purple mountains to the east. Jagged and serrated, unearthly looking, shrouded in mists that boil and curl about their sides, they rise, looking as if they had something ominous about them, hostile to mankind.

The Ossianic heroes still seem to stalk about their corries and peep out from the mists approvingly at their descendants, whose names are cut upon the little, lonely monument, set in its sea of wild flowers, opposite the loch. Far off Quiraing, Blaaven and Bein a Cailleach; the unquiet tide rip opposite Kyle Rhea, Coruisk and Sligachan; all the wild myrtle-scented moors, the black peat haggs, the air of wildness and remoteness from the world that even motors hooting on the road, and charabancs with loads of tourists, four-beplussed *[sic: in plus-fours]*, shingled, and burberried to the eyes, cannot dispel entirely, make a fit setting for a memorial to men bred and begotten in the isle. Most of them served in Scottish regiments, MacAskill Royal Scots, MacMillan London Scottish, McAlister Scottish South Africans, Galbraith New Zealand Infantry, MacPhee Black Watch, McKinnes Scots Guards, McDonald of the Rhodesian Rifles, and many more, all Skye men, whose bones moulder in battle-fields far from the Winged Isle.

That nothing should be wanting to connect the warriors with their sea-roving ancestors, Captain McFarlane and Angus Cumming of the Mercantile Marine sleep with their slumbers soothed by the murmur of the waves above their heads, a fitting resting-place for men born in an island into which the sea-lochs bore to its very heart. Out of what shielings, with their little fields of oats and of potatoes that stretch like chess-boards on the hill-sides, won from the uncongenial soil by the sweat of centuries of work, the humble warriors came, only their families can tell.

It matters little, reared as they were with one foot in the past, one hand on the "Caschrom" *[sic = Gael., crooked spade]* the other on the handle of some up-to-date reaping machine from Birmingham. Those only who had gone out to the Colonies could have known much about the outside world, until the breaking out of the Great War, in which they lost their lives. For them no placards, with their loud appeals to patriotism, could have been necessary. For a thousand years their ancestors had all been warriors, thronging to enlist in the Napoleonic Wars, eager to join Montrose and Claverhouse, and fighting desperately among themselves when there was peace abroad. They fought their fight, giving up all that most of them possessed, their lives. And now, although their bodies are disintegrated in the four quarters of the globe, it well may be their spirits have returned to some Valhalla in the mists that roll round Sligachan.

Seasons will come and go; the ragworts blossom in the fields where stands the monument, wither and die, and flower again next year. Time will roll on. The names carved upon the stone become forgotten. The cross may fall, and the cheap iron railings exfoliate away to nothing. The very wars in which the Islemen fell become but a mere legend, as has happened to all other wars.

Men's eyes will turn more rarely to the memorial in the wind-swept field, and they will ask what it commemorates. Still, the wild hills will not forget, as they have not forgotten the story of the wars fought by the driver of the twin thin-maned, high-mettled, swift-footed, wide-nostriled steeds of the mountains, "Sithfadda and Dusrongeal." *[sic: Gael., Sithfadda and Dubhstron-gheal, Cuchullin's horses]* But if the eyes of men are turned no longer to the plinth, with its long list of names and Gaelic text, when the spring comes, and once again the eyebright springs in the hungry field, the west wind sweeping up the loch will turn a million little eyes towards the cross.

Redeemed

A Hundred in the Shade

The river looked like a stream of oil flowing between the walls of dense, impenetrable woods that fringed its banks. Now and again it eddied strongly and seemed to boil, as some great rock or snag peeped up menacingly. Then it flowed on again resistlessly, bearing upon its yellow flood great trunks of Bongos or of Ceibas, as if they were but reeds. Toucans, looking as if they had been fashioned rather by Gian Baptista Porta than by nature, darted like kingfishers across its face. Parrots screeched harshly, and above the tallest trees, macaws, blue, red and orange, soared like hawks, looking as fitting to their natural surroundings as rooks in England cawing in the elms. Upon the sand-banks great saurians basked, and when they felt the passing steamer's wash, rolled into the stream, as noiselessly as water-rats in a canal.

Now and again a little clearing broke the hostile wall of the fierce-growing vegetation, with a few straw-thatched huts, a mango tree or two, and a small patch of maize or yucca, with an unsubstantial fence of canes. Occasionally, where a stretch of plain intervened between the woods, a lean vaquero on a leaner horse, his hat blown back, forming a sort of aureole of straw behind his head, galloped along the banks after a point of steers, or merely raced the steamer for a few hundred yards and then, checking his horse, wheeled like a bird upon the wing. The steamer, painted a dazzling white, with decks piled one upon another till it looked like a floating house, belched out its thin wood smoke and panted as it fought the powerful, almost invisible current of the oily stream. Upon each side a barge was lashed, carrying a load of cattle that diminished day by day, as one was slaughtered every morning, in full sight of its doomed fellows, whose hooves were dyed red with the blood that flowed upon the deck.

As the boat forced its way up-stream the heat grew daily greater, and the fierce glare from the surface of the water more intense. The sun set in a dull, red orb, and from the banks there rose a thin, white mist. From the recesses of the forests came the cries of wild animals, silent by day, but roused into activity at night. The monkeys howled their full-throated chorus, jaguars and wild cats snarled, and in the stillness the brushwood rustled as some nocturnal animal passed through them stealthily. Clouds of mosquitoes filled the air, rendering sleep impossible. Even the freshness of the evening seemed to wear away as night wore on, and one by one the jaded passengers sought the topmost deck-house to try to catch the breeze.

Sprawling in wicker chairs, as the steamer forged along, the great black banks of vegetation sliding towards her as she passed, the passengers, mopping themselves and killing the mosquitoes now and then with a loud slap, relapsed into a moody silence, as they sipped iced drinks. Now and then someone cursed the heat, and now and then one or another of the perspiring band would walk to the thermometer, hung between the windows of the deck-house, and then exclaim, "Jesus! a hundred in the shade." One of the group of men who looked at him as a shipwrecked sailor might look out for a sail, said, "In the moon, you mean," and sank back on his chair with as much elasticity as a sponge thrown out of a bath rebounds upon the floor.

At last, rounding a bend, a light breeze ruffled the surface of the river and brought a little life into the men lounging in their deck-chairs. No one could think of sleep in such conditions. Talk languished after a few general remarks about the price of cattle, and the usual stories about the prowess of the horses, the best in the whole world, that everyone had owned, for general conversation usually flags in a society of men, when women and horses have been discussed. No one spoke for a considerable time, as the steamer swept along through the dark alley of the woods, illuminated by a thousand million fireflies flashing among the trees. The dark, blue southern sky, and the yellow waters of the stream, lighted up by the powerful port and starboard lights, appeared to frame the vessel in, and cut her off from all the world.

Without preamble, the orchid hunter, a thin, sunburned man, spectacled and bald, took up his parable. He told of having camped alone in Singapore, and being bitten on the forefinger of his left hand by some poisonous snake or other. "I had no antidote of any kind with me. My whisky bottle was quite empty. Not that I think it would have done much good had it been full, for I was so well soaked in it, I should have been obliged to drink a quart before it took effect on me. Yes, well, we orchid hunters as a rule are not teetotallers. Perhaps the damp, the solitude, or God knows what, soon drives most of us to drink. What did I do? Oh, yes, I sawed the finger off with a jack-knife. Of course it hurt; but it was just root hog or die. The worst of it is that the mosquitoes always fasten on the stump." He held up a brown mutilated hand for us to look at and then, after a long pull at his iced drink, sank back again into the silence that had become a second nature to him. Perhaps to those who practise orchid hunting it seems indecent to be talking, in the primeval silence of the woods.

To the disjointed story of the orchid hunter, that seemed to be extracted from him almost against his will, succeeded the impresario of a travelling operetta company, fluent and full of New York slang and jokes designed to please the intelligence of infant cavemen, long before wit or humour humanised the world. Withal not a bad fellow, for a man whose company, by his own confession, was half a brothel, and as difficult to drive as a whole waggon load of apes. A ranche *[sic]* man brought a whiff of purer air into the symposium, and as he sat tapping his leg with an imaginary whip, his thumb turned upwards from constant using of the lazo, his soft and soothing Western voice acted as a soporific on the company. They listened half awake to a long tale about the prowess of a Flathead Indian horse, "a buck-skin and a single footer, why, that yer hoice would pick a animal out of a bunch of steers, he knowed a fat one, too, better than a human, sure he did, that little hoice."

To him succeeded a traveller in a patent medicine that would cure snakebites, shingles, coughs, colds, and rheumatism. "What about earthquakes?" ejaculated someone. "Well, my stuff doesn't lay out to stop 'em; but it does no harm to 'em, anyway, and maybe might do some good to the survivors if they took it soon enough." He told us that he had never taken it himself, preferring good, sound whisky, but added, "I am its prophet, anyhow. 'One God, one Zamolina,' as good a creed as any other as far as I can see, and one a man can hold without much danger to his conscience, as long as the stuff sells."

The laugh that greeted the exposition of the creed of the patent medicine philosopher died away, and it appeared the experiences of the company had been exhausted. Confession, no matter if auricular or *coram publico*, generally extorts confession. Seated in the shade, so that up to the moment of his speaking no one had observed him, there was a quiet man, dressed in immaculate white clothes. His hundred dollar jipi-japa hat lay beside him on the deck. Somewhere about fifty years of age, his thick, dark hair was just beginning to turn grey. Tall and athletic looking, he still had not the look of being used to frontier life, and his quiet voice and manner showed him to have received what for the want of any better word is styled education, a thing that though it can do nothing to improve the faculties, yet now and then gives them the power of self-expression, in natures previously dumb.

"I don't know why I should tell you or anybody," he said, "this tale, experience or what you like to call it, except that as it happened to me twenty years ago to-day, it seems impersonal and as if it had occurred to some one I had known. I was young then." He paused and drew himself up a little, as a well-preserved man of fifty does when he refers to himself as old, all the time feeling women still turn round to look at him as he passes on the street. "I was young then. . . . It was in New Orleans that I met her, an English girl, living alone, *faisant la cocotte* as they say down there. I think it was in the St. Charles Hotel that I first saw her. Tall and red-haired, not too fat, not too thin, as the Arabs say when speaking of a handsome woman. What her real name was I never knew. I liked her far too well ever to wish to pry into her life. Her *nom de guerre* was Daphne Villiers, and by that name I knew and by degrees began to love her. She lived in one of those old streets that run into Lafayette Square, in the French quarter of the town. I forgot to say she spoke all languages, French, Spanish and Italian, German, and God knows what, indifferently well. A rare thing for an Englishwoman, even of her profession.

"Her rooms were furnished, not in the style you might expect, big looking-glasses, Louis Quinze chairs and tables, with reproductions of the Bath of Psyche, Venus and Cupid, French prints of women bathing, as Les Biches à la Mer, or La Puce, showing a girl of ample charms catching a flea upon her leg, but simply and in good taste. Two or three bits of china, good but inexpensive, with one fine piece of Ming, and a Rhodes plate or two were dotted here and there. Upon the walls were a few engravings of French pictures, with one or two water-colours and a pastel of herself, done, as she said, in Paris by a well-known pastelist, with the signature carefully erased. What struck me most about the rooms was a small cabinet of books. Anatole France and Guy de Maupassant, some poetry, with Adah Mencken's verses, and some manuals on china and on furniture, with Manon Lescaut, Dante's *Vita Nuova* and the *Heptameron* are what I recollect.

136

"There was a piano that she said 'of course is necessary in the metier,' on which she played not very well and sang French Creole songs with rather a good voice. Not having much to do at that time, I got to dropping in upon her whenever she was not engaged, not so much as a lover, but to enjoy a talk with someone whose mind did not entirely run upon the price of cotton, the sale of real estate, railway shares, dividends, the things in fact that citizens of God's Own Country chiefly converse about to the exclusion of all else. Curiously enough I was never jealous, although she often had to postpone my visits on account of her work. Of course, after the fashion of most women of her class, she always talked about 'my work.' She said she never drank except when she was working and I rather think that the use of the word kept me from being jealous, for I flattered myself she never used it when speaking of my visits to her.

"Little by little we grew almost indispensable to one another. I lent her books and literary magazines. How well I recollect bringing her *L'Imitation de Jésus* and how she laughed, saying she knew it all by heart. 'Twas only then I found out that she was a Catholic; not that she cared too much for her religion, but as she said, the Mass with all there is about it, lights, incense and the tradition of antiquity, appealed to her on the æsthetic side. Yes, well, yes, I got to love her, and to look forward to our long talks on books and china, pictures and the like. I never took her out to theatres, for she said people would think that she was 'working' if they saw me with her, and she looked upon me as a friend. I liked to hear her say so, for as time went on we had become quite as much friends as lovers, and I used to tell her everything that had happened to me since my last visit to her.

" She on her part used to advise me, as all women will advise the man they love. Though their advice may not be very weighty, yet a man is a fool who does not profit by it. One evening I went to see her, taking a big bunch of flowers, and when she thanked me I said, 'Congratulate me too, this is my birthday.' To my surprise she burst out crying, and for a long time I could not make her tell me the reason of her tears. At last she said, 'I should have liked to give you something, but you know how I live and I am sure you will not take a present from me.' Nothing that I could say would pacify her, although I swore that I would value anything she gave. For a long time she sobbed convulsively, till at last, drying her tears up with a handkerchief, she smiled and coming up to me, threw her arms round my neck and said, 'I have one thing that I can give you,

137

that belongs entirely to me, that is myself.'

"Business kept me from seeing her again for several days. The more I thought about her, the more certain it appeared I could not live without her. So on the first opportunity I sought the curious old winding street in the French quarter of the town. The house looked strangely silent, and after knocking at the door for a long time the coloured girl I knew so well opened it, crying, holding a letter and a little packet in her hand. 'Missy Daphne, she done gone away,' she said, and looked at me reproachfully, as I thought afterwards. The letter told me she had gone off to Tampico with a mining engineer, not a bad fellow, who she thought would marry her. She said she had acted for the best, for both of us, and asked me to accept the little piece of Chinese pottery I so often had admired."

The story-teller ceased his tale just as a bird stops singing, when you expect he will go on. Silence fell on the hearers. It may be some of them had had presents on their birthdays, of less value than the teller's of the tale. No one said anything except the ranche *[sic]* man with the directness of a simple soul, "Reckon you missed the round-up that time, friend." The story-teller nodded at him, and walking up to the thermometer, muttered, "A hundred in the shade."

Writ in Sand

"*Vivo si miro adelante*
Muero si miro hacia atrás
Me columpio en el ahora
Un dia menos, un dia mas."

Salvador de Madariaga

R. B. Cunninghame Graham

To

Louisa Miéville

Introduction to *Writ in Sand* (1932) and *Mirages* (1936)

Writ in Sand (1932)[1] and *Mirages* (1936)[2] are Graham's last two collections of sketches, published when he was 79-80 and 83 years of age.

Comment on each sketch as it appears in each collection would lead to much cross-referral, so the six pieces in *Writ in Sand* are here merged with the ten pieces in *Mirages*, with clusters of two, three or more sketches then brought together under a common theme or approach.

In the Preface to *Writ in Sand* Graham shows jocular contempt for the reader curious about the writer's life. Though most people keep something private, Graham humorously respects the man condemned for sexual deviancy who publicly admitted his actions. If Graham in his writing has revealed something of his own personality, he cares not. These thoughts carry a hint of an approaching end.

The Preface to *Mirages*, addressed to empire-builders, is scathing towards them. In Graham's view, empires, based on military force, bring the gospel truths to "those we impudently call savages" and do horrendous violence to Indian, Arab or Abyssinian villages. Races inferior in arms must – in the name of progress, civilisation and our tripartite deity – be brought up to date with motor-cars, television, our measles and all the poxes. Graham is resigned to such developments. The 1936 references to television and to violence in Abyssinia – where Italy's imperial army used mustard gas – are very up-to-date, though they are used to reinforce Graham's detestation of imperialism and modernity.

Mirages is not for empire-builders, for "all men born of woman are but brief shadows." For Graham all men under the skin are equal, virtue is rarely rewarded, vice is not especially triumphant and death is equally the wages of the sinner and of the saint. This Preface also has the feel of an imminent closure.

Two sketches in particular look back to older and gentler worlds, one off the west coast of Africa, the other in the interior of South America.

"Camara de Lobos" is a suburb of Funchal, in the Portuguese-speaking island of Madeira. The title might be casually read as "Chamber of Wolves." Graham, drawn again to a foreign-language title, fails to explain that 'lobos' here refers to sea-lions. Graham depicts the Ash Wednesday processions where virtually the whole population gathers at the little parish church, hears Mass and then moves in procession up to the hilltop Calvary. The procession returns to town just as night falls.

This sketch has no single individualised character: the community as a whole actively participates in a religious festival. Nor is there any false drama. The local people by nature are quiet, admirably sober folk, quite different to southern Italians and Sevillanos. His affectionate sketch does honour to an old-fashioned community steeped in the rites of its religion.

"The Stationmaster's Horse" is set in Paraguay, on the railway line between Paraguari and the capital Asunción. In the early stages Graham takes delight in showing the comic opera and ramshackle railway service. Seen collectively, the country folk used to the pace of bullock carts are proud of their rickety little symbol of modernity. In the second half the protagonist is Graham, borrowing the horse to pursue the slow-moving train and hand over his letter for delivery in Asunción. His ride back to Paraguari is quite uneventful.

This is a sketch in a minor key, with no grand theme or highly dramatic incident. It is a humdrum little scene set in a remote little country far, far away in place and – for Graham by 1932 – in time. Graham knows well that defeat in war left Paraguay in 1870 with only 28,746 men.[3] Graham does not dwell on this shocking scenario, preferring to show a likeable country people much like the villagers in "Camara de Lobos": where the Madeira villagers are content in their faith, the Paraguayans are content in their simple backward lives. This mood of gentle mellow warmth brings the *Writ in Sand* collection to a wistfully quiet end.

In "Up Stage" Graham contemplates death. The sketch focuses on a headstone – dated 1844 and naming Reginald Montague – near a little church on the Island of Bute in the Firth of Clyde in west Scotland. Graham nearly a century later gives a simple evocation of the church, graveyard and the natural surrounds, a landscape more attractive than those seen in "The Craw Road" and "Caisteal-na-Sithan" (*Charity*, 1912). Local parishioners believe Montague to have been an actor: 'up stage' signals actor movement from front to back stage. Graham does not give the text of the inscription, he cannot explain why Montague was buried near the church but in unconsecrated ground, and he does not know who designed the grave surrounding and brings flowers. Lacking information and drama, the sketch relies on unresolved mystery in a fetching location. Might Graham through Montague be anticipating his own departure from the front stage of life?

More recent or near-contemporary deaths are described in "Musicos!" and "Casas Viejas, 1933", two short items set in Spain. In both cases Graham adopts an impersonal and documentary style of journalistic reportage, close to classic realism.

"Musicos!" describes a Sunday evening performance in an old theatre in the poorest part of Madrid. When a fire is declared, panic breaks out. The conductor tries to calm the panic with music but then leads his orchestra to safety. Three musicians stay behind: "Then the flames consumed the humble heroes whilst in the pit of hell the audience struggled for their lives." Though the event may be sourced to a newspaper, Graham relays it with cool economy and conviction.

"Casas Viejas, 1933" has a strong political background, based on a very recent real event. In the poverty-stricken village of Casas Viejas in Cádiz province, profoundly radical peasants clashed with soldiers. In one burning house five villagers died alongside their leader 'Six Fingers.' The morning after, the troops executed fourteen villagers.

Graham's sketch is true to the political background. Gerald Brenan memorably described the desperate peasants, especially in southern Spain, who believed absolutely in the doctrines and promises of libertarian anarchism.[4] Graham also stays fairly close to the then known facts. Graham's matter-of-fact description of the arrest, shackling and execution of the randomly taken prisoners shows a brutal repression. He does not go beyond reportage into political discussion. He has been drawn – as in the theatre fire - to the drama in the incident and has captured this again economically and fluently.

Graham explores the experience of the expatriate in several sketches, three based in South America, three relating to Tangier in North Africa.

In "Facón Grande" Martín Villalba, the native-born Argentine, perfect gaucho and Indian-fighter, is supported in the perils of frontier life in southern Buenos Aires province in the 1870s by two English brothers who can barely speak Spanish but whose nicknames suggest their preparedness for life in that violent place – 'Big Knife' ('Facón Grande') and 'Little Knife.' Martín is also supported by the fine German horseman Vögel and by the brothers Millburn. These expatriates have become a vital element in the defence and gradual 'civilisation' of the frontier. Such tough characters and the real threat from the Pampas Indians hold the potential for a frontier drama, but the sketch – the last in *Mirages* - becomes instead an old man's gentle *In memoriam* for long-lost companions of the saddle.

"Charlie the Gaucho" is a penetrating study of the transformation of an expatriate and offers much greater drama and resonances than "Facón Grande." The young English midshipman Charles Edward Mitchell comes to identify totally with the gaucho culture of the Uruguayan plains. He spends several years back in Britain but leaves to return to life as a gaucho. At a country store in the grasslands, another gaucho confronts him about his horse's brand. In a furious knife-fight Charlie is killed. Years later the British vice-consul fills Graham in on Charlie's English background.

Graham uses several narrators: himself for the scene-setting, then the Basque store owner, an old gaucho, the vice-consul and himself again in the conclusion. Graham handles the shifting narrative voices well. The dramatic events emerge in reverse chronological order: first a dead body, then the knife-fight, the fight set at the mid-point of the tale, with Charlie's earlier background filled in towards the end.

Graham uses many Spanish-language terms associated with gaucho life – around 300 in 34 pages.[5] Graham usually explains the Hispanisms or embeds them deftly in context so that the narrative flows smoothly.

Graham is clearly familiar with nineteenth-century Argentina's passionate debate about the country's future: whether to favour a native American "barbarism" or an urban European-style "civilization". Graham's educated European twice over rejects Europe for a more primitive American life-style. When Charlie dies a prototypically gaucho death – in a knife-fight in a country store after an argument with another gaucho about a horse - Charlie has opted, whatever the risks, for American "barbarism".

In "Tschiffely's Ride" Graham uses newspaper material to write up an extraordinary adventure. Aimé Tschiffely, a Swiss citizen who spent several years in England before moving to Argentina, there became so well integrated that he could draw from Argentina's still vibrant horse-based culture the idea of riding two Criollo horses overland from Argentina to the United States. This "long ride" he completed (1925-1928) with great common-sense, determination and bravery. The expatriate Tschiffely's name and the names of his two Criollo horses are renowned in Argentina.

In Tangier in the sketch "Bibi" Edward Pio was born into a poor English Catholic family and learned Spanish and Arabic in the streets. A personable rogue, he was nicknamed Bibi by the Moors and himself became almost a Moor: Bibi, like Graham and Charles Edward Mitchell, 'went native.' His appointment as British consular agent increased Bibi's wealth. When a vicious Kaid sought to extort money from one of Bibi's tenant farmer partners, Bibi visited the Kaid, took tea and engaged in a traditional wrestling match: they fought each other to a standstill. Bibi knew that the Kaid would never again threaten his Mahalat. The Tangier mix of races, languages, religions and cultures shapes the distinctive figure of Bibi. His gradual rise from Christian-born rogue to status, wealth and influence for good as understood by Muslims is cleverly and convincingly charted.

"Creeps" is a mischievous sketch of the British painter Joseph Crawhall (1861-1913): "Creeps" was Crawhall's nickname. Crawhall favoured watercolour and pastel for his studies of birds and animals and for figurative work inspired by North Africa and Spain. The artist Sir John Lavery, to whom Graham dedicated *Charity* (1912), and Graham had a high opinion of Crawhall the painter.

This sketch focuses on Crawhall the man, seen in an almost salacious incident. In Tangier Crawhall the man might disappear for days at a time on a bout of drinking. His friends Bibi (see "Bibi") and Bernardino (see "Fin de Race") might find "Creeps" in a local brothel. The girl Relampagos would explain that Crawhall – who never went native - was dressing. Quite unembarrassed, Crawhall would appear, kiss the girl Relampagos and go off with his friends.

Graham invests his description of the malodorous town and Crawhall with gentle humour. Crawhall having died in 1913, Graham has no qualms in 1932 about describing Crawhall's fox-hunts, whisky-drinking or brothel visitations. Crawhall draws a fine charcoal sketch of Relampagos on the wall of her room and she washes and irons his shirt before he leaves: these details round off a disarming vignette of an eccentric and gifted expatriate, a vignette delivered with a fine light narrative touch.

"Fin de Race" chronicles the life of Bernardino de Velasco, born into one of the oldest noble families in Old Castile. The real-life model may be the 16th Duke of Frías (1866-1916).

The narrative line is simple: youthful promise, reckless dissipation of wealth in mainly foreign places, failure to make a fortune in Africa, decline and death. Graham's depiction of a charming and multi-talented young aristocrat and absentee landlord's slow, steady and apparently irreversible decline through gambling and disinterest in the management of his estates is convincingly sustained. This long-term expatriate finally retires to his remaining estate in Spain. Capable even to the last of inspiring devotion and loyalty in the woman Modesta and his estate guards, Bernardino dies from bronchitis and pneumonia, the combination that will kill Graham himself. Bernardino's death is a pathetic end to a life that once held such promise.

In Graham's use of the collective 'race' in the title, Bernardino's decline may reflect that of a caste - the self-indulgent Spanish landed aristocracy. In parallel vein and time, the Spanish poet, Antonio Machado (1875-1939), presented his Don Guido with lilting mocking irony as representative of his class: "¡Oh fin de una aristocracia!" That caste's failure to address its responsibilities contrasts sharply with Graham's own real-life efforts to save the much-indebted estates that he himself had inherited. These lateral resonances add density to Bernardino's wasted life.

In this expatriate cluster the lives and deaths of Charlie the Gaucho and Bernardino are especially striking.

At least five sketches use horses as incidental or supporting features.

In "The Stationmaster's Horse" Graham's ride back to Paraguari in Paraguay as night falls is uneventful: he attends to the horse and goes off with his friends. The Anglo expatriate painter "Creeps" 'rides to hounds' in Tangier. In "Charlie the Gaucho" an argument about a horse leads to a knife-fight in which Charlie the Gaucho, transplanted from England to Uruguay and an accomplished gaucho, dies: his opponent rides off with Charlie's horse in tow. In "Facón Grande" the old-time south-west frontier in Buenos Aires province bred tough characters who to survive had to be excellent horsemen. In the circus performance in the sketch "Writ in Sand" the four superb bay horses "seemed to take a pride in their own beauty."

A more substantial presentation of horses appears in Graham's hugely enthusiastic long review "Tschiffely's Ride". Two native Criollo (Argentine) horses took the Swiss adventurer Tschiffely on his 15,000 mile overland trip from Buenos Aires to the United States in the 1920s. Graham pays full tribute to *Mancha* and *Gato*: the plains-bred horses coped magnificently with scrub-land, hills, mountains, jungles, high plateaus, deserts, burning heat, freezing cold, torrential rains, wild animals and risks from bandits and revolutionaries.

Graham first read of Tschiffely's adventure in newspaper reports before writing this review: he later met Tschiffely and recommended him to his publisher. They became good friends and on his last visit to Argentina in 1936 Graham on behalf of Tschiffely delivered special packets of oats to *Mancha* and *Gato*: within days the two horses would escort Graham's coffin through the streets of Buenos Aires.

In "Inmarcesible" Graham pays a much broader tribute to horses. This rare unexplained Spanish word means 'undying, everlasting.' A Jewish lady of Algoa Bay, next to Port Elizabeth in south-east Africa, "has raised a monument to all the horses killed in the Boer War." Algoa Bay was the main point of disembarkation for the British remounts needed for the Second Boer War (1899-1902). Graham visualises the horrors of the horses' original capture, transportation, disembarkation, training, cross-country marches, battles, woundings and deaths – 200,000 by the end. Graham seeks to make the horses' sufferings more accessible to the human reader – and more noble – through the use of "a common holocaust", "purgatory", "Via Crucis", "Via Dolorosa" and "hell." Though the last lines of "Facón Grande" may hope for a horses' and horsemen's paradise after physical death, in "Inmarcesible" the picture is grim – apart from the single positive note of Mrs Meyer's generosity in raising the everlasting Horse Memorial.

Two sketches blend an interest in performance ritual and a sense of pathos.

The sketch "Writ in Sand" depicts a traditional circus performance in a southern French town. The narrative is straightforward: arrival, preparation, performance, packing up and departure. Graham creates a bustling sense of anticipation that includes the unmistakable odour that he names "Bouquet de Cirque". He revels in the variety of origins and languages of the performers and workers and in the medley of animals, especially in the different breeds of horses. The little town, set between sea and a backdrop of mountains, is skilfully drawn. In the evening the sideshows brim with abnormality. The circus acts are described at a breathless pace, with the bullfight sequence by the clowns generating the magnetism traditionally associated with the circus.

Graham's special feel for animals manipulated by man shows through when he says of the elephant: "To see the monster, with his intelligence, and his docility, so careful not to hurt any of the pygmies, fussing about him, is a sad sight…". And he finds pathos too in the high-wire performers. They perform their feats of daring for an audience where some hoped to witness an accident. The trio accept their applause, "the father's arms about the children's necks as if he recognised that once more they were safe."

"Los Ninos Toreros", set in the bullring in Caracas, Venezuela, delivers perhaps even more action, suspense and pathos.

Over six pages Graham's long run of negatives emphasises the tawdriness of the Caracas bullring. A small touch of grace is provided by three figures in bullfighting costume: a Spanish middle-aged ex-bullfighter with a limp and his two teenage sons. The pale sweating face of the father who knows the dangers his sons are about to confront is already striking. Though Graham in "Aurora La Cujiñi" (1898) and here sees bullfighters as butchers, he puts aside his distaste and convincingly presents the bullfighting ritual as genuinely life-threatening drama in which the two teenagers acquit themselves very well. The danger over, father and sons embrace behind the barrier, their embrace recalling the embrace of the family of high-wire artists in "Writ in Sand."

Two sketches look far back in time and border on the ethereal, almost on the supernatural.

The opening sketch of the final collection, "Mirage", strikes a reflective note, marred slightly by sophisticated vocabulary and references. Graham projects the Latin *Animula* (soul) as an English word. The contrast with luscious water-melons suggests that colocynths are bitter-tasting fruit. **Cafila** comes just after "long trains of camels." Graham does not clarify **sundogs** as 'small rainbows or haloes near the horizon'; *Fata Morgana* as a mirage; or **Hadgi** *[sic = Hadji or Hajji]* as Muslim travellers who have made the pilgrimage to Mecca. The reader has to work with Graham to draw full value from his texts.

Citing the poem addressed to his soul by the dying Emperor Hadrian (76-138 AD), Graham proposes that all life is like Hadrian's soul a mirage, elusive yet dangerous. The mirage is fallacious, yet we believe the mirage. The traveller should not touch the mirage: to touch is to destroy. The traveller should rather enjoy the vision as presented in the mirage. Graham's use of "we" and the second person commands on the last page seek to draw the reader into sharing his thoughts. These musings opening his final collection of sketches may suggest that for the elderly Graham – as for the dying Hadrian – all now is mirage.

In "The Dream of the Magi" Graham reports having seen in an Italian church an unusual medieval depiction of the Three Wise Men - asleep, each in his own bed.[6] In Graham's sketch, the European background in the painting magically dissolves into a Middle Eastern scenario wherein Balthazar becomes a Negro. In Bethlehem they deliver their gifts and gaze long upon the Nativity scene. Again as if by magic, the stable grows dim and disappears, Kings and caravan fade away in another film-like dissolve. The Kings, having dreamt their dream, sleep on in the image in the Italian church.

Watts and Davies in their critical biography suggest that in Graham's last three collections of sketches there is a falling away in quality, that "The Dream of the Magi" is "the most extreme example of the relaxation of Graham's literary nerves and muscles".[7] Yet at the level of surface reality Graham revels in the description of the Magis' sumptuous caravan. At another level he may – inspired by the Italian painting - be experimenting to see if he can capture some of the magic of the traditional Christmas story. And if the whole sketch – embedded in a volume entitled *Mirages* – is framed as a mirage, as a trick of the mind, then perhaps all such stories are mirages…

Six sketches are bright and hopeful ("Camara de Lobos", "The Stationmaster's Horse", "Facón Grande", "Tschiffely's Ride", "Bibi" and "Creeps"). Apart from one phrase ("… half of sorrow as she thought upon his lot as the redeemer of mankind"), "The Dream of the Magi" can be read positively. Death, however, is present in the other nine sketches. The possibility of sudden violent death lurks in both "Writ in Sand" and "Los Ninos Toreros". "Up stage" is a contemplation of a gravestone. "Musicos!" and "Casas Viejas, 1933" record multiple deaths by fire and arbitrary execution. Charlie the Gaucho dies in a dramatic knife-fight. The aristocratic wastrel Bernardino dies pathetically in "Fin de Race". 200,000 horses die in "Inmarcesible". And "Mirage" is based on a dying Emperor's poetic address to his soul. In these two collections there is a significant continuing preoccupation with death and dying. If a yearning for the past is 'a little death' in the sense of an anticipation of finality, then it is important to note that in "The Stationmaster's Horse" and "Facón Grande" Graham rounds off his two final collections of sketches by again stepping back from the modern world into evocations of past worlds, of 'vanished Arcadias'.

1 R. B. Cunninghame Graham: *Writ in Sand* (First edition published London: Heinemann, 1932, reprinted here)

2 R. B. Cunninghame Graham: *Mirages* (First edition published London: Heinemann, 1936, reprinted here)

3 Hubert Herring: *A History of Latin America from the Beginnings to the Present* (New York: Knopf, 1961, second edition, revised, p. 714)

4 Gerard Brenan: *The Spanish Labyrinth – An Account of the Social and Political Background of the Spanish Civil War* (Cambridge University Press, 1943, reprinted)

5 John C. McIntyre: "Spanish-River Plate Vocabulary in R. B. Cunninghame Graham's *Charlie the Gaucho* " Unpublished article.

6 This image found (14.06.2010) at website Flickr > Sant'Abbondio Como > renzodionigi's photostream. Other medieval representations of the Dream of the Magi (three in one bed) can be seen in Canterbury Cathedral (stained glass), Saint Lazare Cathedral in Autun in Burgundy (stone sculpture by Gislebertus) and in the St. Alban's Psalter (devotional book).

7 Cedric Watts and Laurence Davies: *Cunninghame Graham – A Critical Biography* (Cambridge: Cambridge University Press, 1979, p. 282)

150

Contents

Preface

Prefaces are written usually either to disarm the public, or to give a foretaste of the writer's quality. They fail, generally, in both their objects. Your preface-monger is constrained perforce to give himself away, for he speaks as man to man, not through the mouth of any of his characters.

The one advantage we poor footsloggers on the dull paths of prose possess over those who on the wings of verse attempt to scale Olympus, is that we are not forced, as they are, ever to meet our readers really face to face, unless we venture into prefaces, prologues, forewords, or what you call 'em. They, on the contrary, if their verse is to rise to poetry, must put their souls' blood into all they write, or remain stodged for ever in the slough of versifying. This may be the reason why most actors, even the best of them, are usually poor public speakers, for it is vastly different for a man to stand up and utter his own thoughts, and to deliver well-conned-over words already written for him.

Therefore, few writers, nowadays, care to come to close grips with those they write for, fearing perhaps that a half-nelson, or cross-buttock, may leave them sprawling on the ground. Again, your public, avid of details as to a writer's private life, thinking perhaps, but absolutely falsely, that they assist it to understand the man, or perhaps out of mere lewd curiosity — the curse of common minds — seems to imagine that a painter or a poet either must have some secret, or that when pen or brush is laid over, that he is different in essence from any other man.

Nature has so contrived it, and I admit it is annoying of her, that even genius must eat and sleep, endure the pangs of tooth and belly ache, fall into and fall out of love, and fulfil all the functions of any ordinary man, that I refrain from setting down, not wishing to offend the gentlewomen, although I know they are not in especial mealy-mouthed. Thus nothing pleases the "respectable" so consumedly as to read that a writer or a politician drinks or takes drugs in secret, keeps a fat mistress as a foil to a thin wife, changes his socks infrequently, or any other detail of the kind that brings him nearer to themselves. Far fewer care about the workings of his mind, those little self-revealing details that are certain to leak out, in an aside, a preface, footnote or what not, that, generally without his knowledge, force him to drop the mask. The spoken word can be manipulated, so as to conceal the speaker's personality, but when a writer takes his pen in hand, in spite of all that he can do, it is straight manifest.

It is a natural instinct in the majority of men to keep a secret garden in their souls, a something that they do not care to talk about, still less to set down, for the other members of the herd to trample on.

This is most manifest in those who write their own biographies, confessions, memoirs or by whatsoever title publishers palm on them, just as a card-sharper palms a card upon a mug.

Possibly, St. Augustine and Jean Jacques Rousseau imagined that they had unpacked their budget so completely, nothing remained to tell, when they had set down their misdeeds, that after all in neither case were very black, to feed their vanity. A Rabelaisian anecdote of old times in France relates that in the tumbril a murderer and a ratepayer of the Cities of the Plains were going to be hanged. The crowd was little interested in the murderer, but called out vociferously, "Quel est le bougre?" The nonconformist, being a well-mannered man, stood up and doffing his hat courteously, said, "Citoyens, c'est moi." Thus, without need of any preface, in his one flight of oratory that has come down to us, he revealed all that the public had a right to know about him. The opportunity was such as does not fall to every literary man when he sets out to talk about himself. It placed its utterer high in the ranks of those who write, have written, or will write confessions, and overtops them all in spontaneity, lack of premeditation, and in its brevity.

Looking over this, my booklet, with the distaste most writers surely feel for the perusal of their own writing, for few of us can, as is reported of Jehovah, look at their work and say that it is good, I ask my readers to be lenient with "The Stationmaster's Horse."

Sometimes the smell of an orange freshly cut recalls the scent of the wild orange trees in bloom, that night, upon my ride. Then I remember how sticky the piece of rapadura, that I had in my pocket, made my fingers, when I ate a piece of it, and how I gave what remained over to the "Zebruno," when I unsaddled him.

The ride, the horse, the fireflies, the musky odour of the alligators at the "pass," the rustling palm trees, and the Southern Cross that lighted the "Zebruno" and myself in our too brief companionship, were stamped upon my brain, more years ago than, as we say in Scottish phrase, "I care to mind."

The portraits of my two departed friends ("may the earth lay lightly on them!") I wrote because I thought I owed it to them to endeavour to preserve something of their strange personality.

Most likely, in writing of their characters, I have done nothing but reveal my own, without my knowledge.

If so, a "fico" for the revelation; all I can do is to stand up, and taking off my hat salute the public, hoping the tumbril will jog gingerly, to its appointed goal.

R. B. Cunninghame Graham

Writ in Sand

At sundown, long lines of motor vans, as huge as arks, converged upon a sandy waste space of the southern little town. Over it towered the Ligurian Alps, rugged and sun-scorched. The waves of Mare Nostrum just lapped against the sea wall that bounded the neglected piece of ground on which a canvas city was to arise, like Jonah's gourd, during the night. The vans scrunched on the pebbles as they came up in long procession, and formed a great corral.

Each monstrous car took its own place with mathematical precision, for Amar's Circus had been long upon the road, having pushed what it called upon its posters "Une Audacieuse Randonnée" as far as Angora, and was now back again in France.

From the cars came the cries of animals, the miauling of the lions, the grunts of camels, and the stamping of the horses eager to be fed.

The scent that can be best described as "Bouquet de Cirque," compounded of the odours of the various animals, sawdust and orange peel, of petrol, dried perspiration, leather, of cordage, canvas ill laid up when damp, cheap perfumes and cosmetics, all the quintessence of a world apart from any other kind of world, a world where men and women risk their lives daily, and reck nothing of it, a world in which they live, in fellowship with horses, elephants and mules, a fellowship that makes them different to all other kind of men, as sailors were in the old world of wind-jammers, floated out into the night air. An army sprang into existence, as it were, from the ground, composed of workmen, unlike any other workmen, looking for the most part like grooms and chauffeurs out of place, but smart, alert and singularly quick upon their feet. All of them seemed able to turn a somersault, saddle a horse, or swarm up a rope ladder, as well as a smart seaman in an old China tea clipper, when he ran aloft into a top, over the futtock shrouds. Babel itself, when Jahwe, out of jealousy of man set confusion on the tongue of men, was not more polyglot. Russian, American, English, French, Italian, Spanish, Arabic, German, and Czechoslovak jostled one another in their mouths. None spoke the others' language properly, but everyone knew the word for horse, rope, saddle, dance, sawdust, knot, slack or tight wire, handspring and elephant, in the others' tongue. For ordinary purposes, they had formed a lingua franca, out of the various elements of speech of all the languages, shotted with oaths and with indecencies, that worn as smooth as pebbles in the current of their speech had become merely adjectives.

These heterogeneous good companions, for no one better merited the term, like ants, set at once busily to work, under the blue glare of the electric light, that as by magic, others of the band had installed on what an hour ago was a mere sandy waste.

Long tents, to serve as stables, grew up like mushrooms, leaving a vacant space, where the great tent should rise. To them, men in trousers of a horsy cut, or breeches unbuttoned at the knees, muffled in greatcoats with woollen comforters up to their ears, covering their gipsy-looking greasy hair, for far Multan had sent its quota to the kaleidoscopic host, led horses that stepped as quietly and unconcernedly as if the planks down which they walked had been green fields, those fields that they would see no more, for once a circus horse their lot is fixed as the fixed stars.

Piebalds, roans, chestnuts, sorrels, duns, skewbalds, creams with black points, steel-greys, and whites of every shade from purest snow to honey-coloured and that palest shade of cream, known in the Argentine as Duck's Egg, formed an equine flower-bed.

Chiron himself when seated underneath a spreading oak in Thessaly — he chose the finest of the mares to blend with the most beautiful of the young men to form the Centaur, that flight of man's imagination, that for once has outgone nature — could not have found better material to his hand. The equine race of the whole world had furnished representatives, from Shetland ponies up to the heavy Mecklenburger, with his round back, fit to count money on, and his stout legs, that do not seem to feel the strain when six or seven riders poise and caper on him as he canters round the ring. Yukers from the Hungarian puzta, with their fine limbs, light bone and saddle backs, as if nature herself had formed them for the circus, intelligent and docile, their long and flowing manes and tails, full gentle eyes and open nostrils giving them the look of an Arabian steed designed in tapestry upon a banner screen in a Victorian house. In a long line they stepped out of their boxes, as delicately as Agag, with that look of comprehension and disdain performing animals all acquire, as if they felt the difference between an artist and a mere spectator, lolling in his stall, with a fat paunch and well-filled pocket-book.

After the horses had disappeared into their stables, a drove of camels, herded by Algerians, or Moroccans, but perhaps best described as "natives," for in what lone Duar, or in what black tent of camels' hair they had first heard the call to prayers, only themselves and Allah could pronounce with certainty.

Dressed in brown jellabas, or dingy white burnouses, they yet preserved entire their racial look, that almost all the other members of the troupe had shed when they took on their circensian nationality.

When the lions, tigers, seals and all the other wild beasts that made the now rapidly growing canvas town look as if Noah's Ark was delivering her cargo on Mount Ararat, had been caged, slowly the elephant appeared, with the look of peculiar cunning in his little porcine eyes that makes him only just inferior to mankind, as to intelligence, although perhaps superior in bonhomie. He seemed to feel the dignity of his position as a survivor of a prehistoric world. All the time that the animals were being settled in their stables, the work went on, but silently, so that when a great canvas dome slowly was hoisted into position in the middle of the waste piece of ground, it seemed to rise out of its own volition from the sand. Then and then only was the noise of hammers heard, as a platoon of men drove home great iron tent pegs, to tauten up the ropes.

Around the ring they ranged the padded barrier, fencing in its thirteen paces of diameter, that sacramental measurement in which horses and men perform in circuses, all the world over, whether in the centre of great cities or in a field outside a village, in rural England, Poland, or Hungary. Seats, boxes, and electric lights, the high trapezes swinging from the roof, appeared to have been always just where the efficient squads of workers had placed them only half an hour before.

By daybreak all was ready for the next day's performance, and when the ring-master, wrapped in an old, white box-cloth greatcoat with huge bone buttons, and a woollen comforter round his neck, looked at the work, and said, like the great ring-master in Eden, "that it was good," a hoot on an electric whistle summoned all hands to breakfast in the dining tent.

In the real, or the unreal world, according to the point of view of those who live in, or outside, a circus, the false dawn had vanished, and the sun was rising over the mountains and the sea. A white mist hung upon the palm trees, magnifying and ennobling them, just as it does out in the desert, or in the tropic everglades, from whence they had originally been brought. The sun's first rays fell on the lateen sails of the fishing boats as they stole out from every little village port and launched into the sea. From them there came the muffled sounds of oars, of cordage creaking in the old-time wooden blocks, as the great yard, that Latin yard, common to all the boats that sail the Latin sea was hoisted into place. Such yards, and ships not much unlike the fishing boats that now began to feel the morning breeze, the ships of Agamemnon and Ulysses, must have borne when Helen's smile launched them upon the siege of Troy. The fishing boats, their pointed sails giving them an air as of a flight of seabirds, sank by degrees below the horizon, as silently as gulls disappear into the haze, before the eye of man can mark their disappearance. Shoreward, the rippling waves lapped on the pebbly beaches, with a scrunching sound as of the cat-ice crackling on the edges of a pond.

The ragged mountains, dotted with villages grouped round their church, the houses sheltering about it, as it were for protection from the modern world, just caught the morning sun. The panorama, fantastic and unreal, with the white houses of the coastal towns, the imported vegetation, and their look of unreality, seemed designed as an ideal background for the great dome of canvas that billowed gently, shivering a little in the light sea breeze, just as a jellyfish thrown up by the sea shivers upon the sand.

All was in order, by the hour advertised. A van with windows cut at intervals, behind which sat well-dressed girls, as quiet and orderly as typists in a city office, served as the box-office. All seemed as permanent as if the dome of canvas had been the dome of a cathedral, stone-built and pointed, designed to last for centuries. Nothing about it gave an air of instability, but set one thinking that in a fleeting world, where all is changing (but as invisibly as the hands move upon a clock), canvas is the most fit material to build with, for those whose lives are after all passed in a circus, where they perform, even with less volition of their own than the trained animals, and pass away as the smoke of a cigarette dissolves into the air.

Bands blared, and men standing before the side-shows shouted the charms of the bearded lady, pig with five legs, the human skeleton, and the fat woman from Trebizond, certain of custom, for mankind unaware

160

of its own freakishness, delights in abnormalities, seeing in them perhaps, something they can wonder at, despise, and patronize, and leave the tent amused and comforted by their superiority.

A continuous stream of people passed the wicket gate where stood the gigantic negro in a green uniform, with that grin upon his face that makes the people of his race quite as inscrutable as the most enigmatic Japanese or Chinaman. Packed close as sardines in a barrel, the audience had that air of expectation that circus audiences must have manifested since the time of the Romans and the Greeks.

In the reserved seats sat a few tourists, some beautifully dressed in plus-fours, that costume tailors have designed as in derision of humanity. The well-known smell of tan, of horses' urine and of orange peel, with all the various scents, human and those compounded by perfumers, that every audience in the world throws off, luckily unknown to itself, hung in the air, in spite of all the efforts of smartly-dressed attendants, who wielded sprinklers with disinfectants.

Gone were the days when everything was dingy, the coats of horses staring, the performers' dresses dirty or ill-washed. All was as spick and span as in a West-End theatre. Smart girls in velvet coats of Georgian cut, flowered waistcoats, knee-breeches and silk stockings, high-heeled shoes, leaving a train of scent in passing, sold programmes and showed people to their seats, with an air fit for any court, or at least such courts as those of Monaco and Gerolstein. The seats, the boxes and the ring itself were models of neatness and of cleanliness, and that, although the circus had been upon the road for months, travelling in Asia Minor and in Turkey, and only meant to spend three days where they had pitched their tents, and take the road again.

Into the arena bounded a Hungarian horse "en liberté," dark chestnut, with white stockings and a blaze down its face that made it "drink in white," as the Brazilians say.

Coursing round the ring, it seemed to cover miles, although the whole circumference was but a hundred feet. At a sign from the ringmaster, who, dressed in evening clothes, his chambrière with the lash lying on the ground, the fiery courser of the desert (see the handbills) stopped and reversed its course. Then, rising on its hind legs, it fought the air before the whirling lash that never touched it, and following its trainer, to the opening in the barrier, bounded back to its stables, passing through the ranks of the attendants, in their green uniforms, who clapped it on the quarters as it passed.

Men and girls rode, springing from the ground on to their horses' backs as agilely as gauchos. They faced the tail, balanced themselves on one another's shoulders, straddled their horses' necks, and passed beneath their bellies coming up on the other side, vaulted over the hind quarters, were dragged round the arena holding to the tail, whilst all the time the docile animals galloped like clockwork, as if they knew their riders' limbs were in their care, and that as much depended on them as on the men and women in their partnership.

A Caucasian horseman galloped into the ring. About the middle height, handsome and as "wonderly deliver" as was the Knight of the Canterbury Tales, the Caucasian dress suited him to perfection. The long green, fur-trimmed coat, set with its silver cartridge cases on the breast, clung to a waist as slender as a girl's, the red, soft, heelless riding boots, that eastern horsemen all affect, were home into the stirrups, that with their short leathers did not allow the feet to come below the belly, and gave the rider the appearance of standing upright on his horse, in the big peaked Cossack saddle with its pads, like footballs, that support the thighs. You saw at once that he was a Gigit, trained to the tricks of the best school of Gigitofka, in Vladikafkas, or some other mountain town in the recesses of the frosty Caucasus. His Persian lambswool cap, set off his bold and sun-browned features, leaving a few tight curls below it, on his forehead. His light and cutting snaffle bridle, with its thin red reins, he held high, in his left hand, to give a better purchase on the palate, for the Caucasian horsemen use no curb. Holding one hand above his head, his nagaika dangling from his forefinger, he rushed into the arena checking his Anglo-Arab in the centre of the ring, where it stood, turned to stone, for half a second, before he wheeled it once again into full speed. Rising in his short stirrups he stood erect upon the saddle, and then letting himself fall trailed round the ring with his head just brushing on the sand. Agile as a cat, he swung himself again into his seat, threw down a handkerchief, retrieved it from the saddle, with a "back pick-up," and riding gently round the ring, amid thunders of applause, saluted gravely with his hand touching his lambswool cap.

The women looked at him, as if he were a cake in a confectioners, devouring him in anticipation with their eyes. Some said he was a prince in his own country, which may have been the case, for certainly he looked a prince upon his horse. Well did Cervantes say that riding makes some

162

men appear like grooms, others like princes.

Next appeared a troupe of Chinese acrobats; modern Chinese without their pigtails, who had travelled the world over and spoke every language, and yet the instant that they set saucers spinning on a long slender cane, or piled a line of rods on one another, striking away the lowest of the pile and deftly catching the topmost rod upon one finger-point, became as Oriental and inscrutable as if they had never left their native country for an hour. Even in the circus ring they seemed to represent a culture that had existed centuries before Europe had emerged from barbarism.

More graceful if less powerful than their Western brethren, who with their great muscles looked a little crude beside them, they seemed as if their feats were an hieratic ritual from an older world, rather than circus tricks. On her bay thoroughbred, with patterns traced upon its quarters with dandy brush and water, his coat so bright and shining that a man could shave by it, the lady of the Haute Ecole rode gracefully into the ring. Seated in her white buckskin saddle, she held her reins so lightly that they scarcely seemed to move, but with a grip as strong as steel. The smartly fitting habit showed her well-cut patent-leather boot, set off with a bright spur. Holding her long Haute Ecole whip in her right hand, she touched her horse upon the shoulder gently, putting him through all the airs of the manège, the Spanish Walk, the Passage, Volte and Semivolte, making him shift his croup, change feet with his hind legs, rear, plunge, and finally kneel down, whilst she leaned back in the saddle easily, smiling her thanks to the delighted audience. The ring-master, advancing, held her horse as she dismounted at a bound, and bowing to the audience, retired, executing two or three of those little skips without which no feminine performer in a circus ever leaves the ring. Demos must have his jesters just as in older ages emperors and kings kept private fools at courts. In this age of mass production the clowns who have replaced, or perhaps merely succeeded, the jesters of an older world, for nothing changes in man's mental atmosphere, tumbled by platoons into the ring. Their antics, quips, quiddities, and cranks fell rather flat on a French public, too civilised and not attuned to "le gros rire" that so delights a British audience. Perhaps the national lack of bonhomie accounts for it to some extent, but certainly jokes that set audiences in other countries hilarious with delight, were received rather coldly, much in the way one listens to the club bore with his well-worn and pointless platitudes.

163

One turn and only one the clowns apparently held in reserve for all eventualities fairly brought down the house, and dissipated the air of cold reserve and condescension that their first efforts had not availed to thaw.

Dressed as a comic Spanish bull-fighter, mimicking the airs of a Matamoros that bullfighters affect, hollowing his back and strutting, whilst he held his wooden sword in the approved position, over the red cloak doubled on his left arm, a tall thin clown advanced into the ring. Stopping before a pretty girl, perhaps placed there by the ringmaster in the same way that company promoters get a mine "salted" before they give the public the privilege of purchasing their shares, he laid his hand upon his heart, made a mock heroic speech, and with the appropriate gesture flung his "montera" on the ground. Then from the entrance rushed in a great dog, equipped with horns, and hunted him after a few ineffectual passes, all round the ring. Dropping his wooden sword and all his airs of a Torero, the clown rushed about in unavailing efforts to escape the onslaughts of the "bull." At last he fairly fled before his adversary, who seized him by the collar of his jacket, and was borne out struggling, behind the scenes. Then for the first time the audience gave itself up to the magnetism that once started surely affects a crowd, and laughed till tears ran down the rough faces of the peasants from the villages and made respectable and well-dressed bourgeois shake their fat sides with laughter, and wipe their glasses as they leaned back in their seats, vanquished by that one touch of folly that makes the whole world kin. No circus is complete nowadays without its "drug store" cowboys to spin a rope and ride a horse trained to plunge three or four times, without putting up its back, that the audience takes to be a buckjumper. They may or may not have been real cowpunchers, once upon a time, but generally come from some western cow-town, where they have learned to lasso in the local stockyards and corrals. They wore silk shirts, wristlets of patent leather, and round their necks gaudy silk handkerchiefs, artistically knotted, that fell upon their shoulders in two points, forming what is called a golilla by the Mexicans, though the word, no doubt brought over by the Conquistadores, really means a ruff. Their loose rather low riding boots, slashed in the front with red and yellow leather, were stuffed into their trousers, cut tightly, such as the Mexicans affect. Each of them carried a well-coiled lasso in his hands. With wonderful dexterity, they spun their lassos, forming the loop so quickly it seemed a

164

living thing that grew beneath their hands. Gradually it circled up and down, rising and falling round the body of the lassoer, who jumped through the loop, threw a back somersault, lay down and rose again, till finally the fifty feet of the long heavy rope, in a vast ring, was whirling in the air. The other youth spun a rope in each hand, keeping a short cord spinning in his teeth. He cracked a stockwhip, cutting a piece of paper from his companion's hands, at ten or twelve feet off, a feat that would have cost a finger-joint to the man who held the piece of paper, had the lash fallen upon it.

Then a man stood against a shutter, with his arms extended, and the two youths outlined his figure on the boards with butchers' knives, thrown with such force they quivered in the wood.

Nothing appeared to interest the audience so much, for it was something anyone could understand, with the additional element of danger to another's life, so dear to those who pass their own removed from any risk. For the first time, the faces of the youths took on a grave expression, and as they drew the knives out of the shutter, one whispered something to the other, who, glancing for a moment over his shoulder, smiled and spat upon the ground. Then came the turn that showed the difference between circus tricks, however dexterous, and roping on a ranch. In the one case a man depends upon himself, and as a juggler by continual practice performs feats that appear incredible, so does the circus lasso expert make a rope seem almost living in his deft hands. Upon a ranch, or even in a circus, to rope animals is quite another matter, for it is impossible to train a horse into co-operation with the man who wields the rope. All that can be done by the best trainer in the world is to ensure that the horse gallops evenly and does not flinch when the man makes his cast. The knife throwing over, and the trained buckjumper duly ridden, a man in chaparreras, a word the cow-punchers have changed to "chaps," wearing a ten-gallon hat, and all the rest of the indumentaria of his calling, rode into the ring. He put his horse into a slow canter, bearing a little on the bit to make him raise his forehand, whilst the roper, watching his opportunity, stood by to throw and catch the horse by the front feet. He dwelt a little long upon his aim, perhaps through over-care, and as he threw, his cast was just a fraction of a second late, and struck the horse's legs as they touched ground, instead of circling them when in the air. The rope came back into his hand, like a snake recoils upon itself if it has missed its spring — a most annoying thing to happen to a man who knows that he knows how to rope, but that occasionally occurs to the best cattlemen.

His companion muttered something to him that made him frown, and gathering up his lasso after a sign to the man upon the horse, he poised himself again to throw his rope.

This time he tried to do the feat a little differently. Instead of aiming at the forelegs, when in the air, he threw the loop in front of them, intending that the horse should step into the noose, and with a deft twist of his wrist to pull it up upon the legs. Again he was a trifle soon, and only caught one foot, an ugly throw that pulls the limb out in an ungainly position, and in the case of a wild animal, may cause an accident.

The audience not knowing anything about such matters cheered vociferously. Honour was saved, and the two youths retired, dragging their legs a little, with the gait, real or assumed, of men who pass their lives trailing great spurs upon their feet.

No one can tell why the European who generally acts as a mahout to a trained elephant should always be got up as a French explorer in an old-fashioned book of travels, in spotless white, with a sun helmet on his head. Yet so it is, and as the elephant is a discerning animal, it may be that he would not perform if his mahout adopted any other costume. Elephants have performed in circuses ever since the times of ancient Rome, when they walked upon the tight rope, danced, fought in the arena, and perhaps now and then knelt on a Christian, when Nero was in search of novelty.

Educated, or rather civilised spectators — the two states are not identical — must always look with compassion on a performing elephant. Certainly he is not overworked, but somehow he strikes one as though he would be more in his own element piling great logs into position in a teak forest in Burmah, or helping to make roads in Southern India.

To see the monster, with his intelligence, and his docility, so careful not to hurt any of the pygmies, fussing about him, is a sad sight, and sympathy goes out to the elephant. When the mahout orders him to lie down, it is as if the dignity of man, a dignity, if he is worthy of it, that he should share with all the animals, is being outraged. Standing on a tub, it is as if a valued friend was put into the pillory for fools to gape at. When the mahout swings himself upon his head by one of his tremendous ears, and strikes an attitude as if he were defying the stage thunder, it shows at once that there must be some kind of partnership between the man and the huge animal.

But when the trainer makes him stand up, balancing himself on his forelegs, it is a sight as sorry as it would be to see a learned judge, duly bewigged and robed, after delivering his judgment in an important case, turn round and elevate his worshipful posterior in the air for the inspection of the people seated in the court. He waddled off, with his mahout cracking a whip, to stand and muse perhaps in his own quarters on the strange ways of men, or to be wrapped in the contemplation of his travels from the time when, as a calf, he first set out, following his mother, to be a wanderer upon the road. The pity of it is that he cannot write memoirs, for if he could, how many things he might be able to impart about ourselves, that have escaped our eyes!

The cruel spectacle over, cruel, that is, to those who feel that elephants were not intended to be clowns, for without doubt his trainer loved him as the apple of his eye, addressing him in private life as "mon vieux," "old fellow," or "viejito" according to his nationality, and would have braved the flames to save him had the circus taken fire, four bay horses trotted into the ring.

Standing in the centre of the arena, much in the way a hostess in an embassy stands to receive her guests, the ring-master, in immaculate dress-clothes, stood to receive them on their entry. They bowed their heads, pawed gently with their near forefeet, and waited his commands. All were in high condition, with their coats shining, as bright as a horse-chestnut, when in the autumn it falls and bursts its covering on the green moss beneath the trees; their eyes were bright, their manes and tails well combed and dandy-brushed, their feet polished like new cricket-balls, and all were so alike that the best ranchman accustomed to pick out a single horse from amongst hundreds running in a corral might have been puzzled to say which, in the language of his craft, was which, and which the other of them.

At a sign from the ring-master, they ranged themselves like soldiers, and cantered round the ring, and as they passed the opening to the stables, four greys joined them, and then four chestnuts, and four blacks. All were as well matched and as well turned out as the first four, and as they galloped they went so evenly and were in such condition that you might have counted money on their backs without a single piece of it falling to the ground. They wheeled and stopped, changed front, and strung out into a long line, put their feet on the barrier, and came back again into their formation, like well regulated clockwork. All seemed to take a pride in their own beauty, and a pleasure in their work, and now and then in passing, nipped at each other playfully, or threw up their heels as they fell into line.

Taking their trainer as a pivot, at a walk they formed a cartwheel and revolved slowly, the various colours serving as the spokes.

Lastly the trainer raised his chambrière and whirling it about before their noses, they rose on their hind legs, fighting the air with their forefeet, so close to him that he seemed to disappear, lost in the thicket of their flowing manes and tails, with their feet flashing round his head.

He lowered his whip, and forming fours again, they trotted off, each four waiting decorously till it received the signal to advance towards the opening. Then the attendants raked the ring where the horses' feet had churned it up, till it looked like a little sandhill in the desert, after a troup *[sic= troupe]* of camels has passed over it. As one of them unhooked the rope-ladder that dangled from the roof, all heads were turned towards a little platform at the end of the tight wire that stretched high above the ring. Balancing poles were fastened to it, and a white wooden chair. From the back there appeared three figures wrapped in greatcoats, whom hardly anyone had seen enter, as everyone had his eyes fixed upon the wire. "The Perestrello Family, the greatest wire-walkers the world has ever seen, renowned for their amazing feats, that have called forth the admiration of all beholders in both hemispheres," so said the programme, now advanced, shedding their wrappers, to where the ladder hung.

A hum of admiration greeted them when they stood ready to perform, for Latin audiences have never lost their love of beauty in the human form, that has come down to them from their ancestors in Rome, who in their turn received it from the Greeks.

Just for an instant the trio remained motionless, feeling the pride instinctively of their appearance, just as a fine horse appears to feel and to rejoice in his condition, and as unconsciously. With his arms thrown round his children's waists the father looked at them with that air of love and of possession that a fond father feels in something that he has given life to. In this case not only had he given life, but doubly created, by his care in training up to physical perfection those copies of himself.

Not more than five-and-forty years of age, and about five-feet-eight in height, the ideal stature for a perfect athlete of the ring, his crisp brown

168

hair curled low upon his forehead, as the Greeks have depicted in their statues of Olympian victors. His muscles stood out on his arms, but not so much as to amount to a deformity, as is so often seen in athletes who have sacrificed everything to strength but have forgotten symmetry. His neck, round, not too short, but strongly made, was set so well upon his trunk that it left hardly any hollow beneath the clavicle, and the whole man gave the appearance of great strength joined to activity.

His children seeming about nineteen and twenty were not unworthy of their progenitor, and looked like copies of their father, not drawn to scale, but executed by some artist who had seen at a glance all really essential to the picture.

The band that had blared out incessantly, discoursing tangos, jazz and patriotic tunes, the chief performer a stout negro, who on his terrific instrument, that may be best described as a mudhorn, from which no one but a member of his race seems able to extract anything but a metabolic rumbling, now ceased its fury.

A gentleman dressed in a morning coat, striped trousers, with white spats upon his patent-leather shoes, holding his tall hat in his left hand, now begged the audience to refrain from their applause during the Perestrellos' act, for he explained the slightest slip upon the wire would of necessity be fatal, for they performed without a net.

Nothing could possibly have been more pleasing to the audience, who in the way of audiences all the world over, hoped inwardly that it would be their luck to witness one of those accidents that it reads of in the Press, with so much gusto.

The girl, putting her foot into a loop, was run up lightly to the platform at one end of the wire, holding with one hand to the rope and with the other blowing kisses to the audience, as she swung through the air.

Bounding upon the platform with a skip or two, she grasped the chain supporting it and looked down upon the upturned faces, confident, youthful, and as unconscious as is a butterfly when it alights upon a flower. Her brother followed her, running up the ladder as easily as if he had been walking up a stair, his feet finding the rungs almost instinctively, as surely as in Colombia a red howling monkey passes from tree to tree. The father followed his two children, and then the girl, seizing her long white balancing pole, tripped across the wire with so much confidence that one forgot to be afraid. She turned and tripped back to the middle of the wire. Her brother joined her, and they passed one another by a miracle of equilibrium. The father, lightly as his children, ran to the centre of the ring, pretended to make a false step and fall, sat down upon the wire, rose again upon one foot, executing all his feats so easily and with such grace that the whole tent rang with applause.

Balancing a wooden chair upon the wire, the elder Perestrello seated himself upon it, looking as secure as if he had been seated in a well-padded armchair in the window of a club. His son climbed on his shoulders, sat with his legs round his father's neck, drew out a cigarette from his waistband, lighted it and smoked a puff or two, sending the smoke out in a cloud from both his nostrils, and then tossed the stump negligently into the ring. Most people would have thought that they had done enough, and put their lives in peril sufficiently to please even the most avid thrillmonger. With infinite precaution, placing her feet as carefully as a steeple-jack picks his way up a tall chimney on a windy afternoon, the girl climbed like a fly upon a window-pane, so little did her feet appear to move, upon the chair, and from the back of it, on to her brother's shoulders, where she stood upright, waving a little flag. The audience held their breath, as if it were afraid to add any additional vibration to the air. Rough fishermen and peasants held their hands before their eyes, women caught tightly at the arms of those who sat beside them; the well-fed bourgeoisie were frozen in their chairs, and even those who never took their gaze off the performers had a strained look, such as you see come over sailors' faces after a close call. At last the Perestrello Family slid down the ladders to the ground. They did not skip in answer to the applause, but bowed and stood for a moment, the father's arms about the children's necks as if he recognised, that once more they were safe.

With a wild cry a troupe of Arab tumblers bounded in for the last turn. The Chinese had presented types of an old civilisation, long anterior to ours, the Perestrello Family, the poetry of the circus, but the wild-looking Arabs had a charm peculiarly their own. Probably they came from Si Hamed O'Musa in the Sus, that ancient Hollywood of Arab acrobatism that furnishes troupes of Arab tumblers to every circus in the world. Half Arab and half Berber, nothing can ever really civilise them, and though so many of them have performed in London, Paris, New York and Berlin, and speak French, German, English or what not, with perfect fluency, sometimes even marrying European wives, there are but few of them who on their holidays do not go back to the Sus, cast off their European clothes, and enjoy a sun bath of barbarism.

So lithe and active were the younger members of the troupe, so wild and flowing their great mops of hair, that it was difficult to tell which of the whirling figures, bounding and turning catherine-wheels and somersaults upon the sand, was a boy or a girl, or if there was an intermediate india-rubber sex, born in the Sus, to tumble through the world.

The elder men had the grave look that years advancing give to all Arabs, when they begin to think of Allah and interlard their speech with pious phrases. This does not take away the racial characteristic of being able to pass out of repose into the wildest ecstasies of fury. The grave and handsome elder members of the troupe, who had stood quietly whilst the boys and girls performed, occasionally encouraging them with a shrill cry, harsh as a seagull's, suddenly became animated.

Bounding across the ring, leaping and somersaulting so quickly that the eye had as much difficulty in making out their limbs as if they had been spokes of some great swift revolving wheel, they fairly outdid all the younger members of the troupe. Such leaps and such contortions, such quickness on the feet, such self-abandonment, only could be seen from those who in the zowia of Si Hamed pay homage to the saint of acrobats. With a loud cry they left the arena, some of them shaking out the sand from their long hair.

The show was over, and the audience filed out, just before midnight, as orderly and with as great decorum as if they had been coming out of church. Almost before the last of them had left the circus, workmen began to pull down everything. The dome of canvas that had appeared so permanent and as if designed to last a century, fluttered down like a gigantic moth, and men began to fold it, almost before it had ceased fluttering.

Men who but half an hour before had been models of grace and of activity, now moved about in heavy greatcoats, smoking cigarettes. Women, their hair untidy and their faces hardly streaked with the grease-paint of their make-up, flitted from caravan to caravan, or stood chattering in groups. By daybreak all was ready for the road. Nothing remained on the bare space of ground, upon the outskirts of the town, of all that microcosm of human life, its dangers, beauties, disillusions, loves, hatreds, and jealousies. Nothing was left to mark the passage of

171

the great town of canvas that had arisen in a night, fallen in an hour and passed away, like life — nothing, except a ring upon the sand.

Tschiffely's Ride

Tschiffely*, Mancha and Gato. The three names are as indivisible as the three Persons of the Trinity.

They will go down to history in the Argentine with far more certainty than those of many worthy politicians, gold-laced generals, diplomats, and others who have strutted their brief hour upon the stage of the republic.

Tschiffely in his various letters to the Press during his three years' journey from Buenos Aires to New York, reveals his sympathetic personality.

Writing from Washington, on April 26th, 1928, to "La Asociacion Militar de Retirados del Ejercito y Armada," Buenos Aires, he signs, "Tschiffely, Mancha y Gato." On other occasions he says, "remembrances and neighs, from the horses."

Tschiffely, a Swiss long settled in the Argentine, a famous horseman, is a man of iron resolution and infinite resource, as his great feat, perhaps the greatest that man and horses have performed in all the history of the world, is there to show.

As to the horses, their deeds speak better for them than any words.

For the last fifty years, it has been the ambition of most stock-breeders in the Argentine to "improve" the native breed of horse, and above all to add a cubit to his stature by taking thought.

They took the thought, and certainly added a cubit (read "hand") to the native horses' height. Nature, however, had her eye upon their work. By crossing with the thoroughbred, the Arab, the Pecheron, the Cleveland Bay and other strains, they bred a taller horse, faster, and fitter both for polo and parade. But strange as it may sound, polo is not the only thing for which horses are designed. It soon was found that the half-bred (mestizo) horse, though larger, faster, and stronger, was a soft animal unfit for work with cattle, slow to jump off the mark, clumsy in

* I did not know Tschiffely when I wrote this sketch, taking my information from
  Argentine papers and magazines.

turning. . . . At this point, I hear my polo players exclaim, "How can a polo pony be called clumsy at turning round?" True that on a well-levelled polo ground, rolled, watered, and treated almost as a lawn, he lumbers round quite readily. But polo players ride for pleasure, their horses are fed and pampered, almost like "Christians." I use the word, not in the religious, but the Spanish sense.

All that can happen to their riders is a collision, a sudden fall or something of the kind. Most polo players die in their beds, with doctors in attendance, and with the Sacraments of Mother Church, after an old age of drinking cocktails in the club, talking of lip-straps, curbs, martingales, bog and blood spavins, splints and other matters of their mystery. The cattleman rides for his daily bread. His horse eats grass, and he himself, as did "Sir Percivell" (in *The Rhyme of Sir Thopas*), sleeps in his hood (read "poncho") and when on the road drinks, if not "water of the well," the coffee coloured fluid of some "charco" or "arroyo" of the plains. The cattle peon plunges into a sea of wild-eyed longhorns, or light-footed Hereford, where a false touch upon the reins means a wound; a fall means death. He rides swinging his lazo, over the roughest ground, and that upon a horse that perhaps has not tasted food or water since sunrise, and then, work over, has to march behind a troop of cattle, and sleep tied to a stake, upon the Pampa, in an icy winter's night, or in a scorching north wind that shrivels up the grass. Gradually it dawned upon cattlemen that the half-bred was an inferior animal for such work. He was slow to turn, proved a poor weight-carrier, was unsafe when galloping in rough ground, and a cold night or two, without his blanket and his corn, made a poor horse of him indeed.

So they turned back to nature, and procured some horses of the old native stock from El Cacique Liompichon, an Indian chief in Patagonia, and started the Criollo (native) stud book, for the native horse. It was found fourteen-two or fourteen-three was the best height for work, for taller horses, even of pure native stock, were not so fit to stand long days, short commons and hard work.

Then they set about to put their theories into practice and show the world the wonderful endurance of the Criollo horse. Now it was that the famous trio, Tschiffely, Mancha and Gato, came upon the scene.

As soon as the "Asociacion Criadores de Criollo," with its stud book,

174

was instituted, long distance rides were undertaken, to show what the Criollo horse could do. Don Abelardo Piovano, on his horse, Lunarejo Cardal, covered the distance of eight hundred and fifty-seven miles in seventeen days, from Buenos Aires to Mendoza, carrying about thirteen stone.

This was no ride round some great stadium, with grooms always in attendance with water and with corn, rubbers and bandages, and a warm stable every night. The route ran over open plains, sparsely inhabited, where the intrepid pair often slept out alone beneath the stars, the horse tied to a stake-rope cropping the grass, the rider eating such spare provisions as could be carried in his saddle-bags.

The feat was good, in all the circumstances, but not definitive, for it was carried out on the flat plains, in which the horse was born, with little change of climate, and with good grass and water all the way, and corn occasionally.

How, when or wherefore it came into Tschiffely's head to announce his raid from Buenos Aires to New York is to me as unknown as most of the designs of fate.

Immediately the local Babbitry gave tongue. Old babblers and young bletherers rushed into print to show it was impossible. Just as in Salamanca, when the wise reverend fools proved mathematically and theologically that Columbus was a madman, so did the local wiseacres demonstrate Tschiffely was an ass. No horses, so they said, bred in the plains, almost at sea-level, could cross the Andes, still less endure the Tropics, or bear the constant change of climate and of food upon the road. Indians and bandits would attack the rider; wild beasts destroy the horses; their feet would give out on the stony mountain roads. In fact the project was absurd and would bring ridicule upon the country. Tschiffely took no notice of the arm-chair riders and quietly went on with his few preparations for the start. They were soon made, and he proceeded to the south, where the most hardy animals are bred, to choose the horses that became national heroes. He selected two, "Mancha," a skewbald, with white legs and face, and streaked all over with white stripes, stocky and with well-made legs and feet, like those of a male mule, as hard as steel. His second choice was "Gato", a yellow dun, for "gato" is a contraction of the word "gateado" (literally, cat-coloured), the favourite colour of the Gauchos of the plains, who always used to choose that colour for hard work. They have a saying, "Gateado, antes muerto que cansado," a dun horse dies before he tires.

Azara, the Spanish naturalist, writing in 1785 (?), says that the great troops of wild horses, known as Baguales, that in his time roamed all over the Pampas, from San Luis to Patagonia, were nearly all either some shade of dun or brown. "Mancha" was fifteen years of age, and "Gato" fourteen, and neither of them had ever eaten corn or worn a shoe.

The horses had just finished a journey of nine hundred miles, taking a troop of cattle from Sarmiento, far below the Welch *[sic]* settlement of Chibut, to Ayacucho in the province of Buenos Aires, in the month of March.

One road and only one was open to him, across the plains to Mendoza, then over the Andes and along the coast of Chile and Peru, from Ecuador to Colombia and through Panama to Nicaragua and on to Mexico.

Once there, Tschiffely knew, all would be easy and the victory assured, for Mexico presented no essential difficulty with its great open plains, and with a population that adored the horse, almost as much as do the Argentines.

Tschiffely set out from Buenos Aires in April, 1925, riding his Mancha and leading Gato with a pack-saddle carrying his food and clothes. Hardly had he started than he encountered torrential rains that turned the "camps" into a morass. He reached Rosario, with his horses fresh, finishing his first "étape."

The local know-alls found the horses "extremely weak and thin." This pleased them, without doubt, but Dr. Nicholas L. Duro, the veterinary surgeon, saw them with different eyes. After examination he pronounced both horses in "good condition and able to proceed upon their march." In a letter to the local press he said: "It is astonishing that animals of the appearance of these horses, selected for such a journey, and in such disadvantageous conditions, in regard to food, for neither of them has yet learned to eat corn, not only have adapted themselves to the diversity of climate (Rosario is hotter far than Patagonia) but have improved upon the road."

The next eighty leagues were chiefly heavy sand, the water brackish (such water generally purges horses) and the grasses often poisonous, so that the utmost care had to be taken where the horses fed. They crossed the prairies of Santiago del Estero and of Tucuman, and on the twenty-sixth of June arrived at the Bolivian frontier at Perico del Carmen, in the province of Jujuy, having covered twelve hundred miles (400 leagues).

In Tucuman, the curiosity to see the horses and their rider was immense. Somehow or other Mancha's fame as a buck-jumper ("tenia fama de reservado") had preceded him. The officers of the garrison, much against Tschiffely's will, persuaded him to let a soldier, known as a rider, mount the horse. He clapped the spurs into him ("lo buscó"), and then the man, being, in Tschiffely's words, "a dud at the business," after three bucks was thrown into the dirt ("lo basurió"), before the eyes of the whole regiment — not bad work for a grass-fed horse that had just completed more than a thousand miles!

As far as the Bolivian frontier all had been relatively plain sailing for the trio. Although the distance traversed had been great, the horses had been in climates not too widely different from their own. They had not had to swim considerable rivers, and grass and water had been plentiful.

In front of them there lay a Via Crucis.

As they came through the grassy plains, camped underneath the stars by the side of some slow-flowing "arroyo" of the Pampas, Tschiffely, after staking out the horses carefully, would lay down the various pieces of the native saddle ("el recaó") *[sic = el recao]*, heat water for his "maté" at a little fire, eat what he had in his saddle-bags and sit smoking, drinking a "maté" or two, and watching the horses eat. When he felt drowsy, he would take a last look at the horses, examine carefully the knot of the stake-rope, look well to the picket-pin, or the bunch of grass if the ground was too hard to drive a pin into, and then lie down with his face in the direction of the way he had to travel at the first streak of dawn.

Leaning upon his elbow he would listen to the mysterious noises of the night, the bark of the Vizcachas, the grunting noise of the burrowing Tuco-tucos, and the shrill neigh of a wild stallion gathering up his mares.

After having taken off his boots, his knife and his revolver ready to his hand, beneath his head, he would draw up his poncho to protect him from the dew. During the night he would rise frequently to make sure the horses were all right. Each time he rose he would look up and mark the constellations as they moved, the Pleiades, Capella and the Southern Cross, with an especial glance at the Tail of Orion, with its three bright stars, the Gauchos used to call "Las Tres Marias." At the false dawn he would awake, shivering and drenched with dew, revive his fire, drink several "matés," and see his horses, half-dozing on their stake-ropes, resting a hind leg, and with their coats dripping and shiny with the dew. Then he would saddle up, taking care not to draw the cinch too tightly if it was Mancha that he was to ride, remembering his fame as a born buck-jumper. Putting the pack-saddle on whichever of the horses was to serve that day as cargo bearer ("el carguero"), he would take the halter of the led horse in his right hand, gather up the reins, and mounting lightly, without dwelling for an instant on the stirrup, strike into the jog-trot called in the Argentine el "trotecito", that eats the miles up with less fatigue to rider and horse than any other gait.

The difficulties lay in front. Probably at this point Tschiffely taught his horses to eat corn. He had to face the stony Andean roads, high altitudes, bitter mountain winds, snow, ice, and lack of pasture by the way. All these with horses born in the plains of Patagonia, accustomed to but little variations of temperature and perennial good grass.

Writing from La Quiaca, on the Bolivian frontier, on July 29th (1925), Tschiffely says, "The worst part of the road so far was that between Jujuy and La Quiaca." Sometimes his horses had to pass the night with seventeen and eighteen degrees of frost, without food, in the open tied up to a post, with winds that "penetrated to the bones." He says the horses were improving day by day, only he himself had suffered from a poisoned hand, due to a prick from a sharp thorn. His face, from the exposure to the sun and wind, was like "an English pudding." This reference to our national rice (or perhaps tapioca) "pudding" is scarcely worthy of a horseman of his stamp. In spite of all the prophecies that no horse born on the plain could reach La Quiaca, "Here we are," he says, "the horses fatter than when we set out." His own condition seems to have been so bad that everyone in La Quiaca advised him to give up. "But," he says, "little did they know of the affection that I have to my two 'pingos,' the faithful sharers of so many weary leagues of solitude." "No, sir" (he is writing to Dr. Emilio Solanet, of Buenos Aires, the great horse-breeder), "I will not give up unless either I or my horses die. Good-bye now to the Argentine, regards to all who have accompanied me in their thoughts, with neighs from Mancha and Gato, and their remembrances to all. Yrs. Aimé Tschiffely."

A gallant and tender-hearted letter, that showed a man, brought up in the Swiss mountains, tempered and toughened to the consistency of jerked beef by sun and wind upon the plains, and with a heart of steel.

September saw him in La Paz, the capital of Bolivia, at an altitude of twelve thousand feet. His horses still were in the best of spirits, and he himself had got well of his poisoned hand, in the keen mountain air. The roads had been abominable, snowy at times and always stony and precipitous. From Potosi to Curdo the mountain pass was fifteen thousand feet in height. His guide's mule completely petered out, though mountain-bred, accustomed to high altitudes, and man and mule had to be put aboard the first train, for they were completely "knock-out," as Tschiffely says. His horses plodded on, their rider walking occasionally in the worst bits of the road. During the journey in the mountains he had made generally about two-and-twenty miles a day. A mountain mule seldom makes more, upon an average.

The rider had hurt his leg in a fall on the road, and was suffering from malaria, the horses had been badly bitten by the vampire-bats, but otherwise were well.

La Paz turned out en masse to see the horses and their intrepid rider, and the local veterinary pronounced both Mancha and El Gateado "quite sound in wind and limb." Mancha was so fresh that he nearly kicked his box to pieces when they arrived in Lima and rested for a week or two. In three days they had come from the region of eternal snows into the hottest of the tropics. The trio had been five months on the road, and of the three the rider had suffered most in health. The next stage, between Lima and Trujillo, was more terrible than any of the past.

To read Tschiffely's letter from Barranca (Peru), it seems impossible that even such valiant animals as Mancha and Gato could have survived the hardships of the road. The trail ran through the desert of Mata Caballos ("kill horses"), impossible to pass without a guide. No one was willing to risk his life on such a quest, for he was almost certain to "die in the demand," as goes the Spanish phrase. Full eighteen leagues (54 miles) had to be covered, in a sandy desert, before water could be reached, under a temperature of fifty-two degrees Centigrade, or say a hundred and ten Fahrenheit.

Tschiffely saddled up at half-past four and reached his water at half-past six at night. His description of the "étape" shows him with as light a hand upon the pen as on the reins.

"Sand, sand, and sun, lagoons with myriad of gulls, sand, rocks, and still more sand. Not a plant to be seen, no refuge from the sun that there is fire. To compare the region with the Hell of Dante would be inexact, for nature there is dead; the landscape seems unreal. The horses' feet sank deep into the sand, a burning thirst consumed us. When we arrived at

Huecho (where there was a well) the horses, although tired, were going well. My head was like an English 'budin' (this is a variant in spelling, not disagreeable to the eye), my face all the colours of the rainbow, with the skin fit to burst."

There he had to stay a little, for his guide and the mule he rode were quite "knock-out," a favourite phrase of his. As everyone at Huecho knew that the next stage was only possible at night, and to attempt it by day was almost certain failure, there was great difficulty to get a guide willing to undertake the task. Besides the risk of wandering from the right path, or perishing from heat, there was the additional danger, in the next two "étapes" of the dry river-courses swelling to broad torrents impossible to cross, by the sudden melting, up in the Andes, of the snow. This entailed the services of someone who knew the fords, for the unusual heat of the season, extraordinary even in that hell of burning sand, had filled the watercourses a month before the time.

Not finding anyone in Huecho who would affront the perils of the trail, Tschiffely set out on a long tramp of seven leagues, on foot, to a hacienda, where lived a guide who knew the road. He was obliged to go on foot, for on the road there was one of those Andean swinging-rope bridges that no animal could cross. Having found a guide, who in a day or two arrived by a long detour that missed the bridge, riding a mule and leading a horse that carried bread and sardines, with water in four ample flasks. Thirty-two leagues of heavy sand, with neither water nor any food for man or beast, now lay before him. In seventeen hours of "sand and sand and sand" (I quote his letter to *La Nacion* of Buenos Aires, Feb. 16, 1926), almost without a halt, he reached a little Indian village called Huarney. The guide and his two animals were exhausted, but Mancha and El Gateado, when they were unsaddled, rolled in the sand and ate voraciously. Thirty leagues (90 miles) lay between Huarney and Casura, another Indian town. When he arrived at the Casura river it was in high flood, and he was forced to swim. Riding his Gateado and leading Mancha, he plunged into the stream. Swept down the current he was almost drowned with both his horses. The cowardly guide, who after much persuasion tried the ford, did nothing to assist him and almost by a miracle they all reached the bank. That day they travelled twenty hours, with only one hour's rest, after the passage of the ford. His horses, as he wrote (to *La Nacion*), though tired, were not exhausted, but the guide and his horses were nearly dead. The sandy deserts now were passed, but perils of a different nature still lay before him on the road.

Once more he was obliged to plunge into the Andes, for no road ran along the coast to Panama. So he set off for Quito, having already passed by Cuzco, the other Inca capital, on his Andean journey from Bolivia to Peru. By this time notices of the "Raid" began to appear in every city of the Americas. The sporting circles of New York and Mexico received reports of Tschiffely's journey from every wireless station on the way. "Mancha" and "Gato" had become household words in every newspaper.

All unknown to himself, Tschiffely was entering on the most arduous and dangerous portion of his ride. The frost and snows of the high Andes, the burning heat of the coastal sands between Lima and Trujillo, the poisonous pasturage in Jujuy, were all as nothing to what he soon was called on to endure. At least in all the countries he had passed through there had been food for man and beast. Scanty at times, but still sufficient to sustain their strength; water, except between Lima and Trujillo, had never failed, and there had been no danger from wild beasts. Once he left Quito, at an altitude of ten thousand feet, straight from the coast, over the roughest mountain roads, he would be obliged to plunge into the forests of some of the hottest tropics of the world. Those forests swarming with vampire-bats, with every kind of noxious insect, full of dangerous snakes, cut by deep streams, the haunt of alligators and electric eels, with every shallow the abode of stinging rays, that if a horse treads on them, inflict a wound that causes agony and does not heal for months; peopled by shoals of the voracious little fish, the Piranha, that tears to pieces every living thing that has the smallest open wound upon it, constituted an obstacle difficult and dangerous beyond belief. Their recesses sheltered tigers (jaguars) powerful enough to kill a horse with a blow of their paw and drag his body fifty or a hundred yards. Moreover, little grass grows under the dark trees, and in the rare clearings such pasture as there is, is wiry, hard, and carries little nourishment. The leaves of a certain palm tree, called pindó, are eaten by the native animals, but it was quite uncertain whether horses accustomed to the sweet grasses of the Patagonian plains would eat them or, having eaten, thrive upon them.

To reach Quito from Piura, on the coast, an arduous journey lay in front of him, of about three hundred miles. If in Peru and Bolivia the intrepid trio had been objects of interest to all, in Ecuador the enthusiasm reached its height. At the first frontier town the authorities and all the "notables," civil and military alike, turned out to greet "Los fenómenos de las Pampas Argentinas." The country people rivalled the authorities in the warmness of their welcome, and their curiosity.

Mancha and Gato, once the frontier of Ecuador was passed, seem to have been almost deified. Deification, even if spontaneous by the adorers, and involuntary on the part of the subjects, has its inconveniences. Tschiffely, with the "pawky" humour that distinguishes both Scots and Swiss alike, writes in a letter to *La Nacion* that the attention with which his horses and himself were treated made him lose much time, when he had rather have been resting, in answering questions at every place at which they stopped. He had to tell his adventures to all and sundry for a hundred times.

In fact, his progress, through such parts of Ecuador as were inhabited, reminds one of a parliamentary candidate on an election tour, dragged to and fro by his supporters, always obliged to smile and to repeat the self-same "boniment." Even the horses suffered, for the people gathered round to see them feed, and gaze at them with that fixed and apparently uncomprehending stare natural to the Indians of Ecuador and Bolivia.

The road as far as Alausi, some fifty leagues short of the capital, was only to be described as devilish.

It ran beside the railway line from Guayaquil to Quito and was a series of ups and downs after the fashion of a switchback. The heat was terrible, the track a "razorback" bordered on each side by a sea of mud. At night the temperature fell below freezing-point, and the rain was perpetual.

The troops of mules that, since the Conquest, had plied upon the road carrying all merchandise from the coast to Quito, had made a sort of staircase of the track, leaving great steps, called "camellones" locally. Sometimes the descents were so precipitous and slippery in the deep mud that Mancha and Gato slid down them seated on their haunches, with their forefeet stretched out in front of them. This feat the mules born in the country all understand and practise and many of the older books of travel have woodcuts showing them at work.

To Mancha and Gato this was new, but it was wonderful that they at once learned to execute the feat as to the manner born. The wretched halting-places, called by the ancient Inca term of "tambos," were filthy in the extreme, malodorous and full of every flying and crawling insect that made life miserable.

Mules and their drivers, pigs, dogs, asses and chickens, slept promiscuously in the corrals attached to the "tambos." Great care had to be exercised that the horses' forage was not stolen or that they were not kicked by any of the mules. All these inconveniences and the state of the road spun out the journey between the coast and Quito for two months.

The horses reached Quito perfectly well and pulling at their bits, but Tschiffely had suffered greatly in his health from hardships and malaria, bad water and execrable food. He had to stop in Quito for six weeks, most of the time in hospital.

The horses, in a hacienda of a Colonel Sturdy, fed on the best of pasture, and waxed fat, getting into such good condition that when Tschiffely, his health restored, mounted them to give an exhibition of their quality, at the request of the authorities of Quito, they jumped about like colts. Gato went at everything with a rush, passing through mudholes in a plunge or two and crossing rotten bridges without looking at them. Mancha, upon the contrary, if he had to pass a doubtful bridge, tried it with his near front foot, looked at it carefully and only ventured on it after putting down his head to bring his ears and eyes and nostrils on a level with the planks. ("Quel destrier, aveva l'ingegno á maraviglia.")

The first part of the journey to the Colombian frontier, although an eight months' drought had dried up all the pastures, was relatively easy, for there actually were roads.

Through the hot valleys between Pasto and Popayan, unhealthy, mostly composed of forest, where no doubt tigers abounded, and if they camped Tschiffely must have been obliged to light a fire and watch his horses all the night, ready to stand by their heads and quiet them if a tiger's cry were wafted ominously through the woods. From Pasto the route lay through Cali and down the Cauca valley to Medellin, the capital of the State of Antioquia.

All three of the adventurers suffered terribly upon the way. Alternately, sometimes on the same day, they had to climb up into the Andes and endure cold, snow and icy winds, and then descend into the steamy valleys, where the damp heat rendered it hard to breathe, and the perpetual rain rotted the rider's clothes. Writing from Bogotá on the 10th of October, 1926, after eighteen months upon the road, Tschiffely gives an account of all that they endured. He reveals also his undaunted spirit and his sympathetic attitude to the companions of his extraordinary feat.

Eight months of drought, he says, had burned up everything, "and my poor horses used to stand at the pasture gate, waiting for me at sunrise, without having eaten anything. It would be difficult to express what I felt on such occasions, especially when I was saddling up at sunrise. The poor animals looked at me with the eyes of children, and Mancha, always a 'talker' ('charlatán'), neighed, as it were asking me for what I could not give him, perhaps for ten or twelve hours," after an arduous day.

When Medellin was reached Tschiffely received confirmation of what he had already heard in Lima as to the impossibility of travelling by land to Panama.

The Government of Colombia, through the Argentine Legation at Bogotá, sent to inform Tschiffely that the journey was impossible. No roads existed through the virgin forests that had never yet been trodden by the foot of man. Swamps, lakes and rivers, without bridges, swarming with alligators and with banks so swampy that it would prove impossible, even after crossing, ever to emerge upon hard ground alive, set up a barrier impossible to cross. The forests were quite uninhabited, even by wild Indians. In fact few portions of the globe are more inhospitable or more unknown; few more unhealthy.

Tschiffely went by train and mule-back to Bogotá, only to receive the same report from the Colombian Government. Nothing remained but to embark the horses as far as Panama, but before doing so he obtained a statement from the authorities of the district of the Choco that borders on the Gulf of Darien. In it they said that from personal knowledge of the country any journey from their district into Panama must of necessity result in the death both of the rider and the horses. They alleged once more the lack of roads, the denseness of the virgin woods and the fact that they had remained as unknown as at the creation of the world.

During his journey by mule-back to Bogotá, he left his horses in a fenced pasture ("potrero") where there was abundant grass. A river ran through it, and an Indian boy gave them two baths a day, and twice a day they fed on sugar-cane, unrefined sugar ("panela"), bran, and a grass called "pasto imperial" that has great nutritive power.

Forced to perform the journey from Medellin to Panama in a river steamboat, a mere step in comparison with the fifteen thousand miles from Buenos Aires to New York, he arrived safely at the Canal, and after fifteen days of quarantine was once more ready for the road.

His spirits rose, his horses were in good condition after their long rest, and he knew the country that lay ahead of him would prove but child's play after that he had just passed. Writing to *La Nacion*, he says:

"Once I have passed the State of Costa Rica, where I am told there are bits of the road that present difficulties, the rest is easy.

"I hope in eight, or perhaps nine months to be safely in New York.

"For my part I assure you all that I can do, I shall do. I have no fear of the results and I shall never give up, if it is possible to go forward, and the same supplies *[sic = applies?]* to both the horses ('pingos'), I feel sure."

The trio crossed the Canal on a drawbridge, not that they would have been afraid to swim it, for Tschiffely says, " 'We' have swum rivers far wider than the Canal."

Just after crossing the Canal, the first accident occurred, for up till then neither of the horses had hurt itself, or suffered anything particular except cold, hunger, heat and the attacks of vampire-bats.

Riding along a muddy trail, Mancha stepped on a piece of half buried rusty wire and cut his foreleg deeply, but, luckily, not near the tendons. The wound was deep and cost them three weeks of delay till it was healed and Mancha ready for the road.

Although he had been told that difficulties awaited him upon the road to San José de Costa Rica, Tschiffely had no idea that they would be so great. The trail from Panama to the little mountain town of David ran through the forests and was deep in mud. Although he took two guides, they lost the track, and wandered helplessly in the vast jungles, all bound together with lianas, into an almost impenetrable mass.

To regain the lost trail, they were obliged to open what is known as a "picada" with the "machetes" (bush knives) that in those countries every horseman carries at his saddle bow.

Food for the horses there was none except the leaves of a scrub oak and a dwarf palm-tree.

The horses' shoes came off in the thick mud. Tschiffely says with pride, "However, they could travel well enough without them." The rain never ceased for an instant, so that his clothes all became rotten, even his boots rotted off from his feet, and he was obliged to tie the soles on to his feet with strips of hide, for, unlike the horses, he could not travel without shoes.

Malaria once more attacked him, and all he had to fight it off with was the native rum, fiery and raw that, when you swallow it, goes like a torchlight procession down the throat.

When he arrived at San José de Costa Rica in a torrential rain after a forced march of eight leagues, a deputation waited on him with an invitation to a banquet. He was wet to the skin, his boots were sandals tied to his feet with strips of hide. After he had seen Mancha and Gato led off in honour, guests of the Legation of the Argentine, his head whirling with the champagne that he was forced to drink, he staggered to his room in the hotel. A bed with sheets, the first he had seen for months, was so inviting that, wet through as he was, without attempting even to remove his fragmentary boots, he threw himself upon it, and fell asleep. He says he was exhausted, but that the horses were as fresh as when they had started out from Panama.

His health obliged him to remain for several weeks in Panama *[sic = Costa Rica?]*. As Nicaragua was in a state bordering on anarchy, a prey to the contending factions, swarming with bandits and disbanded soldiers, and horses were extremely scarce, and, of course, contraband of war, he was obliged once more to embark his horses a little distance from Puntarenas (Costa Rica) to La Union in Salvador. The journey through that small republic was not difficult, but the heat was so intense that it brought out a new attack of the malaria, and in San Salvador (the capital of the republic of El Salvador) he was laid up another fifteen days. His strength exhausted by the hardships of the road and the attacks of fever that he suffered from, he doubted for the first time since he left Buenos Aires of his ultimate success.

However, when he reached Guatemala City, at an altitude of six thousand feet, he soon revived in spirits and in health.

"We" were warmly welcomed by the inhabitants and the Government; society and the learned institutions all joined in honouring "us." The phrase shows the man's character, as well as a whole volume of his "life and miracles." Mancha and Gato, without doubt, were flattered by the attention of the "cultured institutions," and if they could have spoken would probably have done as well as or better than many orators such institutions endure and suffer under.

Tschiffely now felt certain of success. Mexico was a land where gentlemen and horsemen ("caballero") were synonymous. The country on the whole was not so difficult as any through which he had already passed. His hopes ran high, and in a week or two he thought he would be in the capital (Mexico).

But as the Spanish proverb has it, a hare springs up when you are not expecting her. ("Adonde menos se piensa, salta la lie bre." *[sic = liebre]*)

Not far from the bridge at the frontier Gato went lame for the first time since leaving Buenos Aires. At Tapachula he could go no farther. Luckily there was a military post of cavalry. The veterinary surgeon found that the smith in Guatemala had driven a nail into the foot. He cut it out at once, but the hot climate and the perpetual moisture of the rainy season inflamed the wound so much that Tschiffely passed three or four nights, so to speak, at the bedside of the sufferer, applying fomentations to the foot. Gato was almost well, when some "son of a mother who never yet said No" let loose overnight a strange horse in the stable-yard. Next morning Gato had received so terrible a kick on his near foreleg that he could not lie down. The leg swelled up enormously and everyone told Tschiffely that the best thing that he could do was to shoot Gato and end his misery.

"It was a rude blow and I was overwhelmed with grief, but I would not even entertain the idea of losing the good horse, companion of 'our' perils on the road."

At once he telegraphed to the Argentine Ambassador in the capital, Señor Roberto Labougli, who replied asking him to send the horse by train to Mexico, where he would be cared for by the best veterinaries.

These delays made him lose a month, but nothing daunted, having procured a guide and bought two horses for him, he once more started out upon the road.

Three or four days' journey convinced him that he would never reach the capital alone, for the road swarmed with bandits and with revolutionaries, words that, as he says, in Mexico have the same meaning.

At the next military post the Commandant refused to let him pass, saying he could not respond for his security if he went on alone.

Hearing the case, the President of the Republic, General Elias Calles, sent out a troop of cavalry to escort Tschiffely on the road.

This was a "gesture", as he says, of "the greatest generosity and sympathy to the Argentine Republic never before accorded to a mere traveller." The truth was that Mexico was all agog to see the "heroes" of the raid.

At every town and hamlet that he passed the inhabitants turned out to greet him, patting and making much of Mancha and doing all that lay within their power to help them on their way.

Even in the humble ranchos of the Indians "they did their best to succour and assist us."

The rains delayed the journey, and the cavalry were not well mounted, so that when they reached Oscara, Mancha alone was not exhausted.

The rivers, too, were swollen with the rains and, as there were no bridges, had to be crossed swimming — a dangerous operation, as they swarmed with alligators. As he advanced amidst general rejoicing, encountering a cooler climate day by day, for the interior plateau of the country ("la meseta de Anahuac") stands at an elevation of six thousand feet, the road grew easier.

At Puebla, the people had arranged a festival "to welcome us," but as fate willed it, he had at once to take to bed, for several days prostrated by malaria.

When he reached Mexico his entry was a triumph, and was telegraphed at once to the whole world.

The streets were packed and as he rode along on Mancha, women came out upon the balconies and showered flowers upon him.

"My joy was without limit, and my feelings unforgettable, when I saw 'friend Gato' ('el amigo Gato') led up quite fresh, and as sound as when he was a colt," owing to the care he had received from the State veterinary, Señor Labougle. During his sojourn in the city he received enormous hospitality from all classes of society, the President himself visiting the horses several times and admiring them.

On the 27th of November he set his face towards the frontier of the United States, leaving a host of friends in Mexico, with both his horses fresh and bounding under him. All through Mexico Tschiffely's journey was a triumphal march, for the news of his coming had been telegraphed from Mexico to every town upon the way. His stages were erratic, for at times more than a hundred horsemen turned out to escort him on his way. The smallest hamlet hoisted the Argentine flag, sometimes made out of coloured paper, and the nine hundred miles to New Laredo, the frontier town upon the Rio Grande, was like a street during a carnival, that is to say, when they passed through a town. I, who have ridden the whole distance from San Antonio, Texas, to Mexico, and back again, when all the road was perilous from the attacks of the apaches near the frontier, and of the bandits, nearer Mexico, though I remember every village he passed through, can hardly take in the changed circumstances. Across the frontier the authorities had organized a military pageant in honour of "the brave horseman of the Argentine and his two faithful friends." Tschiffely, mounted on Mancha and holding Gato by his side, took the salute, as the troops with their bands playing passed before him.

It must have been the proudest moment of his life, and have repaid him for all that he had undergone on his fantastic journey of fifteen thousand miles.

Two thousand kilometres still lay between the frontier and his goal, and perils of a sort he had not looked for still awaited him. He had hoped to reach New York in June, but invitations, banquets and interviews rained on him. If he had not protested, escorts of cavalry would have accompanied him all through Texas. In San Antonio he was obliged to stay for fifteen days, the guest of the municipality. The same thing happened in Austin, Houston, Fort Worth and Dallas, and invitations from towns far off his route flowed in upon him. When in Fort Worth a compatriot, Don Gustavo Muñiz Barreto, fitted him out with a complete Gaucho costume, "poncho," and wide Turkish trousers, tucked into high patent-leather boots, with silver trappings for his horse. Public enthusiasm knew no bounds. Mancha, on account of his striking colour, was the idol of "las bellas Yanquis," who flocked to see him every day, patting and petting him. They grew so demonstrative in their affection that Tschiffely had to keep strict guard over Mancha or they would have cut off all his mane and tail to keep as souvenirs.

Mancha, who, as we know, enjoyed "fame as a buckjumper" ("tenia fama de reservado") became so irritable that it was dangerous to go near him but Gato, more apathetic, took everything "con apatia," and was concerned entirely with the good things of the stable, which he consumed with great enthusiasm.

Both of them grew as fat as Jeshurun, but there is no recorded instance of their ever having kicked.

Once more the local wiseacres shook their long ears and solemnly announced that no horse in the world could stand more than a day or two upon the treated roads. In spite of that, Mancha and Gato advanced steadily, doing their thirty miles a day, passing by St. Louis, Missouri, Indianapolis, and Washington.

As they drew nearer to New York the danger that they ran from the continuous stream of automobiles on the roads was as great as on any portion of his adventurous road. As he rode on, in constant peril from the motor traffic, his mind dwelt always on his goal, and on the joy that he would feel when once again he and his horses arrived safely in Buenos Aires, where, after all their perils and hard work, Gato and Mancha could forget for ever girths, bits and saddles, and the hardships of the road. His dream is fulfilled, and the two faithful companions of his wanderings once more are back again in their own country, after having travelled fifteen thousand miles during their three years' raid. Happier than mankind, they have their Trapalanda upon earth, eat the sweet grasses of their native plains, drink the soft, muddy water of some "arroyo," and though they know it not, never again "the cruel spur shall make them weary."

"Creeps"

As he stood in the smoking-room of the Hôtel Continental in Tangier, dressed in a faded red hunting-coat that had turned almost the colour of a mulberry through exposure to the weather and the fierce sun of Northern Africa, holding a velvet cap in one hand, and in the other his crop and a pair of weather-stained rein-worn dog-skin gloves, his face almost as weather-beaten as his gloves, few would have taken him for a great artist and a man of genius. He had the air of a second whip to a provincial pack of hounds down on his luck and looking for a place. His cord riding breeches hardly met his cracked and ill-cleaned boots. His spurs were rusty, and had it not been for his hands, well-shaped and delicate, his sleek dark head, and deep brown, almost chocolate eyes, eyes that impelled you to follow them, he might have gone straight on the stage, without any make-up, to play Tony Lumpkin.

Although he spoke to no one, it was evident that he had seen not only every person in the room, but every object in it. For a considerable time he sat, turning over listlessly the pages of *The Field*, and drinking several stiff whiskies and sodas, that had no effect upon him, except to seem to seal his lips more firmly, not that it seemed a voluntary act, but something born with him, as were his lustrous eyes or his sleek head. His slightly bandy legs he had acquired through early riding, for he was seldom off a horse, holding that Providence would have bestowed four legs on man had he intended him to go afoot. The man was Joseph Crawhall, known to his friends as "Creeps"— why, no one seemed to know.

Unknown all his life to the general public, and even now only appreciated by his fellow artists, he certainly was a man of genius, if any painter ever merited the term. Genius, I take it, is the power of doing anything in such a way that no one else can do it. That (and fifty other things) separates it from talent, for talent merely does in a superior way what other men can do. Thus talent does not excite enmity, as is so often the fate of genius, for we all dislike that a mere man such as ourselves possesses something we can never hope to compass, even by years of unremitting toil.

Those who like myself are quite profane to the pictorial art, holding it as a miracle — but the mind of man is the greatest of all miracles, a miracle of miracles — that by some few strokes on a flat surface of canvas or of paper, a vase looks round and solid, a horse or stag is made to gallop, or a familiar face is reproduced, could see that there was something wonderful in Crawhall's art. Something there was as I see art — but then of course my vision may be more limited than I suspect — that linked him by pictorial succession to the art of the great draughtsmen of the caves of Altamira.

Crawhall, as they did, left out everything not essential, not as some leave out most that is essential, in their search after originality. Whether the prehistoric artists studied, as I think they must have, for I believe no miracles except that cited above, we do not know. Certainly Crawhall had been kept hard to learn the ribs and trucks of his profession (as Joseph Conrad might have said) in his youth, by his father, a book illustrator of repute in Newcastle-on-Tyne. Thus drawing became like thinking to him, and I think just as subconsciously. It was his speech. His pencil was to him what the tongue is to other men. He talked with it, for no sachem of the Iroquois could have been more silent in ordinary life. Lavery used to call him the Great Silence, and no one ever better merited the name. Whether he would have produced more if he had drunk less is a moot question. After all, great production is not always a sign of merit, though it implies, as in the case of Sargent, Luca Giordano, Tiepolo and others, extraordinary vitality of hand and brain. All that "Creeps" did produce was perfect of its kind, and certainly no one before or after him, except the Altamiran artists, have produced anything even remotely resembling his work. It may have been on that account that he so strongly influenced the Glasgow school, a group of painters whose aims were totally dissimilar to his, but who all admired and recognised his genius. No place could have suited him better than the Tangier of those days. In it he found exactly all he wanted for his art. Of course wherever he had lived he would have found congenial subjects, for he was not one of those who sought for any subject in particular, but painted what he saw. If he had been condemned to live in a house that had no view but into a backyard with a great water-butt at one end of it, that water-butt would have appeared exactly rendered, but somehow differently rendered from the way that any other artist would have drawn it. Thus his art had some affinity to the art of Japan, before the knowledge of perspective under European rules took away so much of its originality.

His methods were his own and differed widely from those of any other painter I have known or read about.

He never held up a pencil between his forefinger and his thumb and seemed to measure spaces in the air. Still less did he when he was painting walk up towards his canvas and walk back again, with the look on his face as of an orphaned archangel looking for the door of Paradise, and execute the rhythmic dance that many painters indulge in, and has always impressed me as one of their most intriguing mysteries.

I hardly ever saw him draw direct from nature.

When he had to paint a horse, a dog, a goat, or any other animal, a branch in which he excelled all painters of his time (perhaps of all time), he would go and look at them for a full hour, with a look so intense it seemed to burn a hole into their skin. Then perhaps, but rarely, he would take a pencil or a piece of coloured chalk out of his pocket, and on the back of an old envelope set down cabalistic signs or dabs of colour, much like the Indian hieroglyphics that I once saw carved on a rock in a cañon near Montery [*sic = Monterrey*] in Mexico, and as indecipherable to the profane.

Next day, he might, or he might not, return and gaze another hour, and when one thought he had forgotten all about the animal, produce a painting so life-like, so strangely similar to the drawings of the cave-dwellers, and yet so tuned to modern vision, that it forced one to regard the animal that he had limned just as he must have seen it for ever afterwards. A sunset he would paint in the same way, looking intently at it and drawing a few wavy lines that he filled in with a light wash of water colour.

Afterwards, in his studio, he would produce a sunset so delicate and imaginative it seemed he must have had a hand in the original.

Most artists, even those of the first rank, produce their works with drops of blood wrung from the soul. "Creeps," I feel sure, suffered no pangs of parturition, and I remember once, when someone said all art was difficult, he answered simply, without a trace of boastfulness, but in the tone of one who states a fact, "No, not at all."

He never strove after originality, but painted as a bird sings, without a thought of the effect it makes. That was the reason, probably, that all he did was so original.

No one could have been less like the ordinary painter of those days as when I first encountered him, looking like a second whip down on his luck.

In his ordinary clothes he had an air as of a stud groom, in a moderately good place. Not that he affected anything horsy in his dress; the horsiness in his appearance came from the interior grace.

He did not stand with his feet wide apart, head on one side and eyes screwed up when horses passed him upon the road.

For all the outward signs he gave, he might not have observed them, but very likely he would say next day, "That chestnut that passed us in the Soko yesterday had an old bullet wound upon its neck. I saw it when the wind lifted up its mane."

That was a long speech for him and very probably he would not say another word till dinner-time. Still, he had humour of a peculiar kind, upon occasions, but so deep-seated and dispensed with such economy of speech that it was often unperceived, unless the hearer happened himself to be a humorist.

Unluckily for him, and to the regret of all his friends, he now and then had a bout of drinking and would disappear for a day or two, and come back, as it appeared to me, much like the celebrated president of the Ten Tumbler Club of Cupar Angus in the Scottish story, "michtily refreshed," after his potations. On one occasion he was missed from his accustomed haunts longer than usual with him. His friends grew anxious and, led by Bibi Carleton, Bernardino Frias and others of his admirers, they searched the little Tangier of those days, but without finding him. Anselmo, the old Catalan who kept the New York Hotel upon the beach, could give no tidings of him, although he said, "The horse of Mr. Creeps is in the stable, eating his head off him, and his effects are in his room." Antonio Sotiri, the big Cretan Greek who kept the little café at the corner of the little Soko, where "Creeps" and other commentators were wont to take their "eleven hours," when the sun was over the foreyard, as say the mariners, could give no news of him. Ansaldo at the Continental was as ignorant. As they pursued their search on horseback — for in those days in Tangier no male white Christian ever went afoot — they passed El Rubio, the blind beggar, who sat like Bartimæus begging at the Gate.

That is, he sat there when he had nothing else to do, for although blind, he was accustomed to take back horses to the stables, galloping furiously along the sandy roads, his tattered brown jellab streaming in the wind, his blind eyes staring out on vacancy, and his bare heels drumming on the horse's sides as he flew by shouting out "Balak!" and a stream of oaths in every language. Sometimes he led the tourist to the English church and sometimes to a brothel, for all that came into the Rubio's net was fish, if he was paid for it. The searchers after "Creeps" drew up their horses and exchanged pleasantries more or less indecent with the blind man, who knew them instantly by their voices, exclaiming, "Ah, Bibi, son of the illegitimate, how goes it with you?" or, "Señor Duque," when he spoke to Bernardino Frias, "there is a man with a fine horse from Abda, would you like to look at him?" and asked for his advice. The Rubio answered with a grin, "By Allah, I would try Hueso de Cochino."

The name, that signifies Pig's Bones, being interpreted, was that of an old Spanish lady who entertained, as Shakespeare puts it, ten or a dozen gentlewomen who maintained themselves by needlework.

Hueso de Cochino was, as she said, the daughter of a general, who was obliged to follow the industry by which she lived, through ill-luck, and the poor exchange of Spanish money, but chiefly through the fault of the evil governments in Spain that had omitted to remunerate her father for his services, so that he had fallen upon bad times. "Spain, señor," she would say, "would be an Eden if God had granted it a decent government, but if He had, no one would have cared to leave it, even for Paradise."

Slipping and sliding on the greasy cobblestones, down the chief street and past the mosque, and turning to the left up the street that leads to the Zouia of the Sheriff of Wazan and the Hôtel Continental, the rescue party that had now dwindled down to two, Bibi and Frias, passed by an archway just high enough to let a man on horseback ride underneath it. A filthy lane full of all kinds of refuse, orange skins, entrails of chickens, heads of fish, the flotsam and the jetsam of a Moorish household strewed its pavement, all broken into holes, that in wet weather were filled with water that the passing animals splashed on foot passengers. The refuse in the street mingling with the smell of asafoetida, bunches of fresh mint, dried herbs and spices, in the Moorish shops, produced a scent, pungent but still not disagreeable to the nostrils that had become attuned to it. Leaving their horses with the first Moorish boy they passed, with strict injunctions not to let them fight, for both were stallions, and not to tie

195

them up by the bridles to the knocker of a door or grating of a window, to fall asleep or run away and leave them to their own devices, the riders beat with the handles of their whips upon a door studded with nails and with a little reconnoitring window in the middle of it.

The patroness appeared in person and welcomed in the friends whom she at once recognised for habitual customers. The door led through a little passage six or eight feet long, known as a Zaguan, into a courtyard with rooms all round it, a fountain in the middle, where several girls were dancing with one another to the music of a piano-organ, for it was early in the evening and no man had hired them. She pressed her merchandise upon them, assuring them "upon her health," that she kept no dried tunny or salt codfish in her establishment, but all was fresh and young, wholesome and medically certified.

Filled with an artist's pride in her establishment she stood, a massive figure in a white piqué wrapper, green Moorish slippers on her bare feet, a faded red carnation stuck behind her ear and a wealth of black hair just touched with grey, coarse as a horse's tail, piled high upon her head, with a cheap imitation diamond comb surmounting it.

She had an air of joviality that made her intensely human-looking. At once you saw that she was a kindly creature and that her long experience in the profession had made her tolerant of all the failings of mankind. Born in La Linea de la Concepcion, outside Gibraltar, she spoke a little broken English and at once told her visitors that "Mr. Creeps was in her house, safe, sound and well and at that moment sleeping off the 'wiski' that he had drunk, in the room of a girl from Utrera, Relampagos by name." She added that Relampagos was a good-hearted girl, one who did not lavish her earnings upon some third-rate bull-fighter, and that she was incapable of taking even a centimo out of the purse of anyone in Mr. Creeps' state, for she was a good Christian who went to Mass on Sundays, and upon Saints' days, if she was unoccupied.

She raised her voice and called out, "Relampaguitos, two friends of Mr. Creepsi want to speak to you," and from a room above the courtyard Relampagos appeared. Not too fat, not too thin, as runs the Moorish saying, vivacious as a squirrel, her teeth as white as pearls, her eyes dark, bright and sparkling, her jet-black lustrous hair, powdered an inch or more above her forehead, to soften off the contour of the face, she well deserved the name of Lightning ("Relampagos") for she was always on the move. She, too, "spik litel Inglis," chiefly terms of professional

196

endearment, having, as she said, "worked a whole year in El Peñon de Gibraltar, amongst the Protestants."

"Creeps" would be ready in a moment, so she said, and was just putting on his shirt that she had washed and ironed for him. She added, she would be sorry when he went, for of all the men that she had known he gave least trouble, speaking but little, eating "not more than eats a sparrow; no, señor," drinking much "wiski," and when not asleep had drawn with charcoal, on the walls of her room, pictures of horses, cows, goats and animals of every kind, and a sketch of her own head, better by far than any photograph.

In a few minutes "Creeps" appeared, quite unembarrassed, greeted his friends, said goodbye to the lady patroness, and kissed Relampagos, leaving a mark on her well-powdered cheek, like the print made by a gull's foot when it alights upon the sand.

A few days afterwards, as we walked through the "Soko de la fuera," a blind man seated on the ground begged, raising one hand to heaven as he called upon God's name. "Creeps" gave him half a silver dollar, and when I said the man had never seen himself possessed of so much capital, broke into one of his rare smiles, that lit up his whole face, transfiguring it, as if his inner genius struggled to come forth, and answered, "I too have been blind."

Camara de Lobos

The winding road paved roughly with dark blocks of stone, like tufa, worn shiny and as slippery as ice in a black windless frost, by the sledge-runners of the local bullock carts, ran on a cliff above the sea.

Smiling and treacherous as life, it lay a sheet of burnished silver, under the westing sun. A faint air, tempered by three thousand miles of passage from the Bahamas, played with, yet hardly ruffled, its deceitful surface.

Here and there jagged rocks stuck up, their base encircled by a foam like soapsuds, that gently swayed when the sea breathed but did not move away.

Eastward, the fantastic shapes of the Deserted Isles, the prismatic colouring of the rocks, veiled by the sea haze, looked like a landscape seen in a mirage, when the sun mocks the eye. A homing fishing-boat, its useless sail flapping against the mast, her crew bent to their oars like galley slaves, but served to show the littleness of man against the sea's infinity.

Columbus in his sojourn in Funchal must have looked out upon it wistfully, half-knowing that it held a secret, that perhaps he was destined to disclose. The road ran on, through fields of sugar-cane, swaying in the light breeze with a faint whispering, as when the advanced guard of a flight of locust whirrs through the air, or as the Pacific surges kiss the reef of an atoll. It ran through straggling villages, and past Quintas buried in masses of bright flowering, tropic and sub-tropic shrubs. Jacarandás and Bougainvilleas, Durantas, Crotons, Acalyphas, Poinsettias, Maracujás, Daturas, embowered the dazzling white houses with their red-tiled roofs.

Rosemary and alecrin gave out their pungent perfume and roses trailed from every balcony, uncared for, and rejoiced to find themselves unmanured, unpruned, not tied to sticks, nor crucified with nails against a wall. Oxen toiled patiently, dragging the sledges, that replace carts in the island, or resting, chewed the cud, looking as grave as judges seated on the bench, perhaps arriving at as wise decisions, but fortunately unable to communicate them to mankind.

Now and then motors passed, their strident horns proclaiming progress, that goddess born of hurry and of noise. Along the roads, silent and civil, if a little bovine, trudged endless streams of people, for it was Ash Wednesday, the day of days at Camara de Lobos, the little fishing village that once a year holds the procession of its saint. Most of the men, villagers from the villages that nestle on the skirts of the great hills that form the backbone of the island, wore the dark shapeless coats and jackets, the well-washed unstarched shirts, and flapping wide-brimmed hats, that since the ancient costume fell into disuse have become as it were a uniform both in Madeira and the Canary Islands.

When they met friends, they uncovered gravely and shook hands, calling each other Senhor, for dignity and a high sense of individual value are in the marrow of the race. Some of the more advanced displayed the livery of universal "progress" and wore brown shoes, well-pressed slop suits, soft store hats and neckties of bright colours whose ends dangled and floated in the breeze. None of them wore waistcoats and their open coats disclosed the narrow belly-band complete with imitation silver clasp, that took its origin in the Bowery of New York.

The women, less the slaves of progress than the men, all wore a full dark-coloured petticoat, under a cotton jacket fitting loosely at the hips. Their jet-black hair, coarse as a Shetland pony's tail, looked blacker still against the fine white woollen scarves they wore about their heads, letting one end fall down upon their backs.

The only animal that man has never tamed is woman, declares a modern, wise philosopher. God grant that he may never do so, for a woman really civilised would have to hide her shame with neutral-tinted spectacles and children would be brought into the world concocted in a laboratory.

Dotted along the road were little taverns entitled "Flor de Pichincha," "O salto de Cavallo," and the like; their legend setting forth that Manoel Silva or Domingo Chaves kept good wines and groceries, all of the best class, "Vendas a dinheiro." In latticed summer-houses sat the daughters and the wives of the inhabitants, looking like women in a pious yoshiwara, for even had their inclination moved them to any indiscretion, nature had countered it by features such as made virtue hardly a virtue by its facility.

The crowd grew thicker as from every hamlet contingents of the inhabitants swelled its ranks. In the whole world there could not be a

200

quieter, more well-behaved, or a more docile concourse of mankind. No, not if the garden on the Tigris had been thickly populated before the Fall. All had the look of people adequately, but not generously, fed. Though the majority had driven oxen all their lives, delved in the fields and ploughed industriously — for every cultivable foot of ground was cultivated — their hands were not deformed by toil, or gnarled and knotty, like the hands of labourers in Scotland or Castile. Lost in their Hesperidean island they had never fought for liberty in the past. Barbary Corsairs had not descended on their shores to massacre the villagers in the name of Allah and his prophet, he of the curling hair and teeth like hailstones newly fallen upon the sand. Life had gone on harmoniously, without revolutions, or without social turmoil, since the day when the storm-tossed English lovers with the strange names of D'Arpet and Machin came on the island unawares to find a haven and a grave.

The road wound on, till from a high curve the little port of Camara de Lobos lay disclosed. Shaped like a cockleshell, defended at the mouth by craggy rocks, it broadened out towards the beach. On it, the village boats lay, just afloat, and scarcely swaying in the surge, that set in almost imperceptibly from the calm, glassy sea. They lay as thickly, all touching one another, as pilchards in a barrel, or the canoes in some forgotten river port, in South America.

High-stemmed and brightly painted, they were but little battered by the sea. Hardly a savour either of tar or pitch perfumed the air, and from the taverns by the port no ribald songs or curses belched out of a den thick with tobacco smoke. Occasionally a fado, tinkled on a Portuguese guitar, plaintively pitched in a minor key, broke on the ear. So may the sailors have passed their leisure hours in Ithaca, when once Ulysses was safely off on his adventure to the siege of Troy.

No doubt at times the fishermen must have seen death at a short cable's distance off, for all their draughts could not have been miraculous and they had often toiled all night and taken nothing, as did their prototypes on Galilee. To-day all recollection of the brief fierce storms that spring up, like a harlot's anger (or her tears) lashing the sea into a foamy fury, was banished from their minds. Dressed in their Sunday clothes, they wended to the little village church, dedicated naturally to St. Peter, the most adventurous of the twelve fishermen who left their nets to follow a more arduous career.

Built in the middle of the plaza, towards which four or five winding

201

streets, paved with round cobble-stones converged, it brooded over the peaceful little port as a hen broods over chickens, at once a mother and the protector of all those who seek the shelter of her wings.

Only Madeira and the Canary Islands possess its style of architecture, with the low, square tower and body of the church built like a convent without an ornament to break the façade. A modest temple, yet adequate for the needs of its Arcadian worshippers. The roof, high-pitched and barrel-shaped, was painted gaily in light colours, picked out with gilding that the march of time had toned down and harmonised. The altar, bright with gold, had the twisted barley-sugar-looking columns that proclaim the art of Churriguera, that baroque *in excelsis*, only to be found in Spain and Portugal.

A votive ship or two in the dark aisle, an ostrich egg and a dried crocodile testified to the piety of sailors, who, by the intervention of the patron of the church, had emerged safely from the perils of the deep. The holy-water stoop, set in a dark corner behind the door, gave out an ancient fish-like odour, left by the horny fingers of the pious fishermen.

Although unusual in a church, all was so much in keeping with the place and its inhabitants that the strange perfume may have been acceptable to the Deity the fishermen adored. It was packed full of kneeling women whose white shawls gave them an air of nuns. The men, as it were, "stood by," their hats held in their brown hands, their eyes fixed on the altar with the far-off look with which they gazed on the horizon out upon the sea.

The church, filled with its seafaring parishioners, seemed a great fishing boat, with St Peter at the helm, keeping her "full and by."

The brief Mass over, when the congregation had filed out of the church, the portly priest, still in his vestments, placed himself beneath the purple canopy that was to shelter him on the long tramp with the procession towards the Calvary.

From the dark winding street the bearers of the various saints emerged, carrying upon their shoulders the images that were to be borne in the procession.

The bearers, chosen from the strongest of the younger fishermen, all wore an expression on their faces of pious satisfaction and of resignation to the task that lay before them. They seemed to undertake it in the same spirit that they bent to their oars, when the wind failed them on the sea.

In their rough hands they carried poles, surmounted by a half-moon made of iron, on which to rest their burden when the procession halted for the bearers to get wind. Silently the various companies, devotees of one or other of the saints, fell into line.

Without confusion, and apparently with no directing officers to marshal them, the images took their appointed stands. Heading the procession, grave and dignified, came the patron saint, not the St. Peter who denied his Lord, smote off the ear of the servant of the high priest, or even as when, as the sarcastic witty Apostle to the Gentiles said, he bore a wife about with him. His nets all dried and laid aside for ever, his martyrdom had cleansed him from the weaknesses and follies of the world, but, as his counterfeit presentment showed, had left him still as lovable as when, a fisherman in Galilee, natural laws had proved superior to faith when he essayed to walk upon the lake. Behind him, carrying lighted candles that hardly flickered in the still air, marched a group of women dressed in black. Their faces wore a waxy look, and from their clothes came the stale scent of incense that characterises, in Latin countries, the devout women of the church. Possibly some of them were accomplishing a vow of penitence, but as they all walked barefoot on the stony path, the bystander, even though not a fool, could not distinguish those who had followed Mary Magdalene from those who had not gone astray. Twisting and writhing like a gigantic snake, the procession climbed the mountain path. The saints upon the shoulders of the men nodded at one another like so many china mandarins, as they swam through the air and seemed to float, borne by some invisible agency.

St. Michael, St. Sebastian, St. James, Santa Teresa, and a goodly dozen of the celestial hierarchy, all newly gilt and painted, graced the occasion and moved the piety of the dense crowd of onlookers that thronged the mountain road. Behind each image of a saint came groups of children dressed as angels, barefooted, with their hair streaming down their backs, bound at the forehead by a silver fillet. Their gauzy wings, their naked little feet, their look of pious innocence and the stout hearts that all must have possessed to face such a stiff climb, barefooted, on such a stony road, inclined one to believe they had escaped from heaven for the day, weary of singing in the celestial choirs, to join their fellow children upon earth and play with them.

Children and banners, and the canopy sheltering the priest, formed a symphony in purple, for with natural good taste all the procession was in the same tone of colour, without a jarring note. As it passed by, the onlookers stood up, the men uncovered, and now and then an ancient, wearing the national two-eared cap of the Madeira mountaineers, bent one knee upon the ground. All were devout, without the orgasm of faith that in the south of Italy turns the women to Bacchantes and the men into their pagan ancestors, with staring eyes and mouths distorted in their ecstasy.

Still less did they resemble in their behaviour the ribald piety of the Holy Week in Seville, where, as the bearers of images, when they stop to rest and rub their shoulders, look at their burden and after murmuring, "God curse the heavy block of wood," cross themselves piously and fall amuttering a Hail Mary or a Credo, for their souls' benefit. Upward and upward climbed the long purple serpent, the edges of the path all lined with people, silent and well-behaved, experiencing inwardly, perhaps, a spiritual consolation, not manifest, except to the interior vision, which after all is the most satisfying and not subject to the deceptions that so often cheat those who trust only to what falls upon the retina.

At a turn in the mountain path the last purple banner disappeared. Angels and priest, the high-borne canopy, the gaily painted saints, the pious women draped in their black, the groups of following devout, vanished without a sound, still climbing upwards towards the Calvary. A passing shower obscured the mountains, shrouding them in a veil, such as the dew spreads on a spider's web. On the horizon a sundog just caught the sails of a home-bound fishing-boat, glorifying them for a brief moment, turning them into cloth of gold, before they disappeared. Their pious duty over, the procession turned towards the town, its ranks unbroken, and the companies of fledgling angels plodding along their Via Crucis wearily. The darkness deepened and the faint slurring of the bare feet upon the stones sounded as if a regiment of ghosts was passing.

Fin de Race

Nature and fortune had combined to shower most of the gifts in their possession on Bernardino de Velasco, Duke of Frias, Hereditary Grand Constable of Castile, Count of Oropesa, of Haro and a Grandee of Spain.

These dignities and titles he had inherited from a long line of ancestors. The Count of Haro of those days was made Grand Constable upon the field of Nájera, where the Black Prince and Pedro el Cruel, or el Justiciaro [sic = Justiciero], according to the bent of the historian, defeated Du Guesclin, the great mercenary soldier, and Henry de Trastamara, Don Pedro's bastard brother, and the usurper of his throne. Even in those days, the Velascos were an ancient family, for the saying was, "Before that God was God, or the sun lit up the mountains, the Quiros were Quiros and the Velascos, Velascos."*

These things came to him by inheritance, after he had given himself the trouble to be born, as dignities, titles and estates have come to many a slobbering fool, with piping eunuch's voice, weak knees and weaker mind.

In Bernardino's case, Nature having set her hand to the plough had not looked backwards, but driven a straight furrow, till her task was done. Alert and active as an Arab or a Návajo, his well-shaped hands and feet, his little ears that clung like limpets to his head with its crop of dark brown hair, aquiline nose, small mouth and teeth, as white as, says tradition, were those of Allah's own messenger, our Lord Mahommed, gave him an air of race. When he walked into a room, he looked like a young thoroughbred amongst a bunch of carthorses.

Quick-witted and a good linguist, he spoke Spanish and English indifferently, for he had been at Eton, and his mother was the daughter of Balfe, the composer of the *Bohemian Girl*. French he was quite at home in, and Portuguese from his long residence in Portuguese East

---

* *Antes que Dios fuese Dios ó el sol iluminaba los peñascos, Los Quiros eran Quiros y los Velascos, Velascos.* The Quiros was another ancient family.

Africa, and Arabic enough to swear at camel-drivers, when their animals upset his horse. His father had been a legendary aristocrat, such as Balzac might well have chosen for the hero of one of his minor studies of mankind.

Dumas would have seized upon him with avidity, for he appeared to have walked straight from his novels, or rather, never to have emerged from them.

He started life the owner of great estates, that stretched half over Spain from Cordoba to La Rioja, a palace in Madrid, in Biarritz the Villa Frias, and wonderful old houses in several towns, such as La Casa del Cordon in Burgos, a splendid specimen of a Renaissance mansion of a Spanish gentleman.

All these possessions he proceeded to get rid of, chiefly at the gaming table, and by always living as if the Rand, Golconda, Ouro Preto, Kimberley and the platinum mines of the Choco had been his private property. He died, as befitted a Spanish nobleman of his kidney, greatly impoverished, leaving to his son, Bernardino, but a tithe of his vast properties. What he could not help bequeathing him was his handsome figure and quick wit. His English mother left him her blue eyes and a slight English accent in speaking Spanish that never left him till his dying day. Perhaps it was not quite an accent, but an intonation, for naturally he spoke his native language perfectly.

His English, although perfect, also still had a faint, almost imperceptible tang about it, such as an iron key, to which a leather label is attached, dropped into a whole pipe of wine, is said to leave a tinge of leather and of iron to the fastidious palate of the connoisseur.

His mother left him, in addition to the intonation and blue eyes, musical talent that his friend and master Sarasate used to say, had he but had the spur of poverty, would have made him one of the first violinists of the world, little inferior to himself.

As a child, he used to play upon his grandfather's violin (a fine Amati), almost by instinct, and after Sarasate took him in hand, as a mere lad at Eton, his aptitude was the delight and the despair of the great virtuoso, who stood entranced when after a few lessons his pupil executed passages with ease that others after months of study failed to execute. Upon the other hand, nothing would make him study, or devote the hours to practice that alone gives to natural talent technical success. I do not say that Sarasate tore his hair, for he was far too careful of his appearance, but he used to say, "If but Don Bernardino would devote himself for a whole year to music, under my tuition, with the natural talent that he has, and with the halo of his title encompassing his head, he might go to America, that paradise of snobs, and return home a millionaire." Thus spoke Sarasate, much in the vein of Zarathustra (by the mouth of Nietsche *[sic]*), but it was not to be. Nature had done her best, but even she is powerless before fate.

In every branch of life she had done all she could, for Frias was a perfect horseman, with the hands that only nature gives and that no teaching and all the practice in the world cannot supply, for, in the words of the old Spanish saw, "What nature does not give, Salamanca is powerless to lend." A good shot, excellent fencer and a tireless walker, he had a constitution that only years of dissipation at last undermined. With all these gifts, nature had omitted to endow him with a sense of responsibility. All through his life he acted after the fashion of one of Captain Marryat's midshipmen, or like a child sent into a pastrycook's, without the hand of a controlling nurserymaid. What he fancied he would have, no matter at what cost, and yet he was not wanting in a certain kind of common sense. Like many men of his position, he talked twenty per cent above his real ability, from having mingled on familiar terms with politicians of high rank, great artists, writers, engineers, and leaders of society. He had not the least shadow of a pose, and, like all Spaniards, had the same manner when he addressed a carter or a prince.

Women adored him, for he had that magnetic personality that attracts them, as valerian attracts cats, or jam left on a table is a certain lure to wasps.

Nothing was further from his mind than were ulterior motives, and certainly no man ever sought for personal advantage less than he did, from the cradle to the grave.

'Tis true he never paid his debts, except those falsely called of honour, contracted at the card tables, whereas the only real debts of honour are to the baker, butcher, bootmaker and tailor, that a man owes for value he receives.

As a mere boy just after he left Eton, as Count of Haro, for he was not then Duke of Frias, as his father was alive, he drifted to Tangier, as an unpaid secretary to the Spanish minister.

Those were the days when Tangier was one of the most fascinating places in the whole world to live in; a miniature Constantinople, it had representatives of every Court in Europe, a consul-general from the United States, and ministers or consuls, who behaved like ministers, from many South American Republics. Flags of the various nations fluttered from half a hundred houses in the town. Adventurers who styled themselves presidents of Patagonia, kings of Araucania, and other hypothetic states, hoisted the flags of their fantastic countries, and whilst their money lasted, if they were presentable, spoke "diplomatic French," were not seen drunk in public, or committed any flagrant misdemeanour, were received as cordially in the tolerant society of the place as if they had been representatives of real countries to be found upon the map. The Moors looked on them all with awe, mixed with amusement, and regarded them as amiable madmen who, for some purpose of his own that he had not disclosed, Allah had endowed with the command of fleets and armies, and with mighty engines of destruction, so that it behoved the faithful to walk warily in their dealings with them. Tangier was then one of the dirtiest towns in the whole world, outside of China, but perfectly safe to live in, for robberies were rare and crimes of violence practically unknown, and though most Europeans "packed," as cowpunchers used to say, a pistol, it was quite unnecessary. The advance of progress and international control had not at that time partially cleaned the streets, nor had the scum of the Levant and criminals from Europe made the place nearly as subject to robberies and crimes as are most European towns. Into this pleasant, evil-smelling, picturesque and old-world little town, where every European who could afford five-and-twenty dollars for a horse equipped himself with boots and spurs and rode about splashing the dirty water of the streets on the foot-passengers, with as much disregard of consequences as John the Baptist when he performed mass baptism in the Jordan, the young Count of Haro was propelled, by destiny. From the first day he found himself at home. As if by magic all the Moors seemed to know him. Certainly he was a striking figure on his horse, with the wind blowing up the front brim of the wide grey felt hat that people wore in those days in Tangier, and his air of careless insouciance, for he was at the age when one has bought the world on credit and not received the bill. He never seemed to go to the Legation, which for that matter seemed to go on quite well without him, under the management of one of those staid diplomatists who, at that time in Spain, either finished up their career at some small German Court or at Madrid, as "Ministre des Affaires Inutiles."

But as even the unpaid secretary of a Legation must have a serious object in his life, Frias, who by this time was one of the chief figures of the British colony, passing much more of his time with them than with his countrymen, entered into partnership with Crawhall, the painter, a kindred spirit and as fine a rider as himself, to hunt the Tangier hounds. He constituted himself master, and nominated Crawhall as first whip, and with the assistance of a nondescript youth born in Gibraltar, who maltreated English and Spanish, quite indifferently, but had a good acquaintance with all the oaths and the foul language of both tongues, rode well and boldly, and answered to the name of "Mataburro," he started out on the first serious business of his life. Nothing was stranger than to see Frias — for by his father's death he had succeeded to the dukedom — and Crawhall at a meet of the Tangier pack: Frias immaculately dressed in pink, his whip in a weather-stained mulberry-coloured hunting frock, with "Mataburro" in a pair of tightly-fitting Spanish trousers, patched at the seat with cloth of a different colour, a bull-fighter's flat hat from Cordoba, tied with a bit of greasy black elastic underneath the chin, and *alpargatas* on his feet. The pack was a collection such as it would be difficult to match in any country, with its three couple of mangy-looking foxhounds, from Gibraltar, with several mongrels of undecided race that Mataburro always referred to as the "bastards," and three or four half-bred fox- terriers. Foxes were scarce, and the heterogeneous pack ran wildly, the "bastards" keeping up a perpetual yelping, and at a check, the terriers snapping at the other dogs or fighting fiercely with one another.

Anyone who had a horse came out, and when the run, if there had been one, or in any case the gallop, finished, a cap went round into which Frias always put a sovereign, "to warm it," as he said. It often formed the bulk of the day's takings, for nearly everybody seemed to have forgotten to bring money with him. Some fairly slunk away when they had an opportunity; others remained behind to tighten up their girths, or slacken them, and others cantered off, shouting out, "Adios, Duque, I will send on a sovereign when I get home." Needless to say it never came, but Bernardino cared nothing for it, for by his father's death he found himself, although his father had disposed of most of his estates, with ready money in his pocket that seemed inexhaustible. As they rode home, leaving the pack to be brought back by Mataburro, a duty he performed after having filled his pockets full of stones, to throw at laggers, Frias would show the empty cap to Crawhall with a laugh, and

Crawhall, who spoke but little but when he did so always to the point, would mutter, "What a crowd of sons of bitches," and jog silently along.

These were the halcyon days whilst money lasted, and before Bernardino had turned into the desperate gambler that he afterwards became. Though some of the great family estates had come into his possession, they were but a tithe of those which his father owned. The Villa Frias, in Biarritz, had been sold; most of the lands of El Paular, not far off from Segovia, a domain of mountain and of wood, full of all kinds of game, from wolves, lynxes and wild cats to deer, hares, rabbits and partridges, had gone to satisfy the moneylenders. Gone were the estates in which the mediæval castle of the Frias reared its head upon a rock; the overlordship of the towns that once the family possessed; gone was La Casa del Cordon in Burgos, and the ancestral palace in Madrid. Still, enough had survived that, had Bernardino but possessed a little of that common sense that nature had forgotten to endow him with at birth, he might yet have retrieved his fortunes with good management, for his estates, like those of almost every other Spanish nobleman, were left to an administrator, and produced but a mere fraction of their worth. Care, prudence, management, were things that Bernardino never understood, if indeed he knew that they existed. Slowly but steadily he began to pile up debts, to borrow money from his administrators, to lend to anyone who asked him, and to tread with filial affection the path his father had marked out for him.

Old-fashioned Spaniards nodded their heads and said that it was lucky that El Duque had not been born a woman, for he was unable to say "No."

Everyone liked him, and he went on hunting his mongrel pack of hounds, gambling and losing far more than he could afford, or sometimes pay, except by giving orders on his administrators, who, like the unjust steward in the Bible, invariably wrote fifty in their books when the amount was ten.

Although he never practised, occasionally he played the violin at High Mass in the Franciscan chapel, rising on one side of the choir, immaculately dressed and executing Sarasate's *Habanera*, or some piece of Chopin's with all the grace of a consummate virtuoso, whilst the packed audience of every nationality longed to break out into applause, only restraining their admiration because they thought that it would not be pleasing to the Deity.

210

Outside, the Spanish loafers, Portuguese fishermen, the convicts who had escaped from El Peñon de la Gomera, or from Alhucemas, and the Italian sailors from the port, who had been kneeling in the street, beating their breasts and crossing themselves at the proper places, now and then cursing the hardness of the cobble-stones they kneeled upon, broke into unrestrained applause. Possibly, if he observed them, when he looked down upon the world occasionally, the Deity that the devout were fearful to offend gave them a kindly smile.

It was in Tangier that he met his wife, an English lady who at the time of their marriage was almost as irresponsible as he was himself, and overhead in love with him, as she remained throughout her life, in spite of his long absences, his innumerable infidelities, and his perfect disregard of everything that marriage should imply. The difference between them was that advancing years, and the feeling of impending catastrophe, that always seemed to hover about Bernardino, making you feel that in the Scottish phrase he was "fey," altered her character and made her fit for a long time to struggle with the money difficulties that soon overwhelmed them.

He himself did not seem to feel that there was any danger, or if he did, resigned himself to fate, like the historic Indian who swept over Niagara in a canoe, ceased paddling, folding his arms before the plunge. Tangier became too difficult to live in, for debts accumulated, and to meet them the only way was to borrow at exorbitant interest from usurers in Madrid, or to sell bits of property at any price that they would fetch. Transferred to Vienna as second or third secretary, Tangier saw nothing of him for several years. No place in Europe could have been so dangerous for him as was the Vienna of those days. A gay society, with nearly all its members votaries of high play, women who changed their lovers almost as often as their gowns, everything was there to attract Bernardino Frias and to encourage him to run more desperately into debt.

With Buda-Pesth for an occasional holiday and a run home to Madrid, where he belonged to all the clubs — and in the clubs in those days in Madrid everyone gambled — the long-expected crash that everyone had seen was bound to come took place. A disagreeable business at the card table, the rights and wrongs of which were never brought to light, and Vienna became too hot for him. Madrid was too expensive for a man in his position, a personal friend of the King, Alfonso XII, the father of the Dom Alfonso now dethroned and a wanderer. Moreover it was not congenial to his wife, who cared nothing for society, and at that time spoke little of the language. Once more he drifted back to Tangier, where he had spent so many of his happiest years. Money was scarcer with him than of old. Crawhall came out only in winter, and his old crony Bibi Carleton was settled in Alcázar el Kebir, running a flour mill, and, to the delight of all his friends, consular agent of Great Britain, with an enormous Union Jack above his house.

Frias and his wife settled down at the "New York Hotel" upon the beach, a third-rate caravanserai run by a Catalan, one Don Anselmo, a most long-suffering man as regards payment of his bills, and always ready to supply El Duque with any money he required. Not that Anselmo was a usurer, for I believe he never charged a penny for the relatively large sums with which he "facilitated" Bernardino, as runs the Spanish phrase. Frias and his wife, who was a first-class horsewoman, kept several horses, that Mataburro, now better dressed and less disreputable, looked after, and styled himself "the Duke's stud-groom." They went out pigsticking, for Bernardino was a first-class "spear," riding as if he had a dozen necks to break, and still had one to spare in his coat pocket.

The scandal at the Austrian Court became forgotten, and Tangier Society would have opened wide its tolerant portals to them. His wife cared less and less for any gaiety, and Bernardino, who at that time drank far more whisky than was good for him, played cards with all and sundry, losing more than he could afford, with anyone who cared to play with him.

His love affairs were innumerable, although he always said, I think quite honestly, that he had never really loved another woman than his wife.

Certainly he asked her advice on all occasions, but never followed it. Had he but done so, he would have had a less disastrous ending to his life, for, as the proverb has it, "A woman's advice is of small value, but he who does not take it is a fool."

It never seemed to have occurred to him that he had still two properties in Spain. One, in the province of Cordoba and another in Toledo, just where that province joins Estremadura. The property in Cordoba that was situated on the banks of the Guadalquivir was one of those great flat expanses of alluvial soil common in Andalusia, and was practically a great olive yard. It is quite possible that Bernardino had never seen it in his life, or visited it but once or twice. Though probably encumbered, it was absolutely his own property, inherited from his ancestors. An administrator rack-rented the tenants, and most certainly cheated the owner to the best of his ability. Occasionally Frias would say, I will do this or that "when I receive my olive money." This, I think, was the sole interest he took in the place, for in those days few Spanish noblemen lived on their estates, but spent their rents either in Madrid or Paris, Biarritz, Deauville or Ostend. In such resorts they passed their time, in what is called High Life, with gamesters, pimps and players, with jockeys, cocottes, bull-fighters, and similar indecencies.

These gentry soon consumed most of what had been left of the great Frias properties. Frias still hung about Tangier, living but poorly with his wife in the "New York Hotel" upon the beach, a hostelry that, with the discomforts of a Spanish *fonda* of those times, still lacked the saving grace of picturesqueness. However, we all frequented it, partly because of "Auld lang syne" and partly because the proprietor Anselmo never sent in a bill unless it was demanded of him, and was always willing to oblige with a small loan without security. Our horses lived in a ramshackle stable at the back, and only cost us a peseta for their keep. Mataburro, who was paid irregularly, presided over the Moorish lads, who served as grooms, and stole the horses' corn with regularity, in spite of various double-thongings that Frias, Bibi and Crawhall used to administer when they caught him in the act.

Then he would curse a little, rub his shoulders, and swear by all the saints that one day he would have the blood of some of them. Nobody minded what he said, for all knew that, in the words of Molière, "cinq ou six coups de bâton ne font que regaillardir l'amour," and he well knew he was a universal favourite.

All things, apparently, must have an end, and one day, as I sat with the duchess having the concoction of birch bark that passed as tea, Frias came in, and throwing down his whip upon the table, quite with the air of Brennus when he cast his sword into the scales, called for a whisky and announced briefly: "I am ruined and have not a peseta in the world." We all knew that, so no one spoke, till his wife asked him what he proposed to do.

Nothing would make him listen to his wife's advice, that they should leave Tangier and settle down on his own property in Spain and see that it was properly administered. "No, no," he said, "I could not stand life in the Spanish country, the eternal chaffering with the peasants, or the attending one of the local councils, to debate what price we ought to give for a pair of wolf's ears, when you were certain all the time the man who brought them in had only shot a dog."

It appeared he had heard that in Lisbon the Duke of Albuquerque was going out to Portuguese East Africa, with some kind of an expedition, of which he was the chief. "I'll wire to him," he said, "and see if he can take me with him as deputy administrator, or anything he likes." He framed a telegram, as lawyers say when it figures in your account. Then it appeared he had no money for the telegram.

Anselmo handed him two dollars, and getting on his horse, he said, "I'll take it," and disappeared upon the beach, galloping furiously. An hour passed by and he returned, explaining that he had not sent the telegram, for a poor Spanish woman had begged for alms from him, and as he said. "Whatever could I do?"

Eventually the telegram was sent, and in a day or two the answer came offering him the post of deputy administrator in Mozambique. He sailed from Lisbon, taking with him, luckily as it turned out, a Moor from Sus, known as Abdallah el Susi, who was much attached to him, as personal servant, groom, gun-carrier, or anything that might turn up in a wild country.

Slight and well-made, active, not very dark in colour, and speaking Spanish perfectly, Abdallah had been in a circus, had visited most of the European capitals, and spoke, as well as Spanish, some English and a word or two of French. A strict Mohammedan, who in his life had never taken any drink, or even smoked a cigarette — for drink, of course, his faith prohibited, and smoking he called "drinking the shameful" — he looked on Frias, as he said, as his father, meaning that he admired him for his open-handedness, his generosity, and his wild ways.

"El Duque is a child of the illegitimate," by which he meant he was afraid of nothing, for in Arabic the phrase is used just as the Spaniards in Cervantes' time used "Hideputa," and the Elizabethan English whoreson, either in praise or blame.

After a week in Lisbon and a fortnight in London, getting his colonial outfit of things that generally prove absolutely useless in a colony, Frias, in his new character of deputy administrator, clothed in a khaki uniform, then a new and mysterious fabric, with a sword enclosed in a leather-covered scabbard, and crowned with a slouch hat such as our troops wore in the Boer War, accompanied by Abdallah, sailed for Port Amelia. During the fortnight he had got rid of the last remains of his own and his wife's ready money, and pawned his violin that his friends had to redeem, and must have sailed almost penniless. Luckily his expenses were all paid.

He left his wife to administer his property. After a long dispute and several law-suits, she managed to get the most urgent of the claims against her husband paid, and some of the usurers who had lent money at monstrous rates of interest satisfied.

Most of her private fortune had been already sacrificed to pay the debts her husband had incurred, chiefly at the card-table.

As was to be expected, Frias and Albuquerque, a careful colonial administrator, soon came to loggerheads, and Frias found himself without a penny, in a colony where white men, except the very poorest, never did manual work. However, he was still well under forty, and with Abdallah, now his one friend and his companion, went to work at daily wages on the roads. He must have suffered terribly, not in his pride, for Spaniards are devoid of snobbishness, but in the hard toil under the tropic sun, to which his former life had not accustomed him. His real and praiseworthy pride stopped him from writing to his wife for assistance.

Abdallah probably suffered less, for in his youth he had worked as a boatman on the Moroccan coasts. He found a wife amongst his co-religionists, and then, as Frias used to say, "We had better food and got our shirts washed regularly."

Six months went past, and then Abdallah found a second wife, and things went easier, with the two strangely assorted friends.

They bought a boat, and used to take out cargo to the ships in Port Amelia, toiling, as Frias said, like galley slaves, at the great clumsy oars. For a short time they prospered, and Abdallah hired some negroes to help him in the boat.

Frias obtained a post as manager of a plantation, but soon lost it, as he had no idea of business, hated confinement at a desk, and when his pay came in, used to resort to a little town upon the coast to gamble, indulge in dissipation, and return to the plantation in a miserable state.

Nine years went by, years that he never cared to speak of, but that must have been a hell.

His wife sent money when she could; but he instantly lost it at the gaming-table, drifted once more back to the roads at daily wages, whilst suffering terribly from tropical diseases, the result of working in the sun and rain, with every now and then a trip to Ibo, and its dissipations. By this time Abdallah had become quite a substantial man in a small way. Occasionally he led the prayers in the mosque, began to lard his speech with bits of the Koran, had several children, and was beginning to grow stout.

He never touched an oar, but steered his launch, dressed in immaculate white clothes, with a well-pleated turban on his head, and a stout wooden rosary in his left hand. Nothing impaired his friendship and respect for his old master, for the nine years of hardships and adventure they had passed together had blotted out all difference of rank, of race, almost of religion, though both of them, as often happens in men of their sort, though lax in practice, were staunch believers in their creeds.

How it all happened Frias never was quite sure. Abdallah, had he survived, would have said that "it was written," which after all is perhaps the best way to explain anything.

Coming back from a vessel in the roads upon a stormy day in their launch laden with merchandise, running the surf that they had negotiated a hundred times, their boat upset. The negro crew swam to shore like Newfoundland dogs, emerging on the sand as easily as a Kanaka rides the surf. Frias, though not a very powerful swimmer, got ashore somehow or other, and lay exhausted on the beach. Abdallah never reappeared.

Thus Frias always used to say: "I lost the best friend that I ever had." Probably this was true enough, for, with the exception of the Moor, of "Creeps" and "Bibi," he had no real friends, after the way of men who easily make friends with everybody.

After Abdallah's death, and having wasted nine years of his life, if life spent in adventure and hard work is ever really wasted, finding himself with enough money to pay his passage, second- or third-class, he came back to Europe, as penniless as when he set out.

This was the fashion of his coming home:

Seated one day in my flat in Basil Street, cursing the rain that fell as ceaselessly as when Shakespeare's clown was a very little boy, the maid told me that a foreign sailor-looking man wanted to see me at the door. I looked at him, and for the moment did not recognise him. Dressed in an old blue suit, unshaved and miserably thin, white canvas shoes upon his feet and carrying a bundle and a dilapidated suitcase, I hesitated, till he said: "Dino, Bernardino Frias, don't you recognise me?"

We had what is called in Spanish "un cordial abrazo," that is an embrace, such as you read of in the Bible, when friends met after an

216

absence. An hour passed like a minute, as he told of his nine years' purgatory, from which he had returned, penniless and suffering either from malaria, frambœsia, or some tropical disease or other.

Then he went off to join his wife, who lived some little distance out of town.

The luck had turned, if he had only known how to profit by it. During his absence, his wife had shepherded his estates, so that he had a tolerable income, and thus the nine years of exile had not been wasted. For six months all went well, and then he gradually went back to his old ways. "The wild goat always seeks the wood," the proverb says, and in his case the proverb was unfortunately true. Back in Madrid, he soon became a friend of King Alfonso XIII, joined the best clubs, where play was high, and lived with people far richer than himself.

Named Senator for Cadiz, he tried politics, but had no aptitude for them, and fell back to the life of a man without occupation about Madrid.

Then as his wife hated Madrid and had to educate their daughter, he tried country life, on one of his own properties, and built a shooting lodge, where he lived, often for months together, with several boon companions and a girl rather inappropriately called Modesta, whom he had met at a street corner one night after the theatre.

Not pretty and but moderately faithful to him, she must have cared for him in the way most Spanish women care for the man they live with, treating them half as superior beings and half as children that it is woman's place to work for, put up with their neglect, pardon their infidelities, half to love, half to despise, but not to leave, till they are cast off or till death separates them.

The property "El Deheson del Encinar" had a most curious history, one that in Spain alone would have been possible.

Two hundred and fifty or more years ago, the King of those days borrowed a large sum of money from the Duke of Frias. He gave for his security the lands of the Deheson del Encinar, in the province of Toledo, close to the boundary of Estremadura. Nine miles or so away was situated the castle of Oropesa, an ancestral seat of the Frias family, on a high rock dominating the town of the same name, of which the family were overlords.

The bargain was that the Frias family should own the lands until the debt was paid.

217

These lands were owned or claimed by five small townships, who from the first protested that their rights had been infringed.

Time passed and the Frias family treated the property as their own, drawing the rents, putting in tenants of their own, and building houses for them, sinking wells, and planting what had practically been waste land with olives, cork trees, and with oaks. It became valuable and the five townships went to the courts alleging that the money had been long ago repaid, but taking no notice of the improvements that the family had made.

Justice in those days was not a speedy matter with the Spaniards. It was so leaden-footed that it became a byword, crystallised in the "pawky" sayings: "Paper and ink and little justice," and "Justice if you like, but not in my house." In the outer world the phrase, "May death come to me from Spain," was a proof of the national deliberation in affairs. Sometimes the Courts decided for the towns and sometimes for the family, according to the greater or the lesser influence the contending parties brought to bear. In either case, the loser instantly appealed, and so the thing went on, a perfect instance of the "ganging plea" so dear to Scottish as well as Spanish justice in the great days of old.

Sometimes the matter was allowed to rest for years, but naturally such a gold-mine for the lawyers in Madrid was not permitted to remain long derelict.

The Frias family had never had a house on the estate. Either from prudence, a virtue that few of them possessed, or because they had houses or estates all over Spain, or perhaps because they never visited El Deheson except to shoot, they had but seldom made, in Spanish legal phrase, "an act of presence."

Nine miles from Oropesa, and three miles from the nearest made road, the property was approached by a sandy track that ran through oak woods, passing a considerable stream, just where a little chapel known as El Cristo stood. In summer, the water hardly came up to a horse's knees, and as there was a bottom of hard sand, a carriage or a motor-car could pass it easily. In winter, it was quite another matter, and could be crossed, when it was practicable, only on horseback or in a bullock-cart. At times it was a foaming torrent impossible to cross, and then El Deheson was cut off from the outer world, except by a long detour, for several days. Then the track ran through more wood, and crossed another stream, but smaller than the first, and finally ended quite suddenly in a little clearing, in which stood the house, a long, low, one-storey building, such as a child draws on a slate. All through the woods, silent, deserted, and unearthly-looking after dark, when great moths sailed about and bats flew screaming through the trees, the underwood seemed all alive, just as it does in a primeval forest when night falls and the nocturnal animals set out upon their rounds. Rabbits ran scuttling across the sandy track, hares loped gracefully before the carriage, or the car, dazzled by the lights. Foxes peeped out or barked like jackals in the underwood. Now and then the mewling of a wild cat or a lynx, or an owl's hooting, broke the stillness of the night.

All was so desolate and wild, silent and melancholy under the beams of the Castilian moon that the road might have led to a ranch in Mexico, in the recesses of La Sierra Madre or the Bolson de Mápimi.

In daylight, the house stood stark, surrounded by a few old oaks, without a garden, planted shrubs or anything to soften off the hardness of the Castilian landscape. The fields were not enclosed, but wheat was planted over a vast extent of ground, between the cork trees and the oaks. A stream whose high banks were fringed heavily with willows, ran close to the house. Taking advantage of the cover, in the winter, wolves made their way down from the mountains in their nocturnal raids.

A fence of strong wire-netting, twelve feet at least in height, kept them off from the house. In winter, especially when snow was on the ground, they came and howled outside the barrier, and were answered by the dogs either through terror or by affinity of race. Even in summer they were heard occasionally. Their melancholy, long-drawn-out howl once heard, never to be forgotten, that seems to chill the marrow of the bones, especially when heard alone, far off from houses, with your horse trembling underneath you, was quite in keeping with the wildness of the place.

Grey olive trees and greyer oaks grew out of the red soil. Only the cork trees, when their bark had been stripped off, leaving a bright, red-looking wound, gave a note of colour standing out vividly in the keen atmosphere of the high Castilian plain.

Some ten miles off La Sierra de Gredos stood out as starkly from the steppe as the Rock of Gibraltar juts up from the sea. Its serrated peaks, unearthly-looking as the mountains of the moon, grey and forbidding in the early morning, at sunset, when the sun's declining rays lighted them up before it set, were a great mass of opaline, or jade, and of rose quartz, irradiating a hundred shades of colour like an old crystal chandelier. In its recesses wandered still the Capra Hispanica, deer, lynxes, wild cats, an occasional bear, together with innumerable wolves.

The whole estate, overrun with rabbits, hares, with flocks of partridges, and bands of wild duck in the winter, was a sportsman's paradise.

In it perhaps the owner passed the last year of his life, if not exactly happily, yet to a great extent absolved from care.

His wife and daughter lived in England, and though he never spoke of them without respect and loved them as the poet loved Cynara, faithfully, in his own fashion, he seldom saw them, or at the best on a brief run to Paris or Madrid.

All his dependants loved and imposed upon him to the best of their ability. His friends, and almost every woman, called him Dino, and so he lived much as Don Quixote lived, with a thin horse, plenty of equally thin greyhounds, and for all I know a brace of ferrets, as bold as those owned by the Manchegan knight.

In fact, a veritable "Hidalgo de Gotera," that is, a nobleman with a leaky house. Always in want of money, for though the rents of his two properties were not contemptible, Madrid and its temptations were as fatal to his purse as had been the town of Ibo whilst he lived in Africa.

His guards — for in his time all Spanish gentlemen had guards on their estates, who rode about, looked after poachers, frequently standing in with them, pretended to protect the house at night, which they did sleeping comfortably in their own cottages — all swore by him.

A curious set they were, dressed in green corduroy, with a broad baldric, bearing a brass plate embossed with the Frias arms, crossing their chests, short jackets, and brown gaiters and *alpargatas* on their feet. They all rode mares, as they explained, on account of the produce, and carried some sort of gun fastened to their dilapidated Jerezano saddles.

The chief of them, one Nicolas, a tall, athletic man, and first-class rider, had been a sergeant in the Cuban wars. Courteous and affable he was a rogue in grain, but still in his own way was faithful to the Duke, singing his praises upon all occasions, respecting though invariably cheating him, when opportunity occurred.

The second was a bird of quite another feather, by name Ignacio. Honest and taciturn, just as good a horseman as was Nicolas, and a far better shot, his fellows all respected though they feared him, for it was known that in his youth he had killed someone or another, and escaped going either to Ceuta or to El Peñon de la Gomera, in penal servitude, but by a miracle.

The other two were colourless, and they with one Manuel, a nondescript, whose duties were to go to Oropesa once a day upon his donkey to bring the letters and to collect the news, made up "the guard." These duties, generally, took him nearly all the day, and he returned at nightfall full of excuses for unavoidable delays. Either his donkey had cast a shoe, the train was late, or there were rumours that "bad people" had been seen upon the road, and he had waited to return till he had company. Modesta, helped by a gypsy-looking, untidy girl, ran the house, with one of the guards' wives to do the cooking, serving up thick country soups, stews, seasoned with saffron, and, strange as it may seem, digestible.

Frias, like most Spaniards of his rank, knew and appreciated good cooking, having lived much in Paris, but, like them, was too indolent to bother, or perhaps in his heart despised those who did, and ate all that was set before him without a comment, washing it down with the coarse country wine, almost as strong as brandy, and as intoxicating.

How long this sort of life might have gone on only God knows, and He, as say the Arabs, never tells, so that it does not matter much whether He knows or not, as we are none the wiser for His knowledge.

Had he lived longer, most likely he would have fallen into poverty, for he still gambled wildly on his visits to Madrid, kept no accounts, and went on generally as if Golconda had been his in tail *[sic = entail?]* settled on him and his heirs male.

He kept his looks to the last day he lived, proving the truth of the old Spanish saw: "Figure and genius to the grave."

Always on horseback in all weathers, after long bouts of dissipation in Madrid, one day your damned bronchitis took him, after a common cold.

This, in the keen air of the Castilian uplands, turned to pneumonia. His wild life, joined to the hardships of his nine years in Africa, had broken down a constitution that had been made of iron.

Helped by the gypsy girl, and assisted by an ill country doctor, Modesta tended him up to the last, perhaps with affection, but certainly with a fidelity that in itself was her reward.

If on the night he died the wolves howled in the woods around the house, nothing could have been a more fitting threnody.

221

The Stationmaster's Horse

After the long war in Paraguay, the little railway built by the tyrant Lopez, that ran from Asuncion to Paraguari, only some thirty miles, fell into a semi-ruinous condition.

It still performed a journey on alternate days, and ran, or rather staggered, along on a rough track, almost unballasted. Sleepers had been taken out for firewood, by the country people here and there, or had decayed and never been replaced. The line was quite unfenced, and now and then a bullock strayed upon it and was run down or sometimes was found sleeping on the track. Then the train stopped, if the engine-driver saw the animal in time. He blew his whistle loudly, the passengers all started, and if the bullock refused to move, got down and stoned it off the line. The bridges luckily were few, and were constructed of the hard imperishable woods so plentiful in Paraguay. They had no railings, and when, after the downpours of the tropics, the streams they crossed were flooded, the water lapped up and covered them to the depth of several inches, so that the train appeared to roll upon the waters, and gave the passengers an experience they were not likely to forget. The engine-driver kept his eyes fixed firmly on a tree or any other object on the bank, just as a man crossing a flooded stream on horseback dares not look down upon the rushing waters, but stares in front of him, above his horse's head. Overhead bridges fortunately did not exist, and there was but a single cutting in the thirty miles. It filled with water in the rains, and now and then delayed the trains a day or two, but no one minded, for time was what the people had the most of on their hands, and certainly they were not niggardly in the disposal of it.

The engines that burned wood achieved a maximum of ten miles an hour, but again no one minded, for that was greater than the speed of the bullock carts to which they had been accustomed all their lives.

Thus they looked on the railway as a marvel, and spoke of it as a sign of progress that ennobled man and made him truly only a little lower than the angels and the best beloved creation of the Deity.

Shares, dividends, balance sheets, and all the rest of the mysterious processes without which no railway in these more favoured times can run a yard, were never heard of, for the line was run by Government, who paid the salaries of the engine-drivers, who were all foreigners, when they had any cash in hand. When there was none, the officials, who had all married Paraguayan women, were left dependent on their efforts for a meal.

The telegraph, with the wires sagging like the lianas sagged from tree to tree in the great woods through which the greater portion of the line was built, was seldom in good order, so that as it stopped at the rail-head of the line, the better plan was to entrust a letter to the guard or engine-driver.

Certainly that little line through the primeval forest, with now and then breaks of open plain, dotted here and there, with the dwarf scrubby palms called yatais, was one of the most curious and interesting the world has ever known. The trains in general started an hour or two behind the time that they were supposed to start, picking up passengers like an old-time omnibus. Men standing at the corner of a wood waved coats or handkerchiefs, or in some cases a green palm leaf, to the engine-driver. He generally slowed down his impetuous career to about three miles an hour, and then the signaller, running alongside, was pulled up by a score of willing hands stretched out to him. In the case when the signaller had women with him, or a package too heavy to be thrown upon a truck in motion, the train would stop, the people scramble up, and haul their package up after them. Sometimes a man on horseback, urging his horse up to the train, with shouts, and blows of his flat-lashed "rebenque" that sounded much severer than they really were, and keeping up a ceaseless drumming of his bare heels upon its flanks, would hand a letter or a little packet to the engine-driver or to some travelling friend. At times the train appeared to stop, for no apparent reason, as nobody appeared out of the forest, either to pass the time of day or to enquire the news. Upon inclines, active young men sprinted behind the train until they caught up the last wagons; then, encouraged by the riders — for to call them "passengers" would be an unnecessary euphemism — and placing a brown hand upon the moving truck, they vaulted inboard and lay breathless for a minute, perspiring plentifully. At places such as Luque, Itá and Ipacaray, the little townships through which the harbinger of progress ran, the stops were lengthy.

Women in long white sleeveless smocks (their only garment) went about selling "chipa" — the Paraguayan bread of mandioca flour, flavoured with cheese, as indigestible as an old-fashioned Pitcaithly bannock — pieces of sugar cane, oranges and bananas, rough lumps of dark brown sugar, done up in plantain leaves, and tasting of the lye used in their manufacture, with other delicacies called in Spanish "fruits of the country."* The sun poured down upon the platform, crowded with women, for men were very scarce in Paraguay in those days. They kept up a perpetual shrill chattering in Guarani; occasionally in broken Spanish, plentifully interlarded with interjections, such as Baié pico, Iponaité, Añariu, in their more familiar tongue. Outside the station the donkeys on which the women had brought their merchandise nibbled the waving grass or chased one another in the sand. A scraggy horse or two, looking half starved and saddled with a miserable old native saddle of hide, the stirrups often a mere knot of hide to be held by the naked toes, nodded in the fierce sun with his feet hobbled or fastened to a post. After a longer or a shorter interval, the stationmaster, generally well-dressed in white, his head crowned with an official semi-military cap, his bare feet shoved into carpincho leather slippers down at heel, and smoking a cigar, would appear upon the platform, elbow his way amongst the crowd of women, pinching them and addressing salacious compliments to those he deemed attractive, till he reached the guard or engine-driver, gossip a little with him, and signal to a female porter to ring the starting bell. This she did with a perfunctory air. The engine-driver sounded his whistle shrilly, and the train, in a long series of jerks, as if protesting, bumped off from the platform in a cloud of dust.

Difference of classes may have existed, but only theoretically, like the rights of man, equality, liberty, or any of the other mendacious bywords that mankind loves to write large and disregard. No matter what the passenger unused to Paraguay paid for his ticket, the carriage was at once invaded by the other travellers, smoking and talking volubly and spitting so profusely that it was evident that no matter what diseases Paraguay was subject to, consumption had no place amongst them.

The jolting was terrific, the heat infernal, and the whole train crowded with people, who sat in open trucks, upon the tops of carriages, on footboards, or on anything that would contain them, smoking and chattering, and in their white clothes as the train slowly jolted onwards, looking like a swarm of butterflies. Certainly its progress was not speedy, but as a general rule it reached its destination, though hours behind its time.

* "Frutos del país."

Having to write one day from the railhead at Paraguari to Asuncion, only some thirty miles away, as the train started by a miracle at the hour that it was advertised to start, I missed it, and as the trains ran only on alternate days, the telegraph was not in working order, and no one happened to be going to the capital, someone advised me to borrow a good horse and overtake the train at some of its innumerable stoppages.

The stationmaster lent me his Zebruno, that is a cream colour, so dark as to be almost brown, with a black mane and tail, a colour that in the Argentine is much esteemed as a sure sign of a good constitution in a horse, and staying power.

He proved a little hard to mount, for he was full of corn and seldom ridden, and more than a little hard to stay upon his back for the first few minutes, a little scary, but high-couraged and as sure-footed as a mule.

I overtook the train some ten miles down the line, at a small station — Itá, if I remember rightly — after a wild ride, on a red sandy road, mostly through forest, close to the railway line, so that it was impossible to lose the track, although I did not know a yard of it.

Now and then it emerged upon the plain, and then, taking the Zebruno by the head, who by this time was settling down a little, I touched him with the spur. He answered, snorting, with a bound, and then I made good time.

I gave the letter to the engine-driver, who put it carefully into the pocket of his belt, crumpling it up so that it looked like a dead locust. Then wishing me good luck on my ride home, for night was falling, the road was almost uninhabited, tigers abounded and there was always a chance of meeting with "bad people" ("mala gente"), he cursed the country heartily, lit a cigar, spat with precision on to the track, released his lever and slid into the night.

The cream colour, who had got his second wind and rested, reared as the hind-lights passed him, and as I wheeled him, struck into a steady gallop that, as the phrase goes, "soon eats up the leagues."

A light breeze raised his mane a little and set the palm trees rustling, fireflies came out and lit the clumps of the wild orange trees, looking like spirits of disembodied butterflies as they flitted to and fro. Occasionally we — that is the cream colour and myself — had a slight difference of opinion at the crossing of a stream, when the musky scent of an unseen alligator or an ominous rustling in the thickets startled him.

As we cantered into Paraguari, he was still pulling at his bit, and nearly terminated my career in this vale of tears by a wild rush he made

226

to get into his shed, that was too low to let a man pass underneath on horseback. I thanked the stationmaster for his horse, unsaddled him, emptied a tin mug of water over his sweating back, and threw him down a bundle of fresh Pindó leaves to keep him occupied till he was ready for his maize.

Then I strolled into the station café, where Exaltacion Medina, Joao Ferreira, and, I think, Enrique Clerici were playing billiards, whilst they waited for me.

Mirages

R. B. Cunninghame Graham

To
Don Ramon Perez de Ayala
with
sincere regard, and admiration
of his achievement in
Castilian letters
from
his friend, R. B. Cunninghame Graham

Contents

Mirages

To Empire Builders

I address this little preface, for foreword is a term I cannot away with, holding it to be a dull and Nordic subterfuge for the older word, to empire builders.

As literature, in the Middle Ages, was mainly written in Latin, at least when it was designed for the consumption of the world at large, the approach to it was naturally through the medium of a Latin word. Had it not been for the eruption of the Latins, against all justice and in defiance of the League of Nations of the day, Britons, who were the Abyssinians of those times, might have remained woad-painted, bathless, and in ignorance of Virgil, Horace, Ovid and Petronius Arbiter; long-haired and lousy, and content to rob upon the highway as there is no mention of a stock exchange in Cæsar's "Commentaries."

Now Cæsar without a shadow of a doubt was of the same complexion as were Rhodes, Pizarro and Cortés, all of them empire builders. Cæsar, of course, though that was an unfair advantage as he was born a Roman citizen, knew more Latin, though Rhodes strove to acquire the Oxford dialect of the tongue, that surely would have sounded as strange in Rome as did the jargon of the senator from Córdoba to Cicero. Cortés knew Latin as we learn from the true history that Bernal Diaz del Castillo penned in Guatemala in his old age.

He spoke and "even answered those who spoke it"; but he also made verses, and from a poet all things may be expected.

Pizarro was of the legitimate breed of empire builders, illiterate, brave and a true Christian, for as he lay at the last gasp, he signed the cross upon the ground, traced with his finger dipped in his own blood.

All four were of the tribe of empire builders, or of filibusters, according to which side their chroniclers belonged, whether the vanquished, or those who came in the name of progress or religion to redeem and set them free from savagery. It is not to that class of empire builders that I address this preface, for the tales, essays or whimsy-whamsays in my little book are written from the point of view, that all men born of woman are but brief shadows, strutting their little hour on an unstable stage, on which it is impossible to get firm footing, and hence are equal, or if the reader be a perfect democrat, each one inferior to his brother.

A Maltese saying has it, "You call me smaitch, I smaitch to you, but you smaitch to the king."

This saying, pithy though it is, and heightened generally by the obscene and phallic gesture that accompanies it, I personally agree with, that is if there exists a king who is not, by the very nature of his office, rendered ridiculous and as much a "smaitch" (whatever that may mean) as the Maltese loafer at Valetta, on the "*nix mangiare*" stairs.

I mean no disrespect to kings or beachcombers. Each of them possibly have their uses in a civilisation that to me appears to be founded on mud, cemented well with blood, and sustained precariously upon the points of bayonets. I would not let my readers (if I should chance to have any) think I forget the aids of poison gas, death-dealing bombs, dropped upon Indian, Arab or Abyssinian villages, for they, of course, are the chief means that empire builders use to bring the gospel truths home to the minds of those we impudently style savages, because, as Montaigne said, they wear no "*Haults de Chausses.*" But of his courtesy, I pray the empire builder living securely at Peckham Rye, at Asnières, Potsdam or Porto d'Anzio, not to think I am enamoured of the noble savage, or have met him in my long pilgrimage in this vale of tears.

I know quite well that he uses no poison gas or bombs, simply because he has not got them, and is constrained to do his level best with poisoned arrows, launched from blow-pipe or from bow, and other poor devices hatched in his neolithic brain. It is inevitable that, by degrees, all the inferior races, that is inferior in arms, should be brought up to date. Our empire builders will see to it in the name of progress, of civilisation and our tripartite deity. They will bestow upon all tribes who can contribute something whereby the empire builders can gain anything, our motor-cars, television, our measles (fatal to all primitive peoples), together with the greater and the smaller poxes.

All that I foresee, and though I no more welcome it than I should welcome the sudden acquisition of a good harelip, I am perforce resigned to it, for I well know that though all races of mankind may suffer outward changes, still underneath the skin all men are equal, and the best manicured Nordic variety of the *Homo sapiens*, for all his plumbing, is not really better than the bull-whacker of Haiti, or the herder of the buffalo in the marshes of Ceylon.

So, gentle empire builders, should you by chance stray into the bypaths of unremunerative literature, forsaking for the nonce, best sellers, where the men are all strong, silent, square-jawed filibusters and the women though mostly whorish, yet I confess occasionally attractive despite their epicenity, you will find these little stories writ from a different angle to that reviewers — a genial race enough — acclaim as epoch-making.

Virtue in them is quite as rarely rewarded as it is in real life, nor is vice especially triumphant. But then, although they tell us that death is the wages of the sinner, as far as I can see, it seems to be not very different for the saint.

R. B. Cunningham Graham.

Mirages

Mirage

Hadrian, who had travelled in the East, may have been thinking of a mirage in the Egyptian desert, on his death-bed, when he apostrophised his soul. Nothing is more like life than is a mirage, vague, fleeting, apparently so stable, and yet impossible to grasp and satisfy yourself that it is your own, to use, enjoy, and to dispose of to your heirs.

How often have both cheated those who have put their trust in them. The mirage with its lakes, its mountains, cool refreshing streams, that vanish at the touch of the lost wanderer in the desert, parched with thirst. Life with the parting of the soft vague little essence, the dying emperor apostrophised in his memorable words. Well did he know, he who had travelled all his empire from far-off Britain to the Euphrates, that the animula was a vague mirage, that was as elusive as the phenomen *[sic]* he may have seen upon the Parthian bounds. Unlike the billowing mists of northern climates, the mirage has not its terrifying aspect, nor seems to harbour in its recesses something hostile to mankind. Yet it is just as dangerous, coming with all the graces of a serpent of old Nile.

It spreads its shroud over the burning sands, the black rocks of the desert, fills up the courses of the parched-up rivers, making them look like cool refreshing streams. Dead trunks of palm-trees take on their foliage, clusters of dates hang from their branches and invite the hungry wanderer to eat his fill. Dry tufts of grass are by its magic, forests, waving with green leaves. It turns the colocynths that nestle lowly in the sand, veritable dead sea apples, with their striped yellow rinds, to luscious water-melons. Bones of dead animals that have died of overwork or thirst become the ruins of strange prehistoric beasts. The grey metallic lizards squattering through the sand, appear as fearsome and as large as crocodiles.

All suffers change. Even the desert takes on a fresh and springlike air, as of a pampa in the southern hemisphere, after a storm of rain, and what was but a sandy waste in the white vapour is a grassy plain. A master-builder, it creates a world as beautiful as Eden, before the serpent held out the apple to our mother Eve. A world so tempting that the traveller longs to throw aside his cares, and dwell for ever in it, but as fallacious as the sad world we know.

So lifelike do its lakes appear, with tiny wavelets lapping on the stones, one rides one's horse into its margin to slake his thirst, and finds but an illusion, a jest of nature in her best vein of pleasantry. The tales of travellers and the grave explanations of the men of science have no weight before a mirage in the sands, for no one ever profited, or will profit by the experience of others. We all must put our finger in the Saviour's wounds, before we can believe.

Your mirage is the sworn enemy of reason. When woods hang with their roots upwards in the sky, woods that we know we cannot see for intervening hills, they look so real that reason toils in vain to disabuse us, for we have seen them clearly, and seeing is believing as the old saw avers. Thus if a man firmly believes that he has seen a ghost, that ghost for him becomes as real as if it had been flesh and blood, projected on the retina.

So it may well be after all that the world of the mirage is the real world, and that the world we live in is a mirage. Mankind has always loved to be deceived, to hug illusions to its heart, to fight for them and to commit its direst follies in the name of common sense.

Our mirages are as real to us (the sons of light), as those the desert atmosphere paints for us, with long trains of camels slowly ploughing through the sand, their drivers plodding by their sides, and the conductor bringing up the rear, seated upon his ass.

Who would not like to join their cafila, and make the pilgrimage to the insubstantial Mecca, that region where the rainbow ends, and sun-dogs kennel? Could we but make a landfall at the port, wherein the *Fata Morgana* harbours to refit after her cruises to lure mariners to death, that region where the captain of the locusts leads his myriads, when they disappear across the sea, wafted by the storm, we might arrive at last at something real, leaving illusion to the dull dwellers of the earth.

When, therefore, fellow Hadgi, the mirage spreads its lake before you, do not allow your horse to put his foot in it or it will vanish from your sight.

Behind the mantling vapour rise castles, towers, cathedrals, lines of aerial telegraphs stretching up to the moon, palaces, fantastic ruins, galleons and galleasses that sail bedecked with flags.

All these exist in the mind's eye, the only field of vision where there is no astigmatism.

238

Rein up your horse, before his feet destroy and bring them back again to earth. Why peer behind the veil to see life's desert all befouled with camels' dung, littered with empty sardine tins and broken bottles, and strewed as thick as leaves in Vallombrosa with greasy, sandwich papers?

At any cost preserve your mirage intact and beautiful. If riding in the desert you behold it slowly taking shape, turn and sit sideways in your saddle, pouring a libation of tobacco smoke towards your Mecca and muttering a prayer.

Mirages

Charlie the Gaucho

The pulperia* stood on a little rise, surrounded by a peach orchard. Its whitewashed walls, flat roof and door studded with iron nails, gave it a look as of the houses in Utrera, Ecija or any of the towns in the land of Maria Santisima. There the resemblance stopped, a side door opened into a room, half store, half bar. Hanging from pegs were stirrups, girths, spurs, bits, bridles and horse gear of all kinds. Upon the shelves were rolls of gaudy cotton goods, and ponchos made in Birmingham. Bottles of cheap scent, in those days generally of Agua de Florida, in tall thin flasks, with elongated necks. They had a picture of a red-cheeked girl, with eyes like saucers, and an air of super-harlotry, that to be honest I never have observed amongst the daughters of the Banda Oriental, the name, in those days, of the republic of Uruguay.

Above the wooden bar were rows of bottles; gin, caña, Hesperidina de Bagley, Vermouth, and various syrups, Cassis, Naranjada, and Orchata, known locally as refrescos, and much consumed by the fair, or more properly, the brown sex.

A wooden palisade running up almost to the roof, protected the proprietor, when what was styled "*una barulla de Jésu Criste*," that may be translated or rather paraphrased as "Hell's own Row" arose, after a quarrel, either between two rival guitar players, or two Gauchos as to the brand, one or the other remembered on a horse, ten or twelve years ago. Then the proprietor would retire, and close the wicket through which he served the drinks, in stout and heavy glasses, with enormously thick bottoms, that I never saw again till I arrived years afterwards in Corpus Christi, Texas. There so to speak he "stood by" grasping a bottle, ready to throw, for there was always a good pile of empty bottles, to serve as missiles in the like emergencies.

Outside at a stout post of hardwood, called a palenqué, were tied the horses of the customers; browns, blacks and chestnuts, duns, sorrels, greys of all shades from steel to dappled, and every kind of piebald and

* Country Stores.

241

of skewbald, wild-eyed, and looking only fit for "perches for a hawk," as ran the Gaucho saying, stood looking nervously about at the least noise, or if they happened to be tame, patiently waiting in the sun with half-closed eyes, head hanging down, arid resting a hind leg.

Their owners, dressed in the "chiripá," that curious garment, consisting of a long piece of cloth or linen, held round the waist by a silk, knotted sash, and passed between the legs to form a trouser, with the front lap tucked underneath the sash, that they must have taken in old times from the native Indians; they either had a jacket of some sort or other, a pleated woollen overshirt, or a cheap, reach-me-down alpaca coat. All of them had ponchos that they either carried on one arm, or wore, their long-handled knife sticking them out just as a boom spreads out a sail. Their hats were very small, and seemed to balance on their shock heads of hair, coarse as a horse's tail, and were kept in their place when the wind blew, by a black ribbon from which hung two tassels, generally greasy from long wear. Their wearers, when they dismounted, waddled like alligators upon land, clanking their enormous spurs known as lloronas or as nazarenas, on the ground.

They called for gin, or caña, striking the counter with their whips, or the flat of their long knives. The etiquette was to invite the company, and in all cases to hand the glass to the man nearest to the drinker, who touched it with his lips, handing it back, with a grave "*gracias, caballero,*" or "*amigo*" as the case might be.

A pack of hungry-looking dogs that usually rushed out to seize the horse's tail of any passerby guarded the house, and helped to bring the cattle up into the corral.

An empty bullock cart, straw-thatched and with the heavy pole sticking up like a mast, served as a roosting place or shelter from the sun, to the wild, stringy-looking chickens, or to a gamecock fastened by a string.

As the house stood not far from where a flying raft conveyed the horses of the travellers or troops of cattle over the river Yi, several straw huts inhabited either by Indian-looking girls, or women, who could no longer get a living in the capital, were the abode of those who dealt in "love."

The country people always spoke of them as Las Quitanderas; no one was able to explain the name, so it remains a problem for philologists.

Over the place, upon that morning of Saint Rose of Lima, a season

242

when in Uruguay the country people always expect a storm, there was an air of tension and unusual quiet, such as in every country of the world seems to take hold of people after a tragedy. The side door of the pulperia was deserted, no groups of Gauchos stood at the bar, gravely discoursing of the next revolution, that was certain to break out if the accursed Blancos or Colorados, as the case might be, remained too long in power. No tinkle of a guitar, its strings mended and supplemented by strips of hide cut almost as fine as wire, floated out into the still heavy air. No high-pitched falsetto voice was heard, singing a "Triste," or some such artless effort of a local bard, as "At the door of my house, there is a plate of vinegar. Who laughs at me, laughs at his mother."

No one sat on the ground drawing, or as they called it, "painting" the brands of horses, with his finger in the dust, or scratching them upon the door with the point of his "facón," to clinch his argument. Three or four grave men of middle age, but without a silver hair in their black heads, stood talking in subdued tones to the proprietor.

The shrill laughter of the "Quitanderas" was subdued, and now and then, one of them, with her face unpainted, and a black shawl around her shoulders, peeped out from her rancho as timidly as some wild animal peers out from its lair.

"*Ché*, friend Azcoitia," said one of the group of men who stood about the door of the pulperia, conversing in low voices, "the commissary has not hurried much. The *chasqui* that you sent off at daybreak this morning, after the 'misfortune,' on your best horse, that *zaino* that you got from the Brazilian, for a pair of silver spurs, two dollars and a flask of rum, with orders to the lad Ramon, not to spare the '*rebenque*' or the spurs, could not have taken more than two hours at the most to arrive at the Estancia de los Sarandis, where the commissary lives."

"I know," said the proprietor, "but then the law always walks with a leaden foot.

"Perhaps they could not find the horses, or perhaps news of the revolution had arrived, God alone knows, and He, although He knows, never informs us what He knows, so that to us it matters little what He knows."

"Heretics," said one of the Gauchos, with a smile, and then, holding his hand, as brown as if it had been cut out of mahogany, before his eyes, exclaimed, "*Carai, amigo*, I see three horsemen on the far-off loma galloping this way."

In spite of all his efforts the Basque proprietor saw nothing for at least half a minute, though Don Fulgencio, the old Gaucho, kept on muttering, "*Sí, Señor*, it is the commissary. *Lindo el lobuno!* What a fine gallop, the two poor soldiers with their crop-eared jades keep their '*rebenques*' going like the handle of a pump, to keep them up with him."

The figures of the men and horses by degrees got more distinct, until at last even the proprietor of the pulperia could see them plainly. Enveloped in a cloud of dust, they neared the house, rode up to the palenque and dismounted from their beasts.

Don Exaltacion Rodriguez, commissary of the department of Porongos and the Yi, got slowly off his horse. In early middle age and with the stoutness that office always lends to men in Oriental countries, in South America and Spain, already coming on, he yet was a fine figure on his horse, a dun with a black stripe right down its back, and markings like a zebra on its hocks. He handed his long white well-plaited raw-hide reins, with silver rings at spaces of six inches or a foot, to one of his wild-looking soldiers, who had forced his horse up to the palenque of the pulperia rejoicing in the appellation of "*La Flor de Mayo*," with curses and with blows of his flat whip. The proprietor, a Spanish Basque, strong, muscular, his black hair contrasting strangely with his dark blue eyes, dressed as a Gaucho of the better class in the loose black merino Turkish trouser known as "bombachas" in the republic of Uruguay, a light alpaca coat, white hemp-soled alpargatas on his feet, and on his head the national blue bonnet of the Basque provinces, came out to greet the representative of the law's authority.

"Good morning, Don Exaltacion," he said, "come in and have your eleven hours, I have the finest caña from Brazil, Vermouth, Gin of the Palm Tree brand, dry wine of Spain, and a butt of the best Carlon from Catalonia."

Gravely the Comisario, who had put on "*une tête de circonstance*," returned his greeting, thanked him and said, "First I must see the dead. I hope that no one has touched the body, as the laws of the republic, in these cases, charge its citizens."

"All is in order, Don Exaltacion, the man lies where he fell, for though the fight took place inside the house, he staggered out to the galpon, holding his intestines up with his left hand, still grasping his 'facón,' and died without a word, just as the '*Tigre*' dies, when he is cornered by the dogs, after a dozen wounds."

"Enough, friend," rejoined the man in authority, "you seem to have not badly of the 'syrup of the beak' for one of your nationality, but men of your calling all learn it in the trade."

Without more words the storekeeper led the way to the galpon. Three or four Gauchos, whose horses, sat back on their halters, as the little cortège passed, making the Comisario's horse that stood hobbled and with the reins tied to the cantle of the "*recado*" arching his neck and looking like the knight in chess, rattle his silver gear.

The Gauchos' great iron spurs, trailing on the ground, completed the orchestra.

The air was heavy, the sky lowering, and now and then short gusts of wind raised dust in whirls like little waterspouts, a sure sign that the Pampero was on its way, from the far southern plains.

Signing with his hand for all to stand back, the Comisario, taking off his hat, crossed himself furtively, threw away his black, Brazilian cigarette and drew away the white embroidered cotton handkerchief, that someone, perhaps a Quitandera, had placed upon the dead man's face, in defiance of the law. Azcoitia had spoken truly when he said the man lay just as he had fallen. Dressed in the clothes of a poor Gaucho, a cotton chiripá, dirty white cotton drawers, his feet, that stuck up in the appealing way the feet of those who have died violent deaths so often take, were shod in boots made from the skin of a calf's hind leg, leaving the toes bare.

The man had fallen with his right arm underneath his head. His left still was in the attitude of holding up the intestines, although the fingers were relaxed, and underneath his cotton chiripá the lump was plainly visible where the bowels had escaped and stained his soiled white drawers with blood. Another gaping wound above the heart, that had not bled much, and was already drying on his white pleated shirt, had been the final stroke. Tall, thin and muscular, his long fair hair was spread over his shoulders, for in those days Gauchos all wore long hair, and took a pride in it. His chestnut beard, and sunburned face, showed that he was a European, but one who had lived long upon the plains of Uruguay. His face was calm, save for a little rictus that displayed his teeth, strong and as white as ivory. His hands were muscular and brown, showing several old scars he might have got in other fights, during the course of a wild life.

His staring, wide-opened eyes were grey, and you divined at once that they were eyes accustomed to great open spaces, by the contraction of the muscles at the corners. Flies had begun to buzz about them.

Gravely the Comisario looked at the dead man, almost with admiration, and said, "Pucha, what wounds; see where the hilt of the facón has left a mark upon his shirt; it must have been sufficient to have killed a bullock. How long has he been dead, Azcoitia? Tell me his name, and how he got his death." The Basque, in the curious jargon so many of them speak in Spanish, using feminine adjectives with masculine nouns and vice versa, took up his parable. Three or four Gauchos, the two ragged soldiers, and several of the Quitanderas, who had overcome their fear, stood by to listen to him.

"Señor Comisario, this was a brave man. Everyone knew him as Carlitos el Inglés. For years he wandered up and down the republic, working occasionally as a tropero, or as a horse-breaker despite his five-and-forty years; for him no horse was wild."

A Gaucho interrupted, "No, Señor, it seemed a lie to see him on a colt, with or without a saddle — *pucha,* * *gringo lindo!* He was really more Gaucho than ourselves, and knew more of the camp than Satanás himself, who, you know, knows more, for that he is old, than because he is Satanás."

The other Gauchos who stood round about the body, nodded their heads in affirmation, remarking, "Sí, Señor, Fulgencio only speaks the truth."

"Enough," said the Comisario, who had been taking what he called "dates" in a little dog-eared pocket-book, with a greasy pencil-stump that was as often in his mouth as on the paper, looked up and turning to the Basque Azcoitia, said, "Tell me the manner of his death?"

Azcoitia took up his parable: "Señor Comisario, this Carlitos, who although he was a man of education, knowing the pen, and reading his own tongue the Castilian, and the French, better than any 'dotorcillo' of them all, liked to live with the Gauchos and be one of them. He, as Don Fulgencio has said, was a great horse-breaker, threw the lasso, and the 'boleadoras' better than any of them, but his chief pride was in his skill with the facón. When he heard of some 'valenton' he would ride leagues to meet him, and when they met, usually at a pulperia, Carlitos would salute him as courteously as if he had been an old friend, and leave him generally stretched out, showing his navel, as we say here in the Department of the Yi."

The Comisario, a man who had bad fleas, as say the Gauchos, cut him short, impatiently. "Jesus! what a tongue, long as a lasso! Friend, you

*Pareció mentira *[sic = It seemed a lie]*

should have stayed at home and been a friar. Tell me without flourishes and rodeos, how this Carlitos died, and who it was that killed him; but not here — one should respect the dead."

As they adjourned towards the pulperia, one of the Quitanderas walked into the shed, covered the dead man's face with a silk handkerchief, knelt down, and saying, "Carlitos was a generous man, and valiant; if he had money no one was freer with it." That was his epitaph. Generous and valiant, what more can man desire to be said of him after death?

Crossing herself both on the breast and mouth, she muttered a short prayer, scarce audible, after the fashion of the country. Then rising to her feet, she draped herself in her black shawl, taking on for a moment the dignity that sincerity imparts. Then with a courteous salutation to the Comisario, she walked out of the galpón. As they turned towards the horses, the long-threatened storm broke suddenly. Lightning played continuously, a low green arch that had formed on the horizon was dissolved into a furious rain that ran along the parched-up soil like hail. The thunder seemed to shake the world. The wind swept everything before it. The horses tied to the palenque turned their quarters to the rain, lowered their heads, and stood looking like caricatures of what they had been but a few minutes before the Pampero had caught them and all their little world in its fell sweep. Almost as if by magic the country seemed to become a lake, and through the water, already several inches deep, the Comisario and the rest scuttled to safety, their heavy spurs clanking like fetters on the ground.

When they had shaken the rain from their soaked clothes and had had a glass of caña or of gin, Azcoitia was once more about to start his parable. "No," said the Comisario, "let a son of the country speak and tell us how this Carlitos died, for this man is as long-winded as a well-trained racehorse." The Basque laughed, but, as goes the saying, "with the laugh of a rabbit," that is, a rabbit that is going to be killed.

"It is this way, Señor Comisario," a quiet-looking Gaucho, Eustaquio Medina, began. "Carlitos came into the pulperia last evening, not drunk but with enough gin under his belt to make him foolish. He rode a Pangaré, half tamed, but that already knew the bit. '*Vaya un fleton.*' He had hardly tied him to the palenque than El Nato Vargas the Correntino, a real alligator, like most of his compatriots, who was standing at the door —he had an eye, that Indian, in his scrunched-up face! — walked up to the Inglés, and called out, 'That is my Pangaré. He has the mark of Sigismundo Perez in the Cuchilla de Haedo, from whom I bought him as a colt.' 'You lie,' replied Carlitos, 'he has another brand, a little like that of Don Sigismundo, but different.' 'Yes,' cried El Ñato, 'but you have altered it; see where the scar has scarcely healed.' Before a man could say Jesús, a terrible 'bochinche' started. Both of them 'Tigres,' both men to whom the facón was as familiar as is the pen to a 'cagatinta' of the law. Carlitos was the stronger of the two, the Correntino quicker on his feet. With their light summer ponchos wrapped round their left arms, their heads held low, to protect their bellies, they circled round each other like two cats, or fighting cocks. Pucha! their facóns flashed through the air like torches! There was no trick they left untried; but both of them were old hands at the game. Not two old bulls, Señor Comisario, when they met at the edge of a rodeo, or alone in a clearing of the 'monte,' were more cunning or more fierce. Carlitos first drew blood. Stooping down low he scooped up dust with his left hand, and threw it in El Ñato's eyes, crossing his face with a 'jabeque,'* that he will carry to the grave. Time after time, they came together with their hands meeting in the air, only to jump yards backwards, and to come on guard again, panting, and glaring, watching each other's every move. At last Carlitos, who had been drinking, began to tire. El Ñato drove him backwards, and with a slash opened his belly, but Carlitos, holding up his guts with his left hand, still came at him, like a tiger, till, weakened as he was, El Ñato drove his facón into his chest, till the hilt clinked on the breast-bone. Then, as you know, Carlitos staggered out to the galpon and died without a word. El Ñato, with his face opened like a water-melon, a finger gone from his left hand, and all the poncho that had covered his left arm cut into lace, mounted his horse, and with the Pangaré, 'de tiro,' galloping beside him, went off, perhaps to his own 'pago' in Corrientes, or perhaps to hide himself in some island in the Uruguay."

" 'Tis well," the Comisario remarked, "we can do nothing, but the man must be buried like a Christian."

Azcoitia promised that it should be done and that next morning he would take the body into town, in his own bullock cart, and pay for a mass for the repose of the soul of the dead man.

After an interval the Comisario got upon his horse. The Gauchos mounted, like drops of water sliding down a pane of glass, saluted one another gravely, and struck into the clockwork gallop of the plains,

* 'Jabeque' is from xebec, a Levantine boat, with a pointed sail.

plains, towards their separate ranchos, gradually disappearing into the horizon, their ponchos waving in the wind, and their right arms moving mechanically as they just touched their horses' flanks with their *rebenques* to keep them to their stride.

The Comisario, as he rode past the galpon, where lay the body of Carlitos el Inglés, who had been both the admiration and the terror of the district, raised his forefinger to his hat, murmuring, "Of all the animals God has created, the male Christian is the wildest, but He knew best when He created him," touched his horse with the spur and, followed by his ragged soldiers, breasted a little hill and disappeared.

What I have written, I, sinner that I am, did not see with these eyes the earth will eat, but three days afterwards I passed the pulperia, halted to buy a box of sardines, raisins of Malaga, and bread; and as I drank a glass of caña, heard the story; heard and forgot it, though no doubt it stayed fixed in the brain, just as a photograph is dormant, on the gelatine or glass, before it is revealed.

Everyone in the Banda Oriental knew Charlie the Gaucho, at least by reputation. His adventures, fights, flights from justice, disappearances into hiding, some said amongst the Indians of the Chaco, and others that he knew of an uninhabited island in the Uruguay, to which he would retire, until pursuit had been abandoned. There were not wanting those who were convinced he used to plunge into the depths of the Laguna Yberá in Corrientes, in whose recesses, as every Gaucho knew, there lived a race of dwarfs, unseen but yet believed in fervently, for faith alone works miracles, has done so since the beginning of the world and will do so, to the last day that it exists. There with the hypothetic dwarfs, lighted at night by the Ipétatá, the bird that bears a lantern in its tail, living on game, Carlitos was believed to pass a month or two, and then emerge, to resume his usual life, as justice in those days was little retrospective, and no one troubled to bring criminals to account, after the immediate scandal had died down. In fact they held that, in the words of the old Spanish saw, "the dead and the absent have no friends," to which they might have added, "and no enemies."

Little by little, the fight upon the margin of the Yi, Charlie the Gaucho, even the story that Azcoitia used to tell, with endless repetitions, had become legendary.

No one could tell me anything of Gaucho Charlie's previous life. He seemed to have come into the world of Uruguay armed at all points, just as Minerva issued from the head of Jove. No one remembered him as a poor rider, an indifferent thrower of the lazo or the boleadoras, or before he spoke Spanish perfectly. No one had seen him possessed of any visible means of support, except such money as he earned by breaking in horses and working as a vaquero with the herds of cattle that in those days were always passing to Brazil. Still he had always money to spend at all the pulperias, or lavish on Las Quitanderas, and at all race meetings he was certain to appear.

At times well dressed, in Gaucho fashion, his horse adorned with silver and he himself trailing great silver spurs that dangled from the high-heeled boots the Gauchos used to wear, at others in the clothes in which he died, poncho and chiripá, with potro boots* upon his feet, and a bandana handkerchief tied round his head, beneath his hat.

Years passed, and even in that country of long memories, Charlie the Gaucho's exploits gradually grew dim. Although I always thought "there was a cat shut up in the bag," and that there must have been a mystery, in the life of an educated Englishman, who for years roamed about, amongst the Gauchos, speaking their language perfectly with all its turns of slang, and met his death in a fight in an obscure Boliche, about a horse, that it appeared that he had stolen, no one I met could solve, or even throw a light upon it.

In my case fate was kind. Long afterwards, business called me to the capital.

A Mr. Beckeridge was, I think, our vice-consul in those half-forgotten days. Short, rather stout, with thick dark whiskers, drink had bestowed a nose upon him as red as a beefsteak. The Gauchos, always apt at nicknames, called him "El Farolito," that is, the little lantern. He seemed as proud of the designation as a Habsburg might be proud of his long chin.

Spanish he spoke as easily as English, with all the verbs in the infinitive, and no regard to genders, but understood it perfectly, although his accent was most formidable, so that one never knew, without attention, which language he was speaking, for he had formed a jumble of the two, almost inextricable.

I found him in his dusty office, unswept and strewed with ends of cigarettes, half torn-up letters, and all the flotsam and the jetsam of an untidy bachelor, seated for greater comfort in his shirt-sleeves, smoking

---

* Potro boots are made from the hide of the hind leg of a colt potro.

a Brazilian cigar. His desk was piled with invoices, bills of lading, deeds of charter-party and matters of the kind, and on the walls hung the announcements of ships' sailings, arrivals at the port, rates of exchange, advertisements for missing British subjects, and all the multifarious affairs that in those days, for miserable pay, fell to a consul's lot. Withal a gentleman, both in his bearing and his speech, and as I found when he began to talk, not inefficient at his job.

He welcomed me, as was the fashion of the country and those days, as if we had been friends from boyhood. My trifling business soon dispatched, we fell a-talking over a glass or two of Hesperidina, a liquor fashionable at the time throughout the River Plate, concocted and retailed by an American called Bagley, who had made a fortune out of it. Long did we talk on local topics, the coming revolution, and that just ended, the want of water for the camps, the locusts, and how a Mr. Walker rode from the estancia de Las Arias to "Montyviddeó," as he pronounced the word, two hundred miles at least, in two-and-twenty hours.

These subjects palling, although we did them ample justice, I mentioned Gaucho Charlie, said I just missed his death, and asked the consul if he had ever heard about him. At last I had struck oil. "Charlie the Gaucho!" exclaimed the consul, throwing away the stump of his cigar, and tossing off another glass of the pale yellow Hesperidina, from one of the little barrel-shaped bottles that I so well remember in every pulperia. "Yes, many's the time he has sat in the chair in which you now are sitting. You are right in thinking that he had a curious history. I will read you what the French call his dossier." So saying, he took from a bookshelf a volume bound in soft brown calf. He mopped his face, settled his glasses well on his red nose, poured out another glass, mixed this time with soda water and Angostura bitters, and was about to read. Then, interrupting himself, he said: "All that I am going to read to you, I had from Charlie's lips. After his death one of his family corroborated all that he had said. 'Charles Edward Mitchell was born in Yorkshire of a good family. His family were county gentry, of considerable wealth. Charles, a fine lad, high-spirited and generous, but subject all his life to sudden fits of rage, was sent into the Navy.

" 'He did well there, and as a midshipman of about sixteen was on board a frigate, lying at the time the tragedy occurred at a little port in Uruguay, upon the River Plate. She lay in-shore, not far from land, and as the weather was extremely hot, with all her ports open.'

"You remember the old-fashioned gun-rooms in the frigates of those days; dark, low and smelling of stale rum and cockroaches, with candles stuck in empty gin bottles?"

I did, having seen many of them, with their air of frowsiness, the midshipmen asleep on benches, the steward in a striped linen jacket, and their well-remembered smell.

"What happened only himself could tell with accuracy, but in some argument a furious quarrel arose. Young Mitchell felled his antagonist with a gin bottle, and thinking he was dead, without reflection rushed to the open port and plunged into the sea. As the ship only lay three or four hundred yards off-shore, escape was easy for him. After a search the vessel sailed without him, for he had disappeared, like a stone disappears dropped into the pitch lake of Trinidad, leaving no trace behind.

"Several years passed and the affair was quite forgotten, when one day a tall young man dressed as a Gaucho pretty well-to-do, walked in, and introduced himself to me. His English had grown rusty with disuse, and it was some time before I took in what he had to say, for he spoke very slowly, bringing the words out from the recesses of his brain in jerks, and asking me in Spanish now and then if I understood him properly.

"He told me he was the midshipman who, as he thought, had killed one of his brother officers, and deserted from his ship. When he had swum ashore, still in a panic, he had walked till he was tired, thinking he was pursued. After a night's rest in a wood, he took the road again till he arrived at an estancia.

"The owner took pity on the frightened, hungry boy, and treated him more as a long lost son than as a lad who had come penniless to ask for food. He sent and found the ship had sailed, after a prolonged search for the fugitive, and that the other midshipman had recovered from the blow."

The consul halted in his reading, filled up his glass and said sententiously: "The wild goat always seeks the wood, and so it happened with young Mitchell in this case. From the first day he liked the wild life of the Gauchos, learned to ride a wild horse, and lazo, with the wildest of the lads upon the place. The language seemed to come to him naturally. He let his hair grow long, after the gaucho fashion of the time, adopted all their ways, dressed as they dressed, and in a year or two left the estancia, to the regret of the kind owners of the place, who, being childless, wished to adopt him, to take up the life of a wandering

Gaucho, working at sheep-shearings, breaking in horses and going now and then as a peon, with troops of cattle to Brazil. That, in essentials," said the consul, "was his tale."

He closed the book, put it back more carefully than I expected in the shelf, and after lighting a black Brazilian cigarette, resumed: "But the tale had a "*llapa*," as the Gauchos call the last six feet of their lazo, that as you know is made of a finer plait than the whole body of the rope. As Charlie talked, gradually his English became more fluent, and he was not obliged to think for words.

"I asked him, 'Why did you never write home to your people, in all the years since you had left the ship?' 'Well,' he said, 'in the first place, I was afraid that there might be trouble with the authorities, and as we say in Spanish, "Justice, but not in my house." Then I forgot all about my life in England. You see, I am a Gaucho now. Their ways of life are mine, and though I often thought of going home, working my passage before the mast, I never did so, and I suppose would have forgotten all about England and that I had ever been a midshipman, brass buttons, and a dirk, "*lindo no mas*," ' he said, as if the midshipman had not been the midshipman in question, but some young officer off a British ship whom he had seen in Montevideo, and whose dress he had admired.

"Last week I was at an estancia near Paysandú, belonging to an Englishman, working as a '*domador*,' a horse-breaker, you know. It was years since I had read an English newspaper, and I turned it over listlessly, as nothing interested me. What did I care for Whigs and Tories, for cricket, or for races I should never look at, or the Court Circular! I was glad, for sure, that Queen Victoria was still alive. Her name has a good sound about it, especially in Spanish, and aboard ship we always used to drink her health at dinner-time. I was just putting down the paper, the famous *Times*, I think, when in the corner I came on my own name.' "

He took out of a pocket-book, bought at some pulperia, greasy and ragged-looking, a piece of newspaper, unrolled it carefully, smoothed it on the table, and gave it me to read. "Jesus, María!" the consul exclaimed, "it was a '*Llapa*,' with a vengeance, and took my breath away."

The little cutting contained an advertisement, asking Charles Edward Mitchell, once a midshipman in the Royal Navy, to apply to a firm of solicitors if he were still alive, as he was sole heir to his uncle's estate. The uncle had been dead for full three months.

"*La Puta!* What an occurrence, as they say hereabouts."

Both bottle and cigars were finished, and the consul rose from his chair, looked at himself critically in the looking-glass that hung upon the wall, and after passing a comb through his hair and whiskers, hummed in a low voice: "Jolly red nose. Jolly red nose. How did you come by that jolly red nose?" A song he may have heard at a Victorian music-hall on his last visit home.

His feelings thus relieved, he went back to his tale, saying: "There is little more to tell. I facilitated Charlie, as we say, enough money to pay his passage home. Wonderful to tell, by the next mail I got a cheque from him, with something over to pay the interest, as he said, and a gold watch. Yes, yes, oh, yes, the watch I still have it, and after what you tell me I shall have his name engraved on it, and the date when he was killed. Did I hear any more about him? Well, he wrote once or twice, to say he was the owner of a pretty large estate, member of several clubs in London, and that he rather liked the life. He added, 'The horses have infernally hard mouths.' Years passed, eight, nine or ten, I don't remember — where in hell do the years go when they pass — '*Labuntur anni*,' as we used to say at school?"

I had no answer to the query Postumus seems to have left unanswered, but waited for him to take up his parable again.

"He told me," said the consul, "that the life in England had become intolerable to him, and that he knew there was no other life for him but with Gauchos on the plains. He said: 'I passed over the estate to a first cousin, for a sum of money, intending to return at once to Uruguay. In London, I fell in with several old friends, and after two years there, till women, drink and gambling had run away with the most of my capital. I still have several hundred pounds, and by the first boat to-morrow I shall go back to Paysandú.'

"Years had not touched him in the least except to take away his sunburn, and make him thinner than he was. His English had come back to him entirely, but his eyes, that always looked beyond you, as if they looked across the plains, showed that his spirit was unchanged. We had a night together, and painted 'Montyviddeó' vermilion, and in the morning I saw him to the boat. That was the last time that I set eyes upon him, though of his exploits I heard plenty, and the name Carlitos el Inglés was known to everyone from the Brazilian frontier to the Uruguay."

The consul stopped suddenly, just as a horse stops in his stride when galloping at night, when he sees something that has startled him. He took his hat down from the peg where it was hanging, set it squarely on his head, lighted another cigarette, and said: "What say you to a *paseo*, to the Quilombo, to see if any camp men have come into town?"

I did not go with him, having ridden twenty leagues since sunrise, although the Quilombo was in those days our general rendezvous and club.

"So long!" the consul said, and left me wondering whether, if after all Charlie the Gaucho had not chosen wisely when he went back to chiripá, poncho and potro boots.

Then I reflected that the Gauchos say, the potro boot is not for everybody.

Mirages

Casas Viejas, 1933

Though but two miles from a high-road, on which pass motors, lorries, endless strings of donkeys, and now and then a countryman erect on his high saddle, his legs in leather leggings and his spurs hanging low upon his heels, the tragic village has an air of isolation as complete as if it were an Arab *duar* in Morocco or as some rancheria in El Bolson de Mápimi.

The great Gaditanian steppe, that runs from Cadiz, sweeps by La Barca de Vejer, and finishes in the low range of hills at El Puerto de las Facinas, surrounds the village on all sides, leaving it almost awash in the great sea of grass. Grass and more grass, dotted with herds of cattle and of sheep; the plain, a European pampa, is full of marshes enamelled with white flowers and overgrown with reeds.

The great Laguna de la Janda, almost dry in summer, is the breeding-place of herons, and of white cowbirds that sit on the backs of all the cattle and walk amongst them with a security that puts mankind to shame. Flamingoes spring from amongst the reeds and look as if they came straight from the pictures of the early Florentines, rosy and delicate, giving the banks of the laguna a prehistoric air.

The range of mountains on the east, stern and adust as are the hills above Cape Gardafui, is speckled with white little Arab-looking towns, whose names betray their Arab origin, Alcalá de los Gazules, Medina Sidonia, Grazalema, and half a hundred more. The landscape, peaceful and beautiful, hardly seems the setting for a tragedy.

Still, in the remote villages, with their Moorish names, perched on the rocky hills or sweltering on the plain, life goes on, little changed, much as it always has done in this part of Spain. The people all wear modern clothes, except the herdsmen and now and then a shepherd, who, in a brown cloak, resting upon his staff, stands like a gnomon on a sundial, motionless, his shadow falling sharp upon the ground.

The herdsmen still use the Moorish saddle, with its high cantle and pommel with a "manta" tied behind it, the ends flowing to the rider's feet. Their short tight jackets, broad-brimmed hats, Arab stirrups, the long oxgoad in their hands, and rusty guns tied to the saddle, mark them out as survivals from the past. Nowhere in the world are to be found faces more weather-bleached or more remarkable, faces that Velazquez painted and that have survived to-day to show that Spain can never change beneath the skin.

At daybreak, after a glass of *aguardiente*, the labourers mount their donkeys, or trudge afoot to their work in the fields, often a mile or two away, a relic of the times when all men had to seek shelter behind walls at nightfall and dare not live in isolated farmhouses after the fashion of the north.

Food is not too plentiful, but the people have been accustomed to short commons for generations, and their dash of Oriental blood renders them patient and uncomplaining to an astounding degree. In the little isolated communities every village looks upon itself as an entity and regards everyone not born in its bounds as an outsider, almost an enemy.

Industry of any kind does not exist. The saying runs, "Industry, that which each one has," which, being interpreted, may mean the care of a few goats, a cow or two, some pigs, or a few sheep, often brown, black, or ring-streaked, as those of Jacob in the Scriptures. If there is an apothecary his shop is the gathering place for all the wiseacres of the village, who sit and talk interminably on politics or discuss the prowess of bullfighters whose names they see in newspapers.

In these communities, where only the outside of modern life prevails — for telegraphs, telephones, and electric light go but a little way in altering men's mental outlook — there always has existed a vague Communism.

In such an atmosphere of poverty and isolation, Casas Viejas was ground fitted for Communist propaganda of the most violent kind. Nearly all Spanish villages and little country towns fall under the dominion of some ambitious bully known as a *cacique*, who terrorises the inhabitants and controls the voting for the party that commands his services.

In Casas Viejas one Seis Dedos, so called because he had six fingers on one hand, was the *cacique* of the place. Tall and athletic, he was renowned as a fine marksman, and was generally looked on as a hard-working countryman, who lived quietly with his wife and family in a little straw-thatched house right in the middle of the town. From the first he became imbued with Communistic ideas, which in his case were probably more a hatred of the conditions under which he lived than any definite ideas of politics.

His miserable cottage, now a heap of ruins, became the rallying-place of all those who had a grievance against the ruling powers.

Emissaries from Madrid, smug little men dressed in frayed town clothes, their pockets bulging with creased newspapers, printed in Barcelona, arrived in a mysterious way to interview the "Chief." Sometimes they stayed all night, and sat up talking to the small hours of the morning of the day when "La Tremenda" would arrive. Sometimes they only stayed an hour or two, to rest and eat a bowl of "gazpacho," that thin dish of oil, breadcrumbs, and cucumbers, the usual midday fare of the inhabitants of the land of "Maria Santisima."

In either case they "sowed the seed" — that is, they talked of dispossessing landlords, abolishing taxation, disestablishing the Church, and confiscating all her revenues.

Ten or twelve soldiers drafted into the place irritated, but were not numerous enough to coerce the villagers. Men arrived by night on donkeys or on mules, called at the house of the *cacique*, and left mysterious packages of ammunition. They went as silently as they arrived, slipping off noiselessly into the night. The soldiers, drawn from the same class as the villagers, insensibly made friends with them. Only the sergeant, who had served long in Africa, against the Moors, remained suspicious, and reported to his chiefs that he thought Seis Dedos was a dangerous man, though he could prove nothing definitely. Even if he had searched the house he probably would have found nothing more incriminating against him than the old single-barrelled gun, for Seis Dedos used to shoot partridges, when he found a covey sitting, after the fashion of peasant hunters for the pot. The ammunition that arrived by night was carefully secreted and shared out amongst the villagers, most of whom had guns and pistols of some sort or another, ranging from long, brass-mounted, single-barrelled weapons of a past age to cheap revolvers from Belgium or from France. Daily the spirit of revolt increased.

The relations between the soldiers and the villagers, at first so friendly, gradually changed into a vague hostility. Meetings were held, and speeches every day became more violent. At last a meeting that was to have been held in the little hall of the trade unionists was forbidden. The villagers determined to defy the proclamation, and gathered in the hall. Outside two or three of the soldiers, for the first time equipped for service, carrying their arms, attempted to keep order. How the collision happened no one exactly knows. Each side puts the blame upon the other, but when a soldier fell his comrades opened fire. Shots burst from every house, impossible to answer, as the firers were invisible, firing from windows, doors, the house-tops, or from the corrals where the animals were driven to at night. Had there been any plan, or had Seis Dedos put himself at the head of the villagers and sallied out in force, none of the soldiers could have escaped. As it was, he remained shut up in his house with all his family, who loaded and handed guns to him and to his son, firing out through a loophole in the wall.

The soldiers retreated to their barracks, hard pressed and in great danger of their lives, but standing stoutly to their arms.

Luckily for them they had a wireless and got messages through to Cadiz and Jeréz asking for instant help. The veteran sergeant in command fired steadily, shouting his orders to his men, accompanying each shot with a mouth-filling oath.

The night wore on, the little village and the tower of the church lit up occasionally and outlined against the sky by the sporadic gunfire as in a flash of lightning. At midnight lorries full of troops arrived. One of them carried a small, quick-firing gun that was placed instantly upon some rising ground behind the village. Right underneath lay the outlying mud-built cottages, thatched with straw.

The first few discharges from the quick-firing gun set them all alight. The flames gave the troops a full view of the wretched little house from which Seis Dedos and its occupants still kept up a hot fire.

Soon it began to slacken, and when the roof burst into flames and the whole cottage became a brazier, ceased entirely. The villagers, either cowed or because their ammunition was exhausted, also ceased their fire. Two or three disappeared into the night and never have been caught. Five perished with Seis Dedos in the cottage that they defended to the last.

Here and there in the streets dead men and wounded lay about. Peace reigned, and law and order were once more vindicated in the usual way. Slowly the tragic night wore on to daybreak, the troops standing to arms until the dawn appeared.

The villagers, cowering in their houses, may have thought the bitterness of death was past. If so, they were doomed to disappointment.

Hardly had day appeared than the commanding officer searched the houses and took fourteen prisoners. All these were shackled and driven down to the burnt cottage that contained the blackened bodies of Seis Dedos and the other occupants who had died, bravely fighting, for what they thought was the cause of liberty. There they were executed at once, without examination, in their chains. They all died bravely, as Spaniards always die, have died in the past, and will die as long as Spain is Spain, the sun shines, and the world turns round. Their bodies lie, in a long line of graves, in the village cemetery, and the lone village in the Gaditanian plain has had its martyrs.

As the Moors say, may God have pardoned them!

Mirages

Los Ninos Toreros

All the taurine intelligentsia of Caracas was in the bull-ring. They filled the square unpainted wooden boxes, sat on the stucco steps that, as in a Roman amphitheatre, mount to the top of the vast building, and swarmed in the cheap seats that border on the arena, so closely that the poorer of the "intelligents" can strike the bull if he passes near to them, with their walking-sticks.

The sun turned all to gold. The sand, in the arena, glistened like gold dust under its fierce rays.

Nature had done her best for the vast amphitheatre. No other bull-ring in the world was situated at the foot of steep descending mountains, cut by the rains into sheer gullies, so deep that the tall trees that fringed their sides seemed to cling to them as lichen clusters on a rock. Tall palm-trees almost overhung the walls, and from the upper seats the panorama of the enchanting valley stretched out, buried in tropic vegetation, with dazzling white houses in the clearings, dotting it here and there like islands in a sea of emerald. The cathedral tower, in the clear atmosphere, appeared so close that you could almost count the stones. The palm-trees, the overshadowing mountains and the soft tropic sky, gave an air of unreality to the whole place. There was no noisy crowd such as throngs the approach to any bull-ring throughout Spain. No gangs of ragged boys hung round to see the entrance of the company at the stage door that so often swallows up a bull-fighter, cutting him off from the public and the world when it has closed. No one cried "Agua-a-a," in the harsh Oriental voice that seems to be an inheritance, left by the Arabs to all water-sellers in the peninsula.

There were no barquilleros, with their tube-shaped canisters surmounted by a miniature roulette wheel, containing the crisp, rolled-up wafers, called "barquillas," the delight of children, soldiers and of nurserymaids, in Seville and Madrid.

Nobody sold red-and-yellow paper fans, or peanuts. No girl, black-eyed and roguish-looking, with her coarse black hair piled high upon her head, or, if worn short, disposed about her cheeks in curls, sold lemonade, carrying the bottles in the classical wooden "vasera," with a rose behind her ear.

The wooden boxes held the local aristocracy known to the populace as "El Blancaje," that is, the Whites, together with a sprinkling of oil magnates from Maracaibo, whose business seemed to call for their perpetual presence in the capital. The Spanish that they spoke, generally with all the verbs in the infinitive, and with a fine indifference to genders, cases, and the like, for rules of grammar were not surely made for free-born citizens, conserved the accent of the various States from which they hailed. Drawling and high-pitched in the mouth of the New Englander, it suffered a sun-change if the speaker came from further south, till in the mouths of Georgians and Carolinans, it became little different from the thick jargon of a plantation negro. With the exception of the aforesaid "Blancaje" and the Americans from Maracaibo, the audience was made up of Indian half-breeds.

These formed a striking contrast to the people who in Spain fill the cheap seats of bull-fights, in their demeanour. There was no wealth of gesture, no harsh voices raised in dispute as to the merits of their favourite heroes of the ring. Such few women as were present sat quite unmolested. Nobody pinched them; no one remarked upon their charms, in the same way as a dealer chants the praises of his horse. No oaths were heard, still less obscenity. Even the traditional appearance of the mounted alguazil to demand the key of the toril, provoked no jokes, no comment on himself or on his horse. The slight, dark faces showed no expression of impatience at the customary wait, for never under heaven in Venezuela was a bull-fight known to start in time. No one beat on the seats with walking-sticks, drummed with his feet or shouted imprecations on the president as time slipped by, and still the blinding glare fell on the vacant sand of the arena. All was as quiet and as orderly as when in Mexico, before the conquest, the people waited for the human sacrifice, grouped round the terraced steps of the great Teocalli, that reared itself upon the spot where the cathedral stands.

The blending of two races had given the people the outward visible appearance of their Indian ancestresses, but in their blood still boiled the fiercer passions of their forefathers, the conquistadores, ready to break out when they were aroused. All the parade, the pomp and circumstance of a bull-fight in Spain was lacking. Grouped here and there in knots, the men who should have been all dressed in brilliant costumes stood in old cast-off clothes, bought second-hand, dirty and stained, holding their cloaks that looked like window curtains, no longer serviceable, without a jot of pride. Still in themselves, they were all active, sinewy-looking youths, but evidently country herdsmen, acting as bullfighters for the occasion, and ill at ease on foot, under the public gaze.

The whole scene was more primitive and less rehearsed than it would have been in Spain. The lack of brilliant clothes in the arena, the silent audience, and the absence of the red-and-yellow paper fans that in Spain make a rustling noise, like a flock of pigeons taking wing, as they are ceaselessly shut and opened, made the spectacle more tense, but far less picturesque.

No long procession, with the espada rolled like a sausage in his sash, surrounded by his acolytes scarcely less brilliantly dressed than the chief actor, all swaggering, and monkeyfied, but in a way conscious they were the only true descendants of the gladiators, about to risk their lives, defiled across the sand, amidst the plaudits of the crowd. No miserable horses with one eye blinded, and their ears filled with tow, to prevent them hearing the bull's charge, disgraced the show.

Stripped of the adjuncts of bright dresses, and the old-world ceremonies, that give an air of picturesqueness in Spain to what is really only a sordid butchery, the stage seemed set for some such combat as must have often taken place in prehistoric times, between a man and the wild cattle in a glade of the Caledonian woods. There was no chapel as in Spain, with its attendant priest; no doctor to prevent wounded bullfighters from dying what would be to them a natural death, with anaesthetics and a battery of instruments. All was reduced to the lowest common denominator. The sun, the palm-trees, and the soft atmosphere were the only decorations of the bare bull-ring. One group of men and one alone spoke of old Spain, of Seville, and of its classic suburb of Triana.

Behind the barriers in the full glare of the sun, stood a tall man of middle age, clean-shaven, dressed in the short jacket and tight trousers of the profession, bare-headed, with a red cloak folded on his left arm. He limped a little on one leg, from a wound that had incapacitated him from taking part in his profession as a first actor, but still had left him active and strong enough to face a bull in an inferior capacity.

His face was deadly pale, and now and then his features twisted and beads of sweat stood on his forehead, and ran down his cheeks. In his left hand he held a crucifix, tawdry and cheap, as if bought in a second-hand depository of religious articles. In front of him stood his sons, two boys of fourteen and fifteen years of age. Dressed in the traditional Traje de Luces, all gay in spangles and gold lace, their blue-black hair brushed back and plastered with some inferior cosmetic so closely to their heads that it looked like a cap of pitch, they faced their father, turning their brilliant eyes upon him, with the fixed stare of all performers about to risk their lives before the sovereign public. Then they advanced and sank a knee before the image of their Saviour on His cross, knowing He died for bull-fighters, as well as for all other sinners.

Their father signed them with the cross, and when they stood up, strained them to his chest and kissed them. Then the boys drew themselves up and with their cloaks wrapped round their left arms, strutted into the enormous empty plaza, at the head of their poor, ill-dressed "cuadrilla" with as good an imitation of the best style of Seville or Madrid as they could manage to assume. No blare of music heralded their entrance. The rustle of a thousand fans did not disturb the air. No shouts of welcome encouraged them. The ragged regiment marched out to the middle of the open space. The shabby members of the company took up their places, their gay but tattered cloaks covering their tawdry sweat-stained clothes. A cloak hides all deficiencies, says the Spanish saw, and certainly in their case there was a good store of deficiencies to hide. Nearly all stockings had a ladder in them; some, good honest holes, but darned with cotton. The heelless pumps that bull-fighters all wear when in full dress were held in place, sometimes with elastic bands across the instep, sometimes with bootlaces. One man, a tall gaunt half-bred Indian, shuffled off his shoes, after having placed them carefully behind the barrier, and in his dirty stockings, torn and sweat-soaked, stood prepared to risk his life to gain his livelihood.

The entry of the two boys, followed by their father with his limping leg, the woeful-looking "cuadrilla," and the half-filled seats of the vast amphitheatre, was somehow more impressive than the procession of glittering gladiators, who, headed by their leader, in his gorgeous panoply of silk and gold, struts into the arena at Madrid or Córdoba.

No blare of music announced the advent of the bull from the toril. Two countrymen opened the sliding door, and with a snort a long-horned prairie bull bounded out, receiving as he passed two thrusts from the long ox-goad the herdsmen who presided at the gate bestowed either from the joy of life, or from their lifelong habit of goading any animal that came within their reach. A languid shiver went through the audience, as the long-horn, after a minute of amazement at his unfamiliar surroundings, rushed at the ill-dressed scarecrow who was nearest to him. He, though grotesque-looking as to his exterior, had his heart in the right place, and proved at once that he had graduated in some one of the taurine universities of Spain. Drawing himself to his full height, he executed a skilful pass with his ragged cloak, keeping his feet still, in the best style of Ronda, or of Córdoba.

A lazy "Viva," that sounded like a muffled cry of "Ease her," on a river steamer, floated from the half-filled benches. All the ragged regiment bravely played their part, with their cloaks, but none of them attempted to place the banderillas in the neck of the bull. Then, but without the bugle call that heralds each phase of the "Fiesta Nacional," the elder of the two lads stepped into the middle of the ring carrying the banderillas in his hand. He drew himself to his full height, of five feet three or four, hollowed his back, threw up his head, and stamping with his foot challenged the bull to charge. The company, who knew their business, crept up behind him, and his father, pale and anxious, stood waiting with his cloak. The long-horn came on gallantly, with his head just in the right position, neither too high nor too low, and the brave lad "planted a pair," as well placed as the best bull-fighter in Spain could possibly have done. Then did the half-bred audience for the first time wake up, and change their attitude of apathy for one of furious excitement and applause, just as a tropic storm breaks out, almost without a sign.

Shaking the darts in the folds of his neck, the bull careered through the arena, the shabby-looking men making some tolerable passes with their cloaks. The younger brother placed another pair, as skilfully as the first had done, but far more easily, so easily that his skill was lost on a Caracas audience, although it would have brought forth thunders of applause in Spain. The father, whose face had relaxed under the influence of the plaudits of the crowd, now braced himself for the last act. After the bull had been drawn into a favourable position by the one real bull-fighter in the troop, a dark and sinewy gipsy from Triana, the elder boy advanced to kill. The bull, fresh from the Llanos, was still untired, for he had not exhausted himself upon the miserable horses, or been bled white, with lance-thrusts and repeated pairs of banderillas, as in Spain. Lighter by far upon his feet than any Spanish bull, taller and heavier, he seemed an elephant opposed to the slight lad who faced him. By this time the audience was all alight, and watched each "pass," if not with knowledge, yet with appreciation. Working as quickly as a man of twice his experience, the boy with his sword hidden in the red muleta, executed most of the passes known to the fancy, turning half-round as the bull charged and patting him upon the flank, or reaching out with the hand that held the cloak touched him between the horns. Then, advancing on the furious animal, his arm shot out and took him just in the right place above the shoulder-blade, driving his sword up to the hilt. Stopped in his full career, as if struck by lightning, the bull fell dead, blood gushing in a thick dark stream from both his nostrils. The quiet-looking, rather stocky boy had taken him, half-volley (*de volapié*), just as a tennis player takes the ball upon the rise.

All the time that the boy had been in peril of his life, his father, pale and anxious, the experience of years overcoming his slight limp, had hovered round him, to draw off the bull, in case his son should fail or lose his nerve.

When the team of mules, not decorated with plumes and tassels, as in Spain, but taken from a cart, with ordinary harness, had pulled the dead bull from the arena, he patted his son on the shoulder, and for a moment his air of tense anxiety relaxed.

His relief lasted but for a moment, for his younger boy had to deal with the next bull. Fiercer and taller than the first, the second was a half-bred zebu, so huge that even the apathetic audience called to the younger lad to leave him to his elder brother, and not to risk his life.

After the regular passes had been gone through and the banderillas placed, the younger lad advanced, perfectly calm and master of himself. Great drops of sweat hung on his father's forehead, and in his agony of mind his limp quite disappeared, and he stood straight and active, despite his fifty years, as when in his last fight at Seville he had received the wound that ended his career.

Three or four times his son played with the bull, escaping his most furious charges as by a miracle, in even better style than that his elder had displayed. Then fixing his feet firmly, he waited till it lowered its head as it charged home, and with a thrust between the horns, pithed him with a stroke just in the spinal marrow. The enormous animal sank like a ship sinks, slowly, when engulfed between the waves, without a struggle, and it is to be hoped quite painlessly. Flushed with his triumph, the boy advanced, and placed his foot upon the neck of his late adversary, standing a moment, like a bronze statuette, amidst the yelling of the crowd, who now, excited furiously, threw off the cold exterior they had inherited from their Indian ancestors. Their triumph and their father's agony were over for the day, and in the dust behind the barrier, after a long embrace that somehow gave the trio an air as of the statue of Laocoon, they kissed the crucifix, and no doubt gave thanks to their own Christ, he of El Gran Poder, who from his shrine in the Triana shoots out his lips at all the other Christs in Spain.

Mirages

Músicos!

The ancient theatre, in the poorest quarter of the town, half-built of wood and with its seats reached by long, winding passages, was packed from floor to ceiling. The audience sat as closely as sardines in a tin. Women with babies in their arms, their thick and glossy hair as black as jet, their faces powdered white, their ample busts straining their cheap blouses to the bursting-point, laughed with the abandonment of the South at jokes coeval with the fall of man, for it was then he first began to jest to hide his pain.

As they enjoyed the well-seasoned witticisms brought in the dark ages up from Seville to do duty in Madrid, they showed their teeth, so strong and gleaming that they might well have graced a shark. Their husbands, portly as Roman senators, with blue, fresh-shaven cheeks (for it was Sunday), perspired in their best clothes, stiff and uncomfortable. Sallow young men, their agile figures, the heritage of the peninsula, dressed in well-cut but shoddy clothes, pressed up against their sweethearts to enjoy the thrill the world-old wireless telegraph imparts. Girls bold of eye and speech, but marked by nature to become as stout and as sedate as were their mothers, flirted cheap paper fans as they ate toasted groundnuts or sugared almonds and kept a watchful eye for admiration, as no doubt did Eve in Eden, though she had only Adam and the snake on whom to try her wiles. Up in the gallery the "morenos," tightly trousered, their hair plastered with grease tightly down on their heads, roared their applause if any actress showed a little more of herself than was customary in the dance, or lapsed into a salted phrase. Each one of them believed himself born to be the ruin of the whole female sex, only restrained from action by want of the "metallic" and a generous forbearance. The atmosphere was thick with smoke, cheap scent, and sweat. The enormous audience exuded joy, the simple, elemental joy that Southern Europeans have inherited from their Pagan ancestors. Stout women, laughing till they wept, laid their heads on their neighbours' shoulders, who wiped their tears away with flimsy pocket handkerchiefs, and they, rested and comforted, thanked them, as children might thank an uncle or an aunt.

Upon the stage the actors and actresses, all in modern dress, set forth a reproduction of the life of the audience, with all the shifts and difficulties, expedients, and homely situations of a people that rarely knows how to make two ends meet, but manages, even when poorly fed, to take the sun as if it shone for their convenience alone.

In the long intervals between the acts all the male audience smoked in the entrance, discussing the last bull-fight as seriously as Ministers of State discuss a protocol at the League of Nations, and with as much satisfaction to themselves. All reputations in Madrid, from the throne downwards, were torn to pieces. Virtue was non-existent amongst women. All men had their price. Yet when they had belched out all they could invent to blacken everybody's character they did not seem to hold those that they vilified the worse for what they said, for words and feathers the wind wafts away. After the protracted interval, the students of high politics and Tauromaquia regained their seats, struggling through the old-fashioned passages almost as football players struggle through a scrimmage, reserving the last puff of their cigarettes to breathe it out into the theatre like a solfatara. This showed their knowledge of the world and proved that all mankind is born on an equality.

The second act portrayed a scene in the poor quarters of Madrid. Torn curtains hung before the windows. Long strips of paper floated from the flimsy side-scenes that trembled as the actors walked upon the stage. The wires of the electric lights were all exposed; the light itself, uncertain, flickering and bluish, threw a ghastly glare on the performers when it quivered, threatening to go out. At other times it flared, lighted up the orchestra as a naphtha lamp lights up a stall of vegetables. In their half-subterranean den sat the musicians, those outcasts of Melpomene who gain their livelihood by the sweat of their souls if they love, or have loved music, once upon a time. The hebdomadal clean shirt and collar belied the sordidness of their suits, stained and rejuvenated with benzine till they were grey about the seams. Their trousers bagged at the knee with constant sitting at their instruments. Most of them were middle-aged and bald, with the downtrodden air of men destined by nature to be husbands, fathers of a numerous progeny, free citizens, and slaves. Honourable, hard-working men, who without doubt had cherished in their youth high hopes, worshipping their art, for they had all been

272

young, although to look at them it seemed impossible. Tangos and jazz, the Charleston, Machiche, German waltzes, the light vivacious music in which Madrid excels, Pucini *[sic]*, Verdi, and Flamenco, all was one to them, for most of them were real musicians, grounded in their art. Over them presided, with the batuta in his hand, their leader, a stout, bald-headed man of middle age, well-dressed and clean, and with the dominating air without which no chief of an orchestra can succeed.

He loved and bullied those he presided over. They would have followed him into the wild vagaries of Scriabine or Dalmetchikoff or into hell itself if he had waved his baton at their head. Seated in his high chair, a rock between the ocean of the public and the stage, now tapping energetically upon his desk, and again turning to a lagging violin with a stifled oath between his teeth, or in full sail, a smile upon his face when all went well and even the bass drum boomed out its taradiddles in good time, he rubbed his eyes and fixed them on a piece of scenery from which a strip of hanging paper glowed like a fiery snake.

His doubt was soon resolved as a pale-faced and agitated actor, advancing to the footlights, said in a half-choked voice, "A bit of scenery has caught fire. There is no danger, but we must clear the theatre at once." It was enough. With shouts of "Fire! To the doors!" the audience, in an instant, from their attitude of childish joy had become panic-stricken demoniacs with nothing left but a mad striving to escape.

Just as the cattle and wild animals driven before a prairie fire rush wildly on they know not whither, cows furiously horning their calves if they should come between them and the open space that seems the only chance of safety, so did the audience lose all semblance of humanity in their extremity of fear. Strong men trampled pale screaming girls beneath their feet, only to be trampled on in their turn by those behind them jammed tightly in the death-trap of the winding passages. Bravely the impresario standing on the stage and shouting "Calma! Calma! let the women pass out first!" essayed to stay the rush of the bemaddened crowd. Smoke billowed from behind the scenery, and the sound of falling stucco and of wood mingled with splintering glass as lamps and mirrors burst into fiery heat added to the horror of the scene.

Not for a moment did the band stop playing, their leader, pale but resolute, calling out to the men he had so often led and bullied lovingly, "Keep playing, boys, for your dear lives' sakes. Even yet there is a chance to stay the panic if they see that we are calm."

Bravely they stuck to it, attacking all the liveliest music that they knew with the flames always drawing nearer to them. At last, when their efforts had been prolonged to the limit of endurance, the chief of the orchestra, leading the musicians, left the field of battle, still playing, by a side door into the street.

Three still remained, the saxophone, trumpet, and the kettledrum, ridiculous, heroic Berserkers. With the same fury with which the martyrs were possessed, that fury of self-abnegation, unreasoning, sublime, and foolish, that has impelled mankind to its most gallant deeds, the three devoted men brayed out such music as their instruments could furnish, whilst death stole nearer to them.

Scenery, stalls, and balcony were alight. Great beams fell from the roof, the smoke choked those who were not trampled underfoot. Still the three "músicos" kept on at their task. They had done more than it was possible for men to do, and probably not saved a single life by their self-sacrifice, for no one listened to them. Their instruments dropped from their charred hands. Then the flames claimed the humble heroes whilst in the pit of hell the audience struggled for their lives.

Bibi

Oueld-el-Haram, literally son of the illegitimate, but used by Arabs to signify a wild young devil, just as the mediæval Spaniards employed the phrase of "hideputa" in the same sense, Bibi was a true son of Tangier. Born of a good English family in reduced circumstances, he had been duly sent to the Franciscan school, catholic of the catholics. There he imbibed the religion taught in such schools, as well as Spanish, which he spoke with all the idioms of La Tiera[sic] de Maria Santisima, but with the guttural accent of those born in Africa.

His university was the streets of Tangier, dark, winding, dirty and ill-paved, but still a mine of knowledge of the world. In that ill-smelling Alma Mater, he acquired Arabic so perfectly that when dressed as a Moor, the Arabs never doubted that he owed allegiance to Sidi-bou-Arakia, tutelary saint of Tangier.

His swarthy face, loud but euphonious voice, his walk, his perfect knowledge of all native customs, nothing was wanting to confirm them in their belief. English, that should have been his native tongue, he spoke less readily indeed than his two other native tongues, not with a foreign accent, but with an intonation that made it sound like Arabic, heard from a little distance off.

Everyone knew and loved him, from the Sultan to the loafers on the beach. They looked on him, although they knew he was a Roumi, as the next best thing to a Moor.

Still he did not affect the Moor, or wear the Moorish clothes, except upon necessity. Dressed in cord breeches, leather gaiters, a grey flannel jacket and felt hat, riding upon an English saddle, with a snaffle bridle, there was not at first sight much to distinguish him from other Englishmen, who in those days rode every afternoon upon the beach.

Yet, when you looked more closely at him, there was a carelessness about his seat, a recklessness about his riding on rough ground, and the high hand that marks the man who rides as part of his day's job, and not for pleasure or for sport.

The man is not yet born, or perhaps never has been born, of whom it might be said more truly, than of Bibi, that he had a foot in either camp. Perhaps a soul in either heaven, that of Mahomed with its houris, or that of the Nazarene with its celestial choirs, would express more aptly Bibi's character.

Christened most ineptly Edward Pio, after Pope Pio Nono as he used to say, Mohamed would have suited him far better, or perhaps Mohamed-Pio, for all his life, although a Catholic, he was a subcutaneous Moslem in his mentality.

Mohamed as a Christian name has fallen into disuse amongst the creed-conscious Christians of these latter days, although it was once used in Spain, as many an old deed testifies. It would confer at least as much distinction as a knighthood upon one so designated.

From Fez to Mogador, all called him Bibi, a name the Moors had given him when a child.

Without a penny in his purse, but with the care of an old mother and several sisters on his shoulders; without profession or a trade, and with but little education, his life was even more precarious than it would have been to a young Moor. He could not loaf about the "soko" and deal in horses and in mules, dressed in his European clothes. It was not open to him to have taken to himself a wife or two, who could have made a home for him, and worked embroidery for sale to keep him in clean clothes, new yellow slippers, and in the means "to drink the shameful," that is to smoke the haylike native cigarettes. One calling and one only, that of guide, was open to him. Good guides are born, not made. They are the only true descendants of knight-errantry, and though the wildest flight of fancy could not picture Bibi roaming the land to prove the peerless beauty of one Dulcinea, when even Mahomed allowed the faithful four, yet the uncertainty of the life, its ups and downs and its continual journeyings, suited his temperament. Nature had given him a special aptitude for the profession. Ceaseless good humour, indifference to heat and cold, and the capacity to reduce to order a refractory mule, or insolent camp follower, he possessed in a supreme degree. Tall and athletic, he could throw most of the Moors in wrestling, shoot just as well with their long flintlocks as with a fifty-guinea gun from Bond Street, knock down partridges upon the wing with the curved club used by the mountaineers, or ride the "powder play" dressed in the fleecy haik, the blue selham and multitudinous wrappings of an Arab chief. In

276

fact, to see him at his best was when he rode amongst a group of Arabs, yelling and twisting his gun about his head, firing it underneath his horse's neck; then pulling up short, the wind fluttering his burnoose like a swan's angry wing, ride slowly back with the grave air the Moors put on at Powder play of having deserved well of Allah, amidst the shrill cries of the women on the roofs.

Probably he had no politics in the European sense, but in their stead no one was ever more imbued with the sentiment of Oriental democracy, that makes all men in theory, equal under Allah and his vicegerent upon earth, the Caliph of the hour. Bandying jokes with boatmen on the beach, or serving as interpreter to Europeans before the Sultan, he was equally at home. Not in the least abashed by the formalities of the Moorish court, or holding himself superior to the boatmen, except in so far as his personal strength, his quick wits and better education gave him the superiority.

His want of means, and his distaste for formal ways, cut him off somewhat from the society of Europeans. Amongst Mohamedans, no Christian, not even one who spoke their language as did Bibi, could really be received on equal terms. There remained the Jews, far better educated and more civilised than were the Arabs, and easier of access than the Europeans, who in those days were mostly either diplomats or missionaries, with the exception of the Spanish population, all of which was poor and punctuated plentifully with escaped criminals from the convict settlements on the coast. In all these various "couches sociales" Bibi had his entry, and in all was popular. Diplomats laughed at his broken French, though they themselves spoke it with all the accents known from Stockholm to Madrid, accents so marked that a French bride was overheard to say, "Take me, for heaven's sake, to some place where I shall never hear the diplomatic French."

Majestic Arab Kaids, shrouded like mummies in their white fleecy haiks, stroked their beards and put their hands before their mouths, for it is an indecency to laugh out loud, when from the athletic figure in its boots and breeches came the last new obscenity, gleaned at the soko or the port.

Nicholas Moreno, known as El Zurco, who had escaped from Ceuta, where he was purging a misfortune that had occurred to him in Malaga, owing to a rash citizen having transfixed himself upon a knife that Nicholas had drawn to slice a melon, swore by Bibi, and tried to teach him, with but scant success, the creed of international socialism.

Comrade Quintanilla, a barber and an anarchist professed, whose own particular "misfortune" has never been divulged, used to aver with many and ingenious oaths, reflecting on the virtue of the female bourgeoisie, on the tremendous day (*la tremenda*) that Bibi should be spared. Both these two worthies, hard-working, honest men, at least in Tangier, when asked what kept them in the place, after first spitting from the corner of their mouths, explained that what detained them among so many lice-filled rags and so much dirt, was the desire they felt to spread the light and push on progress in the dark places of the earth. Bibi would lead them artfully up to this declaration of their faith, and laugh consumedly, whilst they, serious and slow-witted, to an extent no one but a Southern Spanish socialist workman ever attains to, rebuked his levity.

Years, if they did not bring him more discretion, as in effect they rarely bring to anyone, for qualities both of the body and the mind are with us at our birth, and stay with us up to the grave, yet brought him more responsibilities.

A good son, attending to the wants both of his mother and his sisters, he yet had time to make himself so much endeared, or perhaps necessary, to the Jewish population, that it was hardly possible for him to ride through the Mellah of almost any Moorish town, without a stout, black-eyed daughter of Israel appearing with a baby in her arms, or child trotting by her side, calling out as she held it up, "Shuf Babak," that is, "Behold your Dad." Bibi would check his horse and with an effort to remember if it was Raquel, Estrella or Miriám, address a word or two to her, pat the child on the head, distribute largesse, and ride on, remarking that he was still quite young, for he was well aware that to the young much is forgiven, by themselves. These "children of the air" were generally known as Beni-Bibi, and certainly, if rumour was correct, were in sufficient numbers to form, if not a clan, at least no inconsiderable sept.

Man, it is alleged, is sent into the world to try and leave it better for his transitory passage through the vale of tears, and Bibi most assuredly contributed his obolus towards the amelioration of the race, and what he gave, seldom or never fell upon unfruitful ground. These amatory passages were, so to speak, all *ultra vires*, entailing nothing upon Bibi of a binding nature, and on the woman only the pledges of his transitory affection in the shape of children, which after all they would have had by someone else had he not intervened, for in Morocco parthenogenesis is unlikely to occur.

Those were his halcyon days when young, athletic, a general favourite amongst Mohamedans, Christians and Jews, he was a figure in the strange little world of Tangier, a world and a society that has passed away quite as irrevocably as that seen in Tahiti by Captain Cook, where, as he tells us, he saw the rites of Venus publicly performed at a native wedding, by the happy bride and bridegroom, the older women standing by to show the neophyte how to perform her part. He adds that Mr. Banks (afterwards Sir Joseph, and perhaps reformed) that night slept with the Queen under the cover of a boat.

Tangier, though not so open in its ways as was Tahiti, yet was a divinely beautiful, immoral little place, a miniature Constantinople, with the advantage that the Arabs were a race of gentlemen, a thing no one could place to the credit of the Turks, upon whose heads the Christian bowler sits with so fine a grace. It possessed ministries of all the powers and principalities. All the dried fruits of all the diplomatic corps of Europe were pitchforked by their Chancelleries into a place where they could do the minimum of harm.

In all these ministries Bibi, at times, held various jobs, until at last, to the delight and amazement of everybody, he was appointed British consular agent in Alcázar-el-Kebir. He did not seem unduly puffed up by his promotion, if promotion it could be called, to the rank of British representative. The Moors at once all called him Consú, and as Consú Bibi he administered injustice, seated at the door of an old Moorish house, dressed in a brown jellaba, his bare feet shoved into yellow Moorish slippers, and with a guimbiri upon his knee, on which he twangled with a bit of palmetto leaf to pass away the time. In the historic town, beneath whose walls Don Sebastian escaped from this illusory life into the firmer realms of history, achieving even a further apotheosis into legend, Bibi at last had found an anchorage, and from henceforth began occasionally to ride a mule, not that he found a horse's paces hard, for he remained a first-class rider at a wild boar, but because consular dignity, in such a town as was Alcázar, required it of him. It was not much for such a town to ask. Set in the middle of a vast-extending plain, flanked on one side by the deep rapid Luccos, that takes a horse-shoe bend half round the orange gardens, its flat-roofed houses dazzlingly white, its mosque tower green-tiled and shining as a lizard's back, outside the walls there stood a mountain of manure, fifty or sixty feet in height. Residents referred to it with the just pride a Roman takes in Mount Testaccio, or as an old-time Jew of Prague might feel a sense of personal possession in the great cobweb curtain in the synagogue, reaching from roof to floor. Progress, that car of Juggernaut that sweeps away old-world abuses, to place more modern evils in their stead, laid its fell hand upon Alcázar's dung-heap and the great natural curtain in the synagogue of Prague. Rome still keeps its Testaccio tumulus, but how long it will endure few care to prophesy.

The hours rolled past for Bibi in Alcázar, almost as quietly as for the storks that sat upon their nests, looking out on the world with the calm of philosophers, and with as slight effect upon its destinies or ways.

He still continued to increase the tribe of Beni-Bibi and his own fortunes, almost imperceptibly, buying a garden here and there, starting a corn-mill, and having Moorish partners in what was known as Mohalata, with whom he pastured animals.

This system, now perhaps passed away, consisted in taking a Moorish farmer under protection, giving him English, French or Spanish nationality, to protect him from the extortions of his Kaid. The protected Moor generally gave his European partner some animals — sheep, cows, or horses — as the price of his protection. Bibi used to relate with gusto how, upon one of his journeys to Tangier, he met a Spanish socialist, who had escaped out of some penal settlement upon the coast, tramping along the road. All that kind of man knew Bibi, and as they talked, in answer to a question as to where he was going, the poor, footsore, ragged, half-starving wretch replied: "To Alcázar, Señor, to find a Moor or two whom I can protect." Bibi's own protection was adequate enough, if perhaps bestowed rather too liberally, for all throughout the Gharb it was impossible to stop at any Arab farmer's house without attention being drawn to Bibi's animals. Still in those days "protection," even such protection as the Spanish socialist ambulant might have been able to extend, was valued by the Moors.

On the point of his protected Moors Bibi was a bar of iron. Possibly, now and then the weight of the British lion's paw may have pressed a little heavily upon these proselytes of the gate, but let a Moorish Kaid try and oppress them and Bibi was at once in arms.

Within a day's ride of Alcázar there lived a Moorish Kaid, one El Khalkhali, who trod the faces of the poor. Strong and athletic, black-bearded, insolent and in the fullness of his strength, he ruled the district that he had bought the privilege of ruling and oppressing, from the Sultan, with a rod of iron. Those he suspected to have money, he tortured and imprisoned, lowering them down into a deep grain silo, called a mazmorra, by a rope fixed to a winch worked by a mule. There they remained to putrefy, till they had disgorged the last penny that they had, in darkness, misery and filth. Others he flogged, or maimed, and if they had wives or daughters in the least desirable, he took them, just in the fashion of a patriarch in the Old Testament. He knew one day the Sultan would come down on him, when he thought he had waxed rich enough, and treat him just as he treated his own subjects, but we are all in Allah's hands. To-morrow is another day. The sea takes the swimmer at the last, but though his fate is sure, the swimmer swims on to the end.

This son of a burnt father, in an evil hour, laid hands upon a Mahalat of Bibi's, and was proceeding to force him to disgorge. Word was brought to Alcázar by a youth, who had pulled up his slipper heels, girt himself tightly with a palmetto cord, and with a stick of hard, wild olive in his hand, had run the thirty miles from the Khalkhali's Kasbah, to lay his father's case before the one man on earth who could do aught for him.

"Consú," he said, "Protector of the Poor, it is this wise with my father. The Kaid, son of a mother who never in her life said No, has taken him. He has suffered many stripes, and will be thrown no doubt into the pit to starve. One word he said to me or rather shaped it with his lips, as they were dragging him away, that word was 'Bibi.' So here I am, oh Consú, and I take refuge with you." As he spoke he bent and kissed Bibi on the shoulder, and remained standing, young and brown, a string of camel's hair wound round his head, his sinewy legs left bare by his short brown jellaba, lithe as a panther, and as like the Apollo Belvedere in figure as was the Indian whom the painter called to mind when on the first sight of the famous statue he exclaimed: "By God, a Mohigan!"

Dressed in cord riding breeches, a white silk shirt, brown leggings and with a broad-brimmed grey felt hat upon his head, Bibi sat listening to the messenger without a word, looking exactly like a high-class Moor who had adopted European clothes. When the young man had finished his appeal, Bibi raised his hand. " 'Tis well!" he said. "Go tell your father that tomorrow I will take El Khalkhali by the beard."

Next morning at the first call to prayers, after a cup of coffee and a piece of gritty bread, toasted upon a fire of charcoal, Bibi and a friend set out to beard the lion in his den. Mounted upon an iron-grey given to him by a well-known cattle-stealer, his friend upon a cream-colour, they left the town, their horses snorting and plunging in the keen morning air. The gate-ward, with the city keys, lighting a pipe of kief at a hot charcoal cinder, stood ready to unbar, just as they reached the walls.

The iron-grey reared up at the delay, and as they passed beneath the arch, the rider's head just missed the masonry. Outside, after a plunge or two on the slippery stones, both horses came back to their riders' hands, and struck into a lope. They passed by rows of kneeling camels, gurgling and evil-smelling, with their high saddles covered by pieces of rough matting. Both horses shied violently and made as wide a circuit as they could to avoid the hated animals. Mules, donkeys, and a stream of white-clad women bending under great loads of brushwood for the bakers' ovens, were coming into town. The sun was rising like a ball of fire. A thin white mist steamed from the plain, and in the distance Gibel Zarzar stood up like an island, blue and mysterious. Two or three Arabs of the Holot tribe, dressed in white rags, mounted upon their wiry little horses, that they rode always on pack saddles . . . "the Holot upon his Kidar" (pony) was a local saying in the Gharb, looked like fishing boats at sea, mere dots upon the plain.

Bibi, with a glance at his friend, shouted Ya Allah, and gave his horse the rein. Half-way across the ten-mile plain, they passed the suppliant messenger, swinging along at the peculiar half-walk, half jog-trot of the Arab on the road. The horses now had slowed down and, for a mile or two, the active youth kept up with them, holding occasionally to Bibi's stirrup leather.

They pushed on steadily and reached the hills. Upon the stony paths the young man overtook and passed them, for no horse upon such roads can keep up with a mountaineer on foot.

About midday they reached the Kasbah of the Kaid. Upon some level ground the little castle stood. Its crenellated walls and gateway, with its horseshoe arch, gave it a mediæval air. Around the gate lounged several followers of the great man, ragged and villainous. Bibi rode through the arch, unchallenged, for Consú Bibi was well known to everybody, and the Kaid's tribesmen probably supposed that he had come upon a friendly visit to their lord. In an inner courtyard the Kaid's horses stood tethered by their feet to pegs in the hard ground. Greys, chestnuts, cream-colours, all with their forelocks falling to their nostrils, their manes flowing to their knees, and their tails sweeping to the ground, they looked as if they had stepped out of a picture of Algerian life, by Fromentin. On all their backs you could have counted money, easily. A black slave, issuing from the door, took both the horses, and another, after some minutes' waiting, ushered Bibi and his friend into the presence of the Kaid. In a room opening upon a little garden where grew mint, rosemary, Marvel of Peru and rue, mandarin orange trees and apricots, the whole pervaded by a murmuring of water that ran in little stuccoed rills, the Kaid received his guests.

Dressed in a fleecy haik, that allowed the plum-coloured selham that he wore underneath to show a little, his hood thrown back and his black beard descending on his chest — "Bibi," he said, "what good wind brings you to my house?" As he stretched out his hand Bibi pretended not to see it, and the two stood for a moment looking into one another's eyes. Both were sons of the country, and knew one another, and the Kaid divined at once why Bibi had come to visit him. Clapping his hands he called for tea, and with a gesture, invited Bibi and his friend to take their seats upon a pile of cushions laid upon the floor.

Two eight-day German clocks, neither of them going, stood in a corner of the room. Six or eight looking-glasses made by the Jews of Fez, their frames fantastically twisted, like the columns on a Churriguerra altar, their glasses dusty-looking, and so contrived as to distort anyone's face who looked into them, adorned the walls. All round the room ran a silk dado about five feet high, worked in a succession of horseshoe arches, and called a Haiti, and in the middle of the floor there smoked a Russian samovar. The Kaid himself made tea, punctiliously, after the fashion of the Moors, in a small pewter dome-shaped teapot, on a brass tray, probably made in Birmingham, but with texts from the Koran superimposed by a skilful brass-worker in Fez. He sipped the tea, having put into it fragments of sugar chopped from a sugar-loaf, garnishing the whole with sweetly-smelling sprigs of mint.

All the time that the Kaid was washing his hands, for he had called for water before commencing operations and had it poured upon them by a black slave girl, Bibi, although appearing unconcerned and careless, watched him as a cat watches at a mouse-hole, so that he should not slip into the tea anything poisonous. The Kaid knew well that he was watched, and smiled on Bibi and his friend, as if he had no greater pleasure in the world than to make tea for the two unbelievers, who no doubt in his heart he consigned to Jehanum, after defiling all the females of their family. Like fencers feeling for the blade, Bibi and El Khalkhali, for at least an hour, beat round the bush, talking of anything, the price of grain, horses, El Raisuli, who at that time was rising into power, or of

El Roghi, a self-elected prophet, who had preached a sort of unofficial Jehad against the Sultan, riding upon an ass.

Long did they talk, consuming innumerable cups of tea, before they came to grips. Outside the camels gurgled, horses occasionally screamed shrilly, and the frogs raised their tinkling melopée. The night wore on, and after several questions and retorts in rapid Arabic, the two men rose, and in an instant Bibi had the Kaid by the beard, who in his turn gripped Bibi by the throat. Both were unarmed, and both were strong athletic men in the prime of their strength, and both unused to fists. Grappling and swaying to and fro, they fell upon the ground, writhing like snakes to get the upper hand. At last by mutual consent they loosed their hold of one another, and rising, in a moment ashamed of their violence, sat down again before the tea-board, panting, but with their fury spent. They looked at one another with the half admiration of men who had proved each other's strength, and the Kaid exclaimed: "By Allah, Bibi, thou art a man, and should be of the faith." Bibi's companion, the one man armed, had watched the struggle with his revolver in his hand, as befits a commentator on such occasions. "Put up your pistol," Bibi whispered, "the Kaid had but to clap his hands, and we were both dead men."

All night they sat, dozing at intervals, talking and drinking tea, and eyeing each other not unsympathetically.

The morning call to prayers woke them up, contrite and rather shame-faced, but almost friends. After a basin of Harira, the thin soup Moors breakfast on, a slave girl poured warm water on their hands, and the Kaid, beckoning with his hand, brought up the horses.

Bibi sprang to the saddle with a bound. El Khalkhali waved him a farewell. Without a word they struck into the plain, just as the rising sun fell on the castle walls, turning them a light rose-pink.

The storks began to chatter on their nests, the world woke up, as it must have done in Eden, silent and beautiful. A mirage hung over the distant palm-trees, midway between the earth and sky, half shrouded in the mist. "Son of a veilless, shameless mother, Kaid El Khalkhali," Bibi said, "but he will never dare to harm my man." Turning round in the saddle he shouted: "Ya Allah," and as he spoke he raised his hand, and touched the cattle-stealer's dark grey stallion lightly with the spur.

The Dream of the Magi

At Como, in the old church of Sant' Abbondio, there is a fourteenth-century picture that the guide-book describes as an unusual subject, showing the Magi in their beds. Painters have portrayed them kneeling in adoration before the Babe of Bethlehem, with ox and ass looking benignly down in equal adoration from their stalls. Outside their horses wait, held by their attendants, horses such as the painters of the Ferrara school have dreamed of, green, yellow and a rich purple-brown not to be equalled, even upon the southern Pampas or in Mexico, where a herd of half-wild horses reflects as many colours as a tulip bed.

Painters have limned the Three Wise Men as they arrived at Bethlehem; upon the road: whilst gazing silently upon the Babe in attitudes of adoration and of ecstasy.

Milton has immortalised them, startled. The gospels have set forth their story for the whole world to love, to make their own, and for the reasoning to still their reason and believe. In the presentments of the painters the black king always has a place to which perhaps he has as little title as the others have to wisdom, although it is the highest wisdom in a king to take his horse and follow where any star doth lead. Pity so few of them have profited by the example of their three predecessors in their guild!

Many have followed the Three Kings upon the road; have seen them talking to the shepherds as they watched their flocks; been with them when they offered up their myrrh and frankincense; have seen them kneel as Mary held the Babe upon her lap, whilst worthy Joseph, with his enigmatic smile of semi-ownership, looked on half-doubtingly, but with an air as if he strove to put the best construction on the case.

Children have marvelled and wise men have gone down upon their knees in sheer delight at the compelling beauty of the tale, and painters have exhausted all their art upon it, so that it has become the best known scene in all the great romance of Christendom. It was reserved for a poor quattrocentista, little skilled in the art that he professed, alone of painters, to depict the Three Wise Men in bed.

They sleep, tucked up in low, substantial-looking beds, all with their crowns upon their heads, as was the wont of kings. Upon the sheets their beards are spread, not curled, but waved like sticks of barley-sugar, their features noble, their noses seemly, and to speak sooth, the three are just as much alike as if they had been run out of one mould. Unluckily, for it shows a lack of imagination, none of the three is black.

A more imaginative painter would have been quick to see that by the introduction of a jet-black king, such a one as figures in so many pictures, he would have secured a most arresting contrast. Nothing was further from his thoughts. He did not think in terms of art, but only those of faith. In a high-panelled chamber on their three beds, so close beside each other that thought transference must have been quite an easy matter, the Three Kings slumber.

At the foot of the middle bed there lies a little white-and-yellow dog. He, too, is wrapt in sleep; but the angel standing at the door, slight, tall and elegant, with his sheeny wings folded about him like a mantle, his yellow hair curled as it had been laid in press, takes no thought of the dog. His business lies with the sleepers in the three comfortable beds. To inspire them and to set their brains a-working, he shot down through the empyrean, ignoring all the laws of gravitation, steering himself by faith, the best of compasses known to aerial navigators, and now stands holding the door slightly ajar, and looking with compunction on the sleepers whose slumbers he had come to impregnate with the most wondrous dream that ever entered into the brain of man. Outside, no doubt, the still Italian night was wrapped in the blue mantle of the sky, ablaze with myriads of stars. Fireflies flashed in the bushes and tall grasses, points of electric light, when electricity lay like a chrysalis in amber, waiting to be rubbed into activity, or showed itself but only in the storm. The waters of the lake plashed languorously against the pebbly beaches, and the cicalas raised their shrill hymns of praise to Pan, for then nothing was known of the great legend that has since filled the world. Even the sleepers were unconscious as the angel stood a-watching them. He raised his hand, and in the middle of the slumbering trinity King Gaspar stirred and murmured. Then his thoughts passed to the brains of his two fellow-kings, and all their minds were focused into one.

"We must arise," said Melchior. "In Bethlehem of Judaea a wondrous thing will come to pass."

"Tell us of it," his fellows said, and in their sleep their faces twitched convulsively although their eyes were closed. So still they lay beneath the blankets and the sheets, with their heads resting on their pillows, their crowns in equilibrium and not a hair of their great beards awry, that they seemed made of wax.

Melchior once again took up his tale, and as he spoke, the angel at the door threw back his wings as a man tosses back a cloak, and stood revealed all shimmering, a celestial dragon-fly.

"The world is full of wickedness," the Magus said in a strange voice that seemed to come out of a cavern, but soon died away into a murmur that penetrated to the souls of his two partners in the triple dream.

"The world has grown so evil that it must be destroyed, burned up with fire, the dreadful fiat has gone forth, unless a babe be born from a pure virgin, to take upon himself the sins of all mankind and suffer on the cross. In Bethlehem a virgin has conceived of the Holy Spirit, and even now awaits the birth of the Redeemer, in a stable, where she sits amongst the kindly beasts, whose healing breath makes a perpetual incense, and who, when night has fallen, and all the sons of men are wrapped in sleep, adore her on their knees.

"Arise, arise, and let us take the road."

Swiftly and noiselessly the Three Kings arose to make their preparations, and as they put on royal robes, a wondrous change was wrought upon the mediæval building where they slept. The dark and massive walls grew dazzlingly white. The high-pitched Gothic roof became an Oriental azotea guarded with flame-shaped battlements. The sculptured doorway was altered to a horseshoe arch, with a great door of palm wood studded with nails, and in the middle hung a knocker fashioned like a ring. The Italian windows disappeared and were replaced by little slits, and in the middle of the house appeared a patio, planted with basil, marjoram and thyme, with sweet geranium, arums and pale-coloured pinks, such as all Easterns love.

A minaret rose from the ground, and, as the Magi robed themselves in trailing Oriental clothes, the call to prayer rang out in the prolonged and guttural notes of the muezzin. Outside the vegetation, that had been oaks and ashes, with Italian elms, was changed to palms, the willow-bushes now were suddra or camel-thorn, and the sweet grass set with a myriad daisies, gentians and fumitory, turned hard and wiry, and the black earth to sand.

But a more wondrous transformation was to be seen in Balthazar, who had become a Moor.

About the gates of the Oriental kasbah sat a horde of beggars, who did not beg with prayers and supplications as they had done before the house in which the Three Kings had lain sleeping in their beds; but murmuring "One God," pointed a finger to the sky.

Long strings of camels passed like ships across the sand, with the conductors perched on little asses, against whose sides their naked heels drummed ceaselessly.

The sun beat down like fire, and out upon the plain great pools of water seemed to lie, that mocked the traveller, ever retreating further off on his advance.

When all was ready and a long train of mules was packed with myrrh and cassia, aloes and frankincense, with sweetly scented gums from Sanaar, amber from the Tyrian coast, and vessels wrought of finest gold from Samarcand, spices and aromatic woods to burn as perfumes, the Magi signed to their attendants to bring up their horses to the mounting-block.

Rearing and plunging, neighing shrilly, attended by black slaves, the horses were led out.

Their tails were long and would have swept the ground had they not been gathered up into a knot below their quarters and plaited carefully. Their manes hung down and almost reached their knees, and their long forelocks nearly concealed their eyes, giving them an air of wildness that their real gentleness belied. Pale green, light canary and a rich plum-coloured brown, they were indeed fit steeds for Eastern kings to ride, in dreams.

Their high-peaked saddles were of richest silk with seven saddle-cloths, the sacramental number without which no horse's back is safe from galls, or rider's life secure from the grave that is ever open for the horseman. Their heavy Arab stirrups were of gold. The reins were long, made of raw silk through which was run gold-twisted thread, and would have touched the ground had not the Magi held them high after the Eastern fashion, throwing the ends over their left shoulders to keep them from the mud.

Their bits were silver, and their broad breastplates set with precious stones, whilst over every horse's eyes dangled a fringe of silk that mingled with his mane. Melchior and Gaspar mounted slowly and carefully as befitted their estate.

Their servants tastefully arranged their clothes, throwing their upper garments back so as to display their snowy under-linen and their fine supple boots of perfumed leather made in Kordofan.

Balthazar chose the green courser that stood fidgeting and snorting beside the mounting-block from which his fellows had got on. Murmuring, "In the name of God," he took up his reins, and wheeling round the horse mounted him in one motion, just as a bird takes wing. He felt his mouth and touched him with the spur, and then with a wild cry put him at once into a gallop, checked him and made him rear and plunge and then circling round like a hawk, dashed back again. Right at the mounting-block he pulled him up and stood just for an instant turned to stone, the rider's white teeth glistening and his horse breathing fire. The women on the castle roof raised a shrill cry of joy. His staid companions looked at him half with indulgence, half with approbation, and the cavalcade set out. The camels and pack mules carrying the precious gifts and the provisions, with the tents of the Three Kings, went first, the muleteers perched high between the packs, the camel-drivers trudging behind the prediluvian-looking beasts, each carrying a cudgel of wild olive wood. The retinues of the Three Kings came next all fully armed with bows and arrows, and with spears.

Lastly the kings themselves, fifty to a hundred paces in the rear to avoid the dust, and as they rode they chatted with the soothsayer, for, as is known to all, no expedition of the kind ever set out without a skilled astrologer, one able to cast horoscopes, foretell eclipses and to reveal the stars.

By this time the kings' chargers had all settled down into a slow and easy amble, so level that they could have held a glass of water and never spilled a drop.

Much did the soothsayer discourse upon the stars, telling about Sohail, upon which hangs the destiny of the whole Arab race; of Alcor, Aldebaran and Algol he had much lore, explaining how they got their names, their influence on mankind, and on each other; but most of all he dwelt upon a wondrous star, bright as a planet, but three times as large. He thought that it had great significance, for it appeared to stand fixed in the sky just above Bethlehem.

As the kings listened, leaning back against the cantles of their saddles, for now the sun had fully risen and his rays poured down like molten lead upon them, they all agreed that what the soothsayer had said appeared most reasonable. That stars are messengers of heaven was a fact that they were well aware of, and what more likely than that an all-wise Power having determined to despatch a saviour to the world, should fix a star above the place where the redeemer should be born to guide men on their way.

When they had heard enough of perihelions and of parallaxes, and the soothsayer, bending down to his saddle-bow, had taken leave of them and joined their other followers, a silence fell upon the kings. The muleteers and camel-drivers, who had at first sung ceaselessly, in a high-pitched key, interminable falsetto songs, interspersed now and then with jokes and laughter and curses when a mule stumbled or lagged behind, or if a pack had shifted, now all were silent as they plodded on, their heads covered up in their hoods, fanning away the flies with a dry palm leaf or a bunch of ostrich feathers. Nothing was heard except the muffled footfalls of the animals, jingling of bits, or the snorting of the kings' destriers, as they jogged quietly along. Brown lizards ran amongst the heated stones, or sat just at the entrance of their holes, their beady eyes sparkling like jewels in the sun. The shadow of an eagle that soared over them was outlined on the sand, and now and then a battlemented tower grew up before them, waxed, waned and disappeared as they approached, but never reached it, just as a man passes his life pursuing happiness, that ever flits before his eyes.

At last in the far distance, standing up starkly as a lighthouse stands up from the sea, appeared some palm-trees and a faint line of vegetation, showing the course of a small river, or at the least a group of wells.

Long did the travellers ride towards it, till about an hour before high noon they reached a small oasis, and dismounting from their beasts, sat down to rest a little and to enjoy the shadow of the trees. In haste their followers set up a shelter and the Three Kings entered it silently, dripping with perspiration, and their slaves, pulling off their riding-boots, kneaded their knees and thighs, for the long ride, perched on their high saddles, had cramped them sorely, as it does every Arab horseman the first day upon the road.

No word they spoke until a slave appeared with water in a brass vessel to pour upon their hands.

"Travel is hell to him who rides," said Melchior, as if, from the stores of wisdom that he had accumulated, he was enunciating a great truth. "It is so," said King Gaspar as he assented gravely; but King Balthazar, the youngest, as he was tallest of the three, said smilingly, "What then must travel be to those who go afoot?" The other kings again assented; and stretching their raxed limbs, drew them up decently beneath them as befits a man of breeding, and once again all three were silent, as they sat resting in the shade.

The muleteers unpacked the baggage animals and turned them loose to feed upon the grass that grew beside the stream. The horses of the kings and their chief followers were fastened by their feet to a long rope of camel's hair stretched between iron pegs, and with their bits hung to their saddle-bows devoured their provender. The little stream that in the winter ran between the date palms, had ceased to flow, and all the water was collected into pools, stagnant and nauseous, in which occasionally a tortoise put up his head for air, and then sank out of sight again in the thick liquid slime. Two or three vultures sat upon the palm-trees, and spread their wings out in the sun with a harsh grating sound.

Some bitter colocynths and a few stunted oleanders was the only vegetation of the oasis — that with its scanty grass and sun-dried palm-trees yet in that desert of grey rocks and sand appeared a paradise.

The star-led kings after a frugal meal of dates and bread, washed down with water from the skins the camels carried, passed the hot hours in sleep, or dozing listened to the quavering music that a lute-player plucked from a rough instrument with a frond of a palmetto leaf.

At the fourth hour all was astir again, and the camp followers packed the baggage animals. When all was ready and the little shelter tents pulled down and stowed upon the mules, once more they took the road.

It led across the plain, well marked by bleaching bones of mules and camels that had fallen by the way. In the far distance ran a line of hills that the conductor of the caravan said they could reach by sundown if they pushed on steadily.

As they emerged once more into the track the kings turned in their saddles and gave a last look at the little clump of palms that they would see no more. The declining sun had moved away from it, leaving it bathed in shadow, looking more green and more refreshing than in the noontide glare.

King Gaspar waved his hand, and turning to his friends said, "By Ashtaroth, it is the very image and epitome of a man's pilgrimage on earth. We are here to-day, to-morrow we may have left the world, as we left this oasis. Just as we go we seem to love that which we leave, better than ever, and to appreciate its full significance. Farewell, oasis, farewell to thy shade."

His two companions looked once more at the green island in the sand, and they too said "Farewell."

They reached the line of hills and finding grass and water for their beasts, camped there and passed the night.

Long did they lie awake after their evening meal, reclining on their carpets, talking about their journey, and listening earnestly when from the distance came the cry of a wild beast, with their hands upon their spears.

Thus did they journey on for several days, enduring noon-tide heat, the sharp chill of the desert morning air, and the dull ache between the shoulders, that makes a long day's ride still longer, as the slow hours pass by.

The star loomed ever brighter, and their way now lay through villages with cultivated fields, and now and then small open plains, on which fed sheep, flocks of brown goats guarded by boys who whiled away the time by playing fitful little airs upon a reed, and troops of camels that browsed upon the thorns.

At last, at nightfall after a weary day upon the road, they reached a little town. It lay beneath them as they camped upon a plain on which some shepherds, seated on the ground, watched their sheep penned in a shelter made of camel-thorns, all whitened by the sun.

"See," said the soothsayer, as they lighted off their beasts, "the star is stationary."

It stood indeed fixed in the heavens and its pale rays shone down, illuminating the white houses of the town with their effulgency.

Now the Three Kings were aware their pilgrimage was over, and on the morrow's morn they could present their precious gifts to the Child born of a pure virgin, who should redeem mankind.

All through the night there was rejoicing in their camp, the horses had a double feed of barley, their manes and tails were plaited, stirrups and bits were burnished, and all the company, even the black slaves, got out rich dresses, and then sat down to meat like a great company of brethren, in the tent of the Three Kings.

Night fell at once, no twilight intervening. The stars shone out and the moon bathed the landscape, casting long shadows on the plain, making a standing figure of a shepherd leaning on his crook, huge as a tree, and the tall canes beside the little pool stand up like lances, tipped with silver in its rays.

Up from the town of Bethlehem, that lay as if cut out of cardboard in the pale moonlight, its row of flat-roofed houses looking like gigantic steps against the hill, there came the ceaseless barking of the dogs, and an occasional wild cry. The notes of a soul-piercing Arab song, prolonged and quavering, the intervals so strange and fitful that it seemed impossible that it could have proceeded from a human throat, were heard occasionally, blending harmoniously with the metallic croaking of the frogs from the still, reed-encircled pool. Then all was silent and night descended on the world as it seemed for the first time since it was instituted.

Much did the kings discourse about their journey: upon the presentation that would take place next day, and much upon the instability of all things human, interspersed with wise saws and proverbs, that they enunciated sententiously, not in the light of sayings, but as if they had been personal experiences of the narrator's life.

Dawn found them seated cross-legged at the entrance of the tent, still talking gravely, whilst all around them their slaves and followers were sleeping with their heads on the pack-saddles of the mules. The horses dozed at their picket ropes, resting a leg, and with one ear pricked forward, the other backward, watchful though somnolent.

The tent and tent ropes all dripped water, for a heavy dew had wetted everything, and by the sheep pen drops glistened on the fleeces of the sheep, and as the sun rose in the east, the great effulgent star appeared to leave the heavens as if under protest, though it knew that its task was over and its duty was performed. They mounted early, dressed in their best robes, and followed by their men leading the animals that bore the precious gifts, they took their way into the town.

Little they said to one another, and even Balthazar rode silently. Their very horses ambled soberly, and as they entered the first sandy street they stopped a passer-by, asking him to direct them to the inn where one called Joseph, a carpenter just come up from Nazareth, had alighted with his wife.

"I know him," said the man, "not a bad joiner, but often out of work, for he neglects his shop occasionally, and sits dreaming in the shade. He married late in life, as I have heard, a woman younger than himself, and beautiful, so beautiful that, as we say, the sheep stop grazing to admire her as she walks across the fields. The neighbours talk, but then so do all neighbours in every quarter of the world, you cannot stop men's tongues . . . . Pardon me, Lords, my own wags on a little over-fast . . . you will find the house beyond the street where men sell leather. Turn to the left, before you reach the market, just at the place where scribes sit writing for the silly country people."

Gravely the kings, when they had thanked him and signed to a follower to give him his reward, rode on, and following his directions, the cavalcade wound through the narrow streets, the people crowding to their doors to see them pass, to wonder and admire.

It was about the third hour of the day when they arrived before the caravanserai and found it full of travellers, but none could give them any tidings of the carpenter.

They turned to go, and in a passage leading to a stable they saw a group of shepherds, some kneeling, others leaning on their crooks, their water-gourds hanging from their shoulders by twisted cords of green palmetto leaves, gazing in ecstasy. The kings alighted, and beckoning to their men, bade them bring forth the precious gifts that they had brought with them, the myrrh, the aloes and the frankincense, and the wrought vessels of fine gold.

In slow procession they advanced, and in a manger wrapped in swaddling clothes they saw a child, that lay as in a cradle, bathed in the breath of oxen and of asses that looked gravely down upon him with their dark lustrous eyes.

As the Three Kings advanced bearing their gifts, his mother, reaching out her arms, took up the babe and placed him on her knee. He laughed and clapped his hands at the three strangers, and upon his mother's face there came a look, half of just pride at the birth of a man-child, and half of sorrow as she thought upon his lot as the redeemer of mankind. Her face was beautiful and calm, her dress that of a Galilean country-woman, and seated on a stool she gazed at the Three Kings with the same quiet air of resignation that the adoring beasts had looked upon the child.

Serious and grave beyond his little span of days, he held his tiny hands towards the kings, and in his large dark eyes there was a look as if the shadow of the cross had fallen on them already and chilled their gaiety.

A venerable old man, white-bearded but still hale, sat in a corner of the stable, now and then stroking the noses of the beasts as if he felt that they and he had more in common with each other than with the other actors in the scene.

The kings advanced and, falling on their knees, adored and worshipped, and then, rising to their feet, rendered their precious gifts.

Melchior, the King of Nubia, gave the rich vessels of wrought gold: gold is for royalty.

Balthazar, King of Chaldea, presented frankincense, and Gaspar, King of Tarshish, offered myrrh, saying, "Myrrh is for death, but in his death this child shall triumph over death, so I present the myrrh."

Long did they gaze, until at last their eyes grew dim with gazing, and by degrees the stable, with all its occupants, gradually disappeared. Then they themselves, their horses and their men were dissolved into nothingness, just as the frost upon a window-pane blurs and then slowly vanishes under the magic of the sun.

All through the night the angel watched the sleeping kings, smiling occasionally as they stirred in their slumbers, and the little white-and-yellow dog whined and barked in a muffled key, as if it too were on the road and saw the passers-by, and the strange incidents of its masters' pilgrimage.

Gradually a faint flush crept up across the sky, announcing the first streaks of dawn, when dreams are ending and when angels must return to the place appointed for them.

The three crowned sleepers' faces took on the placid air as of a dreamless slumber, and then the angel gently closed the door.

A soft, low, swishing sound, as of the waves that kiss the coral reef of an atoll in the Pacific, was wafted back into the chamber where the kings lay sleeping, as he took flight towards the sky.

The Magi still sleep on in Sant' Abbondio, just as the painter limned them five hundred years ago.

They have had their dream:

Gaspar and Melchior and Balthazar.

Mirages

Up Stage

An iron railing with a locked gate surrounds a lonely grave, on the lee side of a little church upon a rocky promontory jutting out to sea in a green island in the Firth of Clyde. There is no churchyard where the dead stretched out in scores, so to speak, keep each other company. I like to fancy that in the long nights of winter, they somehow are a consolation to each other, as they lie enduring rain, frost, snow, and the fierce north wind's blasts, the answering owls chanting their nightly threnody.

No one knows anything of the solitary dead, except his name — Reginald Montague — cut on the headstone, with the date 1844. A text by some friend, wife, mistress, or mother, to serve perhaps as passport to eternal bliss, or perhaps merely a last pathetic gesture of affection, is cut below the name.

Local tradition has it that the lonely tenant of the plot of ground, in mortmain, who for so many years has lain beneath the well-worn turf, on which reposes, under a glass case, a white marble wreath of roses, was an actor.

No one knows any more of the alleged Thespian.

A bush of fuchsia grows at the corner of the little iron corral that guards the grave, in which the actor lies, waiting the call-boy to summon him. Across a whitely gravelled path, where after weekly service, the faithful daunder for a few minutes, of what in other parishes would be the clash o' the kirkyard, sappier and more refreshing to the soul than all the sermons in the world, there is a wilderness of wiry grass, flecked here and there with tormentil and eyebright, and engayed by harebells; menacing fronds of bracken threaten to invade and overwhelm the little paradise. Two or three rowan trees, ragged and stunted by the blast, stand round the ruins of a deserted salt pan, hard by the church. Ivy has covered the soft red stone, biting into it, as the lianas bite into the bark of some great ceiba in the tropics, giving the mouldering stones an air, as of a ruined fort.

The rocks upon the promontory are carpeted with dulse, ware and sea tangle, whose tendrils float in the tide, coiling and recoiling like water snakes. Seals haunt the rocks, their round and human-looking heads bobbing up in the water as they utter a sharp bark, before they disappear into the depths.

The nightly owls, the seals, the lonely church, the wind-wasted trees, the moaning of the sea, the harsh cries of sea-gulls and the honk-honk of the wild geese as they fly southward in a wedge, on winter nights, set the stage fittingly for the sleeper who no more shall tread the boards. Why he was buried in the unconsecrated ground, outside the church, what made him lay his bones beside a fane whose worshippers, Presbyterians of the strictest sect, who looked most likely on his art with contumely, holding it as a wile of Satan to entrap men's souls, no one remains to tell.

Who raised the well-wrought iron railing round the grave, planted the luxuriant fuchsia, and placed the marble wreath, as if they knew, when they had passed away, it would remain to mourn both for the sleeper and themselves, there is no record of them.

Almost a hundred years have passed since he was laid to rest. Was it a mother, who came weeping to the grave, who placed the wreath, emblem of sempiternal sorrow, upon it? Perhaps an actress of the company, mincing along in the full skirt of 1848, lace mittens on her hands, upon her feet low shoes with ribbons curling up her stockings, like sandals, or as she might have said, a Greek cothernus, a curtained bonnet on her head, tied underneath the chin with a silk ribbon, and carrying in her hand a much flounced parasol, paid for the everlasting roses from her scant salary.

She may have had, what were called love passages in those days, with the member of the company who now was "resting," a rest that no advertisement in the *Era* will break with news of an engagement.

Maybe a comrade, who had acted, gambled and drunk with him, put up the railing and the headstone, saying, "Poor Reggie was a damned good fellow, and should not be forgotten, like a dog, if he could help it."

But then, the wreath of roses and the text! Only a woman who had loved him could have thought of such a grave, so quiet, so romantic, and so like the resting-place the man would have desired.

He may himself have chosen his own resting- place; but what the devil brought him to the Isle of Bute?

There could have been no theatre in Rothesay in 1844, or if one had existed, it must have been a place where only barn-stormers strutted their little hour, and, the performance over, counted their exiguous copper gains. 'Tis true that Edmund Kean once owned a villa in the middle of the green Thule, by the borders of a lake. The unknown actor may have been a member of his company. Long Wolf sleeps in the Brompton Cemetery, with his totem sculptured on his headstone, and such another wreath of artificial roses in a cracked glass case upon his grave, placed there by Colonel Cody, ere he too passed to the happy hunting grounds.

Blondin, his tight-rope slackened and his balancing pole long ago chopped up for firewood, though once so certain of his equilibrium in mid-air, had found an even firmer footing in a London cemetery.

Reginald Montague, the name sounds somehow as if he had been, as goes the Spanish phrase, the son of somebody, and whosoever paid for the headstone and the grave, and chose the spot, so well selected, with a southern aspect, with the waves always singing throbbing lullabies, must certainly have been a person of no ordinary taste.

After a life of grease-paint, make-up, the petty jealousies and feuds of Thespian life, the triumphs, failures, and the constant doubt, whether or not a "ghost would walk" on Saturday, all the discomforts of a strolling actor's life, are done with, and he sleeps in a grave fitting for any artist, poet, man of letters, or anyone who in his life has been dependent on a fickle public, but now has reached his port.

Let him sleep on, the fuchsia every spring will put on its glad livery of green, and hang its scarlet flesh-like petals over the iron railings, where he lies. The wind-scarred trees will rustle in the breeze, the wavelets tinkle on the beach, and in the winter out on the rocks the seals will lie and sun themselves upon the dulse. At night the owls will call to one another, with their long quivering Towhit Tohoo, as if they asked a question that required no answer, and the stage still waits.

Mirages

Inmarcesible

The piety of Harriet Meyer, a Jewish lady of Algoa Bay, has raised a monument to all the horses killed in the Boer War. No general, colonel, hard-riding captain, or any one of all the thousands whom these horses carried, in thirst, in hunger, wounded and left to die, has had a thought so generous.

No one, except this Jewish lady. She alone remembered man's partners in every war, from the immortal partnership of Alexander and Bucephalus, down to the present day.

The wind-swept, sun-scorched town, with gardens full of canas, bright as a flock of Brazilian macaws, its streets, planted with jacarandas and flamboyant trees, its sandy suburbs full of oleanders, holds the one monument raised to the memory of horses killed in war. Generals who strutted their brief hour, colonels who clinked their spurs, captains who trailed their sabre scabbards on the stones, brave men whose bones have mouldered, whose fame is long o'er dusted, and whose deeds have been eclipsed by others equally forgotten, have their monuments, in stone, in marble, and in bronze. Peace to their memory, and honour to their deeds; but it was surely fitting that their fellow-heroes should not be forgotten, for they shared all the dangers and suffering. Without them, what a poor figure a hero's statue would present!

The monument stands in the middle of an open space, where four streets cross, so wide, they must have been laid out to give a bullock cart with sixteen yoke of oxen room to turn.

A thirsty horse lowers his head towards a bucket that a trooper, in a spiked helmet, spurred, belted, buckled, gaitered, in the style of thirty years ago, supports upon his knee. On the near side dangles a sword, slung no doubt after long thought, in the war office, in the most inconvenient way that it is possible to sling a sword upon a horse. No strap or buckle of the saddle, but is rendered faithfully, the very nails upon the trooper's shoes, as he kneels holding up the bucket, are as distinct as is the rim of dirt under the nails of many of the personages Holbein, who was a realist of realists, has made more real for us than are thousands of our fellow-citizens, whom we can tell apart but by the buttons of their coats, their hats, their hosen, and the other pieces of their indumentary.

Time, or the marauding street boy, has broken off a stirrup, for I can hardly think the conscientious artist who omitted no one tittle of the saddle-gear, could have soared up to such a height as to turn out a broken stirrup of his own free will.

Still, the whole monument achieves its purpose, as well as if Lycippus had carved it in white Parian. To anybody cursed with imagination, the gift that makes life sometimes almost unbearable, it is infinitely sad.

One sees the thousands upon thousands of bewildered creatures torn from their stables, and their surroundings so dear to horses, from their pampas, prairies, their regimental life, their lush, green fields, their heaths, their upland pasturage, their hunting stables, with their regular hours of feeding, after a terrifying voyage, mute sufferers, enduring agony, unable to be sick, and landed in a country of which the very grass was unfamiliar to them, the water strange, for a horse savours water as keenly as a connoisseur of vintages savours his wine.

Fancy their despair, fastened in horse lines in the scorching sun, and in the chill of early morning, just as alone amongst the crowd of strangers as is a man alone amongst the unfriendly faces of a crowd in a strange city, where he has no friends. Australians, Argentines, Hungarians, French, English, Canadian, Arabs and thoroughbreds, with Irish Hunters, Pecherons [sic = Percherons], all brought together for a common holocaust. Victims about to sacrifice their lives, for reasons incomprehensible to their simple brains. For them no glory, no ideas of patriotism, only the misery of being reft from their well-known surroundings, tortured by flies, stiff from the confinement of the voyage, and bruised by the uneasy movement of the ship. In one thing fortunate. They had no foreboding of the future, no thought of what might be in store for them, happy if food and water came at stated hours, and if their guardians spoke to them kindly, or dressed them over with a wisp of hay. What was it that they had desired? What was their *summum bonum*? Only a little grass and water when they were still unbroken, roaming about with others of their kind, most innocent and harmless of all the animals that tread the earth. Then came the training, with its long hours of repetition of the same movements, a thing naturally repulsive to all animals before association with mankind has turned them into sentient machines.

If the incomprehensible movements must have been irksome to stable horses, broken and bitted and accustomed to man's vagaries, from their earliest years, the training must have been especially severe to the half-wild Argentines shipped in a hurry, carelessly selected, coming from a flat and stoneless country, to South Africa, a land of stones and mountains, with feet that never wore a shoe, blindfolded and securely tied, to find themselves with iron circlets nailed to their hooves when the blind was removed, they must have passed through purgatory.

Snorting and plunging, beaten to give them confidence in man, screamed at and kicked, for the crime of being wild, whereas the kicking and the beating should have been the portion of the rogues who sent half-tamed colts instead of seasoned animals, the Argentines had a foretaste of what was in store for them, that the rest escaped.

The march with its long hours, its scarcity of water, the heavy weights to carry, the jingling sabres beating on their flanks, the girth galls, and the sore backs, for after a sea voyage they necessarily were soft, all these and scanty rations, the infernal buzzing of the myriads of flies, the penetrating dust, the mud in which they stood after a heavy semi-tropic shower, these were their portion, or the Via Crucis they endured, before they entered into the hell from which no saviour ever came down from heaven to save them. Of course they had no souls, as good men tell us, and so were spared the torments that, it appears, so many sad good Christians may reasonably expect.

As the army slowly penetrated into the interior, conditions gradually got harder for the horses. Already many had to be left derelict, without the mercy of a shot to end their misery. Lions and leopards preyed upon them, and hyænas stole out at night to mangle and devour those who could no longer keep upon their feet, vultures that seemed to come from nowhere picked out their eyes, almost before life had left their bodies, and flies settled and buzzed upon the saddle-sores and girth-galls. Sometimes a horse or two would struggle to a water-hole, only to fall and flounder in the mud, before they slaked their thirst for the last time. Uncombed, undressed, with staring coats, with manes and tails a mass of burrs, looking like bottle brushes, with bodies a mere mass of ticks, then, when death released them, they remained milestones upon their Via Dolorosa.

Then suddenly, from behind rocks, from clumps of bushes, and from hills, there came the crackling of sporadic rifle fire. The bullets fired by men who never missed their mark, soon emptied saddles, and the thud when they pierced horses' flanks, broke legs, or stretched an animal dead on the ground, its troubles over, formed the beginning of the tragedy. With manes and tails erect, some ran, so terrified they looked like spirits of horses escaped from the infernal regions, in their flight.

Some dangled broken legs, hopping like wounded birds, and others with great gouts of dried-up blood, mingled with sweat, running down their flanks, staggered about till they sank down, biting their parched tongues that hung out looking like pieces of raw hide. Sometimes a wounded rider, spurred on his wounded horse, until both dropped together, the horse in its death-struggle mangling its rider's limbs. Days grew to weeks, and weeks to months, and months stretched out to years, and still from overseas, from pampas, prairies, steppes, and fresh green pastures, shiploads and shiploads of more victims landed at Table Bay.

Hard work, food they were not accustomed to, and horse-sickness, that left them in a few days mere living skeletons, accounted for the most of them. Death held an equine carnival, such as the world had never known, in any of its wars.

The sandy valleys, the high veldt, the forests, bushy scrub, the mountain trails, the bogs and the morasses, were strewed with bones of horses that placed together in a line would have stretched out from Capetown to Portuguese East Africa.

Perhaps their bodies may have fertilised some backveldt Boers' farms. A dear manure, when one thinks how it was obtained, and the two hundred thousand victims. All dead, forgotten, remembered but by one Jewish lady. I make kidush to her, and hope that where she sits, with Miriam and Deborah listening to dulcimer, to psaltery, to sackbut and all kinds of music, there will be mingled with it now and then, a strain of a soft whinnying.

"Facón Grande"

All the south-western frontier of the province of Buenos Aires, in the far-off days of which I write, was as wild and almost as dangerous as the Apacheria in Arizona. The Pampa Indians who owed little to the Apaches in fierceness, cruelty, skill in horsemanship and general devilry, were the scourge of the whole frontier, from Tapalquen to the Gualichu Tree.

The rare estancias were like islands in the great sea of grass that flowed around them, just as waves surround atolls in the South Seas. Most of the estancia houses, and the pulperias were fortified with a deep ditch, and some of them had a small brass cannon that was chiefly used to signal to the sparse neighbours, for naturally its range was short and the Indians took care not to advance too near, and separated when it was fired, so that it did but little execution on the open plain.

The life, wild, dangerous and lonely, threw off strange characters, for only men of resolution, who held life cheaply, or outcasts from society, cared to settle in a district where the government could give scant protection and a man was ruined in a night, by raiding Indians, who drove his cattle off and left him destitute.

Still there were some who, neither desperate nor outcasts, resolutely took up land and settled down. Of such the most remarkable was a tall Englishman whose name, I think, was Hawker, but better known as "Facón Grande," from the sword bayonet that he wore stuck through his belt and sticking out upon both sides, after the fashion of the lateen yard of fishing-boats in the Levant. Tall, dark and wiry, his hair that he wore long and ragged beard gave him the look of a stage desperado, but in reality he was a brave and prudent man who knew quite well the danger that he lived in, but was determined to hang on, for he had faith in the country's future where he had made his home.

As he had lived for many years upon the frontier, he dressed in Gaucho fashion, with loose black merino trousers tucked into high boots. A white pleated shirt always left open at the neck, a short alpaca jacket, with a broad belt fastened by what was called a "rastra," composed of silver coins that served as buttons, and an Indian poncho, woven in red and black, completed what he called his "indumentary."

He spoke a strange phonetic Spanish, blameless of grammar and full of local words, as easily as English. A short half-league away, his cousin lived, one Ferguson, known to the Gauchos as "Facón Chico," from the smaller size of the yet formidable knife he carried. No greater contrast could be found than that between the cousins. "Facón Chico" was about middle height with sandy hair and a short well-cropped beard. His face was freckled and his hands, mottled like a trout, had once been white, of that unhealthy-looking hue that exposure to the sun often imparts to red-headed or to sandy-coloured men. For all his quiet appearance and meek ways till roused, he was perhaps the bolder and more daring of the two. The Gauchos said, although he looked like an archangel who had lost his wings, that in an Indian skirmish his porcelain-coloured eyes shot fire and he became a perfect devil, the highest compliment in their vocabulary.

Though he had lived for twenty years in the republic, he hardly knew more than a few coherent sentences in Spanish, and those so infamously pronounced that few could understand them.

Curiously enough he spoke Pehuelche fairly fluently, for he had lived some years with an Indian woman, who, when she went back to the Tolderia, had left him as a pledge of their love, or what you call it, a boy the Gaucho humorists had christened Cortaplumas, to the delight, not only of his father, but the whole neighbourhood.

The boy grew up amongst the peons neither exactly tame nor wild. Like other boys born in that outside "camp" upon the frontiers he ran about barefooted, lassoed the dogs and cats, and brought down birds with little "bolas" that he manufactured by himself out of old strips of hide and knuckle-bones.* By the age of six or seven he, like all the other boys, was a good rider, climbing up on the saddle, using the horse's knees as a step-ladder for his bare little toes.

Once mounted, he had come into his kingdom, whirling his whip round his head and drumming ceaselessly with his bare heels upon the horse's side, he would set off at the slow machine-like gallop of the plains, either to help round up the horses for the day's work, or to snare partridges with a noose at the end of a long cane.

* Always called "boleadoras" by the Gauchos, because the shorter word carries a double meaning with it.

306

He naturally, perhaps to prove his lineage, carried a knife large enough for a grown man to use, stuck in the Pampa Indian waist-band, that kept up his ragged "chiripá."† His wiry jet-black hair stuck out below his hat, and fell upon his shoulders like a mane.

In everything he was a perfect type of the half-bred urchin in the outside "camps".‡

Had his Pehuelche mother not gone back to her own people, or his father had not married a douce Scottish Argentine, most likely Cortaplumas would have grown up a Gaucho without education, and perhaps have disappeared one day to join his mother in the "Toldos,"* taking some of his father's best horses with him.

Some years of school in Buenos Aires certainly altered him from the teeth outwards (*de los dientes afuera*), as runs the Spanish saw, and he returned to the estancia a well-mannered silent youth but really little altered, if it is true that character and features go with us to the grave.††

It looked as if he would have had as well known a name upon the frontier as his father and uncle, for the lad had remained as good a rider and as clever with the lazo as when he left his home. Fate had decreed it otherwise, and before he grew to man's estate the medium with which he might have earned his way to fame had disappeared. Little by little the Indians were forced back into the recesses of the valleys of the Andes. A railway was slowly pushed on right to Bahia Blanca. Lands that had but little value rose in price, and Cortaplumas had no field where he could have displayed the talents that I, his only chronicler, am certain, if there is anything in the doctrine of heredity, he must surely have possessed. So was a person born as it were with a silver-handled knife already in his belt, fated to leave behind him only the recollection of his delightful name. In those days when there was an Indian raid it always was announced by the arrival from what was known as the "inside country"** of flocks of ostriches and bands of deer fleeing before the Indians' advance.

† The "chiripá" was the garment the Gauchos inherited from the Indians and consisted of a piece of cloth or linen, belted round the waist and drawn through the hips to form a sort of trouser.
‡ "Camp" used for "country" in the Argentine, by Englishmen. It is from the Spanish "campo" = country.
* Indian tents, teepees in North America.
†† *Genio y figura, hasta la sepultura.*
** *Tierra adentro.*

Luckily for the dwellers in their isolated estancias, the Indians never came by night, either from some superstition that they had, or because, even they, skilled as they were in desert travelling, could not find their way, unless there was a moon. Be that as it may, I never once remember a "malon"† at night.

Unlike the Indians on the borderlands of Texas and of Mexico, the Pampa Indians seldom came in isolated bands of twenty or of thirty, but always raided in full force. Both of them always used to attack, if possible, just as the sun was rising, and though we had no "Facón Grande" in the north, we did as well as we were able with Wild Bill Hitchcock [sic], and other worthies, heroes who wanted but a Homer to have preserved their names, and placed them on a level with Achilles and with Diomed.

Many and various were the types our frontier in the Argentine threw off.

Martin Villalba, at one time Alcalde of Bahia Blanca, rises before me, out of Trapalanda, as I write, that Trapalanda, the mysterious country where good Gauchos and their horses rode, their horses never tiring, sustained by never-failing grass and water, the nectar and ambrosia of the equine race, their riders never ageing and I suppose their saddlery never wearing out.

In that fair land of the imagination Martin Villalba will have by this time become the "compadre" of Don Segundo Sombra, Martin Fierro, and the immortal rider of El Fausto, on his roan and white skewbald, known to all Argentines as "Lindo el overo rosao!"

The said Martin was a short, rather stocky man, dressed always in the style of a better class Gaucho, in loose black merino trousers, tucked into high boots with the feet made of calfskin and the legs of patent leather, embroidered with an eagle, worked in scarlet thread. His spurs were silver with the rowels, almost as big as a small saucer, and worn dangling off his heels, kept in their place by silver chains, clasped on his instep with a lion's head.

Around the waist he wore a red silk netting sash, such as was used by officers in the army when Queen Victoria ruled, covered by a broad belt of "carpincho"* leather, full of pockets, and fastened by silver coins.

Under the belt the tassels and a foot or so of the sash dangled down on the leg and gave a note of colour on the merino "slacks."

† *Malon* was the word used for an Indian incursion.
*The *carpincho* is an amphibious animal about the size of a small pig. It is, I think, the largest of the rodents.

Don Martin, for no one ever called him plain Martin without the Don, always wore a white frilled and pleated shirt, with a high collar, turned down and open at the neck. His short black jacket was of fine alpaca, and over it, spread out into tails, he wore a red silk handkerchief. His hat, known from the Fortin Machado right down to Patagones, was a fine Panama, the only one upon the frontier. He used to say with pride that he acquired it in Buenos Aires, a city that he had visited but once in his career. It had cost him ten sterling pounds of England* and he held the money well laid out.

Strange but unconvincing tales of his experiences in that "Babilonia" he would unpack upon occasion, especially after a glass or two of Brazilian Caña (rum) or Vino Seco, a thick yellow Catalonian wine, that with sardines and biscuits was our banquet at the "camp" pulperias. Our chief dessert was either "raisins of the sun," or the dried peaches, known as "orejones," looking exactly like human ears, that came from Chile and the upper provinces. Over this more or less Gargantuan feast, would Don Martin take up his parable.

Though wedlocked, married in Latin, that is, in a church, as he would say, as far as I know the husband but of a single wife, it would appear in Buenos Aires, in his brief sojourn of a fortnight, he had spent the time in a continual orgy of costly but intensely satisfying love. The names and the appearance of the damsels who had accompanied him in his various pilgrimages to Cytherea, he still remembered, as well, he used to say, as the brands of the various estancias round about Bahia Blanca in the days of his magistrature.

Certainly Don Martin was one of our best leaders against the Indians, and I can see him still, mounted on his skewbald, his rifle hanging from his saddle and his celebrated Panama, the brim blown back by the wind, as he rode from house to house along the Sauce Grande, the Sauce Corto and the Napostá, warning the neighbours to be ready to resist a raid.

Naturally, "Facón Grande" was our general, silent and watchful, his eyes fixed always on the horizon, marking the movements of the cattle, the flight of birds, dust rising on the horizon, reading the Pampa like a book in Braille by little indications invisible to those whose mental sense of touch, life in a city had left dormant.

Mounted on a tall "Pangaré"† with a fawn-coloured nose, his rifle

---

* *Diez esterlinas de Inglaterra.*
† *Pangaré* was a sort of mealy bay, and was a colour much esteemed by the Gauchos.

carried always in his hand, across the saddle-bow, his long black hair gave him a look almost of an Indian and his great height and perfect seat upon his horse made an ideal picture of a frontiersman.

"Facón Chico," always the first to rally to the call, looked in his tweed coat and riding breeches as if he had strayed by accident from some meet of harriers into that wild company.

As talkative as "Facón Grande" was silent, his usual greeting was: "Have you heard this one?" Then he would retail some Rabelaisian story interspersed with Spanish words, wrongly pronounced, or a new Limerick, of his own mintage.

He, like his cousin, carried his rifle in his hand, riding upon an English saddle, for, as he said, "a man ought to show his nationality," although in his case nature had stamped it on him both inside and out.

A hard-riding German, Frederick Vögel by name, but always known as "Pancho Pajaro" to the Gauchos, was sure to join us, although his business was to sell sheep-dip to the "estancieros." His name was a household word amongst the Gauchos, for the long daring rides he had undertaken along the frontier.

Fair and square-built, fatigue of any kind was a thing unknown to him; so, I should think, was fear.

No one could want a better man beside him in a tough place, and when his off stirrup happened to touch yours, you felt assured as long as he had life that "Pancho Pajaro" would not let you down.

These worthies and the brothers Milburn of the Sauce Grande, one a retired sea captain and the other, who was called lieutenant, perhaps because his brother was known as captain, for he had nothing military about him, and several settlers on the Naposta, composed our company.

Most of them had been in Indian skirmishes and heard the Pampa Indians yelling, striking their hands upon their mouths as they came on like a storm cloud, brandishing their spears.

Where they ride now is but a matter of conjecture; no one remembers them but I who write these lines, that I have written *in memoriam*, hoping that some day they will allow an old companion to ride with them, no matter where they ride.

Afterword

"I thanked the stationmaster for his horse, unsaddled him, emptied a tin mug of water over his sweating back, and threw him down a bundle of fresh Pindó leaves to keep him occupied till he was ready for his maize.

Then I strolled into the station café, where Exaltacion Medina, Joao Ferreira, and, I think, Enrique Clerici were playing billiards, whilst they waited for me."

(Writ in Sand, "The Stationmaster's Horse")

Robert Cunninghame Graham left for Argentina in January, 1936. He was welcomed as a returning hero in Buenos Aires, but in the course of his many engagements, he took the time to visit the birthplace of W.H. Hudson. In March he became ill with bronchitis, which turned into a fatal pneumonia. Shortly before his death, he paid a visit to the two horses of his friend, Aimé Tschiffely, and fed them some oats that he had brought specially for them from Britain. The two horses, Mancha and Gato, followed Graham's funeral carriage through Buenos Aires, with his riding boots reversed in the stirrups.

"He kept his looks to the last day he lived, proving the truth of the old Spanish saw, 'Figure and genius to the grave'".

(Writ in Sand, "Fin de Race")

The monument to Robert Cunninghame Graham near the house of Gartmore bears the inscription:
"A Master of Life — A King among Men"

311

An Argentine Child's Wake, with Music and Dancing
– as seen by Alfred Ébélot and R. B. Cunninghame Graham

In 1870 two foreigners landed in Argentina for the first time — the Frenchman Alfred Ébélot and the Scotsman Robert Bontine Cunninghame Graham. In different places each witnessed a traditional child's wake accompanied by music and dancing. This article compares their experiences of Argentina and their literary interpretations of an intriguing piece of Hispano-Argentine folklore.

Alfred Ébélot (1839-1920)[1] had a remarkable career in Argentina. Trained as a civil engineer in Paris, he avoided — as a committed republican — a career in Napoleon III's civil service. After experience with the important journal *Revue des Deux Mondes*, he emigrated to Argentina in 1870, when its population was c.1.8 million, of whom 32,000 were French. A first venture in journalism failed, and he was employed by the Argentine government to survey and define the frontier 300 kilometres south and west of the capital Buenos Aires.

This frontier was porous. Every few years untamed Indians from the south raided north to seize women and children as slaves and to drive off cattle, horses and sheep back to their tented villages in the "desert", the plains beyond the frontier line. Alsina, Minister of War, proposed that a ditch be dug to stop the Indian raiders taking captives and beasts south. The initial plan visualised a ditch 2.6 metres broad, 1.75 metres deep and six hundred kilometres long, linking ninety-two forts and military outposts on a line running from near Bahía Blanca in the south-southwest of the huge Province of Buenos Aires to just south of Córdoba Province towards the northwest. Over 350 kilometres of trench were to be completed.

Ébélot's involvement in this huge nation-building project, known as the Alsina Trench[2], and his work in laying out a town planned to house treaty Indians put him in contact with government ministers, landowners, army officers, ordinary soldiers, storekeepers, gauchos, their women and with Indians, both tame and wild. His extensive knowledge of the frontier and its problems is seen in his long and dramatic article "Une invasion indienne dans la province de Buenos Ayres. Souvenirs et récits de la frontière argentine" in the *Revue des Deux Mondes*, May 1876)[3]: this described the raid in late December 1875 by up to 5,000 Indians in the areas of Tandil, Azul, Tres Arroyos and Alvear when the Indians killed hundreds of settlers and made off with 500 captives and over 150,000 animals.

After this massive raid the government adopted a much more aggressive policy aimed at forcing the Indians south of the Río Negro. In 1879-1880 General Roca, the new Minister of War, led a large military force that 'solved' the Indian problem by exterminating the Indian warrior castes and relocating the Indian women and children to the "civilized" north as virtual slaves. Millions of acres were opened up for settlement and development, and Roca became President.

His engineering skills no longer needed, Ébélot went back to journalism with *Le Courrier de La Plata* and *La Nación*, writing and editorialising with great vigour in French and Spanish for thirty years on Argentine national and international affairs. His long residence, his engineering experience and his high-level journalism gave him ample opportunity to study Argentina's headlong rush to modernisation. Aware that the gaucho culture was being rapidly swept aside, in 1890 Ébélot published *La Pampa. Moeurs argentines* in Paris and the same volume, in his own very able Spanish, as *La Pampa. Costumbres argentinas* in Buenos Aires. The first vignette of fourteen in Ébélot's volume is "El Velorio"[4] (*The Wake*), a description of a child's wake with music and dancing in the heart of the grasslands — the pampa. This event occurred probably in the 1870s.[5]

R. B. Cunninghame Graham (1852-1936) was by age seventeen in early 1870 an accomplished speaker of Spanish and an expert horseman.[6] In his three extended visits to Argentina in the 1870s he gained bruising experience as an apprentice rancher, a promoter of plantations for growing Paraguayan tea and as a horse drover and dealer. He travelled widely in Argentina, Uruguay and Paraguay and acquired a lifelong love of the gaucho cow-herding culture of the open unfenced grasslands. In the late 1870s he travelled in Iceland and West Africa. In 1882 his and his new wife's cattle ranch in Texas was destroyed in an Apache raid: to recoup losses he drove a caravan-load of cotton to Mexico City and stayed on to work for a time as a fencing master. In 1883 his father died and Graham took over the debt-ridden family properties in Scotland. During his six years (1886-1892) as a radical Liberal Member of Parliament, he took special interest in major socialist reforms relating to labour conditions in factories and became a co-founder of the Labour Party. In the 1890s his magazine articles criticised British and United States imperialism and gave support to the principle of Home Rule.

In 1896 Graham published *Mogreb-el-Acksa*, a record of his attempt, in disguise, to reach the forbidden city of Tarudant in Morocco. In 1898, he and his wife Gabriela jointly published the collection of sketches entitled *Father Archangel of Scotland and Other Essays*. Four out of Graham's nine sketches in *Father Archangel of Scotland and Other Essays* were set in Argentina or Spain. In 1899 he published *The Ipané*, his first solo collection of sketches. The third sketch of fifteen in this collection was entitled "Un Angelito" (*A Little Angel*),[7] a description of a child's wake, with music and dancing, at a country store in southern Buenos Aires Province, again probably in the 1870s.

Graham had less continuous residence in Argentina than Ébélot, though he seems to have made up for this in passionate commitment. Graham, the more widely travelled of the two, was familiar with more Spanish-speaking countries than Ébélot. Both men in Argentina had close contact with the pampa and the cow-herding way of life threatened by Argentina's modernisation during the last quarter of the nineteenth century. Both were careful observers and thoughtful commentators. The speculation is that Graham may have used Ébélot's 1890 sketch "El Velorio" to shape his writing in 1899 in "Un Angelito".

In his Spanish-language Preface Ébélot states that his "ciencias positivas" contain his imagination and that his sketches ("bosquejos") are precise. He has lived successfully in the "desert", the untamed pampa beyond the frontier, and for long periods has lived and thought as a gaucho. He is acutely aware of Argentina's rapid process of change: "El indio ya no existe. Antes de diez años, la desapiadada (= despiadada) civilización habrá pulido como con esmeril las anfractuosidades y las líneas toscas de la acentuada figura del gaucho ".[8] (*The Indian no longer exists. Within ten years heartless civilization will have smoothed out the rough coarse edges and lines of the sharply defined figure of the gaucho.*) His notes, he feels, will soon be "documentos pre-históricos".

This writer identifies five sections or phases in Ébélot's "El Velorio".

The opening section (37 lines, to "... llover de lo lindo.") shows Ébélot, commissioned by the Minister for War, journeying with his guide across the pampa. Ébélot's horse-drawn carriage moves very slowly over the roadless grassland. Caught in a rainstorm they head for Torres' store.

In the second phase (85 lines, to "… y de guitarra.") Ébélot and his guide arrive at nightfall, drenched, at Torres' isolated country store. A voice directs them to the kitchen hut. When Torres is brought, he explains that his four-year old son had died the previous day. Torres invites Ébélot to join the wake.

Ébélot's third section (78 lines, to "… el primero que contemplé.") is set in the main hut, a room smelling of candle wax, tobacco and gin. Towards the back, the dead child, dressed in its best clothes, is sitting propped in a little chair set on gin cases on top of the table. On this second night of the wake, green shadow is showing around the child's lips. On one side of the table a seated gaucho holds a guitar: the music and dancing had stopped when Ébélot entered the room. The men stand clasping the women and whispering to them, the women laughing loudly. On the other side of the table is the mother, "la mirada fija y cruzadas las manos" (*the eyes staring and her hands crossed*). Speakers tell her that "el angelito está en el cielo" (*The little angel is in heaven*). She agrees, "y seguía mirando fijamente" (*and carried on staring*). Ébélot, shaking her hand, omits to murmur the expected formulaic phrase "El angelito está en el cielo", and joins the older men in a corner. The dance picks up again. The women dancing shake their hips, bless themselves and cackle loudly as they spin past the dead child. The rain-storm outside momentarily drowns out the guitar, the voices, the feet beating on the floor, the kisses.

Ébélot's third section has two images that to the average reader might seem grotesque. The first is of the dead child — "horroroso y enternecedor" (*horrific and touching*) — sitting up "a manera de pedestal", as if raised on a little throne, and the dancing women blessing themselves and hooting at their partners' "galanterías" (*compliments*) as they pass by the dead body. This is the "horroroso" dimension. The "enternecedor" dimension is suggested in the body's slack arms and dangling legs and in the two flashes of the stricken mother staring fixedly as Ébélot forgets to murmur the standard words of sympathy to her. Ébélot does not dwell long on the mother's grief.

In the fourth section (47 lines, to "… especulación repugnante.") Ébélot opens up a general debate. This custom of celebrating a child's death with music and dancing, according to Ébélot widespread across Spanish America, can be turned to commercial ends. A store-keeper can hire a dead child's body and use it to set up a dance and sell liquor. This may give isolated pampa-dwellers a chance to meet, though the dead child's parents may spend at the store any money gained from renting out their child's body. When the storekeeper tries to keep the body fresh for use on a second or even a third night, Ébélot finds this "bárbaro": he opines that these small dead bodies should not become part of the struggle for money or of "una especulación repugnante". His distrust of religion — evidenced in his closing phrase "los paganos de la pampa" — may blind him to the spiritual and emotional support that the original "angelito" ceremony might have provided for simple believers in times of high child mortality in remote rural areas. His reformer's anxiety to criticise the commercial abuse of the custom perhaps also draws him away from the individual human pain, especially that of the suffering mother.

Ébélot's fifth and final phase (27 lines to the end) recognises that the advance of civilisation will erode "las viejas leyendas". Once given the perspective of time, such customs may take on "una apacible tonalidad de arcaismo (= arcaísmo) pintoresco" (*a gentle toning of picturesque archaism*). As of 1890, though, he concludes:

> Superstición singular, característica mezcla de brutalidad y de poesía [...] el velorio es un genuino rasgo de los antiguos usos y la más curiosa manifestación del catolicismo de los jesuitas interpretado por los paganos de la pampa. (*A remarkable superstition, a characteristic mixture of brutality and poetry [...] the wake is a genuine feature of ancient customs and the strangest manifestation of Jesuit-style Catholicism as interpreted by the pagans of the pampa.*)

Ébélot — trained engineer, experienced journalist, a believer in positivism and rational progress — has witnessed and recorded a curious piece of pampa folklore. His sketch is a fine piece of social observation and thoughtful commentary, perfectly in tune with the sub-title of his collection of sketches — "Costumbres argentinas" or "Argentine Customs".

The literary link between Ébélot and Graham is pinpointed by Watts and Davies in their critical biography of Graham:

He [Graham] was encouraged by Hudson to set down his South American experiences in sketches and essays. In 1894, when Graham was struggling with a projected history of the gauchos, Hudson recommended that, instead of writing at length, he should follow the example of *La Pampa*, a collection of vignettes by Alfred Ébélot. Ébélot, a Frenchman long resident in Argentina, combined depictions of gaucho life — brawling, dancing at wakes, tracking runaways — with speculations on themes close to Graham's heart: biological evolution and the nature of civilisation.[9]

Graham in 1870 was utterly enthralled by the open pampa and by its free-ranging cow-herders, the gauchos. So profound was the pampa's impact on him that of his two hundred-plus sketches and tales in fourteen volumes (1896-1936), several dozen are set on the pampa in Argentina and Uruguay. Blessed with a phenomenal memory, even forty or fifty years after an incident Graham seemed able to recall settings, characters and events in considerable detail.

This writer identifies five phases in Graham's 1899 sketch "Un Angelito".[10]

In the opening section (79 lines, to "… out on the open "camp." "), Graham rides across the pampa in southern Buenos Aires Province from Tandil through the Tres Arroyos area heading towards Bahía Blanca on the Atlantic coast. The horses are described in great detail, and mention is made of the great expanses of grass and sky, the ombú tree, an ostrich, a Patagonian hare, the salty rivers, the rare and very cautious travellers met and the news shared regarding the depredations of the Indians. Ébélot in his horse-drawn carriage offers a less romantic image than Graham on horseback, and Ébélot's comments on horse behaviour are straightforward, almost mundane, whereas Graham's descriptions of landscapes and horses bubble with wonder and enthusiasm.

The second phase (107 lines, to "… uninstructed minds.") shows Graham arriving towards evening at an old fort surrounded by a peach grove. Hitching posts front a house and the great number and variety of horse types tied to them puzzle Graham. He is welcomed at the hitching posts by his acquaintance Eustaquio Medina: the latter reports that his son has died and that folk have gathered for the child's wake, to celebrate the fact that "his soul is with the blest [...] When a child dies it is the signal for a dance to celebrate its entry into bliss". On arriving at Torres' store, Ébélot had been directed to the separate kitchen where meat and fuel were available for the travellers. Torres, told of Ébélot's high government connections, was concerned to pamper his guest — almost even to the point of setting aside his sorrow at his child's death. Graham on the other hand goes straight from the hitching post into the main living space where the wake is being held.

The wake is described in Graham's third section (61 lines, to "Yet so it is: ..."). Fifty people crammed a room filled with candle and cigar smoke. Cotton-gowned women — "Chinas" — sat along the wall. The dead child — the "Angelito" — "sat in a chair upon a table, greenish in colour, and with his hands and feet hanging down limply — horrible, but at the same time fascinating". An old "Gaucho" played the guitar. In a corner old men talked of horses' brands. The younger people performed various popular dances, with the guitarist occasionally bursting into shrill falsetto song. A man recovering from an Indian lance-wound lay poncho-wrapped on a litter. The girls dancing occasionally blessed themselves as they passed the child's body before then breaking into laughter.

The wake scenes in Ébélot and Graham are fairly similar, perhaps necessarily so in that custom would demand that the ceremonial be followed rigorously. Even so, Ébélot's "ligera sombra verdosa" (*faint greenish shadow*) on the child's lips becomes Graham's "greenish in colour". Ébélot's "caídos los brazos, colgando las piernas, horroroso y enternecedor" (*arms and legs dangling, horrific and touching*) is paralleled by Graham's "with his hands and feet hanging down limply — horrible, but at the same time fascinating". Whereas Ébélot's encounter with the grief-stricken mother covers eleven lines, Graham mentions her only in one phrase on the final page: Graham misses the opportunity here to draw out the potential for pathos. Ébélot reports a touch spicily that "una que otra bailarina [...] meneaba las caderas con la provocativa ondulación propia de la habanera o de la zamacueca" (*one or other of the girls dancing [...] wiggled her hips in the provocative sinuous style of the habanera or zamacueca dances*). Graham on the other hand openly reports the girls as for hire: they are prostitutes attached to the country store. The details of the women dancing, blessing themselves and cackling as they pass by the dead body are again very similar across the two sketches.

In Graham's fourth phase (23 lines, to "... I cannot tell:...") "... a commercial element has crept into the scheme". An owner of a pampa store "will beg or borrow the body of a child just dead to use it as an "Angelito" to attract the country people to a revel at his store". Graham does recognise the role of the country store as the "Pampa Club", but does not know the origin of the "Angelito" custom. Where Ébélot the positivist gives nearly twenty per cent of his text to the commercialisation of the wake custom, Graham gives barely eight per cent. Graham had been a great proponent of social reform in his time in Parliament but here in the pampa shows little inclination to promote change. Ébélot is harsher in his extended criticism of the abuse of the folk practice, as in "pulperos, nada propensos a la sensibilidad" (*storekeepers, not at all prone to being sensitive*) and "Este ardid" (*this ruse*). Ébélot recognises that "Su mercantilismo es una mancha en el cuadro, no lo niego, un manchón poco simpático. Hasta concedo que es algo bárbaro" (*Their money-making spirit is a stain in the picture, I do not deny it, a large and not very pleasant stain. I even grant that it is somewhat barbarous.*) Yet he feels obliged to add: "Es de notar sin embargo que no ha sido producido por la barbarie, sino por un rudimento de civilización" (*It is to be noted, however, that it has been produced not by barbarism, but by a rudiment of civilisation*).

In the fifth and final section (47 lines to the end) Graham strikes a fully elegiac note: he does know that all such pampa customs "are doomed to disappear". Progress in the form of barbed wire fences and telegraph poles will break up and destroy the apparently unlimited space of the old pampa. Within Graham's memory the Indians have already gone: "though savages", they will leave a blank that can never be filled. In time gauchos, ostriches, huanacos will all disappear. European nettles and thistles, cities, cabs and railways will occupy the old grasslands.

Graham's final lines emphasise that he can always recall the precise details of that first wake:

> Eustaquio Medina, the wounded man lying smoking on his *catre*, the decomposing "Angelito" in his chair, his mother looking at nothing with her eyes wide open, and the wild music of the cracked guitar seem to revisit me.

In Ébélot's last ten lines he makes slightly distracting reference to his friend Charton, the great editor of "Le Tour du Monde": mention of his death in 1890, the year of publication of *La Pampa*, might be meaningful to an educated French-based reader but perhaps falls rather flat in the Spanish-language version published in Argentina. Ébélot's view that the passage of time will give the original customs and his sketches a veneer of "arcaismo pintoresco" is less impactive than Graham's closing elegy.

Some similarities of presentation may derive from the formulaic nature of the child's wake tradition in remote places and from the fact that both Ébélot and Graham are seeking to record curious scenes witnessed twenty or thirty years previously. Other similarities may occur because Ébélot and Graham are opinionated individuals, both highly educated or extremely well-read and thoughtful witnesses and commentators, mistrustful both of them of organised religion. Ébélot's final phrase "los paganos de la pampa" is mirrored by Graham's biting remarks: "we separated with a fallacious "Go with God," knowing full well our only trust was in our spurs"; "faith, that first infirmity of uninstructed minds"; and — referring to the creeping urbanisation and civilization of the pampa — "His will will be accomplished who, having made the earth a paradise, gave it to us to turn into a purgatory for ourselves and all the dwellers in it". It has to be recognised, however, that the organisation of Graham's 1899 sketch into five phases or sections — the journey across the pampa, arrival at an isolated country store, the wake with music and dancing, the commercialisation of the wake and the sense of loss as the old customs disappear — carries strong echoes of Ébélot's 1890 sketch. Of the two sketches, however, Graham's sketch seems superior.

Whereas Ébélot views the pampa and the gauchos with the eyes and mind of a technically educated (*vide* "... anfractuosidades..." in his Preface), rational and practical man, Graham's intimate feeling for the pampa — its vast sense of space, its horses (in the opening section and even more so at the hitching posts in section two), its flora and fauna, its gauchos — seems all-encompassing. If Ébélot is a careful observer and student of the pampa, Graham is its passionate lover, acceptive of all its splendours and abject realities.

Graham also has an incredibly sharp eye for striking and suggestive detail, as when he illustrates the terrible dangers from the wild Indians: "the body of the owner lying before the door, swollen to the dimensions of an ox, and festering in the sun" and "a woman's body hanging naked to a post, and decorated with leaves torn from a Bible skewered artistically about it where decency required". He understands that the hitching post before an isolated house is an unspoken boundary between public and private space, and that the Christian traveller must approach that pampa house by identifying himself from a distance with the opening words of the Mary prayer. Graham subtly presents the gauchos as very material-minded yet made occasionally proud by being in direct touch with heaven through the death of an "Angelito". As Argentina engages in a cycle of monumental economic, social and political change, Graham logs the signs of the arrival of six million immigrants, listing the presence at the wake of "the ubiquitous Italian with his organ". He shows delicate irony and a measure of compassion in describing the rural prostitutes, the "Chinas", "waiting as patiently for any man to hire them as the eleventh-hour labourers in Holy Writ". His keen eye spots the richer men — with silver-handled knives and spurs — standing just a little apart from the general company. Old men trace out horse-brands with fingers dipped in gin. The men dancing rattle their spurs on the floor. The wounded man on the litter "ate great pieces of beef cooked in the hide, and smoked incessantly". The pulpería, the Pampa Club, is resorted to by "all the elite of frontier ruffianism". Graham's eye is so precise and revealing that a film-maker would find everything he needed in his sketch to re-create this scene perfectly.

Graham seems, then, to have had unlimited empathy with the pampa and gaucho world. His almost uncanny skill in capturing particularly memorable and compelling detail helps him evoke the dying heartbeats of the plains and gaucho culture. Yet Graham's rapid development in the late 1890s as a writer of literary sketches may to some extent derive from the lessons he learned during his extremely deft re-manipulation of Alfred Ébélot's "El Velorio".

Notes

[1] See: Cecilia González Espul: "La conquista del desierto y la zanja de Alsina bajo la dirección de Alfredo Ebelot" at http://www.rebanadasderealidad.com.ar/espul-08-02.htm; Pauline Raquillet-Bordry "Alfred Ébélot, La Pampa", at http://www.univ-paris-diderot.fr/hsal/hsal96/prb96.html [date of death given as 1912]; and María Sáenz Quesdada "Alfred Ébélot, un francés acriollado", at http://www.lanacion.com.ar/nota.asp?nota_id=334247

[2] Spanish Wikipedia = http://es.wikipedia > Zanja de Alsina. The map supplied shows the gradual movement of the frontier towards the south and south-west.

[3] The article is available on the *Revue des Deux Mondes* website at: http://www.revuedesdeuxmondes.fr/user/details.php?author=Ebelot&subject=&title=&month1=1&year1=1829&month2=12&year2=2011&content+&code=63410

[4] Alfred Ébélot: *La pampa. Costumbres argentinas* (Joseph Escary, Buenos Aires, 1890), Preface p. 7 and pages 9-22. Full Spanish-language text readable on screen at: http://www.archive.org/details/lapampa00ebelgoog

[5] A child's wake is illustrated in [the Chilean film] "Largo Viaje" (1967) [directed] by

Patricio Kaulen: http://pasatelapelicula.blogspot.com/search?q=Largo+Viaje+Patricio+Kaulen

[6] See http://en.wikipedia.org/wiki/Robert_Bontine_Cunninghame_Graham

7 R. B. Cunninghame Graham: "Un Angelito", in *The Ipané* (London: T. Fisher Unwin Ltd. [First published 1899, reprinted in this series].

[8] Alfred Ébélot: *op. cit.*, pp. 7 and 9-22.

[9] Watts and Davies (1979), page 155

[10] R. B. Cunninghame Graham *op. cit.*

References

Ébélot, Alfred (1890). *La Pampa. Moeurs argentines*. Paris: Quantin.

Ébélot, Alfred (1890). *La Pampa. Costumbres argentinas*. Buenos Aires: Joseph Escary.

Graham, R. B. Cunninghame (1899). *The Ipané*. London: T. Fisher Unwin.

Watts, Cedric and Davies, Laurence (1979). *Cunninghame Graham - A Critical Biography*. Cambridge: Cambridge University Press.

(JMcI)

This article was originally published in the electronic journal *Fulgor*, Vol.4, Issue 3, Dec 2011, Flinders University, Adelaide, South Australia.

Appendices

Spanish-Argentine Vocabulary in Four Sketches and Tales by R. B. Cunninghame Graham

Cunninghame Graham (1852-1936) made his first trip to South America in 1870. Already an accomplished horseman and speaker of Spanish, Graham was utterly enthralled by the horse-driven world of the great plains - the Pampa - of Argentina and Uruguay. His early literary publications in the 1890s included a depiction of his family lands in Menteith in Scotland, a well-received travelogue set in North Africa and ten sketches and tales set in Scotland, Spain, North Africa and South America. He would by 1936 publish the fourteen volumes of literary sketches and tales in this collection: many of the sketches are set in Texas, Mexico and South America. Graham's South American sketches can deliver a considerable amount of Argentine Spanish, so only four sketches are examined here: three heavily descriptive sketches ("The Horses of the Pampas", "La Pampa" and "Los Indios") and a fourth sketch blending description and dramatic incident ("La Pulperia", also known as "Pampa Store"). In his quest for authenticity, Graham often deploys a range of local place-names and usually typical locations; a further range of personal names and group identities either in the local language or closely based upon it; and a scattering of items in direct speech, sometimes in Spanish or transliterated into English. He is well-informed about the local environment and culture and therefore able to use a range of further lexical items associated with the life of that community. Material taken directly from Graham is set in bold, under four sub-headings and in order as they appear in each sketch or tale: PLACE-NAMES; PERSONAL NAMES AND GROUP IDENTITIES; DIRECT SPEECH; and REMAINING ITEMS. Comment (and corrections to Graham's Spanish) in square brackets in plain type are by this writer.

"The Horses of the Pampas" (in *Father Archangel of Scotland, and Other Essays* (1896)) contains nineteen pages and the following:
PLACE-NAMES AND LOCATIONS: **the Pampas; in the desert** [the uncolonised plains beyond the towns and the frontier]; **great plains**

called **Pampas; the horses of Spanish America; the Pampas horse; the dusky plains; to cross a Pampa ...; upon the Pampas; Great, well-watered, grassy plains, a fine climate, and an almost entire absence of wild beasts ...; all over the Pampas, from the semi-tropical plains of Tucuman** [Tucumán] **and Rioja** [La Rioja] **right down to the Straits of Magellan; Cordoba** [Córdoba, Spain] **was the place from which the conquerors of America took most of their horses; in the New World; the Agricultural College of Santa Catalina near Buenos Aires; in La Plata** (here, the capital of Buenos Aires province); **the 900 miles of territory from Buenos Ayres** [old spelling] **to the Andes; From the frontier of Bolivia to Patagonia** [semi-arid tableland in the deep south, beyond the pampa]; **at the Pulperia** [pulpería: pampa store, gathering place for cow-herders].

"La Pampa" (*Charity*, 1912): This heavily descriptive piece (12 pages) seeks to evoke the spirit of the Argentine and Uruguayan grasslands. PLACE-NAMES AND LOCATIONS: **the Pampa stretched from the *pajonales*** [scrublands] **on the western bank of the Paraná** [river] **right to the stony plain of Uspallata** [village on the road across the Andes], **a thousand miles away. // It stretched from San Luis de la Punta** [western town] **down to Bahia Blanca** [Bahía Blanca (White Bay), major town on east coast of the southern pampa of the huge Buenos Aires province], **and again crossing the Uruguay** [river], **comprised the whole republic of that name and a good half of Rio Grande** [Rio Grande do Sul, southernmost state in Brazil], **then with a loop took in the *misiones*** [Jesuit missions stations during colonial period] **both of the Paraná** [river] **and Paraguay** [river]; **deer stood on the tops of the *cuchillas*** [ranges of hills]; **Down in the south...** [southern pampa of Buenos Aires province]; **Towards the middle region of this great galloping ground, the greatest that God made...; Tigers** [jaguars] **and pumas** [mountains lions, cougars] **inhabited the woods, right from the Estero Ñembuco ... down to the Antarctic beech forests of Sandy Point** [Punta Arenas in deep southern Chile]; ***Por allacito, en los Porongos*** [porongo - gourd for preparing and drinking mate; Los Porongos - location in central Uruguayan pampa; location in Santiago del Estero in far west of Argentina. Graham's speaker may wish to consign the plague of locusts to a far-off place, or to 'anywhere'.]; **in far-off Nabothea** [in Judaea in Old Testament], **that old-world Entre-Rios**

[Entre Ríos - large province in northern Argentina between the Rivers Paraná and Uruguay]; **the Cuchilla de Peralta** [near Bahía Blanca], **by which the mule-trail, used since the Conquest, led winding on its way towards Brazil; the Banda Oriental** [in colonial times the 'Eastern Strip' of Spain's Vice-royalty of La Plata, on the northern/eastern bank of River Plate. Later the independent Republic of Uruguay]; **the Missions of the north; the southern plains; the River Plate; the Pampas of the south; on the open plains; a "pass"** [crossing-place, ford]; **from the Atlantic to the Andes** [major mountain chain]; **where the Pampas joined the stony plains of Patagonia** [arid tableland beyond the pampa] **in the south; Northwards... in the Jesuit Missions; in the dense woods of Paraguay; under those southern skies.**

"Los Indios" (in *A Hatchment*, 1913) is an evocation over 14 pages of the way of life of the wild Indians of the Pampa.

PLACE-NAMES AND LOCATIONS: **the southern Pampa; outside Bahía Blanca** [Bahía Blanca]; **though they** [the wild Indians] **had their Toldos** [tents, encampments] **out on the Salinas Grandes** [the Great Saltpans], **and dotted all the way along the foothills of the Andes right up to the lake of Nahuel-Huapi and down to Cholechél** [Cholechel]; **the inside camps** [Indian territory]; **They either entered the province near the town of Tapalquén, by the great waste between the Romero Grande** [romero - rosemary herb; pilgrim] **and the Cabeza del Buey** [Ox-head], **or through the pass, right at the top of the Sierra de la Ventana** ['Window Range': sierra - range of hills, mountains; ventana - window]; **The terror and romance of the south frontier; the great *estancias* of the south; in the Tolderias** [tolderías - groups of tents, encampments of wild Indians]; **the Gauchos** [cow-herders of the pampas] **of the south; Hurried off to the Toldos** [tents; Indian tribe], **often a hundred leagues away...; ... Indians on the warpath, from San Luis de La Punta, right down to Cholechél. Stretches of "camp"** [colonised pampa] **now under corn were then deserted; A chain of forts, starting upon the Rio Quinto** [River Number Five] **and running north and south; The mysterious territory known by the name of "Tierra Adentro"** [The Land Inside, the inside lands, Indian territory beyond the frontier], **began at Las Salinas Grandes, and stretched right to the Andes, through whose passes the Indians, by the help of their first cousins, the Araucanians, conveyed such of the cattle and the mares they did not want...; Tierra Adentro** served the wilder gauchos for a sure refuge in their times of trouble; out on the Napostá [river]; [quoting from the *Martín Fierro*] **"… las ultimas** [últimas] **poblaciones,"** the *poblaciones* [White settlements] being, if I remember rightly, some low and straw-thatched *ranchos* [huts], **surrounded by a ditch; The serious side of Tierra Adentro was in the refuge it afforded to revolutionary chiefs; in that mysterious Inside Land; at the sack of an** *estancia,* **somewhere near Tapalquén; In the Arcadia of the Tolderias, especially in those close by the apple forests of the Andes; Amongst the Toldos** [tribe of wild Indians] **of the Pampas; At the rejoicings in the Tolderias; the Toldas** [= Toldos - tribe of wild Indians], **those on the edge of the great apple forests of the Andes, and those between Las Salinas Grandes and the Lago Argentino** [Lake Argentine], **are all gone. All the wild riders now ride in Trapalanda** [Indian heaven, perfect for riders and horses], **the mysterious city in which no Christian ever breathes his horse. Over the treacherous Guadál** [guadal - sandy bog], **the Vizcachera** [prairie dog burrows], **or through the middle of a Cangrejál** [cangrejo - crab; cangrejal - marshy, swampy ground, home to black crabs], **no more wild horsemen gallop; Round the Gualichu tree** [Gualichú - tree held in reverence by Indians]; **in some mysterious Trapalanda of his own … from Tapalquén down to the Sauce Grande** [Great Willow River]; **an alarm of Indians at Tapalquén; We camped on the Arroyo de los Huesos** [Stream of Bones], **swam the Quenquen Salado** [Salty Quenquén River], **buried a man we found dead at Las Tres Horquetas** [Three Forks], **and after a week's riding, through camps** [settled pampa space] **swept clear of cattle and mares, came to the Sauce Grande; now the plough breaks up the turf that had remained intact and virgin since the creation of the world.**

"La Pulperia" ("Pampa Store") in *Thirteen Stories* (1900) blends description and drama over 10 pages. It opens with a detailed description of a typical pampa store in southern Buenos Aires province in the 1870s. A gaucho troubadour and a roaming Negro gaucho famed for knife skills engage in a singing contest, taking turns with old Spanish love songs and then with fragments of the gaucho-based narrative poems *Fausto* (1866) by Estanislao del Campo and *Martín Fierro* (1872, 1879) by José Hernández. The two singers eventually fight, the troubadour is wounded, the two men then drink amicably. An aged gaucho moves to centre stage: he had been a bodyguard-cum-executioner for the dictator Rosas [1833-1852]. The young narrator – "with the accumulated wisdom of my twenty years" - provokes the old gaucho into a fit, from which he collapses on the floor of the store. The narrator "either impelled by the strange savagery inherent in men's blood or by some reason I cannot explain, caught the infection…", then mounted his horse and galloped furiously off out on to the plain.

PLACE-NAMES AND LOCATIONS: **la Pulperia** [La Pulpería - pampa store, gathering place for gauchos]; **Flor de Mayo, Rosa del Sur, or Tres de Junio** ['Mayflower', 'Southern Rose', 'Third of June'- typical names of pampa stores], **or again but have been known as the Pulperia** [pulpería] **upon the Huesos** [the River Bones], **or the Esquina** [usually street-corner, here store] **on the Napostá** [river]; **the southern plains; in the districts known as tierra adentro (the inside country); countries such as those in whose vast plains the pulperia** [pulpería] **stands for club, exchange, for meeting-place; went to Buenos Ayres** [old spelling[; **Martin Fierro** [Martín Fierro - main character in the long narrative poem by José Hernández (1872, 1879)], **type of the Gauchos** [cow-herders of the pampas] **on the frontier; they passed the frontier to seek the Indians' tents; at the pass** [ford, crossing-place] **of the Puán** [river]; **have dispatched many a Unitario dog** [term of abuse applied by supporters of dictator Rosas to Rosas' enemies] **either to Trapalanda** [Indian heaven for riders and horses] **or to hell; the women trembled and ran to their "tolderia"** [toldería - collection of tents]; **I, on the contrary, … then shouting "Viva Rosas," galloped out furiously upon the plain.**

PERSONAL NAMES AND GROUP IDENTITIES in "The Horses of the Pampas": **Urquiza, the tyrant of Entre Rios** [Entre Ríos] **had about 180,000 horses; some Gauchos; Don Roberto** [title given to Graham by gauchos]; **the Spaniards; the conquerors of America; To ride like a Cordobese** [a man from Córdoba, Spain]; **the late Edward Losson, a professor …; the Moors; the Emir; the Arabs and the Gauchos; the Indians of the Pampas; In the Pampas he who is not an Indian is a Christian; the Gaucho wakes in which the company, to light of tallow dips and the music of a cracked guitar, through the long summer nights danced round the body of some child to celebrate his entry into Paradise; the hope that in the heaven the Gaucho goes to, his horse may not be separated from him.**

PERSONAL NAMES AND GROUP IDENTITIES in "La Pampa": the **Gauchos** [cow-herders]; **"... there has a Christian died."** **// "Christian" was used more as a racial than a religious term, the Indians usually being called** *Los Bravos* [wild ones, savages], *Los Infieles* [infidels]**,** *Los Tapes,* **the latter usually applied to the descendants of the Charruas** [Charrúa Indians originally based in Uruguay; nickname applied today to Uruguayans] **in the Banda Oriental, or to the Indian Mansos** [indios mansos - tame Indians, here Guaranis] **of the Missions of the north; the aforesaid** *Infieles* **and the** *Tapes*; **the "Infidel we found dwelling in all these plains, when first Don Pedro de Mendoza..."** [leader of first (failed) settlement at Buenos Aires in 1536-1541]; **the influence of the Indians, the Quichuas, and Guaranis, the Pampas and Pehuelches, Charruas** [various Indian groupings] **and the rest of those who once inhabited the land; also did the fierce Gaucho troops who rose under Elio and Linares** [locals defending Buenos Aires 1806] **crash in the skulls of various English, Luteranos** [Lutherans, Protestants] **- for so the good Dean Funes** [Gregorio Funes 1749-1829: priest, educational and political reformer, journalist] **styles them in his history – who under Whitlock** [commander of English invasion force] **had attacked the town** [Buenos Aires]; **None of the Pampa tribes used bows and arrows; where marauding Indians on a** *malón* [Indian raid north, to seize cattle, horses and White women and children]; **at a** *pulperia* [pulpería] **some Infidel or other stole my horse and saddle; in Rioja** [La Rioja, a western province in the "dry pampa"]; **Well did the ancient Quichuas** [Indians] **name the plains, with the word signifying "space," for all was spacious ... .**

PERSONAL NAMES AND GROUP IDENTITIES in "Los Indios": **how constantly the fear of Indians was ever present in men's minds; The Indiada of the old Chief Catriel; on the sly maintained relations with Los Indios Bravos** [the wild Indians]**, such as the Pampas, Ranqueles, Pehuelches, and the rest** [tribal names]**; the Indian tribes; rode the cacique** [Indian chief]**, sometimes upon a silver-mounted saddle; as the Gauchos said; shouting as you rode up...** *"Los Indios "* ["Indians!"] **... a cry which brought every male Christian running to the door; the Gauchos of the south ... never had anything but an old blunderbuss or so...; the Indians themselves, having no arms but spears and bolas** [the Indian throwing weapon, adopted by the

330

gauchos. Also: boleadoras]; "**Christian girl, she more big, more white than Indian**"; the Indian women, who beat and otherwise ill-used them [Christian women captives] **on the sly; Such were the Indians on the warpath; a chain of forts** ... **to hold the Indians in check; the Indians, by the help of their first cousins, the Araucanians...; silver horse-gear, known to the Gauchos by the name of Chafalonia Pampa; little difference between La Indiada Mansa** [the tame Indians] **of the Chief Catriel and their wild brethren of the plains; Tierra Adentro served the wilder Gauchos for a sure refuge in their times of trouble; José Hernandez** [Hernández], **in his celebrated *Martin Fierro*** [*Martín Fierro* - the long narrative poem of 1872 and 1879] **has described how Cruz** [character's name - Cross] **and his friend took refuge with the Indians; The wood engraving, primitive and cheap, in which Cruz and Martin were shown jogging on; the picture of the Conde Duque** [de Olivares, in a Velázquez painting]; **Las Hilanderas** [The Spinners, another Velázquez painting]; [re Tierra Adentro] ... **the refuge it afforded to revolutionary chiefs. The brothers Saá and Colonel Baigoria held a sort of sub-command for years, under the great Cacique Painé, and to them came all the discontented and broken men, whom they formed into a kind of flying squadron, ranging the frontiers with the Indians, as fierce and wild as they; All kinds of Christian women, from the poor China girl** [companion of a gaucho; sometimes a prostitute] ... **to educated women from the towns, and once even a *prima donna*; a lady carried off from San Luis... Throwing herself about Baigoria's neck; the great Chief Painé, who for ten years at least was ruled by a white girl...; a most real faith in the Gualichú, that evil spirit... They lived almost exactly like the Gauchos... The Indian's toldo** [tent] **was but little inferior to the Gaucho's hut... Both Indian and Gaucho wore the same clothes... Their** [the Indians'] **carelessness of life and their contempt of death exceeded that even of their first cousins and deadly enemies, the Gauchos... Cutting of throats was a subject of much joking both amongst Gauchos and the Indians; the Indian children playing carnival, with hearts of sheep and calves for scent bottles, squirting out blood on one another in the most natural way; the amount of mare's flesh that the Indians used to eat was quite phenomenal; all the wild riders now live in Trapalanda, the mysterious city in which no Christian ever breathes his horse.**

PERSONAL NAMES AND GROUP IDENTITIES in "La Pulperia": **some Neapolitan or Basque** [incoming immigrants]; **the improving settler; the flower of the Gauchage** [= Gauchaje - gauchos] **of the district; Gauchos; the women, who always haunt the outskirts of a pulperia ... Indians and semi-whites, mulatresses, and now and then a stray Basque or Italian girl** [recent immigrants]; **the Creator's scheme; a contest of minstrelsy "por contrapunto"** [by counterpoint-singing alternately] **between a Gaucho payador** [troubadour] **and a "matrero negro"** [a roaming or nomad gaucho who is quick with the knife] **of great fame... Negro and payador each sang alternately...;** **the Gaucho Aniceto** [protagonist of *El Fausto* by Estanislao del Campo]; **the strange life of Martin Fierro** [protagonist of *Martín Fierro*, second narrative poem mentioned]; **his friend Don Cruz** [character in *Martín Fierro*]; **the Indian chief ... the captive woman ... the Christian** [Martín] **... her dead child** [characters in *Martín Fierro*]; **La Vuelta de Martin** [*La Vuelta de Martín Fierro*, part II (1879) of the narrative poem by José Hernández]; **Tio** [Tío - uncle; title of respect to older man] **Viscacha, that Pampa cynic** [character in *Martín Fierro*]; **an aged Gaucho ... shouted "Viva Rosas,"** [dictator of Argentina 1833-1852] **though he knew that chieftain had been dead for twenty years; Tio Cabrera** [Tío - uncle; title of respect to older man; cabrero *River Plate colloq.* furious, mad; also goatherd; **the days when Rosas ruled the land... Before the "nations," English, Italian and Neapolitan, with French and all the rest, came here to learn the taste of meat;** Urquiza [landowner and gaucho leader in Entre Ríos province, eventually arch-enemy ofRosas]; **have dispatched many a Unitario dog** [Unitarians - opponents of Rosas].

DIRECT SPEECH in "Horses of the Pampas": **'How often do you feed your horses, Don Roberto, in England? Every day?'; 'God knows, the Argentine horse is a good horse, the second day without food or water, and if not He, why then the devil, for he is very old.'; 'he is useless for the lazo** [lasso], **though perhaps he may do for an Englishman to ride.'** 'Manso como para un Ingles' [un inglés] **(tame enough for an Englishman to ride) is a saying ...;** [from Cervantes] 'he could ride as well as the best Cordobese or Mexican'; 'Yes, he sits well,' was the answer; let us see how he falls'; 'What a pity he did not know how to fall!'... 'But, after all,' remarked a bystander, 'he must have died *de puro delicado* ' (of very delicateness) ...; 'Alazan [Alazán - sorrel] **tostado, mas** [más] **bien muerto que cansado,' says the proverb** [Sorrel horse, sooner dead than tired]; '**He** [a light chestnut horse] **is for Jews,' say the Arabs;** '**Caballo ruano para las putas**" [The roan horse is fit only for whores]; **The Arab dislikes the piebald. 'He is own brother to the cow.';** '**Christian frightening horse, he mount quiet on Indian side.';** ending **in a prolonged Ay** — celebrating the deeds and prowess of some hero of the Independence wars.

DIRECT SPEECH in "La Pampa": "**Where is the Manga?**" [swarm of locusts]; **Por allacito, en los Porongos** [Yonder, in Los Porongos]; "**he who wanders from the trail is lost**"; "**See where the grass grows rank around the bones; there has a Christian died**" [Ahí ha muerto un cristiano?]; "**Work, madre mia,**" [madre mía: exclamation - Mother of mine!] **said the man, "how can I work when I am bankrupt?**" // "**What then,**" the Frenchman said, "**you have been in commerce, and fallen upon a bad affair; poor man, I pity you.**" The Gaucho stared at him and answered, "**In commerce – never in my life, but at a** *pulperia* [pulpería] **some Infidel or other stole my horse and saddle, with** *lazo,* *bolas,* **and a** *cojinillo* [lasso, bolas - throwing weapon favoured by Indians and gauchos, and sheepskin base for saddle] **that I bought up in Rioja, and left me without shade.**" [shade?]; **the proverb said, "The House shall never prosper upon whose roof is thrown the shade of the** *ombú.*"

DIRECT SPEECH in "Los Indios": **their** [the Indians'] **yells, a loud prolonged "Ah, Ah, Ah—a—a," more wild and terrifying; a pingo "fit for God's saddle"**, as the Gauchos said; **shouting as you rode up** ... "Los Indios" ["Indians!"]; "**Christian girl, she more big, more white than Indian,**" they would say; **hear their** [the Indians'] **salutation "Mari-Mari";** "Al fin, por una madrugada clara, viceron [= vieron] **las ultimas** [últimas] **poblaciones**" [recited from the *Martín Fierro*]; **she cried, "Save me,** *compadre* " [friend]; "**poor fellow, how he suffers,**" [from rheumatic fever]; [of a man being executed] "**he put out his tongue when I began to play the violin**" (i.e. with the knife); "**There's a good Christian**"; "**Huinca** [Christian], **he foolish; Auca** [Indian] **do that because first see the sierra**".

DIRECT SPEECH in "La Pulperia": **calling out "Carlon"** [Carlón: a Spanish wine]; **shouts of "Ah bagual!" "Ah Pehuelche!" "Ahijuna!"** [exclamations meaning approximately 'Damned horse!', 'Damned Indian!' and 'Son of a gun!']; **"Negro," "Ahijuna,! "Miente," "carajo,"** [insults - 'Black *******', 'Son of a *****', 'Liar!' and 'Bastard!' - traded between the troubadour and the Negro]; **the negro is a "valiente," "muy guapeton"** [a brave lad, a very tough fellow]; **"Viva Rosas"** ['Long live Rosas!']; **Pucha, compadre** [exclamation based on puta - whore, and compadre - mate, pal], **those were the times, eh?; even the devil knows more because of years than because he is the devil** [Spanish saying - Más sabe el diablo por viejo que por diablo]; **"Muera! ... Viva Rosas,"** [May he [Urquiza] die! Long live Rosas!]; **Viva Rosas! Muera Urquiza dale guasca en la petiza"** [Long live Rosas! May Urquiza die! Give him leather on the xxxxxxxxx! Unit petizo = *Arg.* small; small person; small horse (?)]; **Yes, I, Tio Cabrera, known also as el Cordero** [The Lamb], **tell you I know how to play the violin (a euphemism on the south pampa for cutting throats). In Rosas' time, Viva el General, I was his right-hand man, and have dispatched many a Unitario dog to Trapalanda or to hell. Caña, blood** [rum, blood - exclamations],**Viva Rosas, Muera!"...; the pulpero murmured "salvage"** [savage, brute] **from behind his bars** [grille]; **the guitar players sat dumb .**

REMAINING ITEMS in "The Horses of the Pampas": **Saddled with the *recado*, the American adaptation of the Moorish *enjalma*; his waving poncho; a good horse costs a Spanish ounce (£3: 15s.)** [old colonial coin weighing one ounce (of silver?)]; **the great stock-owners count their *caballadas*** [horse-herds] **by the thousand; has as many blemishes as Petruchio's own mustang** [mesteño]; **or through the green *monte* (wood); the necessaries of desert life** [life on the open pampa]; **the slow gallop and the jogtrot, the Paso Castellano of the Spaniards... is the usual pace; the lazo** [lasso]; **a good tropilla of ten or twelve horses, following their mare** [bell-mare - madrina] **with tinkling brass bell; a *domador*** [horse-tamer]; **a blue and white (*azulejo*) colt; crossed (*cruzado*)** [with a white forefoot and white hind foot]; **The object in life of a rich Gaucho is to have a tropilla of piebalds. The author of 'El Fausto,' a well-known Gaucho poem, makes his hero ride a piebald; see him catch the ostrich with the bolas; the seven wild horses and the stubborn mules which I have so** frequently seen harnessed to a diligence [diligencia - stagecoach]; the races at the Pulperia [pulpería]; the long-drawn melancholy songs of the Payadores, the Gaucho improvisatores.

REMAINING ITEMS in "La Pampa": ostriches (Mirth of the Desert, as the Gauchos called them) [mirto - also means myrtle, a desert plant; desierto - the desert, the as yet uncolonised pampa beyond the then current frontier]; the Patagonian hare, mataco, and the quiriquincho [quirquincho - species of armadillo] scudded away or burrowed in the earth; great armadillos [burrowing mammal covered in horny plates] and iguanas [lizards]; *isletas* [clusters] of hard-wood montés [montes - wooded areas, tree-plantings, often of peach-trees]; ant-eaters (the Tamandua of the Guaranis) and tapirs [large browsing mammals, pig-like in shape] wandered; the "tero-tero" [bird] hovered; Tigers [jaguars] and pumas [cougars, mountain lions] inhabited the woods; In all the rivers nutrias [otters] and lobos [lobos de río - otters] and the carpincho [water-hog] ... swam; Viscachas [burrowing rodents] burrowed, and wise, solemn little owls [lechuzas] sat at the entrance to their burrows; their ponchos [rectangular woollen cloak with hole in middle to pass the head through, leaving arms free]; the pampero [strong wind, from the south, heralding a storm], roaring like a whole *rodeo* [herd of gathered cattle] had taken fright; a white *estancia* [farmhouse, estate headquarters] house, or a straw-coloured *rancheria* [ranchería - collection of huts] or *pulperia* [pulpería], built either at the pass [ford, crossing-place] of some great river or on a hill, as that at the Cuchilla [range of hills] de Peralta; seated upright on their *recaos* [recados - sheep-skin saddle-gear] driving their horses in a bunch [tropilla] in front of them; after first hobbling the mare [bell-mare - madrina], they tied a horse to a long *soga* [rope]; the national costume of the *poncho* and the *chiripá* [gaucho garment worn front to back over trousers]; In the current Pampa speech the words *bagual*, ñandu [ñandú], *ombú* and *vincha, yayu, Tacuara,* and *bacaray,* with almost all the names of plants, of shrubs and trees, recalled the influence of the Indians [bagual - unbroken horse; ñandú - ostrich; ombú - bush/tree of the pampa; vincha - headband; tatú - armadillo; tacuara - bamboo; bacaray - calf born by Caesarean section]; *Las boleadoras* [Indian and gaucho throwing weapon], known to the Gauchos as *Las tres Marias* [Marías: 'The Three Marys']; the bolas [boleadoras], and in especial the single

335

stone, fixed to a plaited thong of hide, and called *la bola perdida*
['the lost ball']; **his** [a gaucho's] **naked toes clutching the stirrups, his
long iron spurs kept in position by a thong of hide … his silver knife
passed through his sash and** *tirador* [strap, braces, belt], **and sticking
out just under his right elbow, his** *pingo* [horse] **with its mane cut
into castles; intent to "ball"** [bolear] **one of a band of fleet ñandus**
[ñandús, ñandúes]; **his huge iron spurs clanking like fetters on the
ground; drawing his** *facon* [facón - long gaucho knife]; **with a** *revés*
[reverse slash] **of the** *facon;* **the troop** [tropilla - bunch] **of dogs that
every Gaucho kept; that portion where distances were great between**
estancias, **and where marauding Indians on a** *malón* [Indian raid]; **in
the Jesuit Missions, clumps of** *yatais* [shrubs] **encroached upon the
plains, which ended finally, in the dense woods of Paraguay; a dark**
ombú, **standing beside some lone** *tapera* [dilapidated hut] **and whose
shade fell on some** *rancho* [hut] **or** *estancia*, **although the proverb
said, "The house shall never prosper upon whose roof is thrown the
shade of the** *ombú* ".

REMAINING ITEMS in "Los Indios": **as suddenly as a** *pampero*
[strong wind] **blew up from the south; All their incursions, known to
the Gauchos as** *malones* [large-scale Indian raids]; **the great** *estancias*
of the south; leaping the small *arroyas* [= arroyos? - streams, water-
courses]; **two or three pairs of** *bolas* ; **Your only chance, unless, as was
unlikely, you had a** *pingo* [horse] **fit for God's saddle, as the Gauchos
said; to muffle up his** [the horse's] **head in the folds of your poncho;
you drew the** *latigo* [= látigo: usually, a whip, here leather?] **of the hide-
cinch; no arms but spears and** *bolas* ; **Stretches of "camp" now under
corn were then deserted or, at the best, roamed over by** *manades*
[= manadas - herds] **of wild mares; silver horse-gear, known to the
Gauchos by the name of Chafalonia Pampa, and highly coveted as
having no alloy; jogging on at the Trotecito** [gentle trot] **wrapped
in their** *ponchos*, **driving the** *tropilla*; **some low and straw-thatched**
ranchos, **surrounded by a ditch; La Vuelta de Martin Fierro** [*La Vuelta
de Martín Fierro*, part II of the *Martín Fierro* in 1879]; **at the sack of
an** *estancia* ; **the Indian's** *toldo* [tent]; **the Gaucho's hut; Amongst
the former** [the gauchos] **it** [the cutting of throats] **was called to "do
the holy office,"** [hacer el Santo Oficio] **and a coward was said to be
mean** [menguar] **about his throat if at the last he showed the slightest
fear; after a successful** *malon* [malón] **or raid in some estancia; for**

caña [rum] was never wanting in the Toldos [Indian tents]; **Round the Gualichu** [Gualichú] **tree; no Indian will tear a piece from off his *poncho* and stick it on a thorn… the tree was a Chañar, if I remember right; except a chance *estancia* surrounded by a ditch; the plaza** [square] **full of men all arming; the *comandante*** [militia commander], **seated in a cane-chair, sat taking *maté;* through camps swept clear of cattle and of mares.**

REMAINING ITEMS in "La Pulpería": **fastening my "redomon"** [horse still wild or only half-broken in] **to the palenque** [hitching-post]; **loosen my facon** [facón - the long gaucho knife]; **calling out "Carlon,"** [Carlón], **receive my measure of heady red Spanish wine in a tin cup; the wooden "reja"** [grille] **where the pulpero** [storekeeper] **stands behind his counter; with paja brava** [a coarse grass] **sticking out of the abode** [= adobe - sun-dried brick] **of the overhanging eaves; ponderous native ploughs hewn from the solid ñandubay** [a hardwood]; **their potro** [colt-skin] **boots; keeping time to the "cielito"** [an Argentine dance-measure] **of the "payador"** [troubadour] **upon his cracked guitar; are piled ponchos from Leeds, ready-made calzoncillos** [underpants], **alpargatas** [rope-soled slippers]; **the "botilleria,"** [bar] **where vermouth, absinthe, square-faced gin, Carlon** [Carlón], **and Vino Seco** [Dry Wine] **stand in a row, with the barrel of Brazilian caña** [rum], **on the top of which the pulpero ostentatiously parades his pistol and knife; Outside, the tracks led through the biscacheras** [vizcacheras - prairie dog burrows]; **at the palenque before the door stood horses tied by strong raw-hide cabrestos** [= cabestros - halters, bridles]; **dressed in black bombachas** [wide, baggy trousers] **and vicuña ponchos** [vicuña - animal similar to the llama; its wool]; **the rush-thatched, mud-walled rancheria** [ranchería - group of huts]; **drink maté** [mate - Paraguayan tea]; **square-faced rum, cachaza** [type of rum], **and the medicated log-wood broth, which on the Pampa passes for "Vino Frances"** [Vino Francés - French Wine]; **taking the cracked "changango"** [gaucho slang for guitar: charango - small five-stringed guitar] **in their lazo-hardened** [lasso-hardened] **hands;** [songs] **in which Frasquita** [woman's name] **rhymed to Chiquita** [Little Darling], **and one Cupido** [Cupid], **whom I never saw in Pampa, loma** [hillock], **rincon** [corner, spot; here bend in a river], **bolson** [bolsón - semi-arid flat valley or depression between hills or mountains], **or medano** [médano - dune, sandbank], **in the Chañares** [species of tree], **amongst the woods of ñandubay** [hardwood trees], **the pajonales** [scrublands]**, sierras** [hills]**, cuchillas** [ranges of hills]**, or in all the land, figured and did nothing special; lost his puñal** [dagger]; **tilting at the wing** [= ring - la sortija - gaucho sport]; **mounted on his Overo rosao** [piebald]; **his "compadre"** [mate, good friend]; **put the "cejilla"** [a small device screwed on to a guitar to alter the pitch] **on the strings; with a stolen tropilla** [group, string] **of good horses, they passed the frontier to seek the Indians' tents; the bolas; to leave off contrapunto** [singing alternately]; **their facons** [gaucho knives]; **the pulpero** [store-owner]; **in his chiripa** [chiripá] **and poncho; potro boots, that is the skin taken off the hind-leg of a horse, the hock-joint forming the heel and the hide softened by pounding with a mallet, the whole tied with a garter of a strange pattern woven by the Indians, leaving the toes protruding to catch the stirrups, which as a domador** [horse-breaker] **he used, made of a knot of hide; his broad belt made of carpincho** [waterhog] **leather; a long facon** [facón - long gaucho knife]; **the "maturangos,"** [people, usually foreigners, who ride badly]; **The pulpero muttered "salvage"** [salvaje] **from behind his bars; "tolderia"** [toldería - huts]; **I ... getting on my horse, a half-wild "redomon"** [half-wild horse] **... struck him with the flat edge of my facon** [facón]**, then shouting "Viva Rosas," galloped out furiously upon the plain.**

This evidence suggests that Graham was intimately familiar with the whole range of vocabulary and expressions associated with the pampa and the gaucho way of life as it still existed in the third quarter of the nineteenth century. Graham's facility for 'explicating' a new Hispanic item by embedding it in a fluently controlled English language narrative and his use over and over of the key elements of this lexis means that the reader lacking Spanish may need initially to concentrate but s/he is seldom left grasping for meaning or understanding. Graham's Hispanic lexis is in fact not an obstacle to understanding but rather a major mechanism for plunging the reader into the very heart of the old pampa world.

(JMcI)

Select Bibliography

Stories, Sketches and Essays, with original publication dates.

Father Archangel of Scotland, and Other Essays (with Gabriela Cunninghame
  Graham), Black, 1896.
Aurora La Cujiñi, A Realistic Sketch in Seville, Smithers, 1898.
The Ipané, Fisher Unwin, 1899.
Thirteen Stories, Heinemann, 1900.
Success, and Other Sketches, Duckworth, 1902.
Progress, and Other Sketches, Duckworth, 1905.
His People, Duckworth, 1906.
Faith, Duckworth, 1909.
Hope, Duckworth, 1910.
Charity, Duckworth, 1912.
A Hatchment, Duckworth, 1913.
Brought Forward, Duckworth, 1916.
Redeemed, and Other Sketches, Heinemann, 1927.
Writ in Sand, Heinemann, 1932.
Mirages, Heinemann, 1936.

Travel, History, Biography.

Notes on the District of Menteith, for Tourists and Others, Black, 1895.
Mogreb-El-Acksa: A Journey in Morocco, Heinemann, 1898.
*A Vanished Arcadia: Being Some Account of the Jesuits in Paraguay, 1607 to
  1767*, Heinemann, 1901.
*Hernando de Soto: Together with an Account of One of his Captains, Gonçalo
  Silvestre*, Heinemann, 1903.
*Bernal Díaz del Castillo: Being Some Account of Him, Taken from His True
  History of the Conquest of New Spain*, Nash, 1915.
A Brazilian Mystic: Being the Life and Miracles of Antonio Conselheiro,
  Heinemann, 1920.
Cartagena and the Banks of the Sinú, Heinemann, 1920.
The Conquest of New Granada: Being the Life of Gonzalo Jiménez de Quesada,
  Heinemann, 1922.

The Conquest of the River Plate, Heinemann, 1924.
Doughty Deeds: An Account of the Life of Robert Graham of Gartmore, Poet and Politician, 1735-1797, drawn from his Letter-books & Correspondence, Heinemann, 1925.
Pedro de Valdivia, Conqueror of Chile, Heinemann, 1926.
José Antonio Páez, Heinemann, 1929.
The Horses of the Conquest, Heinemann, 1930.
Portrait of a Dictator: Francisco Solano López (Paraguay, 1865-1870), Heinemann, 1933.

R.B. Cunninghame Graham Biography.

A Modern Conquistador: Robert Bontine Cunninghame Graham: His Life and Works, H.F. West, Cranley and Day, 1932.
Don Roberto, A.F. Tschiffely, Heinemann, 1937.
Cunninghame Graham: A Critical Biography, Cedric Watts & Laurence Davies, Cambridge University Press, 1979.
R.B. Cunninghame Graham, Cedric Watts, Twayne Publishers Boston, 1983.
Gaucho Laird: The Life of R.B. "Don Roberto" Cunninghame Graham, Jean Cunninghame Graham (Lady Polwarth), The Long Riders' Guild Press, 2004.

Critical Writing.

Cunninghame Graham: A Centenary Study, Hugh MacDiarmid, Caledonian Press, 1952.
"The Scottish Writings of R.B. Cunninghame Graham" (article), John Walker, *International Review of Scottish Studies*, Vol. 13 (1985), 25-33; and at www.irss.uoguelph.ca/article/viewFile/636/1057

Background Reading.

Sketches descriptive of picturesque scenery on the southern confines of Perthshire, Patrick Graham, Peter Hill, 1806.
Facundo – Civilización y Barbarie, Domingo F. Sarmiento (1845), Editorial Sopena Buenos Aires, 1945 (in Spanish).
Martín Fierro, José Hernández, Buenos Aires, 1872, 1879: ed. Luis Saínz de Medrano, Cátedra (Letras Hispánicas), Madrid, 2010 (in Spanish).
Morocco That Was, Walter B. Harris, William Blackwood, 1921.
Tschiffely's Ride, Aimé Tschiffely, Introduction by R.B. Cunninghame Graham, Heinemann, 1933.

South from Granada, Gerald Brenan, Hamish Hamilton, 1957.

Gauchos and the Vanishing Frontier, Richard W. Slatta, University of Nebraska Press, Lincoln and London, 1983, 1992.

Sir John Lavery, Kenneth McKonkey, Canongate Press, 1993.

Moorish Spain, Richard Fletcher, Phoenix, 2001.

Argentina, eds. Deirdre Ball et al., Insight Guides, APA Publications (HK) Ltd, Third Edition, 1997.

Argentina – Eyewitness Travel, W. Bernhardson, Declan McGarvey, Chris Moss, Dorling Kindersley, 2008.

Uruguay, Tim Burford, Bradt Guides, 2010.

Previous Selections of Cunninghame Graham Stories and Sketches.

Scottish Stories, R.B. Cunninghame Graham, Duckworth, 1914.

Thirty Tales and Sketches, R.B. Cunninghame Graham, with introduction by Edward Garnett, Duckworth, 1929.

Rodeo, a Collection of the Tales and Sketches, R.B. Cunninghame Graham, with introduction by Aimé Tschiffely, Heinemann, 1936.

The Essential R.B. Cunninghame Graham, Paul Bloomfield, Jonathan Cape, 1952.

The South American Sketches of R.B. Cunninghame Graham, ed. John Walker, University of Oklahoma Press, 1978.

Beattock for Moffat, and the Best of R.B. Cunninghame Graham, with notes by Alanna Knight, Paul Harris Publishing 1979.

Tales of Horsemen, ed. Alexander Maitland, Canongate Publishing, 1981.

The Scottish Sketches of R.B. Cunninghame Graham, ed. John Walker, Scottish Academic Press, 1982.

The North American Sketches of R.B. Cunninghame Graham, ed. John Walker, Scottish Academic Press, 1986.

Index of Stories in Volume 5

Index of Appendices in *Collected Stories and Sketches.*

Complete Index of Stories and Sketches in *Collected Stories and Sketches of R.B. Cunninghame Graham*

Key (Title, *Collection*, **Volume**):

AH,	A Hatchment
BF,	Brought Forward
C,	Charity
F,	Faith
FAS,	Father Archangel of Scotland, and Other Essays
H,	Hope
HP,	His People
M,	Mirages
NDM,	Notes on the District of Menteith
P,	Progress, and Other Sketches
R,	Redeemed, and Other Sketches
S,	Success, and Other Sketches
TI,	The Ipané
TS,	Thirteen Stories
WS,	Writ in Sand

GCG after a title indicates item by Gabriela Cunninghame Graham.

Lightning Source UK Ltd.
Milton Keynes UK
UKOW032207051012

200112UK00001B/16/P